P9-APZ-062

LUCKY RED

LUCKY RED

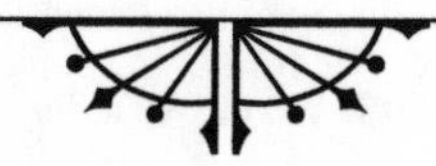

A NOVEL

CLAUDIA CRAVENS

THE DIAL PRESS
New York

Published in the United States by The Dial Press, an imprint of Random House, a division of Penguin Random House LLC, New York.

THE DIAL PRESS is a registered trademark and the colophon is a trademark of Penguin Random House LLC.

LIBRARY OF CONGRESS CATALOGING-IN-PUBLICATION DATA
Names: Cravens, Claudia, author.
Title: Lucky Red: a novel / Claudia Cravens.
Description: First edition. | New York: The Dial Press [2023]
Identifiers: LCCN 2022024060 (print) | LCCN 2022024061 (ebook) | ISBN 9780593498248 (hardcover; acid-free paper) | ISBN 9780593498255 (ebook)
Subjects: LCGFT: Western fiction. | Lesbian fiction. | Novels.
Classification: LCC PS3603.R394 R43 2023 (print) | LCC PS3603.R394 (ebook) | DDC 813/.6—dc23/eng/20220520
LC record available at https://lccn.loc.gov/2022024060
LC ebook record available at https://lccn.loc.gov/2022024061
International edition ISBN 9780593729694

Printed in the United States of America on acid-free paper

randomhousebooks.com

2 4 6 8 9 7 5 3 1

First Edition

Design by Ralph Fowler

CONTENTS

PART ONE | JOURNEY'S END

Chapter 1 . . . 3
Chapter 2 . . . 15
Chapter 3 . . . 24
Chapter 4 . . . 34
Chapter 5 . . . 54
Chapter 6 . . . 70
Chapter 7 . . . 84

PART TWO | FIRST SNOW

Chapter 8 . . . 101
Chapter 9 . . . 119
Chapter 10 . . . 136
Chapter 11 . . . 146
Chapter 12 . . . 160
Chapter 13 . . . 172
Chapter 14 . . . 180
Chapter 15 . . . 208
Chapter 16 . . . 216

PART THREE | HARD RIDING

Chapter 17 . . . 229
Chapter 18 . . . 236
Chapter 19 . . . 253
Chapter 20 . . . 263
Chapter 21 . . . 272
Chapter 22 . . . 279

Epilogue . . . 285

Acknowledgments . . . 291

PART ONE

JOURNEY'S END

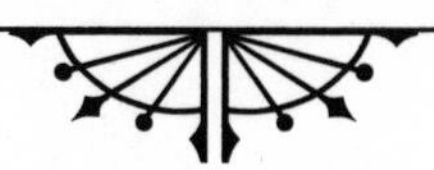

CHAPTER I

Some years ago, in Dodge, I was a sporting woman. This was before I took up my current trade, back when the prairie ran with cattle like a river runs with fish. It's different now, of course, but then, so am I. I didn't mind whoring—it can be good work in the right house—but it demands a great deal of keeping still, and I'm one of those itchy, fidgety sorts who's always looking out the window or glancing toward the door, so it was only a matter of time until I had to move on. Most rambling types like to act as if they just woke up one morning and lit out, turning their backs to all and sundry, but this is just good storytelling. The truth is that making your own way happens piecemeal, like a baby who scoots, then crawls, then eventually toddles her way right out the cabin door where she's as likely to be snatched up by coyotes as she is to seek her fortune; either way, once she gets loose, there'll be no getting her back. All of which is to say that though I ended up a pretty girl in boy's clothes, mounted like a woman and armed like a man, I started much smaller and simpler, and mostly alone.

Before I was a whore in Kansas, I was a poor drunkard's daughter in Arkansas. My pa wasn't a bad man, but it was far too easy for circumstances to get the upper hand on him. He called himself unlucky, but the losing hands dealt him were too frequent and too numerous to be mere turns of fate. I will admit that at times, events truly were beyond his control: first Ma died having me, then came the Brothers War, then he was on the losing side, and then he lost what was left of the farm to nursing his broken heart. But there were other misadventures that showed me, if not him, that there's more to this life than luck, even bad luck.

First there were the mustangs, which he bought cheap and wild but lacked the will to break and was forced to sell off cheaper and wilder. Then the sheep flock, whose feed he let rot so they all went mad when they ate it. When we finally had to slaughter them, the screaming clatter of blood and terror seemed to thrust him back to some Virginian hellscape, for halfway through he threw aside his knife and shot the rest as fast as he could. In between, there were crates of plow-blades that wouldn't hold an edge, barrels of discarded horseshoes, bales of kinked wire, all manner of flotsam that somehow always cost more than it made. He told himself he was getting by on his wits, when most of the time it was my willingness to scrub linens, tote water, and muck out horse barns that kept our souls inside of our bodies.

When I wasn't hiring myself out on odd jobs, I was usually standing in the doorway of our small cabin on the edge of Fort Smith, from whence I watched the sunsets and periodically wondered if my pa had finally gone off for good. He was a restless soul, and his absences always mixed me up bad. There was the fear that comes from being alone—I was just sixteen and getting a little too ripe to be left unguarded—the snapping awake at every shift in the wind outside only to stare into the blue-black darkness and wait with bated breath for nothing to happen. There was the righteous fury at having been forgotten, as though I, his child and only living kin, was no more memorable than a cracked jug or a harness with a broken strap. This fury would surge up unannounced: suddenly I'd find myself slamming down buckets only to slosh water over my feet, wringing wet linens like turkey necks, shoveling horse shit like

I was digging one grave to hold all of my enemies. And then there was relief, the sole proprietorship over my supper, the break from caring for the one person left on this earth who should have cared for me.

We always scraped together just enough to keep us in that little house at the far reaches of the town. I would watch for Pa's return, going about my chores with half an eye on the cabin door, propped open during the warm months to admit the evening. I couldn't tell you what he did when he was gone; he'd just disappear, leaving me to scratch out a few pennies doing other folks' chores, and come back whenever he'd a mind to, half singing a loop of some dirty song he'd learned long ago in the army. He'd roar for cornbread or a fire, but when I couldn't produce them he never got rough, just sad. The cold, blue reflection of the empty hearth would pierce through the fog of liquor in some way that the sun, or I, never could, and for a moment he would understand that he was a disgrace, supported by a daughter who pitched hay and scrubbed petticoats, and greasy, overlarge tears would well up in his eyes. If I didn't move quickly to cheer him up with a song or a joke he'd set to weeping, which only required more soothing and petting to tame down. Once he started crying I'd have to smile and lie right into his face for hours on end, until he calmed enough to pull himself up into the loft, where he'd snore like a full crew of lumberjacks, or toss and shout when his dreams grew too lifelike. Sometimes, as I lay awake after a long evening spent dabbing at his cheeks, I wished he would've just smacked me instead. It was an ungrateful sentiment, but a beating would have been less humiliating than pretending I didn't mind that I'd never been to school, that all I wore were baggy hand-me-downs, that the pretty town girls wouldn't even talk to me.

At five days and counting, this was Pa's longest spree yet: usually his drinking spells only lasted three, four days at most, but now as the sun was easing down to kiss the tops of the pines, he was still nowhere to be seen.

The sun dipped an inch lower, and at last I heard a rattling, then a scrape and holler.

"Bridget!" His voice came from up the track. My whole back prickled like a porcupine, that strange admixture of fury and relief that, once again, he'd survived his own recklessness.

"Where's my little red hen?" came a second shout. I'd swung the kettle out from over the fire and was poking at the contents, willing the possum I'd earned chopping firewood to turn into stew so my stomach could cease its fistlike clenching.

"Come on, Henny Penny, I'm stuck!" he called out again, tacking a hoarse laugh onto the end.

With a stick of firewood I pushed the kettle of possum back over the flames, wiped my hands on my apron, and went outside. It was that hazy, uncertain time of day when the sky can't decide whether to keep its day clothes on, and the lowest-hung tree branches blur together like a mist. A little way down the track that led past our house I found my pa perched on the seat of a rattly little buckboard I hadn't seen before. There were two skinny mules attached, flicking their ears and staring wall-eyed into the trees. The wagon's rear wheel was stuck on a rock, the work of a moment for anyone remotely capable.

"Where'd you get all this?" I said, hands on hips like I was his overworked wife rather than his underfed daughter.

"That's none of your nevermind," he said. He swayed as he spoke, focused on some fixed point in the air. I pursed my lips and went around behind the wagon to dig out the rock, scrabbling at it with my nails while my pa kept his seat, humming that same old song, something about a lady in a red dress. I pulled the rock loose—it stuck up high but wasn't nestled in very deep—and the wagon jolted forward into our yard, leaving me to chase after.

"Where'd you get all this?" I asked again as I caught up to them behind the cabin. He clambered down and started unhitching the mules, tying them up at an empty trough.

"Traded for 'em!" he crowed.

My heart sank, mind searching wildly for something he could have traded away, even for such a lean prize as this.

"Traded what?" I asked him, tensed all over.

"Well, the man who gave 'em to me said he was looking for a gal to care for him and his aging mother," he said, looking up at me. I stopped breathing, staring at him with my mouth wide open. He winked like the joke was obvious. "But I told him I was too attached to my girl to give her up on such terms. So he's taking the cabin instead." He lifted one hand and gestured at our little house.

"You gave him our house?" I gasped. I looked at the mules again. Their hip bones stuck out and one of them still had the shaggy remains of a winter coat patchworked over his flank. "For them?"

"And this," he said, reaching into his jacket and pulling out a folded piece of paper, worn through where it had been folded and refolded too many times. He thrust it at me and I looked at the words, but I was poorly lettered and all I could pick out before he plucked it back from me was *Kansas.*

"Twenty acres, plus these two fine fellows. A fresh start, Bridget! A chance to change our luck!" The dusky shadows hid his face so that he was naught but a blue-gray silhouette. Instinct told me that to be less than jubilant would bring out a storm of tears and drown us both; I smiled and must have said something pleasant, for he drew me close and ushered me inside, complimented my treatment of the stringy, obstinate-tasting possum, and fell asleep still mumbling that song about some far-off pretty girl, long since forgotten.

Much to my surprise, traveling agreed with my pa: he just nipped at a bottle at night, stretched out alongside the fire right in the open air, snores reduced to horselike sighs, and for moments here and there I thought this might not have been a terrible mistake. As we bumped along, the cool forests of Arkansas gradually thinned and gave way to prairie under vast swathes of blue and white sky. It troubled me to come out from under the cover of trees; I'd lived my whole life in the shade and hadn't realized how much I had come to rely on the pines for their uprightness, how under their canopy I'd felt held as by the great, green hand of God. As the woods dissolved, first into groves and then single, isolated trees, I found myself staring hard at them, suppressing the urge to wave sadly as though bidding old friends farewell, not that I'd had any. I began to wonder if each tree I saw would be the last, and to worry that I wouldn't recognize that last one when I saw it.

Of course, there never was a real end to trees, just as there never is a real start to grass. And perhaps there should have been, for in the end it was our shared love of shade trees that got my pa killed. We were well into Kansas by then, just west of Abilene. Some speck on the horizon must have caught his attention, for he swung the mules off the wagon track and into open country, jolting me awake from where I'd been dozing in the mostly empty wagon bed.

"What is it?" I asked him, sitting up and rubbing the back of my head, which felt bruisy after so many days spent bumping in and out of sleep.

"A grove," he said. "And maybe some water."

He swung around and grinned at me. His hat had fallen forward so that I could only see his teeth, flat white and crowded together like passengers pressing toward a train door. "What do you say, Bridget, could you use a little shade?"

"I surely could," I replied. I couldn't see anything when I squinted past his shoulder, but I meant it all the same. We'd been under nothing but beating prairie sun for days; it seemed impossible that we could have traveled so far and still be surrounded by so little.

It was late afternoon by the time we came to the spring, nestled into a little dell that fed down to a creek bed, overhung by a stand of twisted cottonwoods. It wasn't until we were under their shade that I saw the sod house dug into what passed for the hillside, a hairy facade with a silvery wooden door in the middle. I stayed in the wagon while Pa hopped down to take a look. The sun was getting lazy, and the light tilted into a golden syrup that spilled over his back; the grass was tall and yellow around his knees, sighing under the touch of a soft wind that ran over it like a hand over a piece of fine cloth; for the first time, I saw how such country could be beautiful.

Pa called out a hello, then rattled at the door when no one answered, but there came not a sound, not so much as a puff of dust.

"Ain't no one here," he said. "Let's stop for the night."

"In there?"

"No, let's camp out here, just in case. Besides, I've grown fond of sleeping wild, ain't you?"

"What if someone comes?" I said.

"And what if they do? Who would begrudge us, two simple travelers bunked out by a spring?" he said, crossing his arms and grinning at me again. Behind him the clear water of the spring rippled, sending up little stars of reflected sunlight, so I said nothing and climbed down. Our campsite twinkled to life as though laid out by fairies, so eager were we to stretch out and enjoy the cool shade and clear water. The hobbled mules huffed and snuffled as they drank, startling a prairie chicken who scuttled off into the brush before we could catch it. I waded straight into the spring to bathe my bare feet and Pa stretched out long at the base of a tree, pulling his hat down over his face. A fine breeze whispered over the grass and stirred the leaves of the cottonwoods; the sun dawdled overhead, and we drifted under its mindless gaze. Through the dancing leaves I watched the sky, enchanted and yet wondering how something that cared so little for me could so capture my attention. First it was a clear, reeling blue of staggering depth, but as I watched, the color drained away and was replaced by a deep gray as though the sky were turning to stone above us. I watched, fascinated, not realizing that the roiling texture it had taken on was cloud until the breeze suddenly turned cold, then whipped itself up stronger. I sat up when the first thick, heavy drops hit my face and shoulders. A new, fierce wind whipped my hair about my face like a blindfold.

"Pa!" I called out, but it was already dark, and he was already moving. We rolled up our meager camp and hustled toward the sod house. Its crumbling, hairy walls were lit white for a split second before the thunder rang out. I had never heard anything like it: the sound was physical, great hands clapping together as if we were two gnats they meant to smash. A fresh lashing of rain sent me barreling through the dark little mouth of the open doorway, the floor before me flashing around my own cutout shadow, and then the answer to the lightning's question hit me like a whip between the shoulder blades and chased me into a corner where I curled up small in the darkness, waiting for the next crack and roll. We'd had thunderstorms in Arkansas, of course, but this was different, my first taste of real prairie weather that has nothing to give it shape or direct its madness. I pulled myself in closer and shivered.

"Come on now, be brave," said Pa. "Ain't nothing but a little lightning, and you ain't been scared of nothing before this."

For a moment I tightened from brow to shoulders with a sudden desire to spit back all the things I'd been afraid of those countless times he'd left me alone, all the things I prayed against before he came back. But there came another white flash and then the crack, louder this time. A sob burst out of me before I could stop it, and I crouched down, clutching the roll of blankets I'd grabbed on my run inside. What had possessed us to come to such a place?

Pa struck a match but made no further move to comfort me. Instead, he searched out a hearth, which he found at the back of the little house. "Why, some Samaritan has even left us some firewood," he said. I heard sticks breaking and clattering against stone.

The next flash of lightning picked out the frame of a window straining to hold on to its ill-fitted shutter, and I was seized with fresh fear that it would burst open and that the storm, which I now viewed as a living, malevolent creature, would get inside.

"Well, if you ain't going to help, I guess I'll have to do everything," said Pa in his half-joking way. I didn't answer but instead kept my eyes fixed on the window. There was more rustling and shuffling behind me, and then a soft, yellowish glow spread out toward the door. The heat woke up a comforting musk of wet dirt and horses that clung to the walls; as my back warmed I felt the most animal part of my fear begin to dissipate, and a little calm pooled in my chest.

Though I was grateful to be in shelter, the sod house was even worse on the inside than it had looked from the outside. There was a ratty-looking pallet on one side of the hearth, away from the window. On the other, a table and two chairs that looked as though they'd sooner collapse than hold a body off the floor. There came another thunderclap, but this one was steadier, more of a long roll, and when it passed I could actually hear the rain outside, lapping over the grass. It was a pleasant sound, familiar. My hands allowed themselves to unclench, and I soon set to laying out our bedrolls, calming myself with work.

"There now, none the worse for wear," said Pa. He came over and smoothed out the blankets, reaching out one hand to chuck me under the chin. He had deep lines around his mouth where he had spent most of his life smiling, but they hadn't been smiles of happiness, and the resulting grooves were not handsome. Still, I could see he meant well, and smiled back. We shared some crackers and a wedge of cheese while Pa got to work on a bottle he'd bought two days earlier in Abilene—something about being cooped up seemed to bring out the urge in him. The thunder passed and the rain relaxed into a steady pace. Worn out with travel and panic, I pulled a blanket over my head and turned over to let sleep find me.

I woke to Pa's screaming. It had happened plenty of times before, when he'd get caught in a dream of a lost battle, so as my eyes searched for anything at all in the pitch dark, my first sensation was annoyance. But then I realized this was different—these screams were high-pitched and strangled sounding. I knew my pa's voice better than any other, and I'd never heard this shrill, twisted tightness before. It froze my heart in my chest even as I struggled to understand the cause. I groped in the blackness for matches and struck one: in its little circle of light I could see my pa writhing on the ground, clutching his throat and kicking out wildly with both feet. A big, blunt-nosed rattlesnake lifted its fangs out of his throat and sank them once again, this time into the back of his hand. Pa's arm shot out to fling the snake away just as my match went out. In the dark I heard him jump up, still screaming; the next lit match showed him twisting like a dancer, flapping his arm until the snake finally lost its grip and flew off across the room, thudding softly against the sod wall before it scrambled away into the gap left by a missing hearthstone.

The match scorched my fingertips as it went out. I struck a third one and held it up to see that Pa had fallen to his knees, tears streaming down his face. His screams had died to a ragged sound somewhere between breath and sob. On hands and knees, I felt around for the stump of a candle and lit it as I crawled over the mess of tangled bedding to examine his wounds. I threaded one arm around his back and held up the candle. There was a bad bite in his neck, a pair of dark-red, seeping punctures that opened a door between him and the world. I clamped my lips down and pulled hard, filling my mouth with the taste of iron laced with bitter poison, turning to spit over my shoulder. By my third pull, his body had taken on a leaden aspect that chilled me worse than the screaming, worse than his raspy wheeze. I shifted my hold—he was not a large man, but still awkward to handle—and saw a faraway look moving into his eyes.

"Pa," I said, surprised by the catch in my voice.

His eyes flickered up to mine like the ticking of a clock. "Just bad luck, Bridget," he whispered.

I would have thought that two deep bites from a snake as big and mean as that rattler would kill a man outright, but it took almost a full day for Pa to cross over. At first light I dragged him outside and laid him under the cottonwoods, where the grass sparkled and the air was fresh as a whole field of daisies. The veins in his neck and arm stood out purple while red patches grew out from the bite wounds until finally, he just gulped like a catfish. I sat beside him and bathed his face with cool spring water, helplessly clutching at his hand while my pa slid away from me, one breath at a time, each growing more ragged and standing out more clearly against the rustle of the leaves dancing above us. All things being equal, it was a beautiful place to die.

Somewhere in the late afternoon, there came an exhale that was not followed by an inhalation. In the silence that followed, I sat half-way up, leaning forward as though it was only a moment's suspense that I had to weather and not the soundless crossing over into a new, orphaned life. I stood up, dizzy, and stumbled on tingling, half-asleep feet back to the spring, wading in up to my knees before I sank down, submerged to the waist and gazing out across the empty plains. I looked at the dappled shadows on the water's surface and found suddenly that I'd had my fill of shade.

Eventually I chilled and crawled out of the water. I sat up through the night, listening to the sound of my own breathing and feeling that it was both the loudest and the softest sound I'd heard in my life. There was no moon, but the stars picked themselves out one by one against the woolly blackness like a mourning dress, half-sewn, with silver pins still tucked into the seams. Each rising and falling of my chest lay heavy on me as I realized that I was truly alone now, that the periods in which I'd been abandoned previously both had and had not prepared me for this. I imagined my pa waving his hat and wishing me good luck as he placed me in the hands of fate, and felt a crack in the crust of resentment that had grown over my heart. I did not wish myself good luck, and I did not hope that Providence would treat me kindly. Instead, I told myself that it was up to me to keep my chest rising and falling, and that to do so I could not be governed by the world's twists and turns, always whipped about by sad winds as he had been. I had never held out much hope for the places my life's road would take me, for I was the daughter of a poor and feckless man, and in witnessing his thrashing about I had learned to adjust my expectations again and again. But I also found, as I sat under the black wing of the night sky, that I still had some fight left in me, and I made a promise to the indifferent stars above that I would live better than that wet-eyed corpse ever could.

CHAPTER 2

I buried Pa under the cottonwood trees. It took most of the day to dig: though I was strong from plenty of hired work, the prairie soil was hard-packed and laced overtop with such a thick net of sod that it took all I had to scrabble a shallow grave out of it. Before I pushed him in, I rifled Pa's pockets. I found his wallet, which held thirteen dollars—about twelve more than I'd expected—and his pocketknife, which still held an edge. I didn't find the folded piece of greasy paper that was supposed to have secured our future, but twenty acres of grass wouldn't have done me a lick of good anyhow, even if the plot had been real, which I doubted it was.

I dragged and rolled the body into the hole I'd scraped out and piled dirt over it, having neither the time nor the patience to search for rocks. When I was done, mud-streaked and exhausted, I laid one hand upon the mound. I tried to think of something to say, but no words came to me, so I just patted it a couple of times and stood up.

It was afternoon already, but I was eager to move on. I didn't know how far it was to the next town, and all I had was cheese and crackers. I didn't let myself think about how miraculous it was that no one had come up to the spring yet. Neither did I mention to my-self that coyotes would be along shortly to unbury my pa, nor the possibility of those same coyotes gnawing my own self down to bones that would bleach out real nice in the summer sun. I thought it best to keep my reasoning grounded in simple things like food rationing and miles traveled, at least until I got someplace.

The mules had bolted in the storm; though one had vanished without a trace, his partner had come through just fine, and Providence had even seen fit to keep him from wandering. He was just down the creek bed that fed from the spring, drinking the clear water and swishing his tail. Apparently pleased to see a familiar face, he came right up to me so that I could load him up with a bedroll and the remains of our food.

It's hard to say how much time passed after I left the spring. At first, I stuck to the creek bed, following its serpentines approximately westward. The cover of brush and the nearness of water were so comforting that when, after some days' wandering we came to the end of the creek, I all but wept to leave them behind. Still, I turned west out onto the plains. The mule and I traveled another day until we hit a wagon track running north-to-south. Having little idea where I was, I shrugged and chose south. Though I wasn't sure what lay in that direction, I knew north was nothing but Nebraska, which was a much rougher place in those days than it is now.

Those days of traveling were dull in the extreme. I grew skinny and irritable from day after day with no one to talk to, while the mule grew bored and fractious, shuffling sideways when it came time to load him up. I alternated riding and walking, and we traveled without schedule or routine: when one of us got tired, we'd stop and rest. On waking, I'd nibble on some provisions and move us on as quickly as I could.

I hid at every sign of people, whether a dust cloud from a distant cattle herd, fresh horse tracks in the dust, or the creak and stamp of an ox-drawn wagon coming up behind us. Not a soul knew where I was, or even that I existed; I pushed us hard as I dared, hoping to get across the prairie unnoticed. Many years later I met a missionary who'd rode the plains awhile, and he told me that the prairie sky was nothing but God's big blue eye. If that's true, I wonder if He saw me, one little speck creeping like a mouse through that featureless stretch of His creation.

Finally, one morning I crested a small rise—I'd woken in the predawn chill and set out as fast as I could—and saw a cluster of smudgy buildings far off. I went hard that day until I had to stop, too tired to continue, but by the time the prairie shook itself awake the next morning, my mule and I were shuffling into Dodge City.

Dodge was in its prime then, brimming like a stoveful of boiling pots. As I came up the main street, every building seemed to be spilling over with people and sound and activity. After so many days with nothing to see but grass and sky and the twitching ears of my mule, it was a lot to take in. Two gray-faced cowboys supported a third between them who looked heavy as a grain sack; his legs spun crazily under his body as his friends maneuvered him toward a horse that swished its tail and sighed resignedly. Up above, I saw a girl in naught but a camisole lean her forehead against the windowpane, eyes shut. A storekeeper sweeping his chunk of boardwalk looked up and gave me a half nod, which I returned tersely. In the window behind him, I looked like a wraith. Through every window a pretty—or at least pretty-seeming—girl was combing her hair, blowing on a steaming cup of coffee, rolling her eyes at something said within. The sides of every building were lined with booted men, sleeping upright with their hats over their faces; before each one a saddled horse shifted patiently from foot to foot, blowing in the crisp air and nickering softly to each other. Farther off, I heard a train whistle before a blast of steam appeared like pipe smoke over the buildings, dissolving blue and ghostlike into the thin sky, while under it a steady rumble of cattle lowing and stamping was punctuated with the yips and whoops of cowboys already hard at work loading them up. It was completely overwhelming, and completely enchanting, unlike anyplace I had ever been.

That first day in town I sold the mule to a sod-buster who planned to take him straight back out to the plains. Though the sod-buster seemed a decent sort, I found I couldn't bear to watch the mule be led away at the end of a rope. The sale brought my assets up to thirty-three dollars plus the worn-out bedroll and the pocketknife. I considered visiting the land office to try and inquire about the plot my pa had died supposedly possessing, but I couldn't even formulate the question I would ask, or how I would know if the answer was correct.

I sold the knife for two more dollars and gave the bedroll to a ragman for fifty cents, and found myself for the first time in my life with more money than sense. My whole body ached, and I suddenly craved to be indoors worse than I had ever craved anything in the world. It was as if the miles had been waiting until the last possible moment to make themselves known through every bone that had carried me this far. The wind felt like sandpaper against my cheeks, the dirt from the street caking between my toes like mold on old bread.

Working my way south down the main street, I was turned out of seven hotels before I found one that would rent a room to a raggedy, barefooted orphan. I had never stayed in a hotel before, which must have been obvious for I was forced to pay an entire fortnight's room and board in advance. Key in hand, I shut the door to my little room, and at the sight of a real bed—neither a roll of threadbare blankets nor a loud, itchy cornhusk pallet—I stood in the middle of the floor and wept. Then I lay down and slept clear through to the next morning, when I was woken by the *thunk* of the key fob falling from my balled fist.

I ran through every dime I had without ever once leaving the hotel. On waking each morning I'd slither into my dress, a hand-me-down that had started out too big in Arkansas and become a faded pink sack during my travels, and patter down to the dining room. The hotel was little more than a flophouse, but there was a real cook, of sorts, and I think he took pity on me. My days began with great, steaming mugs of coffee with enough cream to make my spoon stand upright, four or five fried eggs layered over thick slabs of toast spread with sun-colored butter, fat glossy sausages with chunks of peppercorn tucked here and there. I ate as though I were packing my soul back into my body, as though I would never be served again. I thrilled at every meat that wasn't possum or squirrel or the meanest hen in a worn-out flock. I'd never mastered the baking of wheat bread, so every slice that crackled and puffed between my teeth was like a fresh start, a sign that I hadn't been dreaming.

Momentarily sated, I'd drift back upstairs and send for a hot bath, ordering buckets of steaming water for hours until I wrinkled up like a little old witch. In those murky, soapy waters I alternated between tears and a buzzy, soft blankness, my head like a hive of woolen bees, letting the misery and terror of that prairie crossing and all that had come before it well up through my chest until it had no place to go but out through my face. When my tears were spent I stared at the sky outside my window or at my callused, crooked toes. As the days passed, I watched years' worth of dirt soak out of them until they grew soft and pink, the nails whitening to milky crescents.

When I wasn't in the tub—and often when I was—I was eating. Hunger wasn't new, of course, but it had always been a source of worry. Now, with my meals paid ahead and the anonymous cook on my side, every whisper of appetite was of interest to me, an invitation to think about not what I lacked but what I would soon have before me. I ate accordingly: double portions of stew to be dabbed at with thick, crumbly biscuits; two or three chops at a time nestled in a lean-to shape against a hillock of steaming potatoes studded with salt crystals; greens boiled silky and toad-colored twining with beans that smelled of molasses and hid chewy burnt ends. I kept bright apples and stout wedges of cheese on my nightstand, let the big crumbs from hunks of cornbread pock into my bathwater, washed everything down with cool buttermilk. With each meal and each well and flow of tears, a bit of gnawing urgency lifted, and gradually I began to feel my feet on the ground once more. In the course of those two weeks, I quite literally ate myself out of house and home: on the fifteenth morning, the self-styled hotelier rapped on my door and demanded either more money or my room key. Having no choice, I turned over the key, loath to take to the streets once more. Now that I had tasted a life of full meals and relatively clean sheets, I hated to give it up.

Outside, I snarled at the dust that leapt up from the thoroughfare like a cloud of fleas to cling in all the deep, familiar places. Lacking any better ideas, I took up the work I knew: doing other people's chores. For a month or so I scrubbed floors, chopped wood, and suffered mightily under the sour gaze of a Mrs. Mackey in her boardinghouse, which overlooked the cattle depot and stank of cow shit. She insisted that I wear a pair of her now-grown son's old boots, which chafed and blistered me while their imagined cost came out of my wages. We hated each other immediately, and though she considered herself a Christian woman for keeping me out of the whorehouses, it only took a week for her to start clouting me with a broom handle whenever she'd a mind to. I tried to bear it as I had borne such things before, but the attic pallet was hard, the food tasteless and insufficiently portioned. More than that, I think something inside me was plumb worn out. I had already spent too much of my life hauling and scrubbing under the pinched face of some stingy matron, and Mrs. Mackey's violent condescension turned out to be the last straw. One day I lost my temper, and when she reared back for a second blow with a stick of firewood I swung the soup ladle I was holding and caught her right on the point of her chin—next thing I knew, I was out on my ass.

For a day and a night I wandered Dodge, taking the place in anew. Though I maybe should have been scared—I was dead broke and fresh out of ideas—the activity that surged and swayed all around filled me with a giddy buoyancy. Everywhere I went, there was music in the air as each saloon's piano strove to be the loudest and most cheerful; every few seconds I'd pass an open door that issued bursts of laughter and conversation like jets of steam from a locomotive. I clung to the shadows but couldn't tear my eyes away. There was every type of person to be seen, though whores and cowboys dominated on the south side of the tracks. The cowboys all shifted from foot to foot just like their horses, while the whores flashed their eyes and showed their teeth, snuggling brightly corseted tits up into their tricks' faces. The street I wandered alternated between mud slick and dust storm, while a rainbow of smells rolled out from between the buildings: now pipe smoke, now piss, now onions frying, all layered over a miasma of dung and cow hair that clung low to the ground. People were coming and going in every direction, and things didn't start to slow until the first gray streaks of dawn crept up from a horizon that seemed very, very far off. By then my wanderings had brought me to the train depot, where I found an out-of-the-way bench and curled up around my empty stomach, too tired to be scared. I slept a few hours until the stationmaster rousted me out, and found myself once more adrift and hungry.

I spent the morning watching the hands work the cattle. There's pleasure to be had in seeing a task properly completed, and despite the noise there was an order to it I admired. It seemed two herds had gotten mixed up into one pen, and the crew were cutting one out to load into boxcars bound for Chicago. There was a terrible racket of the stock lowing and hawing at each other, layered under the yips of the cowboys, who eased their mounts between the cows, shouting and popping at them with their quirts. The cowboys were young and friendly-looking, most not much older than myself, tanned and bright-eyed under their hats. They rode as easily as most people walked, as if each man and his horse were a single creature with four legs and two heads. Every now and then one would spot me watching and duck his chin; the bolder ones tipped their hats, and when I finally smiled back at one, his fellows exploded into a shower of hoots and joshing.

"Well, they sure like you," said a voice over my shoulder.

I started and turned around to see a woman, still young, with black hair pulled up under a smart little top hat. She wasn't tall, but she didn't need to be; under her arched brows, deep-brown eyes held me in sway with a steady gaze that clearly ducked to no one. Her rouged lips looked like a piece of heart-shaped candy, complimented by a deep-red dress that looked far too fine to be worn out in all this dust. I'd never seen anyone so stylish in all my life.

"I . . . I suppose I don't know," I stammered, feeling very young and shabby before her, relieved to be shod.

She chuckled. "Oh, yes you do. They like you plenty, and what's more you know it." I said nothing, and she approached, closing the gap between us in two steps while she looked me up and down. She reached out for a loose lock of my hair, rubbing it between her gloved fingers as if I were a bolt of cloth she might buy. She was looking right into my face, scanning it carefully. I was used to having a woman look me over, but usually it was to judge whether I could lift her Dutch oven out of the fireplace. This one was looking for something else. Like a deer, I found myself getting very still, waiting for a sign as to what I should do next.

"You are a pretty thing," she said. "That red hair of yours sure stands out." She dropped the lock and grabbed my upper arm, running her hand down to my wrist with a series of light squeezes. "You're skinny, though. We'll have to feed you up. What's your name?"

"Bridget," I rasped.

"Bridget what?"

"Shaughnessy."

"You a church-going gal, Bridget Shaughnessy?"

"No, ma'am, not especially."

"Good." She stepped back and took one more look at me, clearly making up her mind. "Well, Bridget, I'm Lila. You looking for work?"

"What kind of work?"

"What kind do you think? Pretty girl like you all on her own."

I said nothing and toed at the dirt between us.

"You look hungry," Lila continued. "Ain't you ready to do a little sporting yet? Or do you want to wait a spell for your prospects to worsen?" She cocked her head like a crow fixing to split open a snail shell.

At that I looked up. "What do you mean?"

"I know we're only just acquainted, but it ain't hard to see you're at the ass end of an ass-kicking," she said. "Or do you have a wealthy suitor stashed up one of those ratty sleeves?"

"Don't suppose I do," I said, twisting my fingers together.

"What's the matter, you disdainful of whoring?"

"Everyone has to eat," I said truthfully.

"Yourself included." She paused to let that sink in, while the scraps of a few sermons I'd heard here and there tussled with my empty belly.

"Tell you what," said Lila. "You come on with me, say hello to Kate, and at least we can get a plate of food into you. I hate to see a girl starve, and you look just about ready to turn scarecrow if we don't get some bacon into you. Maybe a couple of fried eggs, some biscuits? With blackberry jam?" She drew out the *m* of *jam* into a warm little hum, and when she cocked her head the other way I got my first taste of Lila's wry, knowing smile. I remembered the promise I'd made to myself out by the spring and was ready to offer my assent, but before I could speak for myself, my stomach yowled like a cat getting stuffed into a gunnysack. Lila laughed.

"Come on, Bridget," she said, and turned to walk away, beckoning me to follow. Unable to think of a reason not to, I trotted after Lila, out of the cattle yard, up the main drag, and into the Buffalo Queen Saloon.

CHAPTER 3

"Well, look at you, Strawberry Pie," said Kate. Lila's business partner tilted her head, appraising me such that I felt an urge to pull my lips back, prove that I had all my teeth. She looked older than Lila by at least ten years, with full eyebrows and a heavy jaw that came to a perfect square at the joint; gently waving hair was swept up into a pale brown cloud on top of her head. She patted my face and reached around to pull on the bit of twine at the end of my braid to work her fingers through my hair, spreading it loose over my shoulders. The touch was so intimate that it shocked me to stillness; Kate took a handful of my curls and lifted them up for a closer look, and for a moment I thought she was about to smell them. "Good eye, Lila," she added as she stepped back. "She ought to do very nicely."

I saw Lila stretch her neck to preen a little, though she said nothing.

"What about that Sallie, any word?" said Kate.

"Got a letter at the post office, said there was a spot of business to take care of, but she'll be along soon as she can," said Lila.

We were in the upstairs room of the saloon that served as Kate's office, bedroom, and receiving parlor. Slow piano music seeped up through the floorboards like smoke. Hoping to hide my inexperience, I'd stolen but one or two glances as we'd passed through the barroom below and come away with fleeting images: afternoon sunlight glancing off rows of bottles and warming the polished wood of the bar, a couple of girls in red dresses sitting with their chins in their hands, unlit lamps whose globes were black with soot. As we passed the girls, Lila had paused to tug a loose lock of brown hair tumbling down the back of one girl's skinny neck with a sharp admonition to tidy herself up, or didn't she want to make any money tonight.

Now in the parlor Lila had retreated somewhat, letting her partner take over. The shades were drawn against the heat of the day; in the gloom I stood on the carpet before a settee whose crimson upholstery had only just begun to sprout loose threads around the edges, while Lila rummaged through a trunk of red dresses and white underclothes, a tumble of lace and calico from which she plucked up bits and pieces.

"It's a good thing Lila found you before some other shady character came along," said Kate. She circled me, leading with her hips rather than her legs to walk, so that her skirt swung in wide, lazy bell-rings that brushed over the floor. "We're a lot fairer than most of the other jokers you'd meet out on the thoroughfare. Lucky for us too—our last redhead lit out for Chicago, though to be fair she was only pinkish," she chuckled.

"And sickly to boot," Lila added without looking up. "You sickly, Bridget?"

"Not a day in my life," I piped, holding Kate's eye. It occurred to me that she must once have been quite striking; now something in her seemed blurred, smudged like a newspaper photograph that had been thumbed over too many times. In looking me over she seemed to be relying more on experience than sharpness, but even this came as a respite, for I had known so little gentleness in my time.

Kate completed her circle and held me out at arm's length, looking into my face again. "Have you done this type of work before?" she asked.

"Not as late," I replied, trying to sound like a sophisticate rather than a liar. Out of the wind, the still air was like a blanket and I could feel myself getting warm.

Kate raised one eyebrow. "No matter," she said. "These cowboys are going to eat you up—you look like all their fellows' little sisters. Still, we'd best give you a tryout, make sure everything's where it ought to be." She looked over at Lila. "Whose turn is it?"

"Langley's," said Lila, holding up a crumpled chemise. She spat on the cloth and rubbed at a spot with her thumbnail. "But I think he's indisposed today."

Kate sighed. "Roscoe, then?"

Lila nodded. "I'll fetch him." She draped the chemise over the back of one of Kate's parlor chairs and opened the door, letting in a breath of piano music and the smell of bacon frying downstairs, and stuck her head out. "Roscoe!" she shouted.

"Yeah?" came a man's voice from below.

"Come on up here!" Lila answered. The piano music stopped and I heard boots clomping up the stairs. My stomach, already knotted, pulled tighter.

"What's going on?" I asked Kate.

She wrinkled her brow slightly in bemusement. "My dear, we can't just take you in and turn you out without so much as a taste for the house."

"Turn me out?"

She shook her head and turned to Lila. "She is greener than a Texas springtime, isn't she," she said, with another chuckle and a small shake of her head.

Lila shrugged. "Well, do we or don't we need a redhead?"

"We do," said Kate. She looked at me. "Don't mind her. She just likes to remind me that we run a brothel, not an orphanage."

"Damn right we don't," said Lila, casting a sharp eye at me. Roscoe appeared in the doorway. He had the strong shoulders and rounded middle that mark all men whose days of heavy work are behind them, with a dark walrus mustache and brows that seemed to glower, but when I looked at his eyes they were soft, and I realized he was just squinting at me in the half dark, clutching his hat in both hands like he was about to ask my ma if I could come out and play when my chores were done.

"Well, Roscoe, what do you think?" said Lila.

"She's a pretty one all right," said Roscoe.

"We think so too, but we oughtn't to turn her out untried. Care for a slice of pie?" At being talked of so crassly I felt a new fold crease in my stomach but held my ground; whatever they had in mind, it scared me far less than going back out onto the street with an empty belly.

"Well hell, I never say no to that," said Roscoe. He set his hat down on the end table and strode right past me to the bed, loosening his sweat-mottled cravat as he went. I twisted to watch him go by. He had his shirt pulled up halfway over his head before anyone said anything.

"Well, go on, Roscoe won't bite," said Kate.

My feet didn't seem to want to lift just yet. "You want me to . . ."

"You want to work? We won't beg, you know. It's up to you."

I looked back over at the bed, next to which stood Roscoe, now with his naked back to me, showing a shoulder-thatch of dark hair. I felt a strange splitting in that moment; my head filled with a loud, even buzz that blocked out all thought, while my feet carried me toward the bed like a fish on a line. I still wonder about that moment, in which I acted but have no recollection of volition. Maybe it was the way that the still air felt warm around me as the wind outside never could, or maybe it was the first time I'd really acted at no one's mercy but my own, or maybe I was just hungry. Whatever it was, it pulled me, and as I walked toward the bed I was only mildly surprised to feel my hands reaching up behind me to unbutton my dress.

"Just to the petticoats will do," said Lila from behind me. "You ain't gotta get all the way down to your skin."

"Leave them be," Kate said.

"Well, we ain't got all day."

"Don't spoil the moment." I glanced back to see Lila roll her eyes while Kate swatted gently at her arm. Though still mostly clothed, I'd never felt more naked in my entire life.

Roscoe must have seen it in my face. He was out of his shirt and trousers and stripped down to the waist, the sleeves of his union suit dangling like offal around his knees while its lowest buttons strained over a bulge I tried not to notice. He held out his hand to me and I took it, letting him guide me onto the counterpane like a princess who'd been married off to a wild boar. "Don't fret about them," he said. He shoved my petticoats up around my waist and leaned back to let me wriggle out of my drawers. The open air on my snatch made me jump a little, but not nearly so much as Roscoe's hamsteak palm, which was soft and slightly damp as it traveled up my thigh and he pulled himself forward.

I'll admit the sensations were strange that first time through, but once he got into a rhythm, Roscoe was easy to ignore. There was a cluster of knotholes on a ceiling beam that I gazed at absently while he set his post; together they looked like the face of a badger, or a spray of daisies in a jar. At one point I lifted my head and looked over Roscoe's heaving shoulder, where I caught glimpses of Kate and Lila, who were watching us intently from the settee.

"Act like you like it," Roscoe whispered in my ear.

I wasn't quite sure what acting like I liked it entailed, so I took a guess, wrapping one arm around his fuzzy shoulder and placing the other on the back of his head, and kissed the side of his face. It seemed to work: he pushed himself in deeper, forcing a series of corresponding little moans out of my mouth, and I saw Kate and Lila exchange the smallest of glances just before he was brought to bear by my innocent charms and, with a pause and a sigh, slumped off to one side.

I lay on the bedspread while he wriggled back into his clothes. He picked up his hat on the way out and tipped it to me, then Kate and Lila, from the doorway. I propped myself up on my elbows and pushed back a lock of stray hair that his sweat had glued to my forehead.

"Can I have some dinner now, please?" I asked.

They cackled in harmony at my question. "What did I tell you?" said Lila, grabbing at Kate's arm. "Did I find us a natural or didn't I?"

"Not quite," said Kate. "A real natural would have got herself fed before, not after."

They both broke into fresh fits while I buttoned myself back up. From below, I could hear the music resuming, sprightly as a new morning.

A couple of hours later I was at last full-bellied—fried eggs, bacon, and biscuits with blackberry jam, as promised. Seated before a cloudy mirror in my new room, Lila showed me how to put the finishing touches on my face. I dabbed a ringless ring finger into a pot of rouge that smelled of wax and rotting peaches and pressed a gentle blush into the center of my lower lip before sitting back to admire the effect. As Lila had said, I was very pretty, though I hadn't had use for it before. Skinny though I was from rough living, I was strong as a pony, with a scatter of chicken-feed prairie freckles and a head of thick, bright-red hair. I'd never painted my face before either, and was astonished to see that it took just a dab to make me look fresh as the dew, like the type of gal to run and play with the boys even after she'd been scolded to walk like a lady.

"Sit up straight," said Lila from behind me. In the glass, I saw her approach and place her hands on my shoulders, pulling them back. "Didn't your mama teach you nothing? You slouch like a farmhand."

"She died having me, so she didn't have time to teach me much," I said.

"Well, let that be a lesson to you," said Lila. She bent down so our faces were reflected side by side in the glass. "After every screw you wash up good in that basin. If you get in the family way we'll fix you up, but the sooner you say something, the better, you hear?" She licked her finger and smoothed my eyebrows into two smooth flashes, like markings on the face of a bird. I nodded but clenched my jaw under her touch; if she noticed, she said nothing.

I kept my gaze on my reflection, mesmerized. But for translucent shadows in store windows, I hadn't seen this much of myself in a long time. The trials of the crossing had put a touch of age to my face that suited me. Hunger had brought out cheekbones that I'd never lose, while grief and worry had given my eyes a deep-down shine that lent dimension to any merriment that crossed them. Taken all together, I looked pert but world-weary, utterly irresistible.

Beside my own, Lila's face looked waxen in the lamplight. "Look for Constance downstairs—dark hair, probably reading something. She'll show you the ropes." She released my shoulders and stood up to go.

The saloon was just waking up when I came out of my room a moment later. The barroom was dim, and there were a couple of drunks snoozing before the hearth, where the fire had burned down to a low crackle. At one of the card tables, a soft-shouldered man in a blue suit was shuffling a deck of cards that snapped gently when he flicked them. Roscoe was idling at the keys, clearly more of a mind to amuse himself than entertain anyone. He nodded when he saw me but said nothing.

I paused at the foot of the stairs while my eyes sought out a round-faced whore with a bundle of brown curls massed around her head.

She was sitting at the end of the bar reading a clothbound book, from which she looked up as I approached.

"Are you Constance?" I asked.

She snapped her book shut and looked me over. "I suppose I am," she said. "Are you the new girl?" She spoke crisply, like a governess.

"I'm Bridget," I said.

"How do you do, Bridget. Have you done this type of work before?" she asked.

"No."

"Have you been married?" As she spoke, the book-holding hand rooted around her crimson skirts until it finally found a pocket. She smoothed her lap and smiled blandly.

"No."

"Have you had a sweetheart?"

"No."

"Aren't you the conversationalist. Not even a secret beau your pa didn't know about?"

I shook my head. Constance's brow furrowed slightly; she had a small scar on her forehead that gave her frown a little F-shape in the center of her face.

"Well, I can't imagine why even Kate would want a girl so untried as that, though we have been in want of a redhead," she said. "Is that what possessed her to take you on?"

Taken aback at her directness, I felt compelled to defend myself. "I been tried," I said, remembering Roscoe's meaty shoulder bobbing in and out of my field of vision.

"Roscoe doesn't count," said Constance, as if reading my mind. She leaned in half a degree. "Did he tell you to act like you liked it?"

I nodded, swallowing.

Something in her face softened. "He said the same to me," she said, patting my forearm, which looked scrawny under her plump, well-fed hand.

"Well, I may be new, but as long as I'm fed and housed, I'll give it my all," I said stoutly.

Constance laughed, bright and clear like a school bell, and the blandness lifted from her smile like dust being shaken from a frock coat. "You don't have to give it all that," she said. "These jackasses don't want your all anyway. Just stick your tits out and laugh at their jokes, and you'll be fine. Stay by me a few nights, I'll see you through. If you don't mind the tedium, this is the easiest money you'll ever make."

Maybe that first night at the Buffalo Queen should have been special, but it was so typical of the nights that followed that but for the timing I probably wouldn't remember it at all. My first trick, like many who followed, was a cowboy who claimed he was the top hand in his outfit. I'd just as soon he'd said nothing as try to brag—his voice was drowned out by the sound of his boots clumping up the stairs behind me, sounding so much deeper than the secondhand high-button shoes Lila had put me in. There was a little swirl of dust as he hung up his coat on the peg behind my door, and another puff as his hat followed. He paid up without hesitation, and I didn't even take my dress off, just lay back on the counterpane and let him set to. When he was finished, I lay still on the bed while he tugged and wriggled back into his trousers. He was too shy to say anything, though like Roscoe he did tip his hat before slipping out the door. I waited a moment, wondering if I should feel different. Like all young girls I'd had a lecture or two on the preciousness of my virtue, and thought perhaps I would mourn its loss, but instead I found myself counting up all the things I hadn't had even just this morning. My belly was full, with more good smells coming from the kitchen downstairs; I could hear a trail of piano music overlaying a growing thrum of activity. There was money on my washstand, which I sat up and counted, letting the coins clink back and forth in my palm before I slid them into my pocket.

It was early yet, and when I came back downstairs, Constance was waiting for me with Lila and a skinny, whey-faced whore named Arabella.

"Are you all in one piece?" asked Constance.

"She better not be," said Lila; Arabella snorted, holding a handkerchief to her lips.

"Nothing to it," I said. Looking at the faces of my new comrades, I felt like I'd learned some astonishing secret. Did every woman know about this?

Lila nodded, hands on hips. "Right, then. You mind me, and if I'm not around you mind Constance, you hear?"

I nodded, and Lila sashayed back toward the staircase. In passing she smacked my rear, then lifted her palm and looked at it, as though it were stained. "You'd best plump up, skinny-bones," she said.

Constance looked past me to watch her go, then reached over the bar for a bottle, pouring me a little glass of amber whiskey.

"Usually when the house pours we just get cold tea," she said. "No use getting drunk on the job. But I say you've had a long day and you deserve a little something."

And so my first poke for hire was capped with my first swallow of whiskey, which I will say I liked a damn sight better. Though it burned and made my throat thicken up, as soon as it was down I felt warm and mellow, like a horse settling into an easy trot he can keep up for miles. Then the front door opened, new strangers came in, and the night went on.

CHAPTER 4

I took to whorehouse life like a duck takes to water, and within a couple of weeks I was all settled in at the Buffalo Queen. There was a lot that was new to me, and a lot to like: the late nights, the music, the liquor, the being around girls my own age, the strangeness of men. Whoring is like any profession in that there's a knack to it, and it turned out I had the knack. To me, men were like horses, mostly alike but for some notable distinctions, and I cultivated expertise with an eye to increasing my profits. I approached each night's barroom herd like a horse trader appraising new stock: this one looked skittish but could be tamed down with gentle words, this one would balk at a tight rein but run easy under a little slack, that one was likely to kick and not to be ridden at any price.

I could spend some time telling tales of the men I sold pokes to, but when I think of it, there's not much to tell. Though I liked living at the saloon and the encounters ranged from pleasant to awkward, I mostly found the act itself pretty unremarkable. The Buffalo Queen was just expensive enough to weed out the most scraggly and virginal of frolickers: our trade skewed toward tradesmen, cavalry officers, the top hands of a given cow outfit. To me, they were largely a series of hats and mustaches—one set of boots clomping up the stairs behind you sounds very like another. But though they mostly blurred together, there were always a few tricks I liked just as fellows. Many of my buyers had a tendency to blurt out truths if I let them linger a few minutes after the deed was done, which baffled me at first. Some cowboy would lie out full-length while his tool pulled back into itself like a judge shrugging his coat on after adjourning the court, and before I knew it I'd be hearing about how much this one missed his mama back in Texas, how that one's brother drowned crossing a herd through a river, or how some other just wished his fellows wouldn't josh him so bad. At first I marveled at these disclosures. I hadn't known much about men going in, but I'd always thought of them as a rather secretive bunch. As I got used to it, though, I started comparing notes with Constance and some of the other gals, who confirmed that in such moments some just come over all chatty. I didn't mind, and in fact would have liked to talk to a few of them for longer—though my own travels had been difficult, my ears kept pricking up at mention of farther places, my neck craned to glimpse at imagined horizons. But Lila had a sixth sense that would invariably have her rapping on the door within a few minutes of the act's completion, and she was right that I had work to do.

Though the Queen formally belonged to Kate, it was Lila who ran the whoring operation much of the time. Kate herself would mostly stand on the balcony, observing the night's action and sipping daintily from a glass of brandy laced with laudanum, or entertain important customers in her private parlor. But once or twice per evening she'd descend to sweep through the crowd. "This is the Buffalo Queen," she'd declare grandly, eyes blurred, "where every time is a good time." She'd sail around in the barroom with all the triumphant serenity of a swan, patting everyone she passed on the arm, the cheek, the backside; patting people seemed to be the main thing she did.

Still, between the two of them they ran a good house: Kate created an atmosphere, while Lila kept a sharp eye out for laziness or lack of economy. Us girls were all turned out in low-cut dresses of sturdy, bright-red calico, showing off cleavage that ranged from floury to toasted so that when we stood all together our tits looked like a rack of fresh loaves in a baker's window. More important, the red dresses made us easy to spot in the crowd so Lila could keep us from bunching up when we should have been circulating to drum up business. Not that it took much drumming—most of our callers were half-wild from the trails and would've trooped upstairs with a possum if one had flashed a little collarbone. But we'd swirl through the room, laughing too loudly and smiling too much, feeling half-crazy until it got late, helping Kate bring to life her vision of the Queen as an opulent New Orleans bordello on the plains, despite all the dust. To her mind's eye, we were turned out in satin and silks, balancing glasses of champagne between our fingers instead of slinging shot glasses up to our mouths; in our rooms she seemed to imagine us unbuttoning trousers that required no breaking in, made as they were of fine wool rather than duck canvas. This dreaminess was infectious, and more than once I caught myself trying to act the part Kate had imagined for me.

The place wasn't large, but it was well laid out so that it always felt the right amount of full and the music could be heard everywhere. Around three sides of the barroom ran a catwalk lined with eight small rooms that us girls occupied and worked out of, Kate's parlor, and an adjoining room for Lila. The only way up to or down from the rooms was a big staircase that plopped everyone right in the center of the bar. Coming down the stairs, the gamblers took the left-hand side, dominated by the big stone hearth, while the piano and the drinkers took the right. Kate and Lila were known the full length of the cattle trails for keeping a houseful of the prettiest girls in Dodge, but they made sure no one could get up to any mischief without the opportunity of a drink or a game before or after, preferably both.

Like any whorehouse, girls came and went, but a few steadies hung on. There was Constance, who despite being the oldest and openly bookish pulled in more money than any of us, while still finding time to screw the roaming gambler who ran the poker game. Arabella was pale and consumptive-looking, her wan appeal being well ahead of its time; nothing pleased her, but no one paid her displeasure any mind. Henrietta chirped and giggled like a sparrow while keeping herself busy as a whole flock. Then there were others who stopped a spell: merry Jennie, selfish Mariella, lazy Anne-Marie, Betsy the gossip. They'd earn too little or aggravate Lila or get bored with the place and be up and gone one day. It wasn't hard finding replacements: as I well knew, gals without prospects were falling off trains and wagons every day, and picking them up was as easy as picking up apples after a windstorm.

But it takes more than girls to run a brothel, and Kate kept the place well-staffed. There were the bear-sized twins, Virgil and Bartholomew; Bart cooked while Virgil watched the card tables, and they shared the duty of pouring drinks and seeing after us girls. Roscoe and Langley shared responsibility for the piano, though Roscoe did the vast majority of the actual playing. Langley was a dope fiend who spent most of his time lolled out somewhere or other until he got just the right amount of loaded to roll up and shove Roscoe off the piano stool. He looped through the same repertoire of dance hall songs and old favorites, but it was clear from the fluency of his playing that he had once been quite accomplished. His was the only laziness that was ever forgiven, for he was Kate's brother-in-law, and no one never spoke of the late sister who'd left them with naught but each other. And then there was Grace, who swept the floors and kept our washbasins full, rarely speaking or even looking up as she worked, the better to hide a long, glossy scar that pulled her mouth much too far up one cheek.

"What happened to her anyway?" I asked Constance one afternoon. Virgil had brought a crate of apples back to the Queen, and we were sharing one; I speared a fine slice on the tip of my paring knife and pointed it at Grace's retreating back as she stumped out to the yard under a bundle of soiled sheets.

"You mean her face?" Constance plucked the slice from my blade and popped it into her mouth.

I nodded.

"She used to be a whore," said Constance. "If you look between that scar and her frown, you'll see that she's quite pretty. Or was. Sharp as a tack too."

"Oh?" I mumbled around another slice while cutting one for Constance, who took it.

"Thank you. And yes, very much so."

"So what happened?"

Constance sighed and looked at her hands. "Bad trick. It didn't happen here—this was before, when she worked at the Emerald."

I'd heard about the Emerald: it was up the street from the Queen, a big, grand-looking place with games of chance and a full fifteen girls working the men. I couldn't imagine how anyone got a moment's peace around there—such a thing was hard enough to find at the Queen, and there were only the eight of us to stir each other up.

"What'd he do to her?"

"I never got the full story, just that he took a knife to her, and now she looks like that."

She let that settle for a moment. I hadn't taken my eyes off the back door through which Grace had disappeared. I tried to picture the scene of her attack but could only conjure bits and pieces: Grace's hard, blue eyes, a torn camisole, the flash of a skinning knife. Even the blood—and there must have been plenty—eluded my imagination.

"That's a damned shame," I said eventually. It was true, but mostly I just wanted to break the silence.

"It is," said Constance. "And to top it off, her pimp threw her out."

"He didn't," I said.

"He did. Most places would," said Constance. She pinched at the air between us to request another apple slice, which I gave her.

"Seems awfully hard," I said.

"This is a hard business," said Constance. "And a ruined girl is bad for the atmosphere. She turned up on our doorstep and Kate took pity on her, so now she does the housework. And I'm sure Lila finds her useful; those sharp eyes make her good at telling tales."

"Guess I better watch my step, then," I said, not knowing if I was referring to the tricks or to Grace.

"Couldn't hurt," said Constance, biting into the last slice.

I'm fairly certain Constance was the most intelligent person I've ever known. She'd been at the Queen for just over a year before I arrived, and though it was her first foray into perdition, she too had the knack, and more than earned her weekly cut. She'd come from Virginia; her parents had been great believers in education, and Constance's was excellent. They were abolitionists who had got through the war in one piece only to be swept away by flood a few years later, and Constance's inheritance with them. All but starving and in need of a fresh start, she'd married a Yankee coffin-maker and let him take her west, where she kept the accounts for his respectable-enough shop on the north side of Dodge. Then he took a fever and died, and shortly thereafter Constance had discovered she'd been married to a secret gambler who'd mortgaged the coffin shop to finance his habit. When the debts were paid and everything lost their service, she took off her widow's weeds and marched right up to the Buffalo Queen to ask for work.

All of us were allowed to play cards, but Constance was the only one who was really good at it. I only met Pierre, the Queen's soft-shouldered poker dealer, once before he took off on what Constance said were his habitual summer wanderings, leaving her to look up from her book and gaze out the window when she thought no one was watching. Under his tutelage she'd grown into an honest-to-goodness card sharp: to please herself, she'd win big pots, chuckling with glee, then strategically let the tricks take most of it back to smooth things over. What she did keep she liked to save up, then send off to booksellers in Chicago and St. Louis, posing as a lonely bluestocking schoolteacher marooned in a sea of ignorance. It was so close to true that they'd ship out heaving crates of books at a steep discount, and she was never without a volume tucked into her dress pocket. If a spare moment appeared, she'd pop it open and snatch a few pages the way most girls grab a smoke.

"What do you do that for?" I asked her one time, after a couple of weeks of watching her flip some novel open and shut eight or nine times a night. We'd found a few minutes for a break and were out behind the Queen, sheltered in the alley between the street and the outhouse. The wind in Dodge never let up, and even such a rank shelter as that was a welcome alternative to either the smoky fug of the saloon or the whipping blasts off the plains.

She looked up at the navy-blue sky, just a strip between the rooflines, and thought a moment before answering me. "Some time ago, when I was a little younger than you are now, I realized I've only the one life to live. It rankled me then, and it rankles me now," she said. "At least this way I can taste a few others."

"Well, why don't you win big and take off? See the world? You could get yourself a wagon and paint 'Constance, the Traveling Whore' on the side—from the sound of it Pierre would be more than happy to drive you around."

"I have thought about it," she said. "But I've done all the traveling I care to for a time. It wouldn't bestow any more life upon me, and what's more would risk the loss of this one I have, to which I have only lately become accustomed."

That was the thing about Constance: she loved to leave a person with some strange thought to chew over. It was a kindness, really, for her pronouncements gave me something to think about while my tricks were getting their money's worth. Still, she found ways to share what she had, reading to me now and then if we found a quiet moment at the same time. I'd mend camisoles or brush out her hair while she read aloud, or just curl up like a kitten and listen. It was a treat to hear someone read with ease. Pa had been neglectful of my education, and though I could read and spell a bit, I was nowhere close to Constance's fluency with the written word. She read beautifully, with subtle voices for the characters, speeding up and slowing down to set the mood. My favorite was *Ragged Dick,* for he was plucky in ways I understood, but Constance found his cheerful adventures tiresome and generally confined us to the parlors and ballrooms of far-off rich people.

And so, as the spring outside melted into summer, my life settled into a comfortable routine. I'd wake around noon and spend the early afternoon puttering away at easy chores with the girls. Mending dresses and brushing a deep shine into my hair was quite an improvement over shoveling hay and scrubbing sheets; in no time at all my skinny, trail-worn body plumped out like a pigeon. During the daytime, my life felt round and snug. Midafternoons Bart would feed us a plate of something hearty, after which it was time to truss up into our work clothes, layer cakes of bleached muslin under sleeveless red dresses that buttoned up the front, high black stockings, button shoes that my feet only resisted for a week or two before they too melted like butter into the relative ease of their new circumstances. By the time we were all dressed and drifting back downstairs, someone would have struck up a tune, and the night's first revelers would be ready for a drink, a joke, and a poke, as we called it. We'd laugh and chatter and fuck until two or four in the morning, throwing back shots of cold tea until my teeth clattered around in my skull like dice. But I'd just toss my copper curls and give a little lip, and the tricks would take me for spirited, which was very popular out on the trails.

Along with everything else that Lila brought into my life when she picked me up that day—friends, a full belly, not having to fetch my own wash-water—I had something else I'd never had before Dodge: money. Living with my pa it had been impossible to amass more than a few dollars before he'd ferret it out to go on a spree. In those days, cash had made me feel like a corporal at the end of a long campaign, down to his last few foot soldiers, knowing each mud-streaked, battle-worn face as well as my own. Now, by the grace of Lila and the sweat of my brow, I was a general, commanding whole battalions of dollars and cents. Every Saturday morning when our week's earnings were tallied I'd shut the door to my room and lay my growing wealth out on the quilt-top, proudly inspecting my troops on their parade ground. I've run across more than a few people in my time who've never been poor, easily made for the way they throw dollars away like cannon fodder. But I never lost the field commander's intimacy: though I had more than I'd ever had before, I knew each piece individually for the labor it represented.

Not that I was mean with what I had. Every whorehouse contains a labyrinth of debts owed and repaid, sometimes in coin and sometimes in kind. Arabella made almost a full second income off the interest on loans to sporting girls all over the south side of town; when I asked her how she did it she just sniffed and refolded her handkerchief. Meanwhile Henrietta, merry spendthrift that she was, would always come knocking for a half dollar for the bathhouse, which she usually paid back by covering for me when I stepped outside at night. Rather, like a general without a war to fight, it was on myself that I didn't know how to spend my hard-earned cash. The first week I only made a few dollars, Kate and Lila having taken a larger-than-usual cut for turning me out and training me for nothing, but I didn't mind. Bed and board paid for, I took my silver dollars down to a dry goods and came back with three full bags of candy, which I ate all at once in a sugared frenzy. The result was a stomach-twisting afternoon and an evening of smiling wanly into the faces of tricks who thought I was addled when in fact I was trying desperately not to be sick on their boots.

The following payday, Constance took me in hand. She shuffled me down to the bathhouse, where we soaked side by side in twin copper tubs. My last real bath had been in the hotel after coming off the plains, when I'd soaked and cried until the bathwater had been mostly tears. I told Constance about it and she nodded her approval, eyes closed, scrunched down so her chin was touching the water.

"Best place to get some thinking done," she said.

"Or to think about nothing," I replied.

"I prefer both at once when I can get to it." She'd paid the extra dollar to get us a private room, so aside from the lowing of cattle that filtered in through the walls there was no sound but a gentle lapping and splashing as we shifted in the water.

"I didn't realize your father had passed so recently," she said after a moment.

I hadn't thought about it. "I suppose he did."

"If you don't mind my asking, what was he like?"

Before me a shaft of light caught the last curl of steam from the water, turning it into a little white snake. "He was all right," I said. "Never beat on me or nothing like that. But he was a drunkard and couldn't hold on to money to save his life. I been working since I was young to keep us afloat, just chores and egg money, that sort of thing. Not a drop of foresight in him." I felt suddenly very tired thinking about him.

"He doesn't sound too bad," said Constance, looking at the same feather of steam above my knees.

"No, but real unreliable," I said. "Wept like a girl anytime he noticed how poor we were, as if it were nothing but bad luck, and then I had to dry his tears atop everything else." The water blurred before me unexpectedly.

"You can go crazy trying to care for them," she said. "I prefer working for a living."

I nodded and sniffed hard, pulling whatever had welled up in my eyes back into the sockets. There was another brief silence, broken by someone outside shouting, "Get out, you goat-fucker, and don't come back!" We both burst out laughing, watery but full-throated.

"Where'd you say you stayed when you got here?" asked Constance as we were composing ourselves, kindly changing the subject.

"Samuel's Hotel," I said, happy to take the bait. "Up the way."

"I know Samuel's," said Constance. "That's no hotel, that's a flophouse with a kitchen attached. At any rate, you ought to learn something about how to spend this money you're making. You hungry?"

"I could eat."

"Well, come on, then," she said, rising with a *whoosh*.

Underclothes still clinging in a few damp places, we made our way out through air thick with the smells of soap, wet linen, and hot copper. As we paused before the reception desk, the door to another room opened and out spilled three girls, laughing mid-conversation. Like us, they were pink-faced, looking warm as kittens. Immediately, before the thought could even form in my mind, I knew them for whores. It's only those who've lived a sheltered life who think it's face paint and flashy clothes that mark a sporting woman; in reality it's that they look right at a person when most women would duck their heads or flutter their lashes. It's a habit grown from the instinct to openly size a man up before he does the same to you; like any other habit, once established it's all but impossible to break.

One of the girls carried an almost-empty gin bottle, which was snatched away by another whose eye was blacked into a round, ripe plum. The third girl stopped short at the sight of us. "Constance?" she said. She had mousy hair, piled atop her head so haphazardly that it shook every time she moved, but her eyes were bright.

Constance looked up. "Oh, Ida," she said, and smiled. "How are you?"

Ida unslung her arm from around her friend's waist to poke a stray lock into her topknot. "Oh, same as ever," she said, then gestured toward me. "Who's this?"

"I'm Bridget," I said, stepping forward like I was saying my lines in a play. The other two looked me over.

"New gal?" said the one with the black eye.

"New as they come," I replied. To anyone else I would have pretended this wasn't the case, but just as I could tell what they were from their faces, I was sure they would have seen through any lie I told them.

"Well, you're lucky you've got Constance looking after you," said Ida. "She knows what's what."

"She sure does," I said. I looked back at the girl with the black eye who'd addressed me. "We got some comfrey growing in the yard—you need any for that eye?"

"We got some too," she said, looking away.

"That's good. My pa used to get the shit kicked out of him once or twice a week, ain't nothing like a comfrey poultice on a black eye."

"Thanks," she said again. A silence fell; I realized too late that in my eagerness to join the conversation I'd said too much, and shouldn't have brought attention to the girl's face.

"Bad night?" Constance asked.

"Just Hugh being Hugh," said the girl with the black eye. "He's been in a temper on account of the Faro dealer running off with his second-best gal."

"No," said Constance in exaggerated surprise. "Not Pauly?"

The third girl, who'd since recovered the gin bottle, piped up. "Yeah, Pauly. Run off with this gal Rachel, she was real pretty."

The girl with the black eye sniffed. "She wasn't that pretty, just played him right."

Constance grinned. "If she can play a saloon Faro dealer, she doesn't have to be pretty," she said. They all laughed at that, and I smiled, feeling something in the air ease up.

The desk man cleared his throat to get Constance's attention. "This ain't a quilting bee," he said, and pointed toward the door.

"We paid up, didn't we?" said Ida.

"And the next people will pay up just as good," said the desk man. "You gals move along."

"Yeah, yeah," said Ida. She slid her arm back around the waist of the girl with the black eye and took a swig from her other friend's bottle.

"You girls take care," said Constance.

"Thanks," said Ida. "And you," she said to the desk man, "I'm sure we'll be seeing you later." She gave him a theatrical wink while her friends blew kisses, and they turned as one toward the door. I glanced back at the desk man in time to see him blush before Constance led me back into the dust and sunlight outside.

She took me to a little restaurant off the main drag, run by a Mexican woman whose glossy hair reminded me of Lila's; she served us big plates of beans and beef stewed with chilis so tender it didn't even need a knife to cut, with fluffy cornmeal fritters and big mugs of sweet coffee. Everything was dusted with sprigs of green herbs or gratings of cinnamon, and we lingered awhile, dabbing the last swipes of sauce off our plates.

"How'd you know that gal Ida?" I asked. I'd been waiting for Constance to say something about the girls we'd met at the bathhouse, but she hadn't volunteered anything.

"She worked at the Queen for a while but couldn't make her cut. She's at the Emerald now," she said. "Ida's the one who sent Grace over to Kate after . . . well, after everything."

"And Hugh?"

"Hugh Montgomery." She all but spat the name. "He owns the place. Nothing but a jumped-up pimp. You've seen him around, I'm sure, strutting up and down the street in that ridiculous coat like he's mayor of the south side."

I had seen him, a tall man, broad-shouldered. Rain or shine, he wore a bottle-green frock coat that matched the paint on the Emerald's sign, as if anyone could take him for anything but a whoremaster. Just before sunset he liked to take a constitutional up and down the main street, pausing before the other saloons to observe the action with a frankly proprietary air. If he paused for more than a moment or two before the Queen, Lila would sense it like a bloodhound and step outside to stare him down.

"What's he beat on his girls for?" I asked. "She ain't going to make any money looking like that." After a moment I caught myself. "I mean, he oughtn't to do it anyway, of course."

Constance sighed. "Search me," she said. "But the decent men in this business are few and far between."

I had nothing to say to that; truth be told, I hadn't thought much about life in other houses, much less what it might be like to work for a man. I pictured an arm sleeved in green velvet raised up to strike at me, and suppressed a shudder. Kate and Lila never laid a hand on us, nor suffered the tricks to do so either, to the extent they could. All we had to do was turn a profit, and even on a bad week no one could expect worse than a tongue-lashing from Lila and a heavy, disappointed sigh from Kate. I'd been so caught up in my own world, watching the men come and go, learning a new trade, that I hadn't considered how lucky I was that I didn't have to guard against my keepers as well as my buyers.

"Is that true about the comfrey?" Constance broke into my reverie.

"What?"

"What you told Ida's friend, about putting it on a black eye."

I shrugged. "Of course. You didn't know that?"

Constance shrugged back. "I never learned much frontier medicine."

"Always had doctor money is what you're saying," I replied a little too fast, and Constance colored slightly.

"I didn't mean it like that," she said.

I sighed. "I know, you're just not used to rough living."

"I suppose not." She was addressing the contents of her coffee cup and I could see that she wished she hadn't said anything. Even when she annoyed me, I hated for her to feel badly.

"I still got some money left," I said by way of amends. "We got some time before we have to get back?"

"We do," she said. "And cleaned-up or not, you still look like a prairie orphan. Let's get you something a little more presentable to wear on your days off, shall we?"

. . .

She took me to a general store just north of the railroad tracks. I hadn't been that far into Dodge before; though the streets were just as dusty and the wooden sidewalks just as crowded, there was one notable difference: women. The streets on the south side belonged to men; while they wove their way from one carouse to another, it behooved us gals to stay put, waiting in our saloons and parlors like jeweled birds in candlelit cages. But here on the north side, women—wives, mothers, unwed daughters fresh as the dew—were everywhere. Respectable women in modestly dark, high-necked dresses milled about in twos and threes, in and out of stores with their parcels and string bags, while children eddied around them, dashing out and back along the sidewalks.

The change in Constance once we crossed the tracks was immediate: shoulders back, hands folded neatly before her, she tilted her head slightly downward, opposite of the jaunty angle at which she usually held her chin. Trailing after her—we must have looked like a teacher being chased by her most disappointing student—I recalled that this had once been her side of town and wondered how often she wished that she still belonged here. Constance had never been rich, but her family had been comfortable enough; she must have already lowered her expectations to marry the coffin-maker who'd brought her to Dodge, though lowered expectations were common after the war had carried off so many young men. It must have been that same practicality that led her to approach Kate when she was widowed. I had always pictured Constance acting boldly, standing at the center of Kate's parlor in her best shirtwaist while she looked Lila full in the face. But as I followed her through the north side, it occurred to me that it had perhaps been quite different. Maybe she'd been shy, ducked her head, spoken too politely and shown too much breeding. Maybe she'd had to beg for work; maybe she'd sought merely to avoid Hugh Montgomery, who had been known to haunt the funerals of men who'd left young wives behind, the better to judge the comeliness of their widows while he paid his hollow respects. I cocked my head at her, half hoping to be asked what I was looking at so I could press her for the story, but Constance was focused on behaving herself and took no notice.

Constance may have looked the part of a decent young woman, but inside the general store my own raggediness could not be ignored. The whole place made me feel like a child, as if I'd leave fingerprints on anything I touched. Disdain rolled off the shopkeeper's wife like the smell of cow shit rolled off the rail yard, and I left Constance to wait politely while the matron climbed a high, rolling ladder to pull me down some ready-made clothes. Wandering around the shop, I tried to enjoy the novelty of the place, looking over stacks of mixing bowls and flour sifters as though I'd never seen such things in all my life, but I was bored by these tools made for a domestic life that only grew more and more abstract as my own continued down this other, more stimulating track.

What did catch my attention was a row of Bowie knives, lined up by size under glass. I'd worked my way around to the other counter, at right angles to where the shopkeeper's wife was holding up a long, dark skirt so Constance could judge the quality of the stitching. I leaned over to examine the blades, pausing at one about the length of my hand, with a carved handle shaped to a gentle curve that would fit ever so nicely into my palm.

The shopkeeper stepped closer. "Anything you'd like to take a look at, miss?" he asked.

"Oh, not today, my friend is just . . ." I looked up and we caught eyes. I recognized him—just a moment before he recognized me—as a trick from not three nights earlier.

". . . picking me out some things." I gave him my pert whorehouse smile and waited for him to remember where he knew me from. Behind my back I heard paper rustling as Constance waited for my new clothes to be wrapped up.

"Please leave," said the shopkeeper quietly.

"I'm just waiting for my things," I replied, at normal volume.

"Everything all right?" Constance came up beside me, while the shopkeeper's wife followed around the long counter to bring my parcel and settle the bill.

"We was just chatting," I said. I counted out my money and slid the small pile of bills and coins toward the shopkeeper's wife.

"About what?" she asked.

We both looked at her husband at the same time as he went chalk-white from forehead to collar. She reddened at the same pace that he paled, as though all color were draining from his face into hers.

"Nothing," I said. "Just passing the time of day."

"Then you pass it someplace else," she hissed. She snatched back my newly wrapped package just as Constance reached out to pick it up.

"Excuse me," said Constance. "Those are my friend's new clothes. We paid for them."

The shopkeeper's wife shoved the money back toward me. "We don't want your money."

"I beg your pardon, but there must be some sort of misunderstanding," said Constance, gathering her good manners about her like a cloak.

"Oh, I understand perfectly," said the matron. She turned her hard look on me. "And so do you. So you take your ill-gotten gains and get out this instant."

As I gathered my money and folded it into my pocket, she turned to Constance. "I'd expect this type of thing from a poor girl like her, but you, whatever you are, you should know better."

Constance drew back, stunned into silence.

"You take her back where she belongs," the wife snarled. "Where—I assume—you both belong."

"Oh, for . . ." I started to protest, but Constance grabbed me by the wrist.

"Let's go," she said. I'd never seen her like this: her face was flat and blank as a sheet of paper. Just outside the door we all but slammed into one of the small groups of wives we'd passed earlier. Constance started and dropped her handbag, which spilled open so that a few coins and a wadded handkerchief tumbled out over the sidewalk; one of the women stooped to help us until the shopkeeper's wife barked imperiously from her doorway, "Stand up, Mrs. Shaw, she doesn't need your help."

The woman looked up at her friend, then at me and Constance. I saw her face shift as she realized there was something wrong with us, something that placed us beneath her concern. She dropped Constance's handkerchief back on the sidewalk and straightened up.

Constance had frozen, as if without the protective walls of the Queen she were stripped naked. I realized that she was unused to this type of treatment, being looked down upon by matrons, while it was all too familiar to me; I'd spent the majority of my life bearing up under some mixture of pity and contempt from women who thought that because their lives were better, they were better. For a moment I was overcome with the same impulse that had not long before driven me to swing a soup ladle at the face of a boardinghouse keeper, and if not for Constance's sake I might have taken a swipe at any one of the women who were now looking at us like we were no more than mud to be scraped from the heel of a shoe.

Instead, I stooped to pick up Constance's things, tossed my hair back, and linked my arm through my friend's. I all but dragged her down the sidewalk, keeping my head high and looking everyone I passed dead in the eye. Though Constance kept up with me, her gait was just a little unsteady; a block from the Queen I stopped and pulled us into an alley.

"Never mind those stuck-up bitches," I said, as if we were already in the middle of a conversation.

She wasn't crying, but her eyes were rimmed with red. She took a deep breath.

"They're no better than we are," I continued.

She gave a single, dry laugh. "That's not how they'd see it."

"Then they're lying to themselves," I said. "They fuck for bed and board same as we do, only their tricks own them body and soul."

She looked at me for a long moment. "I know you're right," she said. She looked up at the clear, blue sliver of sky visible between the buildings. The alley stank, as all alleys do, this one of rotting onions and horse piss.

"That one who bent to help us, I recognized her," she continued. "We used to say hello at church, though I can't recall her Christian name. Goodness, I can't recall the last time I went to church either."

"What would you do there anyway but lose half your Sunday getting yelled at by the same man who lets himself in by our side door first thing Monday?" I said. Kate allowed men of the cloth to enter the Queen through Bart's kitchen; as a result, a not-insignificant portion of each Monday night's profits were made up of tithes.

"No, I know, it's not that," said Constance. She smoothed back her hair and took another breath. "I recognized her right away, but I can't tell if she knew me at all, or if she just knew what I was."

"It's that you've come down so far," I said.

Constance nodded and turned her head in the direction of the Queen, squinting into the wind. "I allowed myself to forget that this is the best I can hope for," she said. "I ought not to have done that."

I nodded. "It'll only bring you grief."

She raised an eyebrow at me. "It's a stark line of thinking."

"It's how things are," I said. "I've been getting looked at like I was a two-bit, no-account whore since long before I was one. It's just what they're like."

"How do you keep from minding it?"

"Like I said, they're no better than we are. They can think it all they want, but all they've got that we lack is shirts to mend and noses to wipe and runner beans to put up before fall. And for what? They don't seem at all happy with any of it."

Constance smiled at me. "They do not."

"And why should they be? It's nothing but trouble keeping house and looking after a man, you know that even better than I do." I held out my hand to her. "Come on," I said. "Let's go sneak a bottle out of the kitchen before dark so we can fuck all their husbands before sunup."

"I don't know if I can manage all of them," she said, taking my hand.

"Well, I'll do my best to help you out," I said. Her hand in mine, I led us out of the alleyway and back toward home.

CHAPTER 5

It was not long after that Sheriff's Deputy Jim Bonnie took to me. We all had regulars: Lila had the favor of Dodge City's second-best doctor, which came in handy, while a married shopkeeper always brought little bags of candy when treating himself to a visit with Arabella. Henrietta was the cherished dream of a young sprout from the Western Telegraph office with no place else to spend his wages, and Constance had Pierre whenever he was in town, seldom though that was.

And then Jim picked me out, just like he was choosing a fresh mount out of a remuda. I'd been at the Queen a month or two by then; one night as I was taking a breather between tricks, Grace knocked on my door and called me over to Kate's parlor. When I entered, she was sitting opposite a man in a brown wool suit, pouring three glasses of whiskey.

"Come in, Bridget," said Kate. "Come and meet Deputy Bonnie."

"Howdy, Deputy," I said with a nod and a dip of my shoulder; I'd learned early on that men don't shake hands with their whores.

"How do you do, Bridget. Have a drink?" he said, holding out a glass. I reached out and took it, smiling. I hadn't been back to Kate's parlor since the day she'd had Roscoe try me out, but I knew only high-tone customers were invited in to sit on the silk-upholstered chairs. I looked Deputy Bonnie over: he was a good deal older than me, close to forty, with hair graying at the temples that made little stripes under his hat like a badger, but he had a boyish aspect, light-colored eyes with sun-carved lines rayed out around them.

"Deputy Bonnie is an old friend of the Queen," said Kate. "Just now as he was coming up he asked if he could meet that gal with the red hair." She emptied her glass and folded it between her gloved hands as she turned to Jim.

"Bridget's one of our foundlings," she continued. "Plucked right up off the street, not a penny to her name."

"Well, lucky you," said Jim, nodding first at Kate, then at me.

"Lucky me indeed," I said. "And what about you, Deputy? You a lucky man?" I cast one eye at Kate to see if I was being too forward—even in a sporting house, most fellows like to think they're talking you into something—but she tucked in the corner of her mouth and I knew I'd hit the mark.

Jim smiled, impish. "Oh, sometimes, but my luck's liable to turn on a dime," he said. "I don't like to press it. Don't you agree?"

"Oh, I don't know, sometimes it's worth pressing just a little." I emptied my glass and leaned forward to set it down, angling myself just right, and felt a little puff of his breath on the tops of my tits. "Anyway, something tells me your luck will hold tonight. Why don't you come with me and we'll see if we can get a game going, just the two of us."

I looked in his eyes but resisted the urge to wink before straightening up. As I did so, Kate caught my eye just beyond his sight line; she rubbed her fingers together and shook her head, meaning the deputy wasn't to pay for the time. I took Jim's hand and led him along the balcony to my room, where he hung his hat on the peg with all the ease and comfort of a homesteader before I pulled him into my bed.

The next day I rose late. From outside came the sounds of Dodge City by daylight, rippling over each other like light playing over the dancing surface of a pond: cowboys shouting at each other and yipping at their herds; the cows themselves stamping and braying in righteous, impotent fury; the occasional trickle of piano from the few saloons that bothered to have someone play during the daytime. Underlying all of it were the voices of men, inside the Queen and out: called-out greetings, mumbled conferences, the rise and fall of constant haggling over this price or that. The noise didn't bother me; even if it hadn't been muffled by the walls and windows of the saloon, I still would have welcomed it, for it sounded like life. In the rare moments when everything outside seemed to pause for breath at once, I would be reminded of the stillness that had surrounded the cabin back in Arkansas, the dread that grew when I had nothing to listen to but the wind in the pines.

I felt I'd earned a little lying-in, for Deputy Bonnie had taken his time taking his pleasure with me. Not that I necessarily minded—though he was a big man he'd proven rather graceful in the act—but it had amounted to the better part of a night's work all the same. I lay still and listened to the voices of women start to braid themselves in with the men as the girls made their way downstairs for the coffee and biscuits that Bart left out on the bar each morning. Not wanting to miss out on breakfast, I bestirred myself to put my feet on the floor, wrap myself in a shawl, and go down.

At the foot of the stairs, Roscoe was complaining to Lila.

"Ain't had a night off in two weeks," he half whined, half grumbled at her.

"We're doing the best we can, Roscoe," said Lila, arms crossed. She looked up on hearing my feet on the stairs overhead. "Bridget, get yourself a cup and come sit with me over by the fireplace." She jerked her head at the far tables and turned back to Roscoe.

"We need another man," he said. "Langley hasn't . . ." He trailed off. Lila held his gaze for a long moment before leaning in and muttering a response, of which I only caught the words "Kate" and "not today" as I slipped past them to fill my cup.

The hearth was cold, for it was high summer and most nights no fire was needed. I seated myself at one of the card tables and waited for Lila.

"So you met Jim," she said, pausing to stretch her shoulders back before easing herself into one of the gamblers' chairs.

"I did," I said cautiously; I never got the hang of guessing Lila's intentions.

"How was it?" she said.

"What, the screw?"

"What else?"

"It was all right," I said. "Seems to know what he's after and how to go about getting it."

She snorted a laugh into her coffee. "That he does," she said.

"You had him?" I asked, not knowing what she meant.

"Once or twice, but I seem to be too worldly for him," she said.

"He likes the innocent types?"

"To an extent," she said. "I'd wager you're just the right amount: doe-eyed, but with a mouth on you."

"What's that supposed to mean?" I grinned at her.

She ignored me and continued. "But he liked fucking you, you're saying."

"Seemed to—did it to me almost three times before he wore himself out."

"Good," she said, taking a sip from her cup. "Jim's real important to us."

"But he's just a trick," I said.

Lila looked at me seriously for a moment, then sighed and leaned toward me across the table with the air of someone having to explain something very simple to a child. "Look at all of this," she said, gesturing around the room. "You think it keeps itself up? You think the rougher types are keeping themselves away, or locking themselves up after they go too far?"

"But I thought Virgil and Bart—"

Lila cut me off, impatient. "What matters is who comes through that door in the first place, not the limited amount Virgil and Bart can do once they're already inside. You seen how we have lawmen stopping around here nice and regular, stars pinned on and everything? That's Jim's doing. So until he wearies of you, you make him feel real welcome here, got it?"

I nodded. "He didn't pay last night," I said. "How am I supposed to make my cut making him feel so welcome all the time?"

"We'll adjust your cut—I'll talk to Kate about it later." She leaned forward and patted my knee through my nightgown; Lila had strong hands, and I felt like a horse being patted on its hindquarters.

"Is she all right?" I asked.

"Don't you worry about Kate," said Lila, without looking at me. She drained her cup, shutting her eyes as she swallowed. "I know this ain't right, but to this day the thing I hated most about the war was drinking all that goddamned chicory." She stood up and stretched again. "You just do your part," she said, and walked off toward the stairs.

From then on Jim was my regular caller. A few times a week he'd lock up the jailhouse, hand the keys over to Sykes the night watchman, and stroll on down to the Queen to pay me a visit. He liked to set a spell downstairs, telling me stories about the ne'er-do-wells he locked up, or recalling his roustabout years after the surrender, which he claimed to have witnessed personally. We became friends, of a sort. His stories scratched the itch I got from the other tricks' hints at their wild lives, and I liked the whiff of leather and prairie wind that hung about him. I couldn't tell how much to believe, but something told me Jim wasn't lying, at least not all the time.

One night I was leaning against the bar, tossing my head back and forth while some cowboy talked a blue streak without once meeting my eye. Often as not the younger fellows had to work up the nerve to do exactly what we all knew they'd come here to do; at times it bored the life out of me watching and waiting for them, and this was one of those times. I was on the point of breaking in to ask him upstairs myself when the door opened behind him; Jim came in, looking windblown and not a little weary. Ignoring the cowboy, I watched Jim's eyes search the room for me, and enjoyed how they lit up when they landed on mine. On a mixture of size and authority he pushed his way through the crowd. He placed one hand on the cowboy's shoulder to maneuver him out of the way and said, "Why don't you get yourself a drink, son, and let me talk to my best girl here?"

He slapped a few coins onto the bar and signaled to Bart, who produced a bottle and two glasses for us along with a consolation shot for the cowboy. Just past Jim's shoulder I could see the cowboy staring at his glass in confusion as if a spell had been cast and I had been transformed into the very drink before him, before he downed it and stomped off.

"Thanks," I said, raising my own glass to Jim's.

"Serves him right," said Jim. "He ought to have known better than to waste a gal's time like that."

I laughed. "Right you are," I said. Jim poured a fresh round and we drank again. "So, Deputy, how's the big, wide world?"

"Oh, same as always," he said. "Full of outlaws and scallywags."

"Meet any especially bad ones lately?"

"Just come from breaking up a fight down at the Emerald," he said.

"Oh?" I—and he—knew that gossip about Hugh's place would always be welcome at the Queen.

"It's that new Faro dealer," he said. "No crookeder than the old one, but his sleight of hand sure could use some work." He chuckled and picked up the bottle to pour us another round, when from the card tables there came a shout, then the pop and shatter of a bottle hitting the floor.

"Get your own gal!" A man in a brown frock coat was shoving my abandoned cowboy away from a pretty, doll-faced girl named Maggie.

"I'm trying, ain't I?" whined the cowboy, weak chin shaking. "They told me this was a whorehouse but all the gals is spoken for."

"Not spoken for, just not looking to have their time wasted with idle chatter," said Jim. He didn't even rise from his seat, just projected his usual rumble farther across the room; as he spoke he twisted around and caught the eye of another deputy who I hadn't even noticed lounging by the hearth. The junior deputy stepped forward and took the cowboy rather gently by the arm as Langley—in fighting shape, for once—resumed "The Yellow Rose of Texas," which he'd already played twice that night.

Jim turned back to me and looked at his empty glass expectantly. I laughed and poured for us both.

"Why, thank you," he said, raising his to mine. I put my hand on his and smiled; tossing back my shot I glanced up to see Kate looking down at us, face as still and placid as the surface of a lake.

The other gals teased me about Jim something awful, saying that he was my sweetheart and it was only a matter of time 'til he whisked me away to be a jailer's wife. All I cared about was that Jim didn't treat me like I was half-stupid, and he bought good whiskey by the bottle so he could share it with me. Still, something about the jailer's wife talk stuck in my craw, and after a few rounds one night I asked Constance about it.

"I swear, sometimes he does make like we're sweethearts," I said.

"Well, only he knows how he feels about you," said Constance. "What's certain is how Kate and Lila feel about your arrangement. Kate may be hazy much of the time, but she's got a sixth sense for the tastes of respectable men. She has you playing right up to that deputy, hasn't she?"

I shrugged. "More or less."

"Well, you keep at it," she said, gazing around the bar. "I've seen things get messy in this place more than once."

I tried to imagine what she meant, but I'd only seen a few hints at a scuffle. "Messy how?"

"Worse than you've seen it," she said simply. "Kate and Deputy Bonnie go way back—he likes to have a good sweetheart, and Kate likes to line them up for him."

"He can't go spark some gal of his own?"

Constance shrugged. "I'm sure he could, but sparking is for nice girls, and a nice girl wouldn't do half the things you do for him. And Kate likes it this way too. Even when he's between fancies, he makes sure his boys look in on us and that word gets around we're under his wing. And when he's got a girl to call his own, so to speak, that's even better."

"I know, I know," I said. I was getting awfully tired of everyone explaining things to me. "Me fucking Jim is keeping the Queen open."

"We got by just fine before you showed up," said Constance, only a little sharply. "But there's more to it than just the deputy. Haven't you been reading the papers?"

That one stung. "You know I ain't."

"Dodge is trying to get civilized," she said. "Movements on the north side for temperance, suppression of sin, what have you."

I snorted. "Decent, God-fearing women?"

Constance nodded. "Decent, self-deceiving women, though the letter of the law is on their side. Anyway, what it's come to is the city has levied all sorts of fines on brothels, so keeping this place going can't be easy. I imagine your pleasing the law greases the skids."

"Was you ever one of Jim's good sweethearts?"

She shook her head, smiling at some private joke with herself. "No. Kate tried, but he took me for impertinent when all I was doing was holding up my end of the conversation. Just as well, really."

We both laughed at that; Jim was nice enough, but Constance would insist on leveling with a fellow, and not all of them appreciated her frank assessments.

"It's a good thing you can stand him, at least," she continued.

"I guess so," I said. I looked around the room. The Queen was getting sleepy: the card tables were dotted with empty seats, and I could see Constance looking at Pierre's empty chair. Bart was wiping down the bar while Virgil drowsed on his stool by the door, and the whores were draped here and there around the room, looking soft and rumpled as unmade beds. I felt a well of affection for all of it, despite my weariness. The Buffalo Queen had become a home of sorts, the first place I'd ever been looked after, even if it was only with an eye toward my profitability.

"What happens if I lose his favor?" I asked Constance.

"Best not entertain the possibility," she said evenly. "Come on, let's see if we can squeeze in a proper drink before we call it a night." She linked her arm through mine and glided us over to the bar, where Bart was already pouring out glasses of brandy.

A few nights later, Jim reappeared, eyes aglow and with a shadow of a bruise spreading up one cheek.

"My goodness, where'd you get that?" I asked as he plunked down beside me. With two fingers, I turned his head to one side for a better look, then drew my fingertips lightly down along his jaw. Too many men are unused to tenderness—the lighter the touch, the quicker they're undone—and I saw Jim's lashes flutter for half a moment before he came back to himself.

"More trouble at the Emerald," he said.

I shook my head theatrically. "That place, I swear."

He shrugged as Bart put down a bottle between us with two glasses, then waited for Jim to fish a few coins out of his pocket. My time may have been given out gratis, but liquor was liquor, and at the bar Jim paid his way just like any other man. I turned to pour and saw him reach up and touch the spot on his face where my hand had just been.

"How's it look?" he asked.

"Not too bad yet, but it'll be a real sight by morning," I said. "You gonna tell me what happened?"

He continued to knead at his cheek as he spoke. "Remember a couple of weeks ago, when the bank got robbed over in Abilene?"

I nodded, though in truth I recalled no such thing.

"Well, turns out the ringleader goes way back with Hugh Montgomery's Faro dealer."

"The new one who can't cheat worth a damn?"

"That's the one. Him and this outlaw came up like brothers, though they ain't true kin. The outlaw got it in his head that the Emerald would be a good place to hole up and wait for the robbery to blow over."

I glanced around the room, which was already swaying like a ship at sea with the combined merriment of men, whores, and liquor—waiting out the law in such a place didn't strike me as a half-bad idea.

"But it didn't work," I said to Jim.

"It did not," he said. "This outlaw friend seemed a pretty cool customer, but his partner—"

"Not the Faro dealer?"

"No, another fellow, the one he done the robbery with, he couldn't keep his head. Blew his entire take in two nights and then tried to touch the outlaw for some of his share to cover the bill."

I snorted, imagining the look I'd get from Lila if I asked for an advance on my pay. "The hell he do that for?" I said.

Jim frowned slightly, for he didn't like me to curse, and continued. "It went over about as well as you'd imagine: the outlaw refused, the partner took a swing at him in the middle of the barroom, then started bawling out the Faro dealer for making him think the Emerald would be a good hideout."

"Good lord," I said, laughing.

"And while all this is going on, Hugh's sent one of his gals out the back door to come get me and the boys. By the time we got there, the place was practically on fire. Everyone fighting everyone, bottles flying, even Hugh got in a few good licks on the Faro dealer for letting all this happen in the first place."

"Anybody die?"

He shook his head. "Nobody died. Jailhouse sure is full, though."

"You ain't gotta be down there, keeping order?"

"Nah, Sykes has it in hand. They're all worn out from the scrap anyhow."

"And what about your face?" I said. "Who did that?"

"The partner, I think."

"Well, I hope you gave as good as you got," I said.

"Better," said Jim. He emptied his glass and put his hand on my knee. "And what about you, Bridget, you got anything for me?"

I laughed and shook my head; his attempts to be forward were always so ham-fisted, it was almost endearing. "Well, I ain't in no mood to fight, but I'm sure I can think of something," I said, taking his hand. "Let's go on upstairs."

I've said before that most of the screwing I did in those days was unremarkable, and I meant it. But not all. There's something that overtakes a person that I just can't quit, that crossover from just talking to swept away, as though one moment you were simply wading by the shore and the next you're soaked, sputtering and clinging to the riverbank. There's an indrawn breath, and something tenses in the hand that grips your shoulder, and suddenly going back is just so much harder and less appealing than going forward. I've fucked dozens of men that I couldn't tell one from another, couldn't have recognized if they ran up to shake my hand in the street. But if they ran up and took that one gasping breath in my ear, I'd know every goddamned one of them. It doesn't matter how much or how profoundly little you care for the one in the room with you, there's life itself in that one breath, and power, and once you know how to conjure it, there's a part of you that never wants to stop, even if you don't take it yourself.

Even so, when I think of that night, most of what I remember is the story Jim told me. While he got what he came for, I cooed into his ear and let my mind wander, filling in the details of the fight: the meaty smacks of fists into jaws, bright splashes of flying glass, blood flying in thin arcs through the air. I wondered where Hugh's girls had been through the melee, how much they had seen. Behind Jim's shoulder I clenched my hand into a fist and looked at it, trying to picture my little paw shooting forward and connecting with some stranger's grimy face, knuckles scraping on an unshaved chin.

Then one afternoon, there came Sallie. It was the lazy period between our noontime breakfast and the start of business during which we'd loll around, dallying at chores. I was a dab hand with a needle and often called upon to mend bits and pieces, refastening cheap lace to muslin worn pliant and velvety, reinforcing seams in dresses buttoned and unbuttoned so frequently. It was late summer by then; as the light pasted itself over the front windows, blank and white, Kate opened up her porch and we all spilled out to thread our needles in the fresh air overlooking the street. The novelty of whores doing the same things regular women did caused the eyes of the men passing in the thoroughfare to snag on us, dragging their gazes back and up as their legs continued down the street. If we'd been open we'd have done some trade off those looks alone, but Kate believed in holding us back now and then to generate interest. Most every eye that watched us so hungrily had at one point sat in a farmhouse parlor, gazing in adoration at some well-brought-up young lady who looked just enough like one of us to make it worth coming back after sunset.

Suddenly the front doors down below burst open, and we all leaned forward to see Lila run out the door and straight into the arms of a skinny, blond-haired girl in a yellow dress. They swayed and held each other tight for a moment, cooing like doves, faces close as praying hands before they laced their arms around each other's waists and sauntered into the Queen. Our collective gaze followed the sound of their feet through the barroom and up the stairs, waiting for the four-legged, two-smiled beast that appeared on the porch momentarily.

"Gals, this is Sallie," Lila said as they stepped out through the door and into the light.

Sallie's face hit me like the slap of an open hand. She wasn't exactly beautiful, but there was something clear and bright about her features that arrested me immediately. I swallowed.

"Say hello to the gals, Sallie."

"Hello, gals," she said, mouth grinning while her eyes flicked over us, sizing us up. She caught me staring and—I could have sworn—gave me the ghost of a wink. She cast frank, appraising looks over each of us in turn, eyes glittering like jewels in a satin-lined box. I felt her eyes run down me and swallowed again, harder this time.

"Sallie and I worked together awhile back. She's up from San Antone, been working the dance halls," Lila was saying.

"You were a dance hall girl?" said Henrietta.

Hands on hips, Sallie turned like an actress on a stage, knowing how to show she was talking to Henrietta, but cheating out so her whole audience—the rest of us—didn't ever have to stop looking at her face.

"Sure was," she said. "Down at the Number Twelve. You look like you could take a turn—you done dance halls yourself?"

Henrietta pursed her lips in a little silent *moo* of pleasure. "Naw, I ain't had the opportunity," she said. Then she looked at the rest of us and rushed to continue, "Besides, this here's a good house—Kate and Lila sure know what's what." She giggled, like she did at the end of most of her sentences.

Sallie laughed, and I felt a twist of what I now know was gut-level envy, though at the time I thought I was just hungry. "You ain't gotta kiss any asses on my account," she said, and swung her lantern gaze, made brighter by eyes so pale they were almost yellow, around to the rest of us.

"Did you like it, though?" Henrietta piped.

Sallie snapped back to her. "Yeah, it's all right, for those as can keep up," she said, just a touch of sharpness in the edge of her voice.

"Is that why you left?" asked Constance. She was the only one who hadn't pressed forward. She was leaning against the rail of the porch, as always doing two things at once: sizing up Sallie while dangling her fulsome rear over the street, reminding the passersby to come back later.

"Is what why?" said Sallie.

"Couldn't keep up," said Constance, enunciating just a little extra.

Sallie let out another high bubble of a laugh like she was blowing soapsuds off her fingers to waft away in the wind.

"Oh, I was just ready for a change of scenery is all. And didn't I get one?" She relinked arms with Lila and smiled again. I felt the wind shift, cooling a new side of me.

"If I say it myself, they are a pretty bunch," said Lila. We all pshawed on cue, and some tension seemed broken. I ducked my head and half grinned with the rest, but under my lowered lashes I kept one eye on the low arc of the new girl's jawline and the wash of sun above it, the wispy-fine down lit up in a slash of gold.

"Fresh as the dew, you all are. But I sure the hell ain't—Lila, you want to show me someplace to flop?" asked Sallie. She leaned in toward Lila secretively. "And maybe a little something to revive my spirits?"

"Why, of course, my dear," said Lila, and they turned like a team of horses to head inside. A wave of chatter rose after them as the whores pressed forward to see the new arrival to her room, peppering her with questions about dance halls, Texans, the train ride up. Only Constance hung back, watching them go. I waited with her.

"What is it?" I asked.

"Oh, nothing," she said. "I just wonder what she's doing all the way up here if she had such a plum job in San Antonio."

"Maybe Lila invited her," I said.

"Maybe, but I wouldn't trust anyone Lila invited either."

"She invited me, sort of," I said.

Constance shrugged. "That's true. Who's to say, maybe I'm wrong."

Immediately, whether we willed it or no, everyone at the house was fascinated by Sallie. She didn't associate with us so much as she held court, clearly angling to be queen of the Queen.

"This is just a stop for me, you know," she said the second night—she didn't work the first. Leaning in to speak as if in confidence, she murmured to me and Constance while we waited for the night to start.

"You ain't stayin'?" I asked, surprised.

"Oh, I'll stay a spell, but not forever," Sallie answered. "I'm on my way out to San Francisco." She twisted a little as though this were novel, but in those days half the world was headed that way.

"What's in San Francisco?" asked Constance.

"Cool weather, for one thing. I knew a gal went out there, said there's always a breeze coming up off the ocean." She went on to describe the wonders she anticipated. Sallie's fantasy contained no trace of originality; she spoke about the same steep hills, exotic strangers, and ships bobbing in the harbor as anyone else who yearned for California. I paid no attention to the vistas she spun out, instead watching the easy grace with which she slung a brandy glass between her long fingers.

I came back to reality just in time to hear her say, "And when I get there, I'm going on the stage."

"To do what," said Constance. I couldn't quite tell if she was trying to egg Sallie on or cut her down, but I didn't care as long as Sallie kept talking, popping her hip to make a point, passing the glass lazily back and forth from hand to hand.

"Why, to sing, of course. I been singing since I was a little thing. My family was real musical, and we'd sing together day and night."

"Well, let's hear it," Arabella croaked from the end of the bar.

A chorus of "Oh yes" and "Let's do" rose up. Sallie ducked her head but did not blush.

"Oh, I don't know," she said.

"Don't know what?" called out Lila, descending the stairs.

"Sallie would have us believe she's too shy to sing for us," said Constance.

"We only just met is the thing," said Sallie.

"Oh, can it, Sallie, you never been shy a day in your life," said Lila. "Still, it will have to wait for another time. I was just out on the porch and three crews broke off working all at once, not five minutes ago. You gals fan out."

Lila nodded at the doors and as if on command they swung open. A long shaft of light poured in ahead of a cluster of cowhands.

Sallie emptied her glass and set it down. "Best get to it," she said. Constance and I instinctively parted to let her go first, and by the time the doors were shut and the drinks poured, she already had the handsomest one whispering into her ear.

CHAPTER 6

We got nights off for the curse, and Constance and I overlapped for the round after Sallie's arrival. I was lying on Constance's bed, cramping and queasy and an absolute delight to be around, tossing back and forth while she read from *Wuthering Heights*.

"I wish you'd be still," she said. "Or go back to your own room."

"There's nothing to do in my room, and if I go downstairs, Grace will set me to sweeping the storeroom." I flopped over onto my back and sighed loudly. "You seen Sallie today?"

"Why do you ask?" she responded without looking up from her book.

"Oh, what's it to you," I grumbled, and pinched at her ankle.

"I'm serious about throwing you out of here," she said.

"Don't pout, I was only teasing." I reached over to tickle the sole of one stockinged foot, but she yanked it away and tucked it under her skirt.

"I don't care to be teased just now. What do you want with Sallie anyway?"

"Just curious is all," I said. I'd taken to looking for her yellow hair in the evening lamplight, and wondered if it was late enough for the flames to be casting a halo around her head as they only did against the true dark of night.

"I don't have to look for her," said Constance. "She's got the next room, I can hear when she's in there just fine."

I sat up. "The next room?"

Constance closed her book over one finger, keeping her place. "You know she does, what's gotten into you?"

I ignored her and rolled onto my stomach to stare at the wall. It was plain pine boards, just like the rest of the Queen. Good carpenters had been hard to come by when the saloon was built, and there were plenty of small gaps in the seams of the planks. I ran my hand over them as if searching for a heartbeat and shimmied forward to press my eye to a crack.

"What are you doing?" asked Constance.

I didn't answer. I swiveled my eye against the crack to take in as much of Sallie's room as I could. It looked much like the rest of ours did, with a high iron bed made up with a red quilt, a couple of clothes pegs by the door, and a washstand with a mirror over it. There was a silver-backed brush on the washstand, and a cluster of ribbons tied to the bedpost like a spray of bright mushrooms growing out of a fallen log. On the floor near the head of the bed was a bottle at low tide, and an empty carpetbag sagging wistfully behind it. Beyond that, there was no sign that the room belonged to anyone in particular.

I heard feet along the catwalk, and then the door opened to admit Sallie and a trick, a man in a black frock coat who I recognized as an undertaker from the north side of town. I hadn't ever serviced him myself—he took me for unrefined—but I knew him by sight as a stiff, too-upright man who used the length of his nose as a high vantage point from which to stare down at the rest of us. He'd taken a liking to Sallie, however, and had already paid her several calls.

"She's got John Borne," I whispered.

"John Borne can go straight to hell and ask me for a glass of water," said Constance, still refusing to look up. She detested the man, for it had been he who'd held the mortgage on her late husband's business, and had taken no pity on the young widow.

"Right you are," I said out of loyalty.

I glued my eye to the crack in time to see Sallie's work dress fall in a crimson pool around her ankles, which were slender in their black stockings. I followed them up to where they vanished under the shift that she hoisted up to expose wax-white legs. She lifted one at a time as she climbed atop the undertaker, who was shucked of his clothes and lying spread-eagled on the bed with his cock pointing out over his head like a sundial. I watched as Sallie licked her palm, grasped it like a pump handle, and primed it once, twice, thrice before lowering herself down, chemise falling demurely over her knees. All through me something pulled tight, like a skein of ropes that twist together until they creak and split at the outermost fibers. I bit down hard on my lower lip. Sallie let her hair fall forward in a golden curtain and stared right into the eyes of the man before her as she rode him, holding his gaze.

"What's going on?" Constance hissed, in spite of herself. I beckoned and she crawled over to look through the crack for a couple of seconds before relinquishing the vantage to me.

"So that's how she does it," she said in a quiet but matter-of-fact tone, sitting back.

I made no answer. I couldn't tear my eyes away. Through a veil of muslin I could see the point of one hip bone that spelled out the rolling motion of Sallie's body, and the lamp's flame drew out the honey-bronze light from her hair that I had been thinking of just moments before. I spared a glance for the undertaker, who was transfixed before her as a pilgrim bearing witness to a miracle. Then he grasped at her hips and they both arced up high for the finish. She sank down beside him, and I lost sight of her behind his rangy bulk.

I rolled back to find Constance staring at me.

"What're you looking at?" I said.

"You," she said simply.

"Well, you've seen me before."

"Not sure that I have," she said. I could not read her expression.

"She's experienced," I sputtered. "Can't a girl try to learn anything new around here?"

"You can learn anything you want. But next time, study in your own bed. Mine's for sleeping."

"What burr have you got up your ass now?"

"You've gone sweet," said Constance.

"I ain't sweet on that gravedigger," I said. The very idea.

"Of course you aren't."

I opened my mouth, but nothing came out. Every now and then, somebody says something about you that's so true you just can't do a thing about it.

"Shut up," I said after a few flaps of my jawbone.

"Have it your way," she said. She sat back against the headboard and found her place in *Wuthering Heights*. "Do you want me to read or don't you?"

"I've had enough of their stupid problems. Yours too." I jumped off the bed.

"What on earth are you talking about?"

My face felt flaming hot. "You know, you think you know everything, but all you got is book learning, and that ain't all there is to know. You think you're smart but you're just—world-stupid!" Her expression showed bemusement rather than indignation, which only made me madder. I slammed the door and flounced downstairs. Bart gave me a gin, but before I could drink it, Grace caught me with her snarling little smile and sent me back upstairs, for I was not fit to be seen.

I got back to work the next night, feeling exposed as a rabbit who darts into a clearing and then freezes, suddenly fearing the swoop and clutch of a hawk. I'd never been sweet on anyone before, not so far as I could tell anyway, and wasn't aware of how impossible it is to act normal once the realization hits. Coming down the stairs that evening I felt half-scared and half-serious; I tried pinning a grin onto my face, but it kept slipping off, and more than once Lila stepped up next to me and told me to smile, God damn it, or didn't I want to make my cut this week? So I tossed my head and turned a few tricks but heard barely a word spoken to me. Instead I started a tally in my head for every time I scanned the room for that honey-blob of yellow hair; by dark I was up to twenty-seven and stopped counting.

To be clear, though Sallie was decently pretty, it wasn't her looks that did me in. She had bright eyes and sharp-cut features, all fair as if she'd been left out to bleach in the sun after washing. In many ways she looked like Arabella, but shorter and not so uniformly disappointed in life. It was something else in Sallie that drew the eye. She never hurried, moving as though she had all the time in the world, like sap that could run slow or fast but wouldn't be told, and she had a way of making you feel that you were right on the verge of impressing her, that any minute now you'd say or do just the thing to win her over. She was just then wafting slowly through the room, pausing to murmur something to Lila that made them both crack up, while that rope-knot in my center just pulled itself tighter and tighter.

"What daydream are you so wrapped up in?"

I hadn't even noticed Jim Bonnie come in, much less that he'd settled himself behind me at a barstool and was pouring out a couple of drinks. I relaxed; a smile crossed my face and was returned.

"Well, how do, Deputy?" I said. "I do apologize, I must have drifted a moment."

"No apology necessary, my dear," he said, sliding me a glass. We clinked and sipped.

"You ain't answered my question," he said.

"Which?"

"Where you was at just now."

"Oh, nowhere special," I said. Sallie had reached the far end of the bar and was flirting with Virgil for a real drink, pink tongue flashing in her mouth.

Jim poured again. "As long as you ain't dreaming of some long-lost sweetheart," he said.

"Nothing of the sort," I said, with no idea whether I was lying or telling the truth. "Just taking in the scenery is all."

Jim twisted to look around, and for a minute or two we sat without speaking, watching the room. There was nothing special going on at the Queen that night, but I was happy to let the liveliness of the saloon prop me up and give a little comfort: this was a room I belonged in, that people would notice if I left, and I was sitting with someone to whom, for one reason or another, it mattered that I was there beside him.

Roscoe was in fine form, playing all of his favorites and embellishing with little trips and twirls of his right hand while winking theatrically at Gertrude, a newish gal perched right up on the piano top. Outside, summer was starting to curl at the edges, and I felt a cool draft from the door as the shifting wind chased Langley inside. He reeled up to the piano and gave the stool one hard kick with the flat bottom of his foot so that it flipped halfway into the air and sent Roscoe crashing to the floor, cracking his chin on the keys. A silence fell and I watched from the bar as Roscoe picked himself up, jaw set and thunder in his eye.

"What in the devil's hell is wrong with you?" he growled, looking to stand his ground without causing a scene.

Langley pointed one long finger at the keys. "That's my fucking piano," he said.

"The hell it is," said Roscoe, rubbing his jaw.

"You play it like a donkey. Anyhow, I'm the one who brought it here."

"Kate brought it, you mean."

"With me! And I aim to play it!"

"Like you're not too loaded to play it your own self. Everyone knows Kate just keeps you around out of pity anyhow."

"Pity, hell. You owe me your entire piano-playing career, you donkey's ass." He leaned back and brayed, curling his lips back to show great yellow teeth like corncobs.

Roscoe swung at Langley's chin and caught him right on the point, scattering the thin man backward over the floor. He spat blood on the boards and picked himself up, piece by piece.

"Let me tell you something," Langley began, but just then Virgil appeared between them.

"Come on, Lang, he didn't mean it." Virgil placed his dinner-plate hand on Langley's chest and fixed Roscoe with one big, white eyeball that promised further conversation. "What say we take you upstairs?"

A path parted between the piano and the stairway, the crowd murmuring with a mixture of pity and disappointment. Up above, Kate's door opened.

"What's all this?" she asked from the balcony, one eyebrow up nearly to her hairline.

"Nothing, Kate, this one just got a little overexcited," said Virgil, jerking his head at the erstwhile piano player, who was tilting as if caught in a strong wind.

"Well, let's have none of that," answered Kate in her stagiest voice. "We want everyone the right amount of excited, no more, no less. Roscoe, strike us up a tune! Half-price whiskey for fifteen minutes—let's have us some fun!"

She collected Langley and shut her parlor door with a bang matched by Roscoe thumping his stool down on the floor and plunking his ass on top. By unspoken agreement, Jim laced his arm through mine and rose to guide us to the staircase, while customers surged around us to get twice as much whiskey in half as much time. Roscoe tried a few chords before settling on a melody; halfway up the stairs, Sallie's voice rose up over the scrum and stopped me in my tracks, a jewel-bright soprano without the thin, needy edge of her speaking voice. Halfway through the first verse of "California Joe" most of the room was singing with her; Roscoe warmed to Sallie's voice and reined in his foul-tempered clanging. When I turned to look, she'd taken the perch atop the piano, and I saw Gertrude scowling as she worked her way to a new vantage.

"Who's that?" Jim asked.

"That's Sallie," I said. "New gal."

"Hmph," he said. "Be prettier if she could sing in tune."

"She's only here a little while, stopping on her way to San Francisco."

Jim scoffed. "She's no more going to San Francisco than you are."

Shocked at his callousness, I opened my mouth to reply but he had resumed his ascent, tugging on my arm, and I felt no choice but to follow him.

A few hours later, when I'd seen to Jim and the night was winding down, I stopped by Constance's room to say good night, rapping softly before opening the door. She was still up, curled around a fresh book. When she had no obligation to entertain, she'd pull the blankets up into a big lump and throw her winter coat over the top; when she stuck her head out to talk to me she looked like a badger coming out of her set to check the weather.

"You ain't stupid," I said from the doorway.

She nodded sagely. "It's the curse of my life."

"And I didn't mean what I said before."

"I know," she said. There was a beat of silence, through which curled the last of Roscoe's late-night filigree and the clank of Virgil collecting glassware down below.

"Are you all right?" she asked me, after a moment.

"I don't suppose it matters much how I am," I said.

"I suppose not," said Constance. "The heart is a beggar, and always hungry."

I shook my head, but it was a relief to be back on the receiving end of Constance's strange wisdom; like visiting with Jim, it was the sort of normal activity that stood in contrast to the revelations of the day before. "I swear, you may not be stupid but you're at least half crazy."

"Rather half crazy than half in love," she said. "Now shut the door, will you? I get enough of Roscoe's tinkering as it is, I don't need it on my night off." She ruffled the blankets up closer to her chin and turned down the lamp flame so that she looked like a lost traveler, warming herself with one coal against the darkness.

A few nights passed in relative peace, during which I pulled myself together enough to resume turning a profit. I kept my earnings in a wooden cigar box, which I wedged behind my bedpost. Kate had offered to keep it in the safe in her parlor, but I liked having my stash nearby so that I could take it out any time and survey the contents. I didn't have any sort of plan for the money, just liked to see it all lumped up, crouched and ready to spring into action. Stacking and counting—I could figure miles better than I could read—the past grew smaller behind me: the windowless, dirt-floored cabin; matrons looking down their noses in scorn and, worse, pity; squares of dry, unbuttered cornbread sitting lonely and baconless on a tin plate; the jolting of that rattletrap buckboard wagon; my pa's wet eyes begging me for reassurance that somehow it wasn't all his fault. They all shrank and faded, while my small fortune shone softly in the afternoon light, proof that I had what I needed, that I could get it again if I lost it, that if I'd come this far once, I could do it again should the need arise.

But bad luck darkens every doorway every now and then, or perhaps I simply grew careless. One night I was tidying up after a trick, having serviced the man and sent him on his way. I could have sworn I shut the door behind him, but maybe I was mistaken, or maybe he snuck back in. He'd left behind a half-drunk bottle of whiskey, and maybe all he meant to do was come back for it.

Either way, I'd taken out the cigar box, thinking myself alone, and started emptying my pockets into the box from which I would pay Kate and Lila their cut at the end of the week. Between the rattle of coin and the din from below, it was easy for him to creep up behind me. He reached around my body like I was no more than a fence post and grabbed the box, snapping it shut over my fingers. I cried out and wrenched my hand away while scrabbling at the box with the other, grabbing at his wrist. My heart pounded up in my throat.

"Give it!" I yelled at him, hating the girlish squeak in my voice. He wrenched his arm free and clouted me with the box. The corner caught my left eyebrow and opened a cut that showered blood into my eye, catching in my lashes to ring the world in salty red.

He darted from the room, door bouncing in its frame to spring open for me. Feeling only a slight sting on my face, I swept up the whiskey bottle with one hand and leapt after him, thinking only to get back what was mine.

I caught up with him at the top of the stairs and swung the bottle by the neck in a smooth, upward motion, catching him under his ear. The bottle didn't break, so I caught him again on the return blow as he simultaneously turned to look at me. I'll never forget the amusement that crossed his face before I hit him a second time. The bottle didn't break that time either, but I could see that it hurt him, for he threw his arms up over his head as though caught in a storm. Enough liquor had sloshed out to wet my grip, and the bottle slipped away to smash on the catwalk while I reached for the box in his hands, still held over his head.

We lost our footing and tumbled down the stairs together. I caught a rail and stopped halfway while he rolled like a boulder into the barroom. The crowd stepped back politely to give him space to fall, and I caught a white flash of Lila's face at the end of the bar as she whipped around to look first at the falling man, then at me. From my perch I pointed like a haint and caught my breath to screech "Thief!"

I heard Kate's parlor door bang open and Virgil jumped up from his post by the door, but before he could cross the room Jim Bonnie, who I hadn't even known was there, materialized out of the crowd at the bar and gave the thief one great thwack with the side of his fist. The miscreant heaved backward and sprawled ass-over-teacups across the floor, but all I saw was my box bursting open so that my money flew out in a cabbagey spray of greenbacks. Jim stepped forward and grabbed a handful of shirtfront, lifting him up so he was forced to dance on tiptoe.

"Only a yellow dog steals from a woman," Jim said.

"Aw hell, ain't but whore's money," answered the thief in a thin, reedy voice that I would have sworn was fuller back when he'd been in a more secure position.

Jim growled wordlessly.

"What's it to you anyway, you her pimp or something? I'll cut you in."

"Not exactly, no," said Jim. He flipped back the lapel of his coat just enough to show the tin star he usually covered off-duty. The thief sighed.

"Aw hell," he said again. "Just my fuckin' luck."

"Luck ain't got nothing to do with it," said Jim. He looked up at me. "You all right, Bridget?"

I nodded, though I was starting to feel strange. My shoulder throbbed, my snapped-at hand was feeling very hot, and it seemed the room was getting smaller all around me.

"I'll see to her." I heard Sallie's voice behind me, and felt her thin arm wrap around my waist to lift me up. "You go on and see to that rascal, we don't stand for that type of thing here. Collect up the money, will you?" She gave orders easily, and the scuffle of movement down below echoed the extra beats of my heart at the realization that it was her, of all people, whose arm was wrapped around my middle. I tried frantically to memorize the feel of her arm and the smell of her shoulder—an alchemy of sweat, talcum, and whiskey breath—while my feet wheeled under me until I was plunked down on Kate's settee. Lila swept in behind us and closed the door.

Kate dabbed at my face with a bit of cotton rusty with iodine.

"It won't be so bad," she said. "Once it heals, you'll look very rakish. Tilt your hat over that scar and you'll be the most exciting woman west of Chicago." Her words were gentle, but her mouth was a firm line stitched into her soft, powder-rimmed lips, and her eyes were glassy and empty as the windows of a store closed for the night. Lila perched over her shoulder and Sallie sat behind me on the sofa so that my back glowed with proximity.

The door opened and Jim brought in the cigar box, which he handed to Lila. They both looked at me like parents once again baffled by their incorrigible daughter.

"Thank you, Deputy," said Kate.

"Just doing my duty," he said.

"Well, I hate to see something like that," she said. "Bruises the atmosphere. Glad you were there to send the opposing message." She handed around little glasses of silvery gin.

"You were keeping all this in your room?" asked Lila, looking into the box and then down at me.

"You let her keep all that in her room?" asked Jim.

I looked around, feeling small and loomed-over. "It's my money," I said. "I suppose I'll keep it wherever I want."

Kate sighed, looking at Jim and Lila. "I offered to keep it in the safe, but if there's one thing I've learned over the years it's that you can't force a girl to do what's best for her."

"Oh, yes you can," said Jim, jaw set. "I won't see you come to any more harm." He reached out and tapped the top of the box with one thick finger, nail rapping against the wood. "Lila, you put that in the safe."

"Right you are," said Lila.

"Now wait just a minute," I cried out, feeling slow and thick-headed.

"No, you wait just a minute," Lila said sharply. "He's right. Whores come to all sorts of grief over their hard-earned income, but we can't have you turning hellcat at the customers." She marched over to Kate's desk, beside which squatted the safe, took out a slip of paper, and wrote some figures on it before passing it to me.

"I ain't no pimp," she said. "This shows what was in there, and we'll adjust it anytime you add or spend anything. You want any of it, you ain't gotta explain nothing, just ask anytime I'm awake." I looked hard into her face, thinking I'd detect any lie that might be hidden there, but Lila had always been honest with me. I took the paper and tucked it into my bodice, where the sharp corner of the fold poked reassuringly into my breast. Lila nodded and carried my box over to the safe, crouching before it and twirling the dial. "Besides," she continued, "most of the gals already keep theirs in here with ours."

The safe door opened with a squeak, and I could feel Sallie craning her neck to get a better look at the stacked bills and little canvas bags stacked within. I watched my box get nestled in among them, and then the door clanged shut like a jail cell and Lila stood up.

"Tell her, Sallie," she prompted. I turned to look at her, my cut eye seeming to move a little slower than the rest of me.

"It's true," said Sallie. "I keep what I save in there, and most of the others do besides. Ain't no use letting your money sit out where anyone could snatch it up."

I looked back at Lila and nodded my assent for what she'd already done.

"It's settled, then," said Kate, rising to her feet. "Mr. Bonnie, thank you again for coming to our aid this evening. I hope you won't mind if we send Bridget here off to bed—she looks like she's about spent for the evening." She patted Jim on the arm and turned her impenetrable madam's smile up into his face, offering him no other option.

"Of course," he huffed, placing his hat back on his head. "Bridget, you rest up now, and take care." I tried to smile back but just showed my teeth. As Sallie was leading me out, I heard Kate continuing to coo a list of other ways to pass the evening.

Sallie slung me along the balcony to my room. "Don't fret," she said. "We all get stolen from now and then, comes with the territory. In fact, you got real lucky this time around."

"You ever been stole from?" I asked her, feeling drunk and swollen-mouthed, worn out from all the excitement.

"Couple of times, 'til I got wise." She propped me against my own doorway, then stepped in so close that we'd have been touching if I could have just taken a deep enough breath. "Next time you get a little pocket money out of that safe, you ought to get yourself one of these." She tilted at the waist and pulled at the front of her camisole, inviting me to look down her dress. I almost passed out, but instead swallowed and looked. There was something nestled between her perfect tits, but I forgot to notice what it was, given the surroundings.

"What's that?" I croaked.

She rolled her eyes and wriggled her hand down her front, pulling out a little ivory-handled derringer.

I snorted. "I seen cocks bigger than that just this evening," I said.

"Maybe so, but you plug a man, even with one of these, and you see if he still wants to rob you then." She stuffed the gun back in among the layers of lace and muslin that clung to her skin, then reached past me to open my door.

"Now go to bed, you look like six kinds of hell," she said, and went downstairs without so much as a backward glance, while I leaned against the doorframe, limp as a rag doll.

CHAPTER 7

Through the last of the late-summer nights, I took to stealing into Constance's room to peek through the crack in the wall and watch Sallie at work. It soon became clear that the performance I'd witnessed with John Borne was her standard procedure, but she had a way of making it seem special every time—I certainly never got tired of it. I'd let a trick traipse downstairs ahead of me before checking if Constance's room was empty and Sallie's was full, which was the case at least once per evening. Sometimes I'd come in at the middle, and when I pressed my eye to the crack I'd be greeted with her rolling hips and tumbling locks. Sometimes I'd catch the aftermath, in which she'd let them lie a moment and catch their breath, sweeping golden strands off her forehead. Twice I caught the very beginning, her dress falling in a pool around her feet only to be kicked carelessly to one side while she stepped out of shoes she never buttoned all the way up. Then the lift and arc of each foot was the real start of the show.

I started copying her moves on my own. I hadn't the nerve to just climb astride a fellow uninvited, but I could hold his gaze while I shimmied out of my dress. The effect of even this small change was immediate: the first time I did it, it was like the floor tilted under my feet and the trick, the bed, everything in the room just came sliding right up to me. My caller, a cavalryman who just moments ago had been flashing his epaulets to verify a tale of his own bravery, was utterly cowed. He watched me with great intensity, eyes shrinking to little glowing coals in his face. The music and chatter from down below filled the air between us like a perfume, and when I came up close to him, he curled an arm around my back and pulled me down under him in a way that was almost tender. That was the first screw of my life that I really enjoyed. I was used to thinking of myself as a tool for some foreign endeavor, or the performer of a useful service like a pickaxe or a postal clerk. That time, I felt a surge of my own presence, the spark that two can strike against each other. Though it wasn't the same as pleasure, which I wouldn't come to know until later, it still woke me up, alerted me to new possibilities.

Though I knew I was running the risk of being obvious, I tried copying other things from her as well. I would have told anyone who asked that I just wanted to do as well as she did, for Sallie made money hand over fist, but in truth I was just making that simple mistake that all girls in love make, that if I could be more like the object of my affection, this would somehow draw her to me. First I tried out her way of only half buttoning her shoes, but they kept slipping around my ankles and after the third time I tripped on my own feet, Arabella picked me up and warned me to knock it off before Grace started telling tales that I was drunk. The next night I tried her lazy way of leaning back and tossing her head, mouth screwed up to one side in almost a half smile; I can't imagine how I actually looked but it can't have been good, for when Constance caught my eye her brow was knit in frank confusion.

But there was something else Sallie did that I had only seen through the wall: after sliding from her dress she'd reach one hand up toward the ceiling, arc it back behind her head to grasp two pins buried in her hair, and pull them out in one smooth motion so that her golden mane tumbled down in one perfect, shining curtain. I was as transfixed as her callers were—we tensed as one as it fell to its full length and bounced slightly, swaying as in a summer breeze.

I'd have given anything to be the one to reach up from the bed and run my fingers down its shining length; more than that, I wanted to know how it felt to take an admirer's eyes and put them right where I wanted them, to pull the gaze where I felt it ought to be.

The trouble was, I couldn't figure out how she did it. Before coming to the Queen, I'd never thought about how I looked except whether I was clean. I hadn't even worn my hair up, just braided it down my back so I could get work done. Pinned up, Sallie's hair looked no different than mine, but try as I might I couldn't find which two pins to pull.

"Shit," I muttered into the mirror. It was well before opening time, on the type of early-fall afternoon where the light thickens to honey and oozes in through the window, and I was seated before the glass with a mouthful of pins, hair half-fallen down one side of my face like I'd done wrong and had my ears boxed.

"What're you doing?" came Sallie's voice from behind me. I jumped, and a miniature hailstorm of pins fell from my mouth as I twisted around. She was leaning on the doorframe, wearing her yellow day dress and dangling a glass of gin from one hand.

"Jesus, Sallie, you scared the hell out of me," I said. My face was flushed and I felt myself crackling from my outside inward, like a log that's just caught fire along the edges.

She shrugged and took a drink. "Door was open," she said.

She had me there. I took a breath, willing myself not to stammer as I looked at the bones of her wrist, how despite pointing outward they still led the eye down to her fingertips.

"Just trying something with my hair," I said.

She took a step inside, nodding. "Smart," she said. "You don't make nearly enough of it." She came forward and stood behind me in the glass, leaning forward to set down her tumbler on the tabletop, and for a moment I caught her scent of sweat and talc and old cotton, overlying some deeper essence I couldn't have put a name to. She put her hands on the back of my head and poked through the half knot still remaining, extracting a handful of pins that she stuck in her mouth as I had done a moment before. I would have expected her touch to be rough, but though businesslike she was gentle, handling my hair not as something beautiful in its own right, but as the valuable object it was. She pulled it out to its full length and before I could stop myself I closed my eyes; she combed through it with her fingers, slowing as I took a breath before fanning it out over my shoulders. She picked up my brush and went to work on the ends and I let myself drift just a moment too long.

"Feels good, doesn't it," she said, voice dropping into a deeper tone from its usual high register.

"Sure does." Eyes half-closed, I looked at her reflection.

She nodded. "My sister used to brush mine for me," she said.

"You have a sister?"

"Used to."

I opened my mouth to ask what she meant but pulled myself up short; I didn't dare say anything that might make her stop touching me.

"What're you trying to get it to do anyway?" she asked.

"Get what to do?"

"Your hair." She lifted her eyes to meet mine in the glass.

"I want it so it'll fall all at once when I've got a trick with me," I said.

"How so?"

"Just reach up, and . . ." I raised one hand up toward the ceiling and reached for the back of my head just as gracefully as I could.

Sallie paused in her brushing to watch me. "Hm," she said. "Where'd you come up with that?"

The stammer I'd been holding back pushed its way forward in my mouth. "I . . . I suppose I thought . . ." I could feel the heat coming off her body behind me, longed to twirl around and put my hands on her waist and slide them up, cup the underside of her jaw. She waited in silence, however, offering me nothing.

I pulled myself together and swallowed. "I mean, they picked out a redheaded gal, shouldn't they get one?" I finally said.

Sallie looked at my reflected face with its patchwork of glowing pink for one more long moment, then shrugged in assent. She leaned forward, arm brushing past my shoulder as she picked up her glass and drained it.

"Couldn't hurt," she said. "You're new at this work, right?"

I nodded.

"Here's what you do," she said. She showed me how to roll my hair up from the bottom and pin it with an X against the back of my skull.

"You might need one more," she said, "for your hair's thicker than mine, but mark my words: you give those pins a yank and shake out those curls and you can add two, three dollars to your asking price."

"That much?" I was shocked at such a quantity.

"Why not? You've got the goods, you ought to take these fools for all they're worth." She paused and gave me a long look in the glass. "Just don't take nothing else from *me,* got it?"

I gulped. "I . . . I didn't . . ."

She took hold of my shoulders and leaned down, lips brushing my ear as she whispered into it. "You know I can hear through my walls same as everyone else, right? You may be littler than Constance, but she's a damned sight more light-footed than you are."

Suddenly the room felt ice cold; I feared that if I looked at Sallie's hands on my shoulders they would be rimed with frost.

"I don't . . ."

"Sure you don't." Her tongue shot out in a pink flash and flicked at the tip of my earlobe. I let out a tiny gasp; before I could catch my breath she'd pressed on my shoulders to right herself and swept over to the doorway, where she paused to look me over.

"Best pick those up," she said, pointing at the pins I'd dropped when she'd startled me earlier. "You know Lila doesn't like a mess. And take that glass down for me when you go, will you?"

She shut the door on her way out, and a moment later I could hear her feet on the stairs as she made her own way down to the bar.

I thought about Sallie's warning all night: had she really known I was watching her, and did she really care? I couldn't imagine that she was anything more than slightly annoyed, for nothing pleased her more than being paid attention to. I steered clear of Constance's room for a few nights, but Sallie had a hold on me, and I wasn't ready to be let go.

After a few nights' abstention, I came out of my room in time to see Sallie leading a man up the stairs; he looked well-kept, beard trimmed and eyes bright, gloved hands on her waist. He must have been a gambler, plucked from one of the tables. I hung back to let them pass; before I could think twice I peered over the balcony to locate Constance, who was engrossed in a card game down below. I slipped into her room and lay down on the bed, wriggling up to the wall to press my eye to the crack. It was like always going back to the same theater, always seeing the same show. There was the soft *whump* of her dress dropping to the floor, and next the gentle step out of her half-unbuttoned shoes, first the left, then the right, while the trick slid out of his own clothes. This one acted fussy, pulling off his yellow chamois gloves one at a time, laying his jacket and trousers over the bedframe so they wouldn't crease. His union suit was clean, with just a ghost of a tea stain under the arms. He held on to the gloves, slapping them against his thigh and reaching out with the other hand to spin the rowel of a spur that he remembered too late wasn't there. A scratched gold signet ring shone on his finger and glinted as he placed a stack of coins on the washstand. When Sallie stepped forward to collect them, he flung out the hand that held the gloves and there was a pop of leather on skin.

Unruffled, Sallie lifted a hand to her cheek. "Now, George, that's a little more than you paid for, you know."

"And?" he growled.

"And if you don't either pay up or slow down, you'll have to leave."

He rummaged in his nearby trouser pocket and slapped another coin onto the stand, eyes fixed on her face. On my side of the wall I grew tense, hearing a sharp whine at the back of my mind like a far-off mosquito. Sallie nodded at the larger pile and approached him for the next part of her performance, in which I expected her to gently push him onto his back and climb up. As soon as she got close enough he smacked her again, this time with his hand, and grabbed her by one slender wrist. "Don't you sass me," he said. "I'll get what I came for."

"Of course you will," she said. He was still seated on the bed; between his parted legs she stood in her stocking feet. Her voice hadn't changed, but with her back to me I couldn't see her expression.

"Shut up," he snarled. He gave a yank and flipped her down onto the bed. "I won't be bucked." He cuffed her a third time and shoved her shift up high around her waist. She didn't fight, but when she turned her face to my wall I could see where his ring had caught and there was a trickle of blood in the corner of her mouth, livid against her cheeks, whose creamy pallor had gone chalky and flat. He placed one hand on her throat, fine hand bones pushing out against the skin, and pushed up so her chin lifted in terrifying false pride, but the rest of her seemed limp. Her teeth were pink, and there was a faraway look in her eye, as though she were a passenger gazing out from a train she hoped would take her away from all this.

Without thinking I rushed out of Constance's room, grabbing the doorframe so I swung wide like a child playing crack-the-whip, and ripped open the door to Sallie's room. The trick was into her now with oddly spaced, deep thrusts. For a split second my gaze lighted on the cluster of ribbons tied to the bedrail, the groove the iron posts were carving into the floor—I thought, absurdly, that Lila wouldn't be too happy to see those. Then I ran the three paces over to the bed and grabbed at the man's shoulder, round and sweaty as a wrapped ham. I yanked at him and he reared back and shook me off without breaking his strange rhythm. Some men are like that, their blood gets up and it's like a fit, they can't tell the difference between fighting and fucking. I grabbed at him again with both hands and bit him, right where the shoulder turns into the neck. I felt a crunch of sinew between my teeth. There was a roar and a feeling of being lifted up, and then I was on the floor and there were two bursts of light: one from the back of my head where it hit the floor and one in my cheekbone shaped just like the back of his bony hand, followed by a singing, metallic pain on the return blow.

All I heard was his breath, as loud and focused and uneven as his thrusting had been just moments before. He must have lived his whole life that way, off-kilter and staggering. There came a pressure on my throat and white lights bloomed up before me; the whine that had been at the back of my mind came flying up as a scream that bubbled and snared in my mouth. I tried to move but nothing seemed to happen; darkness rose up around me like I was falling backward down a well. I had a vision of Sallie out on the prairie, running off ahead of me toward the distant smudge of a cottonwood grove, bleached-straw hair swirling around her as she turned back to me and her face dissolved.

Then there was a grunt and a scream, and then a gunshot like a whip cracking against my ear. The pressure lifted from my windpipe and I gasped in great, heaving breaths as the saloon crashed back over me. The man twisted up toward Sallie, deep red spreading along the back of his union suit. Just beyond him, Sallie reloaded the little cock-sized derringer that stuck out of her fist like a too-large pointer finger. It rang out again and the man dropped to his knees, wheezing. Hands lifted me up and dragged me away, while all around me was a welter of voices and shouts, many feet in many boots, and no music to be heard anywhere.

I must have fainted, or perhaps there is just a gap in my memory, but the next thing I remember hearing clearly was Henrietta's voice, saying my name softly. I opened my eyes to see her sitting on the edge of my bed. As soon as she came into focus everything else started to spin, and I clapped my eyes shut again.

"You're awake," she chirped.

"What happened?" The words had to climb and roll their way out over a jaw that ached like a rocky stream bed.

"Sallie shot that trick that was beating on you," she said, and giggled. Her voice cut through the air and landed sharp on my ears. There was a little pause where I knew she would be shaking her head, though I didn't open my eyes to check.

"I'm glad you're all right, but she oughtn't to shot him. He's an officer, and his pa's in Congress." She leaned in closer to whisper. "They're saying he's like to die."

"Is Sallie okay?" I mumbled.

"Yep, she's okay," said Henrietta. "She's in a heap of trouble, though."

My heart gave a sickening guilt-leap. I sat up and pulled my eyes open as a tide of swamp green rose through my cheeks. Henrietta, always quick on her feet, had the washbasin under me before I even knew I was going to puke. She patted me gently over my shoulder.

"You got a bad few whacks on the head there," she said. "Doc says you gotta rest awhile, ain't nothing else for it."

"I gotta talk to her," I said.

Henrietta set the basin down and pushed me gently backward. I found I could not resist the pull of the mattress, whose stable grasp I welcomed after the miserable spinning of sitting upright. I heard her saying something else, but darkness closed over me like the lid of a box, and her voice relaxed into a flow of sound that I could not distinguish.

The shot trick must have struck me bad, for I don't recall much of the time that followed. For a time I drifted as a leaf in a stream of meltwater, unaware of waking or sleeping. Waves of heat and cold passed over me, which I took for the rising and setting of the sun. Sometimes the past reared up before my eyes, and I would be a tiny speck confronted by my pa's marble teeth under the shadow of his hat before the tears rolled off his cheeks and filled a bathtub that I soaked in up to my neck. Then I'd be whisked off in the gentle hiss of the wind in the cottonwood trees, landing tiny among the trampling feet of the cattle in their pens, shoving and mooing as they waited to be sent off to slaughter. Other times I came almost all the way back to my room. I'd catch the tail of a bit of music from below, a half sentence of conversation, and I'd grab hold of it like a drowning man grabs the last end of a rope before the sea pulls him under. But then the song would change, or Sallie would lean forward to show me her gun, mouth oozing blood, and I'd sink once more into the dark eye of a storm where thunder rolled eternally but lightning never struck.

Finally, I rose up to a room full of mellow lamplight, and when I looked around it seemed solid and present, not likely to dissolve if I reached out to touch anything. I lifted one hand and ran it over the quilt, which felt strangely rough but stayed put.

"Welcome back," said Constance, looking up from her book. "If you are, that is. You've been talking some very strange talk, I must say."

I eased myself half-upright. My head ached, but it was the dull, familiar ache of the living, not the railroad spike that had pinned me down before. From below I could hear someone playing "Beautiful Dreamer" on the piano—I wish I'd thought to laugh at the coincidence.

"How long's it been?" I asked.

"Oh, just a couple of days," she said. She kept her tone light. "You hungry?"

I thought a moment, but my body seemed very far away from my head. "I'm thirsty as hell is what I am."

She poured a glass of water and handed it to me, then rose and moved toward the door. "You've had the whole place on tenterhooks. Bart's got a whole teakettle's worth of his cure-all waiting for you, and I already secured you the week off. Jim Bonnie's probably down there too—he's been pacing the boards like a madman ever since the fight. Would you like to see him?"

I shook my head.

"Well, I'll tell him you're out of the woods anyway. He'll be relieved to hear it."

I heard her going down the stairs. A minute later Kate and Lila appeared in the open doorway. Kate looked vague, distressed—the rouge on her cheeks stood out for artifice, and when she moved it seemed like little puffs of face powder were left in her wake. Lila followed like a crow perched on her shoulder as they approached the bed and stood over me.

"Are you all right?" asked Kate.

I nodded. "What happened?"

Kate perched herself on the edge of my bed in an almost motherly fashion, clasping her hands and looking with just-too-bright eyes out the window beside my bed; when she spoke there was a bitter note of laudanum on her breath.

"I won't ask you how you knew what was going on in that room," she said. "I despise these . . . specialists who think that money pays down being so vile, and Sallie should have known better than to permit that type of nonsense, extra or no extra. As if hurt can be bought and sold like railroad stocks. He had a Bowie knife the size of an opium pipe in his boot—lord only knows what would have happened if he'd been left to his own devices." She sighed and looked at her hands, then at Lila, who stood silent, hands on hips, her jaw working side to side.

"Still, she didn't have to shoot him again," Kate continued. "That first pop was plenty. I suppose you heard his pa's in politics—you can't just go around shooting people like that, especially in a place like this." Seeing her habitual equanimity tipped over into distress like this, I felt a fresh sweat breaking out all over.

"Is she okay?" I asked hoarsely.

"She's fine. Jim pulled some strings with a judge he came up with so she won't go to jail—our debts to him certainly keep mounting—but she's going to clear out for a while, try her luck up in Cheyenne."

The room seemed to darken, as though some unseen hand had snuffed out the lamp. "She wanted to go to San Francisco," I rasped, tongue thick in my mouth. Behind Kate, Lila looked at the ceiling and re-gritted her teeth.

Kate patted the bedclothes beside my arm. "So do a lot of people, my dear, but it's an expensive trip. Cheyenne will have to do."

She rose and stood again beside Lila. "Like I said, we won't ask how you knew what was going on the other night, but Bridget, this better not happen again. You've caused plenty of scenes for the time being—to say nothing of the costs involved. Let this be a warning to learn some discretion. Pull yourself together, and change your ways before Jim gets a notion of what's really going on in that pretty little head of yours." She touched Lila gently on the arm. "Lila, I feel another headache coming on—will you take me to bed, please?" She held out one hand and let Lila lead her out of the room.

As soon as they were gone, I pulled myself up and swung my legs carefully over the edge of the bed. My entire body was suffused with a lank, sweaty ache like dirty linen, and my feet felt like knobbly potatoes against the floorboards. I made my slow and leaning way out of my room and along the balcony to Sallie's door, which was open a crack. She was seated before the mirror, braiding her hair, holding it up with one hand to swig from a whiskey bottle.

"Sallie?" I croaked from the doorway.

"What do you want?" she said without looking up.

"Can I come in a minute?"

She dropped her half-done hair so it fell in one flap like a curtain over a dirty window. "Why not," she said. I pushed the door open and stepped inside, shutting it behind me and leaning on it. I looked like a schoolgirl who'd snuck out of her dormitory in the middle of the night: barefoot, hair loose, nightgown hanging limp around my body.

"I heard you was leaving," I said.

Sallie picked up a half-smoked cigarette from a saucer on the table and lit it, the rasp of the match all but drowning out my voice.

"I am," she said, puffing hard to pull a spark back into the paper. "Apparently I'm a liability, endangering the business, or their protection agreement, I forget which. If only that lawman cared for blondes instead of redheads, it'd be me staying cozy and snug and you bumping your ass over to the godforsaken Territory."

"What about San Francisco?"

"What about it?"

"You ain't going there no more?"

"I was," she said, voice rising. "What do you think that extra money was for he was paying me? I assume you saw the whole thing." She waved her cigarette at me and took another pull, followed by another drink.

"But that's gone, and most of the rest besides. Stingy cunts wouldn't but chip in for a stage." She pointed her chin right through me in the direction of Kate's parlor. "So it's back to square one, screwing my way up from the bottom once again."

"I was trying to help," I said, feeling smaller and smaller with each passing moment.

"Well, you didn't help, did you," she said. "I would've rode it out and lived to see another day. You think that was the first trick wanted to get cranky with me? You think that's all it takes to bring me down? Hell." She spat on the floor, and I felt myself recoil slightly, shocked at the coarseness of the gesture. She sneered up at me. "He and I had a deal. But no, you and your little secrets. Like everyone can't see you beaming out unnatural thoughts from the fuckin' moon."

"Kate said he had a knife," I all but whispered, desperate to smooth the sharp edge from her voice, lift the furious gleam from her eye, but she ignored me.

"Well, of course he did. They all do. You think this is just a job, just more chores to do, don't you. You toss your head and service a few cowboys and keep the law's balls drained so this whole damned house will leap to your rescue the moment anything goes awry. Your best friend reads you stories and your pennies go for candy like a good girl's should, and it's all nice as pie, isn't it? You don't see the first thing about this, though, do you. They *all* have a knife, Bridget. They all have a gun, and they were all born with two fists on the ends of their arms. You think you've got this all figured out, but any single one of 'em could take a swipe at you some night and you'd be dead before you hit the ground."

She stubbed her cigarette out with a shaking hand that caused the saucer to buck and toss ash over the tabletop and took another swig from her bottle. "I'd have rode it out," she said again, looking into its amber contents. "I've rode out worse. And so will you."

She looked up at me, and for the first time I saw the real hardness in her yellow-brown eyes, flat and white with stone slabs in the center.

"I'm sorry," I said, as if it could mean anything to her.

"Oh, well then."

"I wish you didn't have to go."

"Me too," she said, twirling on her stool to face the mirror again, picking up the silver-backed brush. "Me fuckin' too."

I slipped out and just made it back to bed before a wave of sorrow crashed over me. I shoved myself deep under the covers and pulled my arm into my sleeve, cramming the cuff into my mouth to soak up the sobs that seemed to ripple up from my legs and out through my mouth. I was like a tunnel, a portal through which some otherworldly awfulness passed into this one. It went so much deeper than the pain in my head or Sallie's imminent departure, or even the fact that it was all my own fault. I couldn't have put a name to what I felt for her, but it was so strong, like my heart had been trying to push its way out through my ribs; with Sallie gone, if it did escape it would have nowhere to go. My own misapprehension, my lack of ties to this world—the knowledge that she was right and it would take but one swipe to end me, one strong wave to wash away my footprints, leaving only some vague memories flickering behind a few men's eyes—the notion that despite all the distance I had traveled, I was destined merely to pass through the lives of others, what was to be done with such a thought? All of this came out in round, perfect howls that spent themselves in a sodden wad of cloth, my teeth clenched over it so tight I felt sparks in my jawbone, until I ran out of steam and fell into a deep and silent sleep.

When I woke the next day, Sallie was already gone. Constance said she left smiling, though she had little more than the yellow dress and sagging carpetbag she came in with. When I went to look in on her empty room, there was nothing left but a saucer marked with a sooty thumbprint and a yellow ribbon under the bed, already furring with dust.

PART TWO

FIRST SNOW

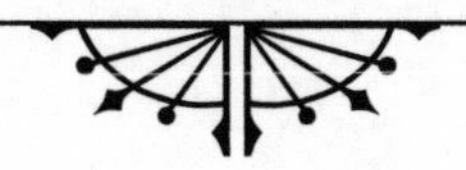

CHAPTER 8

I got back to work a few days after Sallie left. The loss of Sallie cost me a week's wages, paid forward in the subpar whoring I was guaranteed to do with a broken heart and busted head; Constance made a bulldog face when I told her, but I didn't fight it. All I wanted was a semblance of routine again, for life to take a shape more fully formed than the head-throbbing drift of lying abed. And so the first night my room wasn't actively spinning, I brushed my hair, put my work clothes on, and headed downstairs to turn a trick or two. It was my first heartbreak, and so I was genuinely shocked to discover that life had gone on: despite the gloom that, to my eye, seeped through the saloon like a feverish miasma, the lamps at the Queen flickered just as warmly as ever they had done.

Aching for normalcy and desperate for something to do, I focused on the small things all around me and tried to be as helpful as possible. I worked hard during the day, pitching in on chores I hadn't done since Mrs. Mackey last made faces at me. It had the additional effect of taking the edge off Lila's ire—rightly or wrongly, she blamed me for the fracas with Sallie. So I polished every speck of soot from the lamp chimneys, waxed the scratches out of Roscoe's piano, scoured Bart's heavy pots with sand, carried Kate's rug down the stairs and out into the yard where I beat out great clouds of dust that swooped away on the wind like flocks of brown birds. I helped Constance crate up some books she'd finished with and lugged the boxes down to the storeroom; she raised one eyebrow when I offered to help, but then just shrugged and stood aside.

When the next wash day came I manned the tub, toting buckets of scalding water out from the kitchen. It felt good to be working outside again. Our red dresses ran something awful, staining the water crimson as the Nile and leaving a pink crust around my fingernails. At first, Grace hung around to supervise, watching like a skinny goose for chances to peck at me, but when it became clear that I knew what I was doing she clucked, huffed something I didn't catch, and stumped off inside to look for more trouble. I knelt in the yard, sleeves rolled up and stray hairs plastering themselves to my forehead, hoping to wear myself out with simple labors. It was harsh but refreshing. The yard stank like every other yard in Dodge from its proximity to cow pens that were only gradually quieting as the last herds of the year were loaded up and shipped off, but the sky above was clearer than glass, and the sun was bright. Scrubbing felt like atonement, letting the water scald my arms and rough up my hands, while autumnal gusts off the plains were cold enough to raise prickling gooseflesh across my shoulders. Sitting back on my heels, I thought maybe this was where I belonged, out back where I would be neither seen nor looked at, and where I could get in nobody's way.

I heard a man's voice shouting inside the saloon, and moments later an upwelling of coos from the whores. I marked the sound and knew that it likely signaled some new exciting arrival, but given how the last one had turned out I was in no rush to learn more. With a sweaty grunt and a heave, I tipped up the tub and let it run out over the dirt, trickling in miniature scarlet gullies between tufts of grass before it sank into the earth. I wrung our dresses one by one and pegged them up onto the clothesline to flap wetly and sag under their own weight. Washing always seemed to take exactly the right amount of time, getting done just as I was getting sick of it.

"There she is," said Constance from behind me. I turned to see her standing just outside the back door with the same neat, soft-shouldered man I'd seen my first night at the Queen, and understood what all the fuss had been: Pierre was back.

Pierre was a Frenchman who'd gambled his way from New York to Denver, and despite his penchant for soft beds and good brandy he seemed to have taken a liking to the prairie. Summers, he crisscrossed the cattle trails between San Antonio and Ogallala, infuriating Texans by beating them at poker; on one of those crossings he'd made the acquaintance of Constance, who was just about the only French-speaking whore west of New Orleans. Though their association was born from Pierre's homesickness for his native tongue, they'd become quite good friends, and he liked to blow into Dodge now and then to rest a spell. He rented a little room on the ground floor behind the bar, but it was rarely more than a storage closet for his luggage. In practice, he shacked up with Constance, helping himself to half her bed just about every night he was in town. It was an unusual arrangement—no one else was allowed overnight lodgers—but everyone at the Queen liked Pierre. His reputation drew in enough aspiring card sharps to more than cover his room and board, he complimented Bart's cooking and brought new sheet music for Langley and, by ear, Roscoe. But more than that, he spread good humor among the whores, tweaking our noses and sproinging at our curls as if we were his own spoiled daughters whom he had long given up trying to keep on the straight and narrow.

I dried my hands on my skirt and went over to say hello. He put his arms out and pulled me in for a kiss on each cheek. Though his frock coat was faded from black to bruise-purple and its shoulder seams were sprouting loose threads, his mustache was soft and there was a slight whiff of toilet water over the usual potpourri of horse and human.

"Brigitte," he said with a smile. "How wonderful to see you again, and looking so well!"

I blushed. I hadn't expected to be remembered after our brief meeting before he'd taken off for the bulk of the summer, much less greeted so warmly. "It's nice to see you, Pierre," I said. "Will you be here long?"

"Pierre's going to overwinter with us," said Constance. As she spoke, he slipped an arm around her waist and I felt dull envy growing like mold along the bottom of my stomach. "Come inside, we're celebrating." She reached out and grabbed my forearm, eyes aglow.

I looked around the yard, seeking some excuse to get away from their bubbling joy, but my work was done, so I followed them into the saloon. It was the grayish time of afternoon before Grace set to lighting the lamps; in the mossy dark I could see the whores clustered around the bar while Bart poured out glasses of something relatively worthwhile. Pierre and Constance took their rightful place at the center of the group.

"How was the trail? Were you lucky?" Henrietta asked.

"Very much so," said Pierre. "I have arrived with a heavy purse, which I'm sure mademoiselle will help me increase." He goosed Constance at the waist and she giggled like Henrietta, slapping his hand gently. He murmured something in her ear and she blushed. Arabella had drifted up beside me, and I caught her eye before she went in for her own kisses and brandy glass, the both of us frankly fascinated to see Constance so undone before a man.

I stepped back and took little sips while the whores all said their hellos. He greeted each girl by name, drawing it out in his lush, floral accent. In his mouth we were each briefly transformed, from short-legged Bridget to elegant Brigitte, from lank-haired Arabella to lissome Arabelle, from glassy-eyed Kate to dreamy Katrine.

"I came back expecting a full house, but there are so few of you here, has someone gone away?" he asked. It was odd to hear a man taking such an interest in whorehouse business.

"Oh, we lost one just a little while ago," said Constance, a little caution in her voice. The rotten feeling in my middle thickened.

Pierre asked Constance a question in French; from her reply the only word I could pick out was Cheyenne. It tugged at me to think of Sallie out on the road, swaying in a stagecoach, gaze sweeping back and forth over the endless plains.

"Quel dommage." He paused to light a cigar, puffing at a lamp that Constance held up for him, chimney tilted back to expose the flame. He said something else; when Constance answered him, she added a tiny jerk of her head in my direction. Pierre raised his eyebrows, but Constance gave a half nod that seemed to contain some sort of promise, and his brows returned to their posts. He smiled and picked up the bottle, pouring more for all of us. I held out my glass mechanically, and when I brought it to my lips I tasted nothing of its contents.

"Venez, venez ici, mes belles!" Pierre said, gesturing expansively, holding the bottle by the neck, and the whores pressed in, cooing like scarlet doves. "I must tell you, I met the most extraordinary person," he said. "In Abilene, a gunfighter, which is of course quite an ordinary thing to be in Abilene, but this one was a woman!"

The whores burst out in laughs and snorts like this was some tremendous joke, reeling back as one. Though I knew they meant it, they looked false, as though they couldn't stop playing to men even when they liked them. "Come on, tell us another one, Pierre," said Henrietta.

"It is true!" cried Pierre. "We played stud poker at the saloon Yellow Stud, and she lost. Terrible card player, no head for strategy, but what do you expect." Behind him Arabella gave a silent scoff and Constance pinched her arm. "Dressed as a man, and fought like a man too, I must say," he continued.

He went on to tell a routine frontier story of integrity questioned, guns drawn, and this woman gunfighter drawing second but firing first, fast as a snake. I drained my glass and pushed past Henrietta and up the stairs.

"Where's she going?" I heard someone say, but Pierre was already moving on to his next tale over Constance's laughter.

Lila was waiting on the balcony, rolling a cigarette. "How long's he aim to stay this time?"

"How the fuck should I know," I said, forgetting that Constance had already told me.

"Don't be tetchy with me, it's Kate who's asking," she said, licking the paper to twist it shut.

"I know who's asking," I said. "Her being the one wanting to know just won't make me know any better is all."

She looked at me sidelong. "Buck up, will you? Or are you jealous of him now too?"

I snorted. "I just don't like how they play up to him is all."

"I'd have thought you'd be pleased to see Constance so chipper," she said. "She ain't got many regulars."

"Ain't many can keep up with her," I said.

Lila nodded. "She's pretty enough, but I wish she wouldn't be so free with her smarts." She struck a match and lit the cigarette. "Why grudge her this one?"

I sighed, remembering that the rot coating my insides had nothing to do with Constance. "Where'd he come from anyway?" I asked, by way of apology.

"France," said Lila, blowing smoke in my face. "So mind your fuckin' manners." Slapping my rear, she sauntered past and down the stairs, empty hand already out for Pierre to kiss it.

Autumn that year was mostly warm spells broken up by fits of stormy weather. Like a child throwing a fit, the skies would drop buckets of rain or odd little snow flurries, then heat up to make the streets run with mud that would harden into ruts like cobblestones in a city wracked by earthquakes. The whole town was off-kilter from being jerked back and forth, and it seemed everyone wanted to shake off the pall of uncertainty with as much drinking, gambling, and whoring as their time and purse would allow.

The fall storms were unwelcome to cattle drivers and homesteaders, but each one packed the Queen with men who wanted to shelter from the night surrounded by warm and smiling company. Roscoe would bang away at his favorites and every few minutes the door would swing open, gusts of wind blowing in some fellow who'd stand there stamping and blowing like a steer, looking astonished that he wasn't the only one who'd had the idea that a saloon was a better place to hide from a storm than a tent or a damned sod house. They all complained relentlessly about the cold and damp while they steamed in their coats and Bart ladled out his Sunday Brew, the noxious mix of odds and ends that he stirred together with molasses and tea every Sabbath and sold for ten cents a glass to anyone willing to find out what was in it.

Fresh clouds had been gathering all day; knowing it would be a long and repetitive evening, I slipped out the front door to take a breath and watch the storm come in. The wind snatched my breath right out of me, but I didn't care. I'd come to love the cold, the way it sliced right through my clothes to prickle at my skin, the way it rushed past me, incapable of caring. Back in Fort Smith, there'd been a woman who'd steal anything she came across; the postmaster's pencil, buttons on a shop counter, worn-out horseshoes, they just jumped into her hand as if pulled by a magnet. Everyone knew it was a kind of madness, as she'd had four boys, a husband, and two brothers go off with General Lee and not a one come home, and the townsfolk tried to be patient with her. All the same, it was aggravating, and so every now and then someone would call the sheriff and she'd get drug off to jail for a few days, where she'd cry until that too became aggravating and the deputy would let her out with a stern warning. I thought of her sometimes in Dodge, where the wind was the same as she had been: unthinking, unwanting, just snatching at everything, wailing at nothing. It was movement that could not be stopped because it had no goal and neither ending nor beginning.

The changes that the wind brought to the sky were some of the most beautiful things I'd ever seen. Great, billowing clouds that seemed as though nothing could ever induce them to move would be suddenly swept aside, pulled carelessly across the sky like a gambler raking in his winnings. Then out of nowhere, the reeling, endless blue would be scudded up with high wisps that threw the heavens' depth into terrifying relief. But the storms, those were truly magnificent, the sky's color changing to iron gray for thunder, pearly translucent white for snow, or feverish frog-belly green before a twister—though I'd only seen that once. I've never felt more sure of the existence of God than I did in those moments, watching Him prepare the sky to deliver some fresh chaos into our lives.

I shivered where I stood. It had gone white earlier this afternoon, which was how we knew a blizzard was coming—first of the year, and early, for it was but October—but now the clouds were finally gathering, piling up stern and sharp-edged just outside of town. From the far end of the street came a train whistle, no doubt telling anyone still working to hurry it up and finish loading so the cargo could get to Chicago and the loaders to the saloons before the sky broke open. I looked up instinctively—I don't think there's anyone on this earth who can ignore a train whistle—and then I saw them.

Astride a big bay mare came a rider in a heavy canvas coat buttoned up high to the collar, hat pulled low against the wind so that no face was visible. A rope, secured on one end to the saddle horn, was wrapped around the wrists of a man on the other, tying him into his seat on a dun gelding. The man and his horse both looked defeated—the man was hunkered into himself as far as he could get, and when a fresh blast of wind came barreling down the street he scrunched up tighter. I'd seen plenty of marshals, posses, and even a few enterprising citizens bringing bandits into town before, and they usually weren't worth much interest until they chose an establishment in which to dispose of their reward money. But something about his captor caught my attention and I could not look away. Maybe it was the ease with which such a small person—for the lead rider looked fairly light-boned under all those layers—rode such a large horse, or that the quarry looked so thoroughly licked. Or maybe I just knew, from all the way down the street, that in a town full of novelties, this really was something new.

The rider passed me by without stopping, but the captive looked up for a moment as the door of the Queen opened, spilling music and golden lamplight out onto the sidewalk, to admit some new shelter-seeker. Through a veil of scraggly hair, two small eyes picked me out and he spat into the mud between us. Behind the angry gesture, there was a hunger in that gaze that frightened me, some unfillable emptiness that struck an echo in me like a hammer to a bell. I'd seen it before—if he were a horse he'd be a ruined horse, fit only for soap. Then the door behind me fell shut and I was thrown into darkness again; the sky had gone leaden and the first flakes were blowing sideways up the street as though they too would like to stop somewhere for a drink and some merry conversation. The two riders blurred into the gloom, so I turned and slipped back inside, chilled to the bone.

A great shiver ran up from the soles of my feet to the top of my head as soon as I came into the barroom, before the heat enveloped me once more in a heavy blanket of smoke and wet leather. In the great stone hearth a fire was burning brightly, and clustered around it were the most recent arrivals at the Queen. A mist hung around them as their coats steamed; against the firelight they were but cutouts in scratchy wool and well-worn leather. I gave one more shiver and made my way over to the bar, where a small group of cowboys were talking. I hung just outside their field of vision and waved at Bart, who shook his head and nodded at the cowboys.

"I seen him being drug in just now," said a cowboy with a brown mustache. "That sheriff sure won't be happy to have him."

"Why not?" said one of his fellows, tall and sandy-haired, while the third one, little and squirrelly-looking, nodded emphatically. "He's been raising hell around here for months. Everyone knows Ottis Shy, but I'll wager no one wants to."

"You mean that rough-looking scallywag I seen just outside?" I saw my opening and appeared between their elbows, and all three looked at me in happy surprise, as if a songbird had just lighted on their saddle horn.

"You seen him?" said the one with the mustache.

"Skinny, real scraggly-looking?" I said.

"That's the one," said Sandy Hair.

"A rider brought him just now, up the street." I tilted my chin up at the one with the mustache, for his shirt was newest-looking, and made my eyes wide. "Scared me about half to death."

"Well, how about something to steady those nerves of yours," said Mustache. He signaled to Bart, who poured me a shot of cold tea that tasted like rust.

"Anyway, it ain't catching Ottis that's the trouble, it's his brothers you have to watch out for," Mustache explained. "You think those two are really going to let their own baby brother get hung by some dern judge?"

"They sure ain't," said Sandy Hair.

"Didn't you hear?" said Squirrelly. "Them brothers is dead. Scalped."

"By, who, Indians?" said Sandy Hair.

"Nah, it was them Lee boys," said Squirrelly.

"And that wildcat sister they let ride with 'em," said Mustache; I felt a little match-strike of curiosity and drew in closer.

"Who's this Lee gang?" I said, pushing in between Mustache and Squirrelly, who jumped like a prairie chicken at the sound of my voice. He looked even younger up close. I would have wagered good money that I was the first gal who'd spoken to—or even toward—him who wasn't his own relation.

Mustache, however, was unbothered. He wasn't too tall, but still managed to affect a vantage point as he looked me over.

"You must be new in town," he said.

"No, sir, not especially."

"Well, you must not listen to your customers very much then, if you've been in Dodge that long and ain't heard of the Lees."

"Can't say that I have," I said, taking a delicate sip from my glass. On a slower night I would have liked him to tell me a tale or two, but the Queen was brimming and I felt compelled to keep things moving.

Mustache leaned toward me to cut his fellows out of the conversation, and I could see them backing away out of the corner of my eye. I just caught Sandy Hair muttering, "Damned Stew, always takes the best ones for himself."

"Then I guess it won't do me no good to tell you, if you don't listen," said Stew. He set his hat on the bar; a half smile twitched under his mustache while I assessed him. A lively mount, not apt to throw a rider, but not without spirit either. There are worse ways to start a night's work.

"Well," I said, "if you ain't talking and I ain't listening, what do you say we go upstairs?"

"I say why not." He drained his glass and plucked his hat off the bar as I grabbed him by the wrist and led him upstairs. Below me, Roscoe burst into an especially lusty rendition of "What a Friend We Have in Jesus," which he had just learned.

After the trick, I lingered a moment at the top of the stairs to let the cowboy troop down ahead of me. I liked to stop sometimes and watch the action, to see how it developed over the course of an evening. Below, there was a constant swirl that would have been dizzying to anyone unused to it, but I had my landmarks to look for as my gaze swept left to right across the room. By the hearth, the card players were scowling purposefully into their hands; at the corner table, Pierre was shuffling a red-backed deck with easy grace, clean hands flashing. At another table, Arabella was draped over the back of one man's chair. She looked up and caught my eye; I smiled at her and shrugged, and she cast her eyes heavenward in response. She was popular with the gamblers, for she could be still and quiet for ages at a time; it seemed like easy work, but I'd done it myself and found the tedium unbearable, and I always got chased off for being fidgety.

Toward the center of the room, the cards petered out; the right side of the Queen was devoted solely to drinking and whoring, and although it was chillier, it was the far merrier place to be. I spotted Constance leaning against the bar and talking to some man, her expression relaxed and easy; beside her, Henrietta was giggling but watching the door, no doubt hoping her favorite caller would find his way through the storm and into her arms. I didn't see Lila, but sailing back and forth between the two camps was Kate, making one of her evening tours of the house. She was resplendent in her favorite wine-red dress, hair piled high, neck ringed in bright paste. Kate had gotten edgier the closer we got to the drives being done for the season, watching the skies like a farmer as the season threatened to turn at any moment and leave us all but deserted for the winter. Under my feet, Roscoe was striking up "Red River Valley," and sitting at the bar, watching me, was Jim.

"How do, Deputy?" I asked him when I came downstairs. He still had his coat on, old but good buffalo hide, with snowflakes melting into water droplets that shimmered on the collar.

There were two glasses and a whiskey bottle before him, and when I spoke he filled the second one and passed it to me with a smile, his square, grayish teeth spread all in a row.

"Well, if it isn't my lucky penny," he said with a chuckle. He wasn't the only one who called me that, but it didn't grate so much when he did it. "You all snugged in for the storm?"

I picked up the glass and gestured at the room, which was full not quite to the rafters but close enough. "As a bug in a rug," I said. "You planning to pass the evening here with us?"

"Just passing by, thought I'd stop to hear a little music. And besides, someone's got to protect you all from marauding outlaws on nights like this."

I craned my neck past him to look out the window, where I could see snow flying sideways against the black.

"Well, isn't that just my good luck that you was passing by," I said, and took a drink. From the first sip I could feel the sharp edges of my boredom starting to melt off.

"I heard you got a real bad outlaw up in your jailhouse," I continued.

"What'd you hear this time?"

"They're saying you got one—Ottis something—locked up this very minute."

Jim cocked his head to one side. "Now where'd you hear a thing like that?" he asked. Despite where we were and how we knew each other, he was very attached to my innocence, long-lost though it was.

I kept my tone light. "Oh, just heard some cowboys talking is all. They were all wound up about some rascal got drug up here."

He nodded, satisfied. "Yeah, we got Ottis locked up. He's a mean customer, I'll say that much."

"What's he done?" I asked.

"It'd spoil my evening to tell you," he said simply.

"What about that Lee gang that caught him?" I said.

"What about 'em?"

I shrugged. "Just curious. These boys made like they was real famous."

Jim nodded. "Yeah, it's two brothers and a sister."

I laughed. "They let their sister catch outlaws with 'em?"

It was Jim's turn to shrug. "Not the tack I would take, I'll say that much. But it was her brought in the bounty, plus the scalps for the others. Maybe she's gone her own way."

I bit the inside of my lip, thinking about the small-framed rider I'd seen coming up the street.

"But you don't need to worry about them, or any other bunch of ruffians," Jim continued. "In a couple days the circuit judge'll be by and Ottis'll take his hanging."

He drained his glass, shoved the cork into the bottle, and tucked it under his arm, clearly ready to change the subject. "What do you say, lucky penny? Got time for an old man before Lila comes around to give you the evil eye?"

"Old man money spends as good as a young one's," I said, and took his hand to lead him upstairs.

As soon as I shut the door to my room, Jim shuffled out of his buffalo coat and hung it on the peg, then sat on the edge of the bed to wrench his boots off like a homesteader preparing to take comfort in the arms of his loving wife.

"Don't settle in too much, Bonnie," I said. I liked to call him by his surname; he hated its girlishness, so it was an easy way to josh him. "You saw the bar, I'm going to be busy tonight."

He paused with one boot off and the other clutched in both hands, looking up from his figure-four shape. "Hell, Bridget, can't a man take his damn boots off?"

"Sure he can," I said. "He just can't get to playing husbands-and-wives on a night like this."

His half-booted foot clumped to the floor. "Well shit, Bridget." I'd swear before God Himself that there's nothing He made more delicate than a man's pride. One wrong touch and it withers up like a daisy. For a split second I flashed to my pa's sad eyes in the low point of a drunk, and my guts tightened in resentment before I reminded myself that Jim hadn't actually done anything wrong.

"Sorry, Jim, I don't know what came over me," I said.

"I thought you'd be happy to have a break from all those braggarts downstairs is all," he said. "But I can move it along if you want me to."

"No, no need for that," I said. "Kate's in a state, is all, over the drive season wrapping up," I continued, thinking to mollify him with some insider's gossip. "You know how she gets—one thing goes askew and she's wringing her hands, then Lila gets cranky and before you know it we're all in Dutch." I knelt down and took hold of the half-stuck-on boot. One good wrench from me had it off, though I pulled too hard and the recoil splayed me backward a little; Jim laughed as I picked myself up.

"All right," he said. "But no more of your lip, young lady. I come to pay you a call, after all." He held out his hand, which I took, and pulled me upright. Sitting still dressed on the edge of my bed, he placed one hand on my middle—he could just about span my waist with his wolf's paws—and looked up into my face. With his free hand, he brushed back a loose strand of my hair and ran his thumb over the scar my would-be robber had left above my brow. A silence fell between us; through it I could hear the general roar of the bar, whatever passed for conversation down there rippling like a river in flood, while Roscoe went to town on "My Bonnie Lies over the Ocean," already the second time that night.

"What is it?" I asked him at last.

"Why, nothing," he said. "But I look at so many ruffians all day I'd just as soon take a moment when something pretty crosses my path."

I smiled my wry, working smile, all pushed to one side of my face, but it was a nice thing to say.

"Well, Deputy," I said, "let's make you feel as good as I look, shall we?"

I unbuttoned his shirt and kept going, shucking him of his clothes layer by layer. His union suit had once been red but was now splotchy pink, with a hole along the button placket through which a tuft of salt-and-pepper chest hair sprouted. He put one hand to the back of my head—I'd have to repin my hair—and pulled me down to his face, but I turned quick at the last moment and he wound up planting a kiss behind my ear instead. He continued down toward my collarbone while I worked on the buttons of my dress, letting it fall in a scarlet pool around my feet.

Jim liked me to climb on top of him first to get things started, but once I'd ridden for a minute or two, he'd awkwardly flip us over and cover me like a tent. There was a care with which he held himself over me, as though afraid he'd squish me against the mattress, that I was grateful for. Plenty of tricks would be drawn to my littleness and then forget all about it in their passion, pinning me against the ticking 'til I squeaked like a mouse, but Jim was considerate in that regard, keeping himself propped on one elbow. It could be disquieting, though, the way he'd try to stare into my eyes through the remainder of the act, as though he really were mine and I his.

After, when his clothes were back on and he should have been sated, he sat on the edge of my bed. He looked nervous all of a sudden, twirling his hat like a missionary about to ask for a donation.

"Bridget, you ain't tired of all this?" he asked suddenly.

I turned around, still half-buttoned. "Tired of what?"

He lifted his hat, gestured at the room. "All . . . all this."

"My room? I suppose it could use a little cheer, but it'll be winter before too long, so I don't expect any cheer's coming," I said lightly.

He looked down, chuffled henlike at his knees.

"What I mean is, this life."

"You mean whoring?"

"I suppose I do."

I did up my last button and let my hands drop as a knot formed in my middle. The question seemed silly, the childish musing of someone accustomed to a warm fire and a full belly. Before this, I'd been scratching a living out of disappointment, thinking hard about my next meal. Now that those fears were allayed, it hadn't occurred to me to consider what I thought of it, beyond the immediate pleasures to be bought and sold.

"I ain't given it much thought," I said. "And besides, I ain't been here that long."

"But you're still, well, you're so lively," he said.

I didn't have an answer for that; the lead coating that had grown over my heart when Sallie left was only just chipping away, but the idea that this had been invisible to Jim was unsettling, given how much time he liked to spend in my company.

"Aw, hell, I'll just say it," he said after a moment. "Bridget, I want you to marry me."

I heard a laugh jump out of my mouth before I had a chance to stop it. I clapped both hands over my mouth, but that just pushed tears up into my eyes.

"What?" I finally said, pressing each cheek with the back of my wrist.

"I mean it. Marry me. I'll take you out of here."

"I'm sorry, Jim," I said. "You just caught me by surprise is all. Here I thought you were here for the usual, and then you spring this on me."

He looked down at his hat again. "I know," he said. "But I mean it."

A silence fell between us, a real one this time. I looked at his face, or what I could see of it, tucked down into his shirt collar as it was. It was red, more boyish than ever.

"What on earth would we do?" I asked. "Everyone in town would know you married a whore."

"Then we could leave. Go anywhere you want. Denver, Chicago, San Francisco, make a new start. No one would know what you were."

That last bristled me. "You'd know," I said.

"Be honest with yourself, what's in store for you here? How many good years you got left?" A pleading note crept into his voice and something welled up in me that was half annoyance, half disgust.

"I don't like your tone," I said. "That ain't none of your never-mind. I expect I've got as many years as I make out."

"What about Sallie?" he said.

"What about her?" My chest tightened as I wondered what sort of stories he'd been hearing about me.

"How long 'til something like that happens to you?"

The question rocked me back on my heels. "What the hell do you know about that?"

"You know that every gal in, well, in your profession comes to something like that sooner or later. I know it too. I ain't as young as I look." He chuckled. He was trying to lighten the mood, but I was in no frame of mind to be lightened.

"Your time's up," I said. I strode to the door and wrenched it open. The noise from downstairs flooded in, a ragged tide of men's voices and horsey, girlish laughter, glasses thudding onto tabletops, Roscoe banging away, exhausted. Jim stood up.

"I know I done took you by surprise," he said, standing so close to me in the doorway that I could feel the heat coming off his torso like a stove. "I ain't sore that you laughed at me. But think about it, will you? I could give you a good life."

I looked up into his face. It was red and gleaming, but I was too tight-chested to feel a shred of sympathy for him. "Go on downstairs and have a drink," I said. "Like I told you, I got work to do."

He put his hat on and edged out past me, the thump of his feet on the stair treads audible over the mix of three songs that Roscoe was playing all at once. There was the shove and crash of a gambler leaping out of his chair, and Virgil appearing out of nowhere to make him lower his drawn pistol, the music playing on as though no one had risked their lives just now. What before had looked bustling now looked grimy and chaotic. I looked around at the roaring faces of the drunks, the yawning, tooth-lined mouths that spewed nonsense or rotten air or sometimes just spewed, the grubby hands being laid on my friends. I heard a door open to my left and Constance ushered a trick out of her room; he winked at me as he passed, but behind him Constance's smile dropped as soon as his back was turned. She rolled her eyes at me, and then we linked arms without a word and went back downstairs to get back to work.

CHAPTER 9

The storm kept up for two days and three nights, a hellishly uneven mixture of rain and snow. First the rain would drum low and fierce on the roof and the boardwalk, then soften into snow that would give us brief moments of quiet before the wind picked back up, howling like an entire starving wolf pack was invading the town. It had been a long few days of men bursting through the door in gusts of cold air, clumps of snow melting all over the floor, and uneven, overly raucous laughter bursting out of all corners. Times like this we just got naps, not a full night's rest, for it was important to make the most of any opportunities that presented themselves before Dodge bedded down for the winter. Roscoe was going wall-eyed, but Langley was out of dope and worse than useless, leaving Roscoe alone to wring an atmosphere out of the keyboard.

I spent the little free time we had at the bar, trying and failing to chat with Arabella and Constance. Though we'd been trapped indoors for days and there was little enough to talk about, I couldn't quite bring myself around to telling anyone about Jim's proposal. Instead I chewed on it like a cow chews her cud, neither swallowing nor spitting it out.

To pass the time, I tried imagining married life. Accepting Jim was the sensible choice, for he was a decent man with a good job, but something about the whole proposition wedged in my chest, like a piece of furniture that can't be got through a doorway. When I tried to picture the tender moments that such a life might offer, I instead found my mind's eye wandering around the house he would build for me. I put myself in its sunlit kitchen, at a scrubbed table, stove in the corner with plenty of firewood piled high. Through the doorway, a parlor with high-backed chairs, side tables that I would polish every week, heavy curtains to keep out drafts in the wintertime. Upstairs, a high wooden bed—surely Jim would want something substantial—piled with quilts and pillows. Everything I pictured was orderly and solid, the type of house a good woman could keep well, but it only looked nice when I wasn't in it: floating like a ghost through this imaginary home, I felt twinges of longing for the life it represented. But as soon as I placed myself inside that house, the chores pressed back in: who but me would scrub that table, brush those curtains, make that bed? And with these questions returned the constant straying of my eye toward the door, tensing at any hint that it would open and fretting at the possibility that it would not. Try though I might, I could conjure up no cheery domestic scene; instead all that came up was the familiar, strangled sensation of sweating over a stove with nothing to do but wait for a man to come back. Perhaps I should have asked Constance whether that was a feeling that would wear off with time, but instead I avoided the conversation, fearful she'd advise me to accept.

Through the storm, the trade had been brisk but the tricks unremarkable, most buying pokes for want of anything else to do, and the mood was restive and seething. By the third night everyone in the Queen was bored to screaming. Constance wasn't even trying to read, just trailing her finger around the edge of a smudgy glass, absently watching Pierre make a fortune off a couple of rubes across the room, though he did so with none of his habitual glee. Sitting beside the card table, a man who'd lost all of his money was trying to raise a fresh stake by holding up a carpetbag with a cat inside, giving everyone within earshot the hard sell on the tom within, as if, to a man, they hadn't already refused to buy the animal. Us gals leaned on the bar and forced out half sentences now and then just to keep a semblance of conversation going, but there was tension in the air, everyone waiting for something—anything—to happen.

Finally, in came a crew whose boss had unwisely kept them from the last couple of towns, so that by the time they fought their way through the weather to hit Dodge, they were wild-eyed and restless, ready to jump on anything that looked softer than prairie scrub. They boiled in all at once, drunk already and talking loud. From the corner of my eye I saw Pierre look up in annoyance at their hooting as they dripped and stomped muddy clumps onto the floor. The cat man half lifted his carpetbag, which pulsed with movement from within as though the tom were eager to join up and trail cattle. Constance looked over my shoulder at the cowboys.

"They look about as trail-broke as deer," she said. "Let's get to it—a couple rounds with these fellows and Kate should relax for a few nights." She patted the back of her hair and fluffed the curly sprig that hung over her forehead, then swung her legs around and hopped off her barstool, bright smile already pasted to her face. I turned to follow and was appraising the cowboys when Lila appeared beside me.

"Why ain't you working?" she asked immediately.

"Why, hello, Lila, how's your evening going? Mine's just lovely, thank you," I answered without looking at her, taking a dainty sip from my coffee cup.

"Don't start with me," she said. "Kate's got a headache coming on and I can't find Langley anywhere."

"He's poorly," I said. "Dope supply ran out, I think."

"Shit, that's just what I need," said Lila. "You know where he is?"

"This ain't a big place—he can't have got far."

She snorted. "Don't play with me tonight, I'm in no mood."

"Ain't nobody in no kind of mood," I said. "We've been stuck in here for days, Lila."

"What would you have me do?" she snapped. "Throw out the men and lock the doors, tell everyone the whores are taking a holiday?" She gave me one flash of her eyes. "The drives'll be done before you know it and then you'll be lucky to catch two fucks a night. See if you sass me then. I catch you lazing around here again I'll tan your hide."

"All right, all right," I said. "I'm going."

As I turned away she grabbed my arm so she could speak low and clear into my face. "You do that," she said. "You get going with these fellows, or if that doesn't appeal to you, you can go right on upstairs and pack your things and go on and try this attitude of yours out at another house. See how your lip plays up the street with Mr. Montgomery."

I yanked my arm from her grasp, smoothed my skirt, and patted my hair. I tilted my chin and smiled. "Better?" I asked.

"Much," she said dryly, and flounced off toward the back room, presumably to verify Langley's incapacitation. I searched the crowd for Constance to see if she'd witnessed the scene, but all I could see was jacketed shoulders and the backs of my friends' heads.

Then there was a high yowling sound, and a chair crashed to the ground as the center of the room erupted. The failed gambler's cat had finally escaped his carpetbag prison—I caught a blur of orange fur as he twisted out of his jailer's hands and flew through the air toward the bar. There was a sense of palpable relief, as if everyone had been waiting for such an explosion. There were two competing surges as half the room rushed after the cat, which was streaking along the bar, and the other half wriggled out of their way. Someone threw a glass at the poor animal and I ducked just in time; the shards showered over my head and shoulders. Still crouched, I crawled behind the bar. Arabella was back there already. Her hair was half-down where someone must have pulled on her comb.

"All this over a cat?" she asked me.

I shrugged. "They are hard to come by out here."

She sighed. "All the same you'd think they'd just let the poor thing go." She talked the way city people talk about the weather, as though men were merely a shared inconvenience.

There was a thud and a fresh spate of screeches from the cat, followed by cheers. I peeked up over the bar to see the cat being held aloft by its triumphant owner, and felt a moment's kinship with this small, roughly handled thing. As it was being stuffed back into the carpetbag, Kate's voice boomed out from over the railing. "Now boys, what's all this?" she said. She never shouted, her voice just carried over all the space it needed to cover, though I detected a quavering note this time. "I leave you gentlemen alone for five minutes and you're rolling around like dogs." There was a ripple of murmuring, and I chuckled, imagining a roomful of rough riders kicking the floor, shamed as if they'd been acting up in church.

"Dawkins's cat sprung loose," someone answered.

There was a beat of silence in which I pictured a bemused expression crossing Kate's face.

"Well, did you catch him? Or is he going to raise more hell as soon as my back is turned?" she said.

"We caught him."

"All right," Kate replied. "Let's drink to poor Tom, then, shall we? And half-price pokes in his honor for half an hour."

A roar went up and I looked at Arabella, who shuddered and wrenched out the wayward comb, loosing a matted tumble of brown hair.

Before I could say anything to her, a voice over my shoulder said, "You gals all right?" I twisted around to look, and there was the most beautiful person I'd ever seen. I say person because even though I heard a woman's voice, I saw a man's hat and coat, and was momentarily displaced by the mismatch. She held out one hand, which I took, and helped me up.

"You all right?" she asked me again. "Your hand is trembling."

"Oh, that weren't nothing," I heard myself saying. "Just a cat got out." Behind me, I heard Arabella straighten herself up and slip past me, her long skirt dragging through a pile of broken glass.

"Well, I'd hate to see this place in a real fight if that's how worked up you all get over one loose pussycat," she said, though I barely heard her; the rest of the barroom fell away into a hazy patchwork of muffled sound. My hand pulled itself back from hers and I found myself rubbing the spot where she'd touched me, as if to spread it further. She had deep-brown eyes that shone brightly, so that I thought she must have been able to see clear through dust storms or heavy rain. She was as tanned as a cowboy, with hair-fine lines around the eyes and mouth, though she didn't look terribly much older than me. She had small, finely cut features that grouped together in a line down her face, which ended in a point of chin.

I realized I hadn't answered her and that now some time had passed. The room snapped back into action around me: men were clambering over each other like crabs in a bucket trying to get their half-price pokes. Someone grabbed my arm and a dragon's breath of whiskey plumed into my face with a "Come on, sweetheart, let's go up."

"Hey!" The woman grabbed my other arm. "This is *my* half-price pussy," she snarled.

"The hell it is, who do you think you are?"

Without a word the woman grabbed a fistful of greasy hair on the side of the man's head, knocking his hat off. She shifted her grip to his ear so she could yank him in close and snarl into his face.

"I'll tell you who I think I am. I think I'm Spartan Lee, I think I'm here to get Ottis Shy hung, and if you lay one more hand on my whore I think I'll break your goddamned jaw," she said. She gave the ear she held a twist and turned the man loose so hard he staggered back, clutching at the side of his head.

His grip on my arm loosened and fell away so that the only thing I felt was Spartan's hand on the other, palm and fingers banded with calluses. I watched her face as the man slunk off and vanished into the wall of noise behind me; the curl of her lip relaxed from its fighting snarl and regained its half grin as she turned back to me.

"You're that gunfighter who drug in that outlaw," I said.

"That's true," she said.

"I saw you bringing him in. Before the storm started. He as bad as they say?"

"Well, he ain't good, that's for sure," she said.

"Is it true you killed his brothers?"

She nodded. "Came to that, in the end." She ran one hand down my arm, raising all the hairs in its wake. "We goin' up?" she asked.

"I don't know if it's allowed," I stammered.

"Why wouldn't it be? Or ain't my money as green as theirs?"

She looked past me to the door, which was closed for now. I suddenly feared it would open and a whisper of wind would call her back out into the night.

"I'm on thin ice is the thing," I heard myself say.

"What for?"

"Oh, all sorts of things."

She leaned back and laughed, but I didn't feel mocked. She reached up to touch my face, but I caught her by the cuff of her jacket.

"I have to go," I said. I turned and let a relatively clean cowboy grab hold of me. As he led me up the stairs, all I felt were the bounty hunter's eyes on the back of my head.

It turned out the circuit judge had beat the storm into town, and, while we'd been cooped up in the Queen, Ottis Shy had been tried and sentenced to hang as soon as the weather let up. After three days of howling rain and snow, the fourth day dawned clear and bright as summertime. The town was already full of people who'd come in to watch the hanging, and with the night so unseasonably warm, a party broke out all through Dodge. The snow had melted and filled the streets with fine, silken mud that everyone slipped around in, hooting and cackling. The saloons threw their doors open so that it felt like summertime again. Virgil pushed the piano out onto the sidewalk in front of the Queen, but Roscoe slipped away before he could be called to the keys, and through the afternoon a series of passersby took it as an invitation to try their hand at whorehouse piano playing.

As the sun was preparing to set and the air outside was laced with fiddlers and guitar players tuning their instruments, Kate called us all together for a word. She stood halfway up the stairs like Mother Superior addressing the novices. "You all go on and enjoy yourselves, but don't be giving too much away for free—remember, you're professionals." She smirked at us, and we all chuckled obligingly. "No wearing your work clothes out either. There's no time for a wash day, so anyone who muddies up something I gave you won't be around for the next one."

She paused a moment, letting a slow grin seep across her mouth. "One more thing. I see seven of you right now, I better see at least seven of you in the morning. No running off with any handsome strangers." She winked, then turned and swept up the stairs.

I couldn't remember the last time I'd gone out looking for fun. There had been a couple of dances and barn raisings back in Fort Smith, but I was just a kid then, and my pa was so useless at those sorts of things we stopped getting invited after a while. In a way, living in the Buffalo Queen was like living in a party, but it was a party I worked at, not a party I was invited to, and certainly not one I could leave when my feet got tired.

Because Constance and I had been thrown out of the store before we'd been able to buy anything, I had nothing that could pass for party clothes. Wriggling back into my only dress—the faded calico that I'd worn over the plains—I felt a stab of frustration. It had bagged around me when I'd last had it on, but since then I'd been fattened like a calf for slaughter. Anyhow, it was a girl's dress, shapeless and yet somehow too tight, buttons straining across the back and seams clutching around my arms, stiff and tight as old sausage casing. I'd grown used to some freedom of movement in my new life of sleeveless dresses and worn-in muslin. I looked in the mirror and saw the penniless country gal who'd washed up by the cow pens just this past spring, all the worse for wear, my own poor relation.

Constance rapped on my door. "Hurry up," she called.

I opened the door to let her in. Constance looked wonderful in a dark green dress, hair braided and pinned up tight to last all night. She was already pink-cheeked with excitement: all bookish girls secretly love to dance.

"I ain't going," I said.

"Why on earth not?"

"Look at me," I said. "I look like I just fell off the back of a wagon train."

She burst out laughing. "You look like you fell right into the mule shit," she said. She plucked at the shoulder seam of my dress, where the threads stood out like ivory comb teeth. "This one's ready for the rag bag, or maybe we can stuff a mattress with it."

I felt myself coloring. Constance slowed her laugh. "Oh, don't be so glum," she said. "Not that it matters what we look like anyway—don't you want a night off from being pretty?"

"Easy for you to say," I said. "You ain't the one who fell in the mule shit."

"Oh, come on," she said. She grabbed my wrist and dragged me down the walkway to her room. "You can wear my old spare." From the hook behind the door she pulled down a loose dress of dark-blue cotton sprigged with pink flowers. She gave it a sharp shake and passed it to me. "But be quick, Pierre's already at the party," she said.

My old dress wouldn't even stand to be taken off: as if they'd been awaiting this opportunity, the sleeve seams popped with a nasty tearing sound, and I shuddered at the thought of it happening in front of . . . I caught myself. In front of who, exactly? Jim Bonnie would just take it as another sign he needed to rescue me. The woman bounty hunter's face flashed before my inner eye but I banished it with a slight shake and slipped into the dress. It was too big, but Constance lent me a tooled leather belt she'd won at cards and I cinched it tight around my waist before looking at my reflection.

I hardly knew the person looking back at me. I was used to looking like a girl, or a whore, but that was the first time I ever saw a woman looking out of the glass. Maybe it was the high neckline and dark shade of the dress, or the simple way I'd braided and pinned up my hair, or maybe I'd just finally learned to stand up straight. Or maybe it was the accumulated mileage, the losses that had tried to ruin me and failed, but under the same old snub nose and prairie freckles I looked ready for anything.

"That's a good color on you," said Constance from over my shoulder. "You can keep that one if you want, I never wear it."

"Thank you."

"But come on, that's enough preening—I don't want to miss another reel on account of your vanity!" She threw her arm around my shoulders to pull me from the room. I caught my face one last time in the mirror as she leaned over to blow out the candle, and watched it vanish into darkness as the light went out.

It was like a fever had gripped the town, as if everyone knew that we had to snatch up the last scraps of joy before they flew off in the wind. At the end of the street, the two livery stables had taken the barn doors off their hinges and laid them in the street to make dance floors that rattled and thumped under the stomping feet of the revelers, who were already red-faced and giddy with liquor and song. Along one edge, three fiddlers, two guitar players, and a man with an accordion were sawing and strumming and squeezing away at their instruments as if possessed. Ringing the dancers, a crowd of women and men alike took swigs from bottles and passed them along to their neighbors. Dodge was a torchlit sea of gaping mouths, grasping fingers, and yellow-flashing eyes seeking each other out.

It was overwhelming, and the crowd made me leery, but Constance was thrilled. She slipped out from my grasp as soon as we got close to the fray, and in the next moment I saw her skipping over the boards, hand-clasped with a stranger. A bottle appeared in my left hand, so I took a fiery drink and passed it to my right, where two and a half grubby fingers materialized to grasp the neck and whisk it away. When I looked over my shoulder, ranks of faces had appeared behind me, and I started to sweat in the press of bodies.

Then I heard someone say my name, and when I whipped my gaze back around, I saw Jim Bonnie in the sea of faces, smiling the same gentle, solid smile I knew so well. He held out his hand; without thinking I took it and followed him out to join the reel. I had never really learned to dance, but it didn't seem to matter. He was like a bear who had been enchanted by a sorcerer—he knew every step and led me so well I barely noticed that he was doing all of the work, tilting and tossing me this way and that so that all I did was skip and be twirled in and out of his arms. I tripped over my own toes and Jim caught me with one great paw, setting me to rights like a teapot. "Ho, careful Bridget" was all I caught before we were off again, whirling over the boards. Sweat oozed out from under my hairline, and I felt my face getting warmer with every step.

There were no songs, just an endless flow of music, so I have no idea how long we danced. At one point I know we whirled past Pierre and Constance, who were laughing and red-faced like two apples come to life. Constance caught my gaze and stuck her tongue out as she sped past in the arms of her friend. I was tacky with sweat and much too hot in her old dress, which stuck unevenly to the skin of my chest. The months of sitting and standing around in the Queen had melted some of my old country-girl strength, made my body soft and unreliable. Suddenly Jim's hands were iron weights and I felt as if I'd stood too long beside the stove, wheezing in the heat coming off him. I craned my neck to look for a still point, but we were moving too fast and my eyes couldn't catch anything; my ears felt muffled. Whenever I missed a step and bumped into Jim's chest, he felt warm and solid, a snug house with bright windows. But something in me still scrabbled and clawed like an animal, something small and wild that belonged outside; I understood with a flash that the door of that warm little house might be open, but I would never be content inside. I broke Jim's hold to make my weaving, stumbling way out of the press of dancers. At the edge of the floor I ran smack into Arabella, who half crouched to peer into my face like a crane who'd speared a frog on the end of her beak.

"You all right, Bridget?" she asked me.

I shook my head and felt the curls stuck to my forehead. "Where's Constance?" I asked feverishly.

She brushed my hair back with one white skeleton hand. "You look pale, come get a glass of punch," she said, and pulled me through the spectators to a table where Grace was ladling out cups of Sunday Brew.

"What's wrong with her?" asked Grace.

"Nothing," snapped Arabella. "Too many folks in love with her is all." She snatched a cup from Grace and pressed it into my hand.

"Where's Constance?" I asked again. "I can't find her."

"She's fine, out there having a lovely time, and you won't go spoiling it," said Arabella. "Drink up."

I did as I was told. Usually the Brew was pretty awful, but this week's had the last of some apple butter that had been about to go over, and tasted like autumn would have tasted in a place with trees. I sipped and felt my heart slowing a little.

"Thank you," I said, giving back the cup.

Arabella led me away from the table, though I could feel Grace's hungry little eyes still on our backs. "What do you want Constance for anyway? Let her have a moment to herself."

I shook my head. "Just wondered where she was is all." Glumness settled over me like a cape. "I hate parties," I said crossly.

"No, you don't," said Arabella mildly. "Anyway, it's too late now, you're already here." She gave my hand a stiff pat. "You ready for more dancing? I was thinking I might try to steal that beau of yours, though I suppose I'm too tall for him."

I forced a chuckle. "No, you go ahead," I said. "I've had enough for now, but it's good dancing to be had, if you can keep up the pace."

She slid away into the crowd. I drifted around the edges awhile, watching fear of the future and pleasure at the present ripple over faces that flickered in the torchlight. I let my gaze drift over the dancers, tossing each other back and forth, and the drinkers, weaving through their own choreography as they filled their cups and clapped them together, smiling and snarling in equal measure. Then my eye snagged on a face I hadn't even known I'd been seeking, and my heart skidded to a stop as Spartan Lee looked right up, caught my eye from across the street, and smiled.

She appeared through a cloud of cigarillo smoke that she exhaled not quite into my face. "Who you looking for?" she asked.

"My friend Constance," I answered.

"Which one is she?" Whenever she was about to speak she maneuvered the cigarillo over to the corner of her mouth, but worked it back to center as soon as she hit the end of a thought; in conversation it gave the impression of impatience, a little brown-suited banker pacing back and forth behind his desk.

"Well, I can't see her right now," I said. She shifted her weight and I was aware of the rustle of her waxed canvas coat, the small sigh of sweat and tobacco smoke that rose from her person. I was afraid to look at her and pretended to search the crowd. "Curly hair, dark eyes."

"She the one runs with that Frenchman?"

"That's her," I said, looking down at my hands. "She's real smart."

"Not too smart, I hope."

I watched the toe of her boot dig into the mud between us. "What's that mean?"

"Nothing," she said. I looked up, but now she was the one scanning the crowd. She plucked the cigarillo from her mouth and smushed it into the mud between us.

"How about a stroll, Red?" As she spoke, she turned back to me and I froze under her gaze like a deer.

"What's the matter?" she said. "Had too much excitement?"

I shook my head. Somewhere in the back of my mind a voice told me to wake the hell up, to either turn her like a trick or get rid of her, but nothing seemed to get through.

"Never in my life," I said, after just too long.

She laughed then, a laugh even lower than her speaking voice; when she smiled at me it was crooked, with all the lines that sun and hard riding had carved into her face pulled into relief, and it was the best thing I had seen in a very long time. "I can see that," she said. "Let's go take in the scenery, shall we?"

And so we walked together, bobbing around the edges of the crowd, not touching, but close enough to brush every few paces. We must have chatted about something, though I can't for the life of me remember what. Spartan had fished a pint bottle from her coat pocket and we shared sips as we poked around. Around us, the party had taken on a life of its own, but I felt like we were apart from it, like it couldn't touch us. We were visitors in a museum of revels, amused by the exhibits but separate from their contents. Here, a charming scene of soon-to-be homesteaders clustered around a sizable, near-empty bottle. And in the next tableau, the wives leaning on each other, whispering in each other's ears and bursting into gales of laughter, children long having scampered off to weave between the grown-ups' legs and hunt up God-knows-what. Around the corner, dancers swinging each other over the mud to time kept by pounding against the wall of a building; just beyond, meat hitting a blazing griddle over an outdoor fire, sending billows of mouthwatering smoke up into the sky.

"Bridget!" I heard my name from behind us and turned my head to see Jim Bonnie weaving our way.

"Oh Christ," I said without thinking. "Not again." The party crashed back to life like a brass band; I'd rather three more days of aimless wandering with this new stranger than three more minutes of dancing with Jim. Even from far off, he seemed big and sweaty, glistening in the torchlight, while in these few minutes I'd already become accustomed to Spartan's dry, dusty presence, wreathed in sweet-smelling smoke. She followed my gaze.

"What's wrong?"

"It's Jim. Deputy Bonnie," I said, feeling suddenly pathetic.

She craned her neck to get a look at him. "Been dogging you?"

"A bit."

She smiled and grabbed my wrist, pulling me into an alley and around to the back of a storehouse so that the party was suddenly very far away. Away from the torches and fires, the light shifted from golden orange to moon blue, and the shadows went to cool black on her face.

"Thanks," I said.

"Not so fond of the deputy?"

"Jim's fine," I said, "but he's aiming to marry me."

She chuckled and slipped a hand over the back of my neck. "And I'll bet he's just having the worst of luck," she said. And then she kissed me.

I'd been kissed a few times before, but never like that. I'd let a few tricks kiss me because they paid extra, or they wanted something more for their money, or they wanted to express their own selves. They hadn't been all bad kisses, but they had been born of someone else's wanting, desire moving all in one direction, from them to me. This was the first time I'd felt pulled, drawn in, drawn out. Spartan Lee was the first person who ever kissed me because she wanted me—and no one else—to kiss her back.

Her mouth tasted of sweet tobacco undercut with a sour tang that only made me want more. She clutched me tighter and pushed me against the side of the building so that my shoulder scraped on the wooden siding, but I barely felt it. My right hand was wrapped around her shoulder while the left slipped inside her jacket and pulled at the tuck of her shirt until it came loose, searching for any bit of skin like I was lost in the desert and ready to die but for the smallest sip of water. My palm found the bare back of her waist and I gasped at the softness of it, pulled hard so that our hip bones ground into each other. She seemed to take this as a sign and started hitching up my skirt with her free hand; the rush of cold air raised the hairs on my thigh, but the hand that followed made me shiver all over as it slid its way up along the line of my leg, which had no drawers to keep any eager hands away.

The bounty hunter chuckled at the discovery. "You town girls sure are wild," she murmured into the back of my neck, and a moment later she slipped two fingers inside me. I swallowed a cry but arced like lightning striking once, twice, and again at the open face of the plains. I felt my nails biting into the skin I had felt but not seen, and her hot breath down the back of my neck; in the midst of it all I was stunned by the solidity of this other person, that she of all people should be with me and no one else, and that all of it was real. Then all thought was swept away and I just barely kept the good sense to bury my face in her jacket so that when I couldn't help but sob with pleasure it stayed just between us, and the stars went black, and a moment later I was leaning back against the side of some stranger's storehouse, prickling all over as my sweat cooled in the night air. I could not have said which was brighter, the glow of the moon or the look in her eyes, shining out from the black shadow on her face. Though we had not released each other, our grips grew slack, foreheads pressed together, and I kissed her again out of the fear that when we let go the whole town would dissolve and leave me stranded on the barren plains, alone.

"Hush, come on," I heard a voice say, and we froze in our shadowy corner.

"What if someone sees us?"

"Ain't no one going to see a thing," said the first voice, a girl.

"I don't want you getting in trouble is all," said the second voice.

"You're awful sweet to care so much about my reputation." I bit down hard on my cheek to keep from laughing as I recognized, somehow, Grace. She and her co-conspirator were making their way to our same spot, or close enough.

"Oh, it ain't that," he replied, more breath in his voice now.

"You worry too much," said Grace. Over Spartan's shoulder I could see them now, blue-black forms that melded with the shadows as some unknown figure pushed his would-be sweetheart against the side of the neighboring storehouse, as had just been done to me. There was some muffled moaning and shuffling—no different from all the moaning and shuffling I'd heard a thousand times before, but with an arresting furtiveness—and a brief pause as they came up for air.

"What about Lila? She'll tan my hide if she catches wind of this," said the man. Without warning, I placed the voice as belonging to Roscoe—you could have knocked me over with a feather.

"The hell she will," said Grace. "She can't get by without the two of us anyway."

The shuffling took on a greater sense of urgency, and I stood frozen, but a pull on my wrist and a push on my shoulder got me moving, and I followed Spartan away to leave the lovers to their sport.

CHAPTER 10

Just like the rest of the town, the warm air staggered off before dawn, chased home by an icy wind that blew in from the northern prairie. I woke to the rattle of my windowpane under an especially forceful blast. Outside, I could hear a man bawling out the livery keeper over a half-dozen sheep that had slipped out and spent the night in the cold.

"Quit your bellyachin'," I heard the livery man say. "Only two of 'em died, and you oughtn't to had sheep in this country anyhow." I turned over and pulled the pillow over my head. The light coming in through my window was as pallid and greasy-faced as the rest of the world, and I had no desire for any of it. I pulled the quilt around me tight and scrunched up in a ball.

After we'd slipped away unnoticed from the young lovers, I'd tried to pull Spartan Lee into another dark shadow for a fresh go-round, but the threat of discovery must have cooled her passion, for she just smiled her same sly smile and shook my hand from hers before she tipped her hat and headed back to the party. With her back turned, I stomped my foot in the mud but had to admit defeat. What else could I do: chase after her, grab her by the arm and, what, exactly? Beg her to do that—whatever that had been—again? The scene was too pathetic to even begin imagining. So I'd wandered back to the sidewalk in front of the Queen and taken Virgil's place at the punch table, turning him loose to the dance floor. I smiled and giggled and doled out ladlefuls of Sunday Brew, stealing larger and larger nips for myself until the forced merriment of liquor and sugar welled up in me, and I felt like I was watching the party through a fogged-up window. Then the wind picked up, and the musicians' fingers got stiff. The torchlight lost its battle with the dawn, and at last it was time to sway my way up to my little hideout, where now I lay deader than a possum, crushed half to death under the weight of two quilts and a swirl of memories from the night before.

First, there was Jim. We hadn't ever seen each other outside the Queen before, but the overwrought feeling our dance had brought out in me was confusing. It should have been nothing but fun to dance with a friend who wanted to care for me as he did. It should have been the start of something kind and safe, but it had left me feeling strangled. It had been as if the searching look I sometimes saw in his eyes when I bedded him was coming out of his whole body, trying to lay claim to something I hadn't even known I possessed. My head throbbed out of time with my heartbeat, and trying to parse out my resistance only made things worse, so I set the question aside to mull over when I was feeling steadier.

Then there was Grace, who I hadn't seen the rest of the night. Beyond gossip, I hadn't given much thought to the other gals' private lives, much less hers. To my mind she was just Grace, who sulked and swept and hovered in corners, not someone whose heart ever beat for anyone but herself. It hadn't occurred to me that she might pulse with wanting for someone, that she too would sigh and gasp, undone, at the touch of another. I was struck with the realization that everyone around me had, at least at one time, had all the depth it takes to give themselves away. It was troubling in a way; I rolled the other gals over in my mind, and the sleeping Queen suddenly felt very crowded with so many beating hearts. I let the thought blur away as a fresh bubble of dizziness swelled through me.

Pressed between those encounters, the final memory of the night was bright and sharp as cut glass. I held it to me like a nugget of gold, feeling a little of the knot behind my forehead start to relax. Spartan Lee, first a smile, then a whiff of tobacco, then a kiss, and then—I didn't know what to call the rest, but I waded into the memory as into a cool river on a hot day. I could have washed my face in it, swum in it, wrapped myself up in a silk-lined fur coat and driven clear to San Francisco on the strength of our hip bones knocking together and her hand sliding up my thigh. It gave me a shiver that I liked so much I called up the memory again, just to let it ripple over me.

From the end of the street came the plaintive whistle of a train ready to depart—even the trains sounded hungover. When I lifted up the edge of my pillow, the light hadn't improved but the argument outside seemed to be over. I sat up carefully and immediately regretted it—that Sunday Brew was a notorious bitch on a Monday morning, though as I recall it was actually a Thursday. As soon as my feet hit the floor, I was down on all fours heaving into the chamber pot, which I remembered too late was not quite empty. I considered collapsing to the floor entirely, but it was too cold. Icy needles of air were working their way through cracks in the siding, along with a frigid glare that pushed through the windowpane. I pulled myself up the bedframe and worked my way carefully back into Constance's old dress, looking now extremely rumpled, and in the daylight I could see that the navy calico was faded to dusky gray at the shoulders. I cinched the belt and pulled my shawl down from its peg. I paused to look at my face in the mirror, searching my pale cheeks for some sign of all that had passed. It seemed impossible that I could have felt so much in so short a time and still look the same, but all that appeared in the glass was my same old face, surrounded by hair that looked downright garish in the wan light.

Downstairs, the other girls looked like a funeral party, clustered around one end of the bar and curled over steaming coffee cups. I drifted up to the group and Bart slid a cup gently toward me. It was only half-full, but he made a show of stirring in a big splash of brandy and a spoonful of molasses before relinquishing the beverage to my care. The gals were all silent, squinting into their cups.

"Aw, look at these poor lambs," said Lila, coming down the stairs. "Fine bunch of wayward girls you are—you'd think I never let you have any fun."

"You don't," said Arabella, caressing her temple with two delicate fingers. Lila drew up beside her at the bar, and Arabella flicked her eyes to Lila's face and back down. "At least, not that much," she added.

"And nor should I, from the looks of things," said Lila.

"Besides," said Henrietta, "we aren't usually drinking all that damnable Sunday Brew—sorry, Bart—plus whatever everyone else was passing around."

There was a general moan of assent from the congregation.

"Now, don't go blaming Bart for your troubles," said Lila. She accepted a cup of coffee from him and took a sip, pausing for her habitual slow smile over the rim. "Not his fault if you can't hold your liquor."

Arabella rolled her eyes and stood up to seek the relative peace and quiet of the hearth, leaving me exposed to Lila's gaze. As if in response, Lila slid down one spot and I half wondered if she intended to work her way through the room to irritate us all one by one.

"Bridget, I daresay I hadn't expected to see you up so bright and early," she said. "Though I suppose you usually spend more time with the deputy than you did last night."

I felt a jolt of either nausea or alarm, while under my dress a beady layer of sweat formed across my chest.

"What do you mean?" I said.

"You sure had Jim all tied up in knots, dancing with him so wild and then running off into the night. Like to break his heart, you are," she said.

I forbore to sigh with relief while my stomach relaxed enough to admit a sip of sweet, brandied coffee. It wasn't that I was ashamed of what I'd gotten up to the night before, but the memory of how much trouble I'd caused over Sallie lingered like smoke over a doused fire, and in my present weakened state I couldn't divine how Lila would react to the truth of what I'd gotten up to behind that storehouse.

She leaned in closer but only lowered her voice halfway, breath sharp with cigarette smoke and oversweetened coffee.

"You better not have some secret lover stashed down your bodice, sweetheart." She took my chin in her hand and peered into my face. "We can't have ol' Jim in a jealous fit now, can we."

She let me go and I pulled my head back. "It was just too much dancing," I said.

"Good."

"Lila, that's enough," said Constance. "It's ten o'clock in the morning, give the girl some peace." She set her mug down on the bar. "Thank you for the coffee, Bart," she said, and swept toward the staircase, grabbing my arm as she passed and pulling me along with. She bade me lie in her bed and sleep off what I could, while she sat up and read, finishing my own still-warm cup while we waited for the hanging to start.

The scaffold had been set up halfway between the Queen and the railroad tracks. We could have stood out front and craned our necks to watch the proceedings, but in light of the special occasion we were invited up onto Kate's porch. We clustered like quail, cooing and jostling for a better spot. I didn't own a winter coat; I'd outgrown my last one before leaving Fort Smith, and now that I lived an indoor life I hadn't thought to replace it. As soon as I got outside wrapped in naught but a shawl, I wished sorely I'd taken the trouble to get myself something worthwhile. Though the cold was bracing, the wind cut through my clothes and straight to the skin, raising gooseflesh all over.

I wedged myself in tight between Constance and a girl named Elizabeth, who I usually ignored for being so soft-spoken I could barely make out a word she said. She was broad-sided, however, and blocked the wind from hitting me so directly. From up above, the rutted street looked as ruined and hungover as the rest of the town. People drifted up slowly at first, in twos and threes, shivering and stamping in the air, gray from head to toe with cold and last night's liquor, until the streets were packed tight with unwashed clothes and greasy hair, which somehow looked even worse from up on high. By contrast, the gallows stood bright and true, its pine planking still yellow despite the relative frequency with which it was used. Usually it was out behind the jailhouse, but some enterprising crew had dismantled it in the wee hours of the morning and reassembled it a few doors down from the Queen, smack in the middle of the south side of town where it was guaranteed to draw a crowd. They must have still been drunk when they did it, for the scaffold swayed in the wind. Still, the small structure shone against the mud that had frozen to the texture of a slate roof from all the shoe prints of the night before. Letting my gaze trail down the street I could even see the frosted, rectangular imprints where the livery doors had made the dance floor, the Z-shape of the cross-braces pressed into the leaden thoroughfare.

The bell tower in the courthouse struck noon, each strike quelling more murmuring until we all fell silent. From the north end of the street came the creak of a wagon and the dull footfalls of horses. First came Spartan on horseback, sitting tall and proud as though she'd just conquered the whole damned Territory. She was the only person in Dodge who could stand to hold their head up against the silver gleam of the sky, and my eyes were fixed upon her, waiting for even just the slightest glance upward, the vaguest acknowledgment, but none came.

Behind her came the wagon, driven by old Sykes, the night watchman, and in it stood Ottis Shy, hands bound. He looked mangy, like a dog no one wanted, liable to bite any hand that came within range of his jaws. As he passed down the street, a wave of hisses and murmurs rose around him. I stared hard at him, trying to see the crimes of which he was guilty written somewhere on his person, but his hair fell in a curtain of frayed ropes to hide his face from the crowd. Seated behind him was a preacher in a tattered frock coat, ruffling the corner of his Bible with the pad of one thumb. Behind the wagon was Jim on his broad gray horse, looking solemn as befitted the occasion, and Judge Harris, who had passed sentence and stayed to see it carried out.

The column drew rein before the steps of the scaffold, and while Spartan stayed in her saddle, Jim, the judge, and the preacher dismounted, leaving their horses looking like any bored horses in any old town, limp-reined and untethered, shifting lazily from foot to foot and switching their ears. Jim unfastened Ottis from the wagon, and he shook his filthy hair back to take in the spectators. A slow smile crept over his face, wood-colored teeth jumbled together under thin, cracked lips. He turned his gaze upward; at the sight of a porchful of whores he licked his upper lip, showing off his tongue's gleaming, fleshy backside. I felt us all recoil as one.

Jim led Ottis up the few short steps to the platform, where the judge and the preacher were waiting. The judge read out the crimes and we all craned forward for the awful details: Ottis, in league with his two brothers, now deceased, had set upon a party of settlers, robbed them, raped the women and girls, and set the wagons afire, leaving none alive.

"Good lord," I heard Henrietta whisper from Constance's far side. "Who could do something like that?"

"He could," murmured Constance, jerking her chin toward the scaffold before someone hissed at her to be quiet. I looked at Ottis, picturing him standing not before a hushed crowd on a gray morning but a wall of flame in the night, the stench of blood, the scream of horses running for their lives. It was hard to believe that so much violence could live in the body of one man, which now seemed quite small compared to the evil deeds it had performed. Jim positioned

Ottis over the trapdoor and set the noose around his neck; for half a moment I imagined that same weight on my own collarbone, wondered what it would be like to hear the last things anyone would ever say to me. Then the judge wished Ottis the best of luck in the next life and the crowd rustled with excitement as the reverend stepped forward to pray over the condemned.

Ottis raised his clasped hands. A fresh silence fell as everyone strained to hear the last words of the notorious criminal. But there were no last words to be heard. Instead, Ottis clenched his bound hands into a single, giant fist and smashed them like a tomahawk into the preacher's forehead, then swung them up like a club into the point of Jim's chin. Jim crashed onto the deck of the scaffold while Ottis slipped out of the noose and leapt over the edge onto the deputy's idle mare. The horse reared and screamed, but Ottis kept his seat and spurred hard at the flanks, and a moment later he was clattering over the hard-packed street.

A roar came up from the crowd; at the end of the street they started to close in like the Red Sea over Pharaoh's army. The judge ran down the steps of the scaffold, but it was too late. The only one who reacted in time was Spartan, whose big mare was already running. She took her hands from the reins and leaned forward, rising up in the stirrups as she drew her gun and fired between her horse's ears. The first two shots missed, but the third struck home and a wet, red flower bloomed over Ottis's back, right between his shoulder blades. The horse reared again, and this time he could not stay on. He fell in a rag-doll heap but scrambled to his feet and grabbed at the rein of Spartan's horse as she came even with him. The mare shrieked as she was yanked down, whipped around with the sheer momentum of his pull, tumbling Spartan into the street. I screamed, but the whole town screamed with me.

Spartan barely seemed to touch the ground; she curled and landed in a roll so that her feet found the earth almost immediately, and before Ottis could loose his raised fists she had fired again, this one lodging in his chest and sending him tumbling backward. She could have stopped there, for he was surely dead or close enough, but it was as if the gun pulled her forward and as he fell back she followed onto one knee, tossing the gun in a quick flip so that the barrel was in her hand and the butt raised up to strike. She slammed the ivory handle into one corner of his forehead, then the other, then back to the first side, where it found its target now soft and yielding as a rotten apple. After the third blow, she stopped and looked around. Her hat had come off and as she rose to her feet I could see her face, now sweat-streaked but utterly composed. She wiped the bloodied butt of her pistol against her pant leg and holstered it, then leaned over to pick up her fallen hat like a dancer picking up a rose tossed from the audience.

"Someone see to this," she said, gesturing toward the corpse. It was like the breaking of a spell: all around some mixture of shouts and cheers broke out, as everyone in town rushed to either ask or tell what had happened. The crowd surged forward to clap her on the back or shake her hand; before I lost her in the churn of bodies I saw Hugh Montgomery in his bottle-green frock coat taking her by the shoulder to lead her away to his saloon.

"Everyone downstairs quick," said Lila, chivvying us along. "Get your work clothes on, in five minutes the whole place is going to be hotter than hell on payday." As we came through Kate's parlor and back along the walkway I could hear Roscoe already pounding away and men's excited voices filling up the room.

"Too bad it wasn't a proper hanging," I heard Arabella saying to Constance.

"What for? If you ask me he got what he deserved."

Arabella sniffed. "It was cowardly to run. He should have taken his punishment."

"Well, the important thing is he's dead," said Constance. She looked over the railing at the barroom, which was already a sea of hats and wild chatter. "And buck up, you're about to make a lot of money, my dear."

I could have sworn I heard Arabella's eyes rolling in their sockets as her door clattered shut, and I slipped into my room to change and grab a last moment's peace. Leaning against the door, I pressed both hands against my heart to see if I could feel its clanging against my breastbone. I thought of the practiced, easy strength with which Spartan Lee had stood up in her stirrups to shoot, the effortless flip of the gun in her grasp. I held up my own palm and looked at it, wondered how much a Colt weighed anyway, and if the barrel had felt warm or cool when she grabbed it. My gut tightened up like a rag at the memory of that killing blow; I chalked that up to last night's liquor, ignoring the shiver that longed to work its way through me. There came a rap on the wall from Constance's room. "You about ready?" she called out.

"Yeah," I called back. I glanced in the mirror to confirm that I looked as hellish as I felt and buttoned into my red working dress to meet Constance on the walkway. I was halfway down the stairs before it occurred to me to wonder if Jim was okay.

CHAPTER II

It wasn't until the next night that Spartan showed back up at the Buffalo Queen. I'd gone wall-eyed from watching the door; I knew she was now too notorious to slip in and out of saloons unnoticed, but my insides churned like a barrel of snakes as I feared the night before the hanging might have meant more to me than it had to her. I was waiting with bated breath for the moment when the doors of the saloon would open and she would be the one stepping inside, wrapped in a gust of wind. There's nothing lust enjoys more than secrecy, and I hadn't told even Constance what had passed between me and the gunfighter. Or, as I disliked to recall, about Jim's proposal.

She and I were at the bar together getting talked at by a couple of scouts from a cavalry unit, on leave from persecuting the Sioux. They had a good strategy going: one would tell a story about the valiant deeds of the other, who would duck his head and truckle like a schoolboy, and then they'd switch places. I could see Constance enjoying their game; in the corner of my eye she was smiling her widest, most knowing smile, for it was the type of human folly that amused her. I was bored halfway to sobs, sipping my cold tea and wishing it was whiskey, tilting my head back and forth and laughing at all the right times. Between the scouts' shoulders I could see the front door, and I was casually keeping an eye on it, pretending to all and sundry that I was just waiting for Jim, about whom the rumors had been promising.

And yet when she did arrive, she seemed not to notice me at all. The cold wind finally blew Spartan Lee through our door and I all but froze in my tracks, my muscles tightening and aching as if frostbitten. I wasn't familiar with the fascination, which I'm told is quite common, of watching your lover when they don't know you can see them, the intrigue of seeing their mannerisms unfettered, untainted by the feel of your eye. Out of the wind, she cupped her hands to light one of those little cigarillos she liked to smoke, raising the match and tilting her head to the side rather than down so that she never lost her view of the room. She threw the match on the floor and tucked the matchbook into the breast pocket of her gold-striped shirt, pushing her jacket back to show her Colt with its newly pink-stained ivory handle. She let her gaze drift in a slow semicircle around the room and I tensed, waiting for her to spot me, but her eyes moved right past without so much as a flicker.

Constance elbowed me hard—one of the scouts was saying something.

"Why, certainly," I said without thinking.

"What's that?" said the scout, startled.

I laughed. "I'm sorry, what were you saying?"

"He was asking if you've ever been shot with an arrow," said Constance, one eyebrow raised.

I laughed harder. "Oh my, no, and I hope I never shall." I put both hands on the arm of the scout and looked all the way up into his face. He was reasonable looking, equally sun- and windburned from the prairie. "Come on, enough stories. I know you been ridin' hard—why don't you come upstairs with me and rest a spell?" Behind him I could see Spartan Lee walking over to the bar. She glanced in my direction and I was certain that she saw me, but she made no sign of acknowledgment. I would have screamed in frustration if I'd thought it would get her attention, but somehow I doubted it would.

"Lee!" She turned to look behind her, rotating away from me, and I followed the line of her gaze to where Branch Cody from the Western Telegraph office was waving his arm. He came by most nights to play cards with Pierre and listen to Henrietta giggle, while only working up the nerve to buy her about twice a week. With a flush of envy I wondered how someone as unassuming as he had become friends with a renowned bounty hunter. The scout said something else that I had missed, but luckily he was already leading us toward the staircase. I went up arm in arm with him, but Spartan didn't so much as look up at me as I passed. From the top of the stairs I saw the crown of her hat move through the room and take her place at the card table, Branch Cody's arms swinging open like barn doors to force the others to make space for her while Pierre stood up to shake her hand, smiling under his mustache.

Things went on like that half the night. Watching Spartan for any sign of recognition cut badly into my profits, as I kept forgetting to act interested in anything being said to me. To me she was like a beacon, and I wondered how anyone could look at anything else. I saw others mark her presence and go over to shake her hand. She'd already been decently well-known before the hanging—as Pierre had pointed out, a woman gunfighter was far from ordinary, even in Kansas—but that stunt with Ottis Shy had sealed her fate.

I watched from the balcony as the scout I'd tumbled just an hour before went over with his fellow to tap her on the shoulder and shake her hand. She was gracious, or so it appeared from above, leaving her hat on and shaking hands hard like a man. Without fail each man took his hand away and looked at it in apparent surprise at her grip, which rankled me. Most of them had started out as farm boys after all—more than likely any one of their mamas had held him to her teat with hands strong enough to drive a twenty-mule team. Yet there they were, each and every one looking at his palm like he'd just shook hands with Daniel Boone.

I made my way back down and found Henrietta at the bar, collecting a fresh bottle of whiskey.

"How's your evening?" I asked her.

"Same as always," she said.

"Ol' Branch looks just about ready to snap," I said, though I had observed no such thing.

"He'll survive."

"Why don't you put him out of his misery and invite him upstairs?"

She shrugged. "I tried it once, he got so embarrassed he didn't come back for a week. Lila said to lay off and play it his way."

"Well, I sure hope he gets around to playing it his way sooner or later," I said. "You been sitting there with him all evening."

"Game keeps getting interrupted on account of his infamous opponent," said Henrietta. She sighed and looked over at the poker table, where Branch Cody, Spartan, and a couple of rough-looking buffalo hunters were studying their hands; Pierre had taken Constance and retired for the evening. "I sure hope she don't win. Cody wouldn't fuss, but I don't like the looks of those other two."

"Want me to fetch Virgil?" I asked.

"Nah, it's all right. I got my beau to protect me," she chortled, grabbing the whiskey bottle by the neck to sashay off, swaying her hips so her skirt swung like a church bell. Now that I looked at him, Branch Cody did look strained—I could see the muscle under his jaw pulled tight. Spartan was facing away from me, but I looked at her so hard she had to have felt my eyes boring into her shoulders. They were playing draw poker; I watched the cloth of her coat shift and buckle just slightly as she reached out to give two cards to the dealer and take two more, holding the discards lightly between her first two fingers.

"Would you knock it off?" Arabella appeared beside me.

"Would you knock off sneaking up on people?" I replied.

"An elephant could sneak up on you the way you're mooning over that gunfighter," said Arabella.

"I ain't doing any such thing."

"You are, and if I can see it so can anyone."

I sighed and turned away to lean on the bar. Arabella waved at Bart and leaned forward to whisper in his ear. He blushed half a shade and gave a terse nod; a moment later he gave us two brandied coffees.

"Well, this is nice," I said.

"I told him I felt the curse coming on and needed a pick-me-up," she said.

"Do you?"

She cocked her head as if listening for distant thunder. "You know, I couldn't say. But I am out of sorts, and Bart doesn't keep track of such goings-on anyway." She took up her cup and sipped slowly, smiling into the dark liquid. "It is nice, though, isn't it. Bitter."

"You're crazy," I said.

Lila came up behind us. "You two making enough money to earn a little break?" she said.

"Even if I weren't, Lila, wouldn't a cup of coffee just make me all the more efficient?" Arabella didn't turn to face Lila until the end of her question.

Lila raised her eyebrows, but she waved at Bart, who brought a third cup. She mirrored Arabella's gesture from a moment before, taking a sip and breathing in a deep sniff. "Bart does make good coffee," she said. "Though it costs a pretty penny."

Arabella sighed and was about to speak when there came a scream from across the room. There was a crash of four chairs hitting the floor as Spartan, Branch Cody, and their rough-looking counterparts leapt to their feet. One of the two had Henrietta clasped to him with his hand over her mouth.

"Turn her loose!" Cody yelled, his voice shaking.

"Or what?" said the one holding her, showing a mouth with six teeth missing in front, making a ragged hole at the center of his face.

"I said turn her loose!" He clenched his fists, but he was a small man, and unarmed. The buffalo hunters, on the other hand, were well-equipped, each with a pistol and a long Bowie knife. The one not holding Henrietta took his out and pointed it at Cody.

"Come on now," said Spartan, voice low and even. "You've had your fun."

The knife swung over to point at her, along with every eyeball in the room.

"Had our fun? We ain't even started having fun."

The one holding Henrietta yanked up her skirt, showing one biscuit-dough leg, and squeezed it hard. Henrietta jerked at him and bit his hand so he yelped and let her go in surprise. Before she could get away the other one swung his empty hand back and caught her across the face. She grabbed her nose but blood was already pouring out from under her hands.

Spartan ducked and charged at the center of the second man, sending him flying backward into his friend. She jumped on the one with the knife and grabbed him by the hair, smacking the back of his head against the floorboards. His companion tried to get her from behind in a bear hug, but she shot one elbow back and caught him just below the ear—across the room I could hear the crack against his jawbone. He grabbed at his face and howled as she whirled to face him, but before she could do anything, Bart and Virgil materialized with a sheriff's deputy who had been relaxing by the fire when the ruckus started. Virgil grabbed Spartan while the deputy grabbed one of the buffalo hunters and manhandled him out the door while Bart grabbed the other.

"What about her?" the deputy called to Virgil, who looked around.

"We'll see to her," called Kate from up above. I hadn't seen her come out of her parlor, but she had a way of appearing when things got rough, so I wasn't surprised to hear her voice calling out from above the fray. The deputy nodded and left.

"You can let go," said Spartan. "I'm all right."

Virgil released her and turned his attentions to Henrietta, who had buried her face in Branch Cody's shoulder and was sobbing freely into it. Virgil made no attempt to separate them but guided both up to Kate's parlor. Grace trailed over to right the chairs and pick up the cards, while Spartan collected the money from the center of the table.

"Bart, a round for the house! Roscoe, give us a tune!" called Kate, descending the stairs, and "Camptown Races" bloomed up around her. She and Spartan converged at the bar just down from where Arabella and I were still standing with Lila. A bottle of the good stuff awaited them with two fresh glasses.

"Thank you for your intervention," said Kate with an air of elaborate gentility, though I couldn't tell how serious she was. I felt my ears straining to catch what was being said.

"Apologies for the scene," said Spartan.

"Nonsense, that could have been a lot worse. I'll take a scene over a stabbing any day."

"I don't like that type of selfish behavior in a man."

"You said a mouthful." Kate poured; they raised their glasses and drank.

"You're the gunfighter who sent that outlaw to meet the devil," said Kate. "Lee, is it?"

"That's right."

"Well, I hate to see any of my girls in distress. Thank you for stepping in."

"You're welcome."

Kate poured again and glanced around the room, which was teeming with revelers. I felt an inexplicable urge to hide from her gaze. "So," she said. "It appears you draw a bit of a crowd."

"It appears I do."

"What would it take for you to keep drawing that crowd awhile longer?"

"You mean an appearance fee?" Spartan raised her eyebrows.

"Why not? Why not build yourself a little stake while you're in town?"

Spartan thought a moment, tapping at the bar with two fingers. "What'd you have in mind?"

"Forty dollars a night, and as much of this as you can handle." Kate raised her glass. "It's the real thing, you know, all the way from Kentucky. Not that sod-busters' corn mash we make do with most of the time."

"Not bad. Since you mention it, I was fixing to stop in town a week or two. I wouldn't mind having a place to do my card playing." My stomach dropped.

"By all means."

"Only I'm told my money's no good here, if you take my meaning."

Kate leaned back. "You mean the girls?"

Spartan nodded; even the blood in my veins ground to a halt as all of me waited for Kate's reply. She narrowed her eyes just slightly, looking around again, and I could see her adding up the drinks she was selling purely on the strength of a notorious presence in the saloon. I didn't care what she was seeing; from the heat rising off my skin I could have sailed up the stairs like a hot-air balloon.

"Usually you'd be right," she said at last. "I'm broad-minded, but I can't have questions going around about my girls' tastes. You understand."

Spartan took a drink without acknowledging the remark.

"But I think I can make an exception, provided you keep this barroom full to the rafters." Kate set her glass down. "But you be discreet, you hear me? Use the back stairs, and don't let anyone see you come out of any of my rooms with some self-satisfied look on your face."

Spartan set her glass down. She reached into her coat pocket and took out the bundle of coins and bills that had been at the center of the poker table ten minutes before.

"Tell you what," she said. "You take this, and I'll keep myself and that little redhead out of sight 'til sunup." My mouth fell open and I all but caught fire where I stood.

"Tomorrow you pay me my forty dollars, before the start of business, and I won't lose at cards nowhere else. Deal?" Spartan stuck her hand out to shake.

Kate appraised the pile on the bar. "Deal," she said. They shook.

Spartan swung around, snatching up the whiskey bottle by the neck, and at last her gaze landed on me like a bolt of lightning striking a cow.

"Come on, Red," she said. "You're coming with me."

We barely made it to my room before she whirled me against the back of the door and kissed me so hard our teeth crashed together; it was like being eaten alive, and before I had a chance to think about it I was trying to devour her right back. I could feel the blood rushing in both our veins as if we were one connected system, feeding each other. I flipped her jacket off and set to work on her shirt, finding beneath it a union suit that made me snort with frustration at its mere existence. I groaned and sank my teeth into her shoulder while my hands went to work on the buttons. I have no memory of how she got my clothes off but I do remember the first brush of her skin, radiating heat and just as astonishingly soft as it had been two nights before, only now I had all of it, and I pressed every spare inch of myself into her. I hadn't ever been naked for a trick before—though she was a trick in name only—and I felt small and exposed and big as all outdoors at the same time. I pulled on her neck and we tumbled into bed.

No one had taught me any of this; nothing I had learned from months of screwing every night of the week had prepared me to fuck for pure wanting, for the plain, overwhelming desire to get as close as I could to another person and then closer still. If I could have passed entirely into her body I would have. If I could have melted us together like two chunks of lead thrown into a crucible I would have melted so fast we'd be gone before you could blink. As it was, I scrambled over her like a lizard scrambles over a rock, kissing everything I could get hold of. I worked my way down from her collarbone, pausing between her breasts to inhale her smell of leather and sweat, underlaid with something earthy, trail-worn. A zip of salt hit my tongue and I followed it farther down, slinging her leg over my shoulder and grabbing her thigh for purchase as I buried my face in her cunt. She rocked her hips while the leg wrapped over my back pulled me in tighter so I could feel every muscle she'd used to mount her horse, rise in her saddle, climb the stairs to this very room shifting under the skin. I heard a gasp, and her hand that had been tangled in my hair flew up to grab the bedpost so hard I heard the whole frame whack against the wall, and I lost all notion of any world beyond its borders.

And then later there was the afterglow, yet another novel sensation. We twined together muddled, half-asleep and half-awake. Stuck together with a layer of sweat and sugary weariness we nestled under the quilts in a haze of distant piano music and murmured bits of conversation, talking of nothing in fits and starts. I felt I could have stayed forever like that: though in truth we were probably grimy and sour, to me she felt silky all over, and running my hand up her arm or down her side over the dip in her waist was like running my hand over the hide of some rare and wondrous beast whose coat is sought by kings the world over. I curled up when she threw one arm around me, pulling myself small and tight into the dark crook under her chin. Outside my door came the occasional spray of music or some shout, but it was far, far off. I felt like someone who'd been starved so long they'd forgotten they were hungry, now fed and full at last.

As promised, we stayed out of sight until sunup. In the early morning I slipped down the back stairs for a pot of coffee and a handkerchief full of yesterday's biscuits, which we tore at ravenously, working crumbs into the sheets.

"What's it mean, anyway, that you're a gunfighter?" I said around a mouthful.

"Mostly that I killed a few people who needed killing," she said. "Why do you ask?"

"Just, what do you do with your time?" I said. "I mean, I've only ever had but one job, and it's pretty straightforward." I gestured at the room.

"What you see, mostly. Go to hangings, play cards, ruin reputations." She leaned over and kissed me just below the ear. "You know, the usual."

I wriggled with pleasure, feeling warm all over, but my curiosity remained unassuaged. Being around her made me feel awake and bright-eyed as a cottontail.

"So do you just ride around looking for people who need shooting, then?" I asked.

She laughed, the low, gravelly chuckle I already adored. "In a manner of speaking, yes," she said.

"How do you know where to go?"

"I just follow the wind, I suppose," she said, this time kissing the spot between my breasts and working her way down to my navel, where she rested her head so that her short-cropped hair tickled my belly. It was my turn to laugh.

"But what'd you do before this?" I asked.

"Oh, this and that. Me and my two brothers traveled together for a spell, but we couldn't agree on nothing and split up awhile back."

"I heard you were all in a crew together."

"Not at the moment."

"What happened?"

"We spent too many days tracking a couple of outlaws. Dumb sons of bitches should've rode north, though I hear the Sioux are keeping the plains all but impassable beyond Ogallala. But for one reason or another they stuck to Kansas, going around in circles like they couldn't make up their minds. Tracking men is hard enough work when they're going in a straight line, but something about tracking them in a circle is much more aggravating."

I nodded. "You could probably just find a spot to wait and save yourself the mileage."

"That's what I say, but I'm sure the one time I do, they'll have a sudden moment of clarity and find their way at last."

I laughed. "What'd they do to get you after anyway?"

"Nothing special—robbed a few small-town banks. Ain't hardly worth the trouble, for it's naught but settlers out there and most of 'em don't have shit to begin with, but in the last one they shot a banker with family back east and the reward went up. So we're tracking 'em and tracking 'em—they're mostly going along this creek bed, making little sallies into the prairie but always coming back to the water within a day. Thought one of 'em might be sick, or maybe they just lost their nerve."

"Lost it how? They already killed a man."

"That's what I mean," she said. "Some can't take it when they do that."

I shrugged. "So did you catch them?" I asked.

"Eventually. I was the one who figured out what they were doing. I said to my older brother, they're low on water, that's why they keep going in circles. He didn't believe me, he never does, but my little brother backed me up. They were working their way along this winding little creek, upstream back toward the source. I could see why they didn't want to leave it, for it was the only water for miles, and it had that feeling about it, like it was the last good place to stop. So we rode up to get the drop on 'em. Lovely spot, really, nice stand of cottonwood trees and everything."

Spartan's voice had lowered another register as I watched her get into the telling of her story. I enjoyed the sight of her hands gesturing off at the imaginary spring; they swept low to show the graceful dip of the cottonwood grove, taking the same path through the air that they'd run down my side. As she spoke I recalled that the plains only appeared bare and flat, when really they had all the curves and hollows of a girl.

"But as soon as we come upon it, we see the real reason they been making all these trips out—they were stealing horses, just a few at a time, and had the better part of a remuda collected up around the spring. Now my older brother, he hates a horse thief, and he wanted to lie in wait and hang 'em, but that's a lawman's job and we weren't no lawmen. I just wanted to round them boys up and take 'em back to Abilene, my younger brother said we should just shoot 'em and sell the horses ourselves, but of course that would make us horse thieves too, and I ain't looking to be hung for no horse thief. Anyway, we got to arguing so long and eventually so loud that the actual horse thieves heard us as they was coming back. They gave us the slip and made off with their lives, though they did abandon the stock. After that we each of us decided the other two were bad for business and went our separate ways a spell."

"Sorry to hear it," I said. "They always that argumentative?"

"Mostly. You know what boys are like," she said. "They do so love to be right." She rolled her eyes at me dramatically and I laughed.

"I used to wish I had a brother," I said.

"They're more trouble than they're worth, most of the time. No sisters either?"

"Nah, it was just me and my pa, until he died."

"What happened?"

"Snakebit, out on the plains."

"Hard way to go," she said. "What'd you do?"

I shrugged. "Walked until I got here," I said.

"Your wagon get stolen?"

"There was a storm and one of the mules run off, so I only had the one other. I was afraid of wearing him out, though, for I had no notion of where I was going." For a rueful moment I imagined what a difference it would have made to have a proper horse back then—we could have likely covered the distance to Dodge in a day or two if we'd just known where we were going.

"How'd you find your way?" she asked.

"Kept on until I hit a wagon track, chose south instead of north, and here I am."

"Jesus, Red, you're lucky to be alive," she said. I couldn't tell the shade of wonder in her voice: was she proud of me, or just amazed that I'd survived my own bad luck? "What if you'd missed that wagon track—you ever think of that?"

"Not really," I said. It was true, but all the same I enjoyed playing it off to her as nothing.

"It's dangerous out there," she said. "That prairie's the biggest place there is: get a few miles from town and there's nothing but yourself between the grass and the sky."

I remembered that selfsame feeling and nodded.

"How do you keep from being swallowed up in it?" I heard myself ask.

"By having someplace to get to, even if it's not a place you want to be."

I considered this. "You don't seem like you go anyplace you don't want to be," I said.

She took a breath like she was about to say something, then caught herself and laughed instead. She touched my cheek with a hand that smelled of tobacco smoke. "Doing all right so far," she said. She cupped the back of my head in one hand and kissed me, and I pulled the quilt up over our heads so we were engulfed in fresh darkness.

CHAPTER 12

Two knocks, then Lila calling, "Bridget!" from beyond my door. I groaned—it was late afternoon and this was our second warning, but I didn't feel any more inclined to obey than I had the first time. I stretched and all different parts of me rubbed against all different parts of Spartan: arm to shoulder, stomach to breast, calf to thigh. She chuckled at me. "Ain't you had enough?" she said.

"I don't believe there is such a thing," I replied, rolling over to look into her face. She had that beatific expression that I was used to seeing on the faces of men I'd just let screw me, and to my surprise could feel on my own face as well.

"No, I don't suppose there is," she said. She chucked me under the chin. "But all the same, sounds like you'd best be getting back to work." She swung herself out of the bed and stretched up long.

"Why don't you just lay a few more dollars on that washstand and we can stay right where we are?"

She laughed again. "No, I think I've done enough damage to your reputation," she said, rustling into her clothes. "Besides, I made a deal with your madam, and if I don't keep up my end how do you expect me to pay for such fine company?" She winked, big and roguish.

There came another knock, louder this time.

"Just a minute!" I yelled at the door, which swung open to admit Lila's face. I pulled the sheets up to my chin as she looked around.

"Jesus, this place is a pigsty. Hurry it up and get downstairs, Jim Bonnie's waiting for you."

"It'll take a minute to get it presentable in here."

"Grace'll do it. You keep Jim busy for twenty minutes or so."

"Grace?" Usually she never did anything for anyone.

"Don't get used to it. Jim's in a lather over your forsaking of him while he was injured, so get this so-called gunfighter the hell out of here." Lila jerked her chin at Spartan, who curled her lip in response but kept right on dressing as if nothing had been said.

"What was I supposed to have done?" I asked. "Sat wailing at his sickbed?"

"Oh Christ, who knows," Lila griped. "Just get your ass downstairs and on that barstool before he decides that you can go to hell and the entire Queen with it."

"All right, all right," I said.

"I'll be waiting," Lila sneered as she shut the door.

"Ain't she a peach," said Spartan as soon as the door was shut.

"Ain't she, though?" I said. I slid out from under the covers, feeling suddenly self-conscious to be the only naked person in the room. I laughed.

"What's funny?"

"Oh, just that I feel so shy of a sudden," I said. "I don't usually disrobe for a customer."

"If you did you'd make a fortune." She pulled me close and kissed me on the mouth. Under my bare feet the floorboards were cold, and I could feel a rough spot that wanted to give me a splinter, but I didn't care.

"You'd better go," she said, stepping back. "I do hate to endanger a lady's gainful employment." She plucked her hat off the peg and tipped it to me like a cowboy on her way out. The room felt extremely empty without her. The bed was a rumpled heap—usually no one but myself got past the top layer. I shivered and began pulling on my clothes. With one foot on the stool to button my shoes, I caught sight of myself in the mirror and paused. I had always heard that love would make me misty, but instead I felt clear-eyed and sure-footed as an antelope. In the weak light from the window, I watched the buttonhook flash as my hands did their work swiftly.

Langley was taking his sweet time through "Loch Lomond," adding flourishes and rich little filigrees everywhere he could, while around him the barroom of the Queen bustled softly; there were a couple of poker games going over by the hearth, and in the amber light the other gals looked like roses studded over silk wallpaper. Of their own accord my eyes flew to Spartan at the far end of the bar, drinking a glass of whiskey and tucking into a plate of beefsteak, though she didn't look up. In the foreground, Jim Bonnie was sitting like a bump on a log in his usual spot, the glass and stool beside him both conspicuously empty.

"Well, how do, Deputy?" I sashayed into my place beside him with my best winning smile, tilting my head to make sure its rays would beam up under his hat. "How's that head of yours?"

He looked up with a smile that was only a little forced.

"Why, there you are," he said. "If it isn't my lucky penny."

"I hope you haven't been waiting long," I said.

"Not at all," he replied, filling my glass. "Besides, who wouldn't be willing to wait for such company as yours?" They were all his usual, merry openings, but there was something hollow in his manner, a sullenness that made my chest tighten up.

"You seem like you're feeling better," I said, hoping to push my way through whatever hung between us in the air.

"Yeah, I'm fine," he said. "Just a knock on the head, and lord knows I've had my share of those."

"Well, I'm glad to see you're on the mend." I put one hand on his arm and looked up at him through my lashes.

"Are you, now?" He glanced at me sideways, looking for all the world like a shaggy bear with a bramble caught in its ass-fur. I supposed he had a right to be a little put out, for I hadn't so much as tried to see him while he was injured, but in the moment he struck me—not for the first time—as childish. To think of a grown man this bent out of shape over a whore less than half his age.

"Good lord, Jim, what a thing to say," I said; I was going for coquettish indignation, but we both heard a hard edge along the bottom of my voice. Jim looked at me a moment and shrugged, letting a silence fall between us. I didn't know what more to say, so I took a drink instead. The whiskey burned my throat and hit my stomach with a thud that reminded me I'd missed supper. Annoyed with both of us, I straightened up and sallied forth once more.

"How're things down at the jailhouse? Any exciting ruffians?" I asked, hoping to herd the conversation forward.

"Oh, just the usual. Sal Johnson's back—got drunk and slugged some card player up at the Emerald, and you know Hugh don't take kindly to that sort of behavior."

"He sure don't," I said with a rush of relief, grasping at the possibility of indulging in whorehouse gossip. "Remember that time," I said, "when those bank robbers rode into town and tried to take over the place?"

Jim shook his head and gave one rueful laugh. "Them boys was crazy," he said.

"You had to deputize half the town to roust 'em out of there," I said, slapping his shoulder as I laughed, but Jim didn't react. I slowed myself down. "Well, I suppose we're just lucky they didn't try to set up shop in here instead."

Jim looked at me fixedly for a moment too long. "Luck had nothing to do with it," he said. A coldness steeled over me, and I recalled Lila's warnings to play nice with the deputy. He turned his face forward and drank. The glass looked almost comically small in his big paw as it rose up and disappeared under his hat. Over his shoulder I could see Lila, tossing her head carelessly and laughing for some stranger. Her eyes flickered over to me, dark and hard as river stones, then back to her own work. I instinctively sat up straighter.

Jim's glass clacked back down onto the bar. "Well then," he said, "shall we?"

I drew back for a moment, surprised by this new businesslike aspect, but let it pass, looping my arm through his to lead him upstairs. When we got to my room it was neat as a pin, with nothing out of place but the buttonhook that was still left on the dressing table.

Upstairs, Jim was better than he'd been down below. Though he became no more cheerful, his sulks lost some of their stiffness once it was just the two of us. I shut the door and started my routine as usual, fixing him with first my gaze, then a warm, slow smile as though I'd been waiting all night for just this moment. I rested my eyes on his face and stepped toward him slowly. In later years I met a dancer who described touring with her company and doing the same show night after night in town after town, 'til it got to where she would step onstage at the beginning, then blink and wake up to a cheering audience and roses landing at her feet. I didn't tell her how much we had in common, for likeness with whores offends too many women, but it did give me a laugh.

All of which is to say that Jim got what he came for, as he had a hundred times before. He searched my face the entire time, going over me the way one goes over the carpet in search of a dropped pin. It unnerved me, but I tried to let it be, telling myself he was just shaken from the week's events. After, we lay back atop the counterpane, me staring up at the ceiling, him on his side, broad as the side of a barn, head on one hand while the other stroked up and down my torso.

I looked up at his half-sleepy, half-worried face with a small wave of fondness. After all, it wasn't his fault I didn't love him. I smiled.

"There you are," he said.

"What do you mean?"

"I've been waiting all night to get a look at your real face is all."

I laughed. "I ain't got but the one, you know."

"But you were so distracted before." His hand slid over my corset and into the top of my chemise to cup my breast.

I sighed. "Just working hard, is all," I said.

"What's that mean?"

I shrugged. "Work is work," I said. "Ain't you never had a long week chasing drunks and bandits down the thoroughfare?"

"Well, you know I don't like to see you working so hard."

"That's life," I said.

"It doesn't have to be," he said, with a little squeeze of his hand.

"Oh, Jim, I don't know," I said.

His hand froze. "What don't you know?"

I shrugged again. "What kind of a life it'd be, is all. I can't do much of what wives are meant to do." I laughed. "I sew all right, but my cleaning is uneven and my cooking unbearable."

"There's more to being a wife than that," he said with a smile that I imagine he thought was roguish.

I rolled my eyes. "You're already getting that, and for a damn sight less trouble than any wife would cause you. And I promise, I'd cause you a heap." Despite my playful tone I felt a growing dread that somehow he would see in my face all the other new types of mischief I'd been getting up to. I wasn't sure what he would do if he knew he had a rival, or who it was.

"I don't know that you're as much trouble as you claim."

"Oh, you'd be surprised."

"What are you saying?"

A gust of exasperation blew through me. "I'm saying, why trouble the waters? We've got a good thing going here. You're my favorite caller and a friend to boot. Don't I always see to you first?"

He snorted. "See to."

"Oh, come on, you know what I mean. Don't we have a good time together? Why spoil it with preachers and houses and such?"

"Why, because I love you."

I opened my mouth but nothing came out. The silence thickened like syrup and crystallized in the air between us. Though Jim didn't move, I felt him stiffen all over. Under his hand I felt suddenly like a piece of bone china.

"Is it someone else?" he said at last.

"No, no one," I said hastily. I could hear my blood rushing in my ears; any previous frustration or sympathy I had felt was gone, and all I wanted in the world was to get him out of that room.

"No card sharp caught your eye? Some cavalry officer, is that it?"

"That ain't it."

"Not that damn foreigner, is it?"

"I already told you," I said, "I simply ain't wife material."

He sat up in a rush and leaned forward, wrist to forehead like he was feeling himself for a fever. He seemed to be breathing hard, blinking heavily; on my chest where his hand had been I felt a cool mitten of absent pressure.

"You all right?" I said in a small voice. I'd never seen him like that. I sat up too, but kept myself behind him, knees up to my chest.

"I'm just surprised is all," he said. "You'd really rather take this life and all its dangers over one with me? Am I that disgusting to you?"

"Oh, not in the slightest," I said. I felt a clamoring urge to soothe, to pet him and tame him back down, to stroke his nose and feed him sugar cubes; some deeper instinct told me to stay put, keep out of the way, try to say the right thing. "It ain't your fault, I'm just not cut out for the life you want. It's me that isn't good enough for you, not the other way around."

He stood up and dressed hastily without looking at me. His hands shook buttoning his trousers, but I made no move to help. There was a heat coming off him like a locomotive, and I didn't want to be in the way of any sudden blast of steam. He wrenched his coat on and opened the door, then looked back at me from the doorway with thunder in his face.

"You been lucky, Bridget, real lucky. But everyone's luck runs out sometime, and when yours does, you just come and find me and we'll see what happens then." Then he was gone, leaving the door swaying on its hinge, letting in a trickle of Langley's uneven, warped piano music.

Arabella caught me halfway down the stairs. "What did you do?" she asked in a low voice.

"What do you mean?"

"I just saw that beau of yours storming out of here, looking for someone to smack," she said. "What've you done now?"

"I ain't done nothing," I said, bridling.

"Well, I'd watch it if I were you," she said.

I felt a small thread snap inside me. What business of hers could any of this possibly be? "The fuck do you mean by that?"

"I mean, Lila saw him leaving, so watch your back is all."

"Ain't none of your nevermind what I watch."

"Have it your way," she said, dipping her shoulder in a pale imitation of Sallie's long-lost half-curtsey. "But don't say I didn't warn you." She made a show of squeezing past me up the stairs. I let her go, steaming like a teakettle at her gall. I knew that Arabella was right, that I'd be in trouble again within the week, but the thought was just a veil overlaying a larger swell of indignation at her, Jim, Lila, the whole damned world. I felt like a doll that was always getting played with and left behind by careless children—my pa, Lila, Sallie, Jim—yet somehow I was the one to blame for not tidying myself away into the toy chest. I just wished we could all agree on what should be done with me.

But the night was young, and I had more to do before I could crawl into bed and wait for Spartan to come and let herself into my room. From the staircase, I scanned the room and saw her presiding at the table closest to the hearth, back to the fire. She'd told me that having spent so much time outdoors, she liked to warm up whenever the opportunity arose, as if the heat could be stored like grain for winter. She was down to her shirtsleeves, coat draped over the back of her chair, and when she reached out to curl a gentle hand around her whiskey glass I could see—or at least vividly imagine—

the lean muscles of her shoulders sliding under her shirt. She blew a puff of smoke right into the face of the man beside her as she rearranged her cards, pinching one between the first two fingers of her right hand and sliding it into place between its fellows, then reached out with those same two fingers to pluck up a couple of chips for the pot, where they landed with a click I swear I could hear over the last bars of "My Bonnie Lies over the Ocean."

She looked up and we caught eyes over the oblivious heads below. She didn't nod or smile, or even wink at me, just looked. I was used to feeling eyes on me, gazes pressing and grasping onto different pieces of me as the looker made their choice. This was different: maybe no one had thought to take me in as a whole before, or maybe I'd just always been too close-up for them to do so. Her gaze touched all of me at once, and it was like stepping into the sun after a harsh winter and feeling that spring has finally arrived. It only lasted a few seconds before her eyes flickered back down to the cards in her hand and Langley struck up a new tune under my feet. I remembered where I was and continued my descent, looking for someone to bat my lashes at.

Later, upstairs, she ran her hand down over my shoulder, lips following in its path.

"You took me by surprise, you know," I said.

"I don't doubt it," she murmured into the flat space under my collarbone.

"Oh? You done that to a lot of gals, then?"

"One or two, here and there."

"Just those, huh?"

She didn't answer, working her way lower down.

"How'd you know?" I asked.

"Know what?" Her voice was muffled.

"How'd you know that I'd, well, go off with you the other night?"

"Lucky guess."

"No one's that lucky."

She looked up, chin nestled in a cloudy pile of my gauzy white petticoats.

"I just knew is all."

"But how?"

She shrugged. "Saw it in you."

"Saw what, though?"

She tilted her head, considering. "That you'd had your heart broke, but couldn't show it. That you'd wagered big and lost big." She grinned. "Or maybe it was just that you couldn't take those big lanterny doe eyes off me," she said. "You wouldn't believe how you stare at a person."

I blushed. "Sorry," I said.

"Not a thing in this world I want you to be sorry for, Red."

"You never shot a pistol?" A while later, still in the deep darkness before the sky even starts to think about daylight, we were stretched out on my bed talking of nothing in particular. I hadn't bothered to refill the lamp and in the near-pitch blackness, I was aware of her only as someone to touch, hear, smell.

"Nope," I said. "I ain't never had the opportunity to learn. And besides, who would I shoot?"

Spartan snorted. "In your line of work? Who wouldn't you shoot?"

I laughed at that. "It ain't so bad most of the time," I said. "Most of 'em understand there's rules to an operation like this, and those who aren't old enough to know better are so excited to be in the room with a real live sporting woman that they'd do backflips if I made it a requirement."

"You've got me there," she said. She leaned over to fish around in the discarded clothing for her smokes, draping across me soft and heavy as a cat. She lit one and leaned back against the headboard.

"Besides, shooting people only leads to trouble," I said.

"In my experience it solves more problems than it causes, but I'll own that may not be the case for everyone." I watched the glowing coal at the tip of her cigarillo flare and fade, followed by a deep exhalation and a sweet, wood-smelling cloud that swelled and faded into the black air.

"What was it like?" I asked.

"What was what like?"

"Killing Ottis Shy."

She took a moment to answer, and I worried I'd overstepped my bounds.

"It was easy," she said at last. "Came natural as walking, and anyway, it seemed logical, in a way." She chuckled, blew a cloud of smoke. "I brought him all this way, after all."

I nodded in the dark, thinking about all the work I'd done over the years that had been more trouble than it was worth. It sounds cold, but I could see the sense of what she was saying.

"What about the brothers?"

"That was different. They fought like hell."

"What happened?"

"I can't really remember in a way that I could tell it to you, but it was bloody, and hard, I mean how work is hard. Heavy, and I came away tired. Maybe that's why it was so easy to keep Ottis from getting away. I hate having my time wasted by men."

"You'd be a terrible whore, then."

"Aw, shoot, you really think so?" We fell to laughing.

"My friend shot a man," I said when we died down, a little surprised to hear myself saying it, for the upset with Sallie now felt long past. "Trick got rough with her, and when I pulled him off she whipped out a derringer and shot him. Twice."

"She kill him?"

I nodded, forgetting she couldn't see. "Not right away. First one got him in the shoulder, second right at the base of the neck. Would've been better if he'd been killed outright, I suppose, but he lingered a spell."

"Sounds to me like he deserved it. Only a dog beats on a whore like that."

"Well, that's what I think, but I guess the man had family someplace. Jim Bonnie settled 'em down, but she still had to go," I said. "Kate and Lila sent her up to Cheyenne, work for a friend of theirs. Damn shame, and all my fault too."

"How's it your fault?"

"Not my fault he was beating on her, but I oughtn't to interfered," I said. "She'd have rode it out, she said."

"Maybe so, but maybe not." Her arm snaked over me and tapped the end of her smoke into a saucer on the washstand. "How'd you know she was in trouble anyway? You all got spy-holes in these little rooms of yours?"

I could feel my whole body blush hot red. "Oh, nothing special. I was passing on the balcony, heard the scuffle."

She tsked me with a low laugh, and I could feel her shaking her head beside me. "I'll tell you what, Red, you sure sound pretty when you lie."

"Aw, hell. She'd have done the same for me."

"Would she?"

I didn't know how to answer. Her arm reached across me again, this time twirling the end of the cigarillo against the lip of the saucer, working the coal out to cool on its own and preserve the second half. She pulled me in close again so we were forehead-to-forehead.

"Answer me this, at least: were you as sweet to her as you are to me?" she asked.

"Not even close," I said. We kissed.

"All the same," said Spartan. "A lady needs to know how to fire a gun. You go to sleep, and tomorrow afternoon I'll take you out, give you a lesson. Never know what kind of riffraff will show up in a place like this." With one last kiss on my forehead, she climbed out of my bed. She dressed by feel with the ease of long practice and disappeared without a word, leaving me to drift off in the press of the dark.

CHAPTER 13

"Kate wants you," said Grace in her high, reedy voice. She liked to stand stiffly in doorways when she was relaying orders, mouth scrunched up like a wadded handkerchief, hands stuffed into her apron pockets.

"What for?" I asked, looking at her in the glass rather than directly. I tugged at the sleeves of Constance's old dress to fasten the cuffs.

"She didn't say what for, just that she wants you."

"Well, tell her I've gone out," I said. I pulled on a stiff wool overcoat, borrowed from Henrietta, and plopped my hat on top of my head.

"That would be lying."

"It'll be true in a minute, less if you get out of my way," I said.

"It's about your deputy," she said.

I forbore to sigh wearily, though Jim was the last person I wanted to think about, much less discuss with anyone.

"Don't matter what it's about, I've someplace to be and I can't wait. Tell Kate I went out and I'll come see her when I get back."

"Might not catch her then, you know how her headaches come on in the afternoons."

"I'll take my chances. Or Lila can tell me whatever it is," I said.

Even a week before, I never would have considered refusing Kate, but I felt Spartan waiting for me, pulling me out into the wind, and little else seemed to matter.

"You sure you'd rather hear it from Lila?"

"What I'd rather hear is you going off to tell Kate I ain't in," I said. I moved toward the doorway and she nipped out of the way just in time.

Downstairs was all but deserted; Pierre and Constance were sitting at one end of the bar, hands of cards laid out open-faced between them. They were murmuring softly in a tumbling mixture of languages; Constance nodded and watched intently as he tapped one card, then slid another forward. They glanced up as I passed, and waved as I heard the door to Kate's parlor open and shut, and Grace mumbling within.

Outside, the air burned just slightly in my nostrils, and I shrugged inside my coat a few times to build up some heat. I turned right to head toward the livery near the south edge of town. Making my way down the sidewalk, I felt the trappings of the Queen fall away from me like shingles off the roof of a house. Though the overcast sky gave but a dull, papery light, I felt wakeful and alert. Catching my reflection in the window of a freight office, I looked completely respectable: bare-faced and buttoned up, I could have been any tradesman's daughter, out buying butter and spools of thread while Ma was stuck at home with the little ones. With a pang I wondered if that was the life I'd been meant to have, before the winds of fate blew my family so far off course. In that life, I'd be spending the afternoon on a buggy ride with some son of my parents' friends. I shook my head to clear the useless thought and looked again at my reflection, noting with pride that anywhere but Dodge I'd be the prettiest girl in town.

Spartan was waiting for me at the livery, holding two saddled horses by the reins. One was her big bay mare, who she called Davey, and the other was a light-footed black gelding, rented for the afternoon.

"The hostler calls him Little Blue," said Spartan. "I sure hope you can ride."

"Of course I can ride," I said, affecting a touch of haughtiness, though in truth it had been awhile. My heart skipped at the possibility that I might have forgotten, and be exposed for a town mouse. However, when I strode up to Little Blue he let me mount without so much as a nicker, and I kept my head up as though there had never been a doubt in my mind.

"Well, all right, then," said Spartan. She mounted up and we rode out side by side.

We rode north out of Dodge, the direction from which I'd come when first I'd arrived, and taking that same route was like watching my own life in reverse. I'd come in footsore, leading a skinny mule loaded with my whole life, which had consisted of practically nothing. I'd been barely able to hold my head up, and yet everything had loomed over me: hotels, storefronts, saloons, and whorehouses crowding in like the ribs of a ship closing under the hull. We passed the hotel where I'd spent the profits from the sale of my mule; the place that had once looked grand and imposing was revealed as shabby and unkempt, nowhere an innocent young girl ought to stop, much less for a fortnight. Now well mounted and decently dressed, I felt part of this place. I understood the expression on every face I passed: the whores lighting each other's cigarettes and tugging at their stockings, the street cooks stoking up their fires, the hungover cowboys wishing they were still asleep as they hauled themselves up into their saddles. All of it was entirely ordinary, of course, but it's the ordinary things that make up life, and in being a part of them I felt a part of life itself.

Ahead of us a crew was rounding themselves up to get back to their herd, horses jostling and blocking the road. They were young and had clearly far outpaced themselves the night before: as they eased their mounts forward the nearest one leaned over and puked down his horse's front leg. The horse whinnied and sidestepped indignantly, nearly bumping into Little Blue and me as we passed.

"Hey, you boys watch it now," Spartan called out.

All of the cowboys except the sick one looked up. They looked at Spartan, then they looked at me, and one of them tipped his hat.

"Apologies, miss," he said to me, not knowing how to address my companion. "Jasper can't hold his liquor at all."

I nodded. "It's all right, you just get him where he needs to go," I said.

"Much obliged, miss." The cowboys tipped their hats as the one who had spoken reached forward and grabbed the reins of the sick man's horse. I heard one of them say to the others, "Did you see who that was?"

"Look at you all respectable," said Spartan as we rode down the street. "Any one of those boys would've married you this very afternoon."

I snorted. "And they'd live to regret it. What about you? You're downright notorious in these parts."

"Oh, that don't matter none," she said. "You see the looks on their faces? They didn't know whether to tip their hats or try to hire me on to their outfit."

I laughed out loud, trying to picture infamous bounty hunter Spartan Lee steering that locomotive-sized horse of hers through a stinking cow pen on a sweltering afternoon.

"What's so funny?" she said.

"You are."

She shook her head. "Whatever you say."

We'd come to the edge of town, where the buildings dropped off abruptly, and there was the prairie, wide and sudden as the ocean lapping at the shoreline. The grass had died off for the year, leaving what I had last seen as a green and waving landscape now a dull tan, stiff and scrubby. Spartan pointed off northeast.

"There's a little gully up yonder, a few miles out," she said. "Let's let 'em run."

Before I could respond she was off, blazing over the plains. I didn't even spur my horse, just loosened my grip on the reins a little, and he took it as permission to follow, breaking immediately into a full gallop. For a moment I was terrified, gripping my saddle horn and fighting to keep my eyes open. The fear in speed isn't in the movement, but rather that you'll keep going faster and faster until you freeze or catch fire. But Little Blue was just an animal, and it was only a few seconds before I could feel that he was running as fast as he cared to, pounding out a swift, steady beat against the packed earth. His joy in pure movement was infectious: he was doing exactly what he was put on this earth to do, and I sat up taller, letting the grass unroll before us while the cold bit and clawed at my cheeks. The feeling I'd had in town of something falling away strengthened to a bittersweet ache all down my center and up into my jaw. The wind sang against my ears and my hands stung in the cold, but I would have let that little horse run clear to the end of the world just to keep sharing his sense of freedom, his peace at doing only what he ought to be doing while the world rushed past, unseen and unseeing.

All too soon Little Blue slowed as we approached a dip, and there was a creek bed with a stand of scraggly half trees, under which Spartan had already drawn rein and hobbled Davey. I dismounted and did the same.

"Not that there's anyone to hit all the way out here, but at least we're in shelter," said Spartan, as though picking up a conversation we'd left off. She unholstered her revolver and showed it to me, pointing the muzzle away down the creek wash toward a bend in the bank.

"It's simple, really," she said. "Just pull the hammer back like this to cock it, then squeeze the trigger. Watch my hand."

The gun lifted and her thumb pulled the hammer back with a click, and then her pointer eased in toward her palm, as if she were slowly and smoothly closing her fist. The Colt roared and twenty yards away a puff of dirt exploded on the wall of the creek bank.

"Then see how the chamber moves, and you're ready to start all over again." I looked and saw that the gusseted chamber had already spun a fresh round into position.

"Now you try it," she said. She offered the gun to me handle-first, and I took it, keeping the barrel carefully pointed at the earth or away downstream.

"It's so heavy," I said stupidly.

"It ought to be," she said. "It's got a lot of responsibilities."

She wrapped her hand over mine and stood right behind me, holding my hand out steady before us both. We fit together perfectly, like a sock into a shoe, and I moved my head to brush her cheek with mine but she didn't respond in kind; while my heart crumpled just a touch, I held myself still. I felt her gaze running right past me, down to the gun sight glinting at the tip of the barrel and then beyond. She wrapped her finger over mine and grabbed my thumb with hers.

"What do you do first?" she said.

"Pull back the hammer," I answered, lifting both our thumbs together and cocking the gun with a click that seemed louder than the last time, maybe because I was closer to it, maybe because we were working together on it.

"Good," she said, speaking softly into my ear. "Don't ever pull that hammer back unless you're ready to take a life, you hear me?"

Against my back I could feel the press of her front, the movement of her chest breathing up and down. Matched against it, my own breath felt uneven, shallow, scared. But she was steady as a rock, on solid enough ground to be solid ground for me as well, and I drew some of that steadiness into me. Even though I'd seen her beat a man to death not one week earlier, and she'd called it easy just the night before, it hadn't occurred to me until that moment that I loved a killer.

"When you're ready, just squeeze," she said.

I curled my finger in one single motion, as I'd seen her do. There was a deafening sound that rocked me back against her chest, and a fresh explosion from the creek bank, right beside the pockmark left by the first.

"Good," she said in a low voice. "You're real steady."

"Let me try it on my own," I said.

She stepped back. "Plant your feet," she said. "That recoil's going to knock you on your ass."

I tossed my head, unbelieving, but when the echo of the gun's next report cleared I was right where she'd said I'd be, on my ass in the dirt. She pulled me up but didn't laugh at me.

"Here," she said. "Put one foot back a little, like you're going to haul off and slug a fellow." She shuffled her feet a little like a boxer, and I followed suit. "Good. Now try again."

I kept my feet that time, and was so pleased with myself that I shot the last two rounds right after, keeping upright the whole time, though by the time the last shot was fired my arm was tingling from the jolts of the gunshots.

"Nice shootin', Red," she said. She marched bowlegged down the creek, splashing a little in the trickle of water, and inspected the cluster of shots. "Real nice and tight, you got a good eye, girl."

I smiled, feeling something akin to the sure-footedness I'd felt the first time I ushered this selfsame gunfighter out of my room.

"Show me how to reload it," I said. "I want to try again."

We practiced through the afternoon, her showing me how to steady my hand, choose a target wisely, pull the trigger on an exhaled breath. I picked out different spots to aim at, my mind transforming them into things I would have liked to shoot: blunt-nosed rattlesnakes, empty soup pots, the quaver in my voice as I soothed some stranger's wounded pride, which I reduced to a stone stuck into the dirt wall of the gully and struck on my fourth try. By the time the sun had finished its arc and was easing its pale and blurry way on down toward the horizon, I was showing signs of becoming a decent shot.

"The key is to not let the little things throw you off," she said.

"Let the world fall away so there's nothing but you and what you're aiming at."

I nodded, shivering. The wind had turned harsh, and with the last pretense of day seeing itself out, the chill was working into me now.

Spartan took my face in one hand. "Poor Red, you're all a-shiver."

"I'm all right," I said.

"You look about half-froze, we'd best be getting you back."

We mounted up and turned back toward Dodge. Having had enough wind for one day, our horses broke into a steady lope, both ready for a barn and a hayrick. As I swayed in the saddle, the day tumbled within me like unused shells rattling in their cartridge box until Dodge began to pick itself out against the deepening gloom, and I remembered that I was about to be in trouble again.

CHAPTER 14

It was full dark by the time I got back to the Queen, where I found Lila waiting for me at the bar when I walked in.

"Upstairs, now," she said, marching me up to Kate's parlor like I was a schoolgirl who'd been caught with her beau in the carriage house.

Kate was nestled on her settee as always, looking hazy-eyed but firm about the mouth. She didn't ask me to sit down but left me standing on the carpet while Lila paced the room like a tiger.

"What's gone on between you and Deputy Bonnie?" Kate asked.

"Nothing," I said.

Lila marched right up and smacked me clear across the face so that my ears rang. "Don't" was all she said.

"Lila, was that really necessary?" said Kate.

Lila stepped back. "Maybe not, but certainly deserved."

I put my hand to my cheek, which smarted, but didn't say anything.

"What's gone on between you and Deputy Bonnie?" Kate asked again.

"He asked me to marry him," I said.

"When?" said Kate.

"Little over a week ago."

"I see. And what did you say?"

"When he asked me?"

"When he asked you." Kate's voice was low and steady. Lila stopped her pacing and watched me.

"I said I'd have to think about it," I said.

"And have you thought about it?" asked Kate.

"I have."

"And what have you decided?"

"I said no," I said after a pause. Lila heaved a great sigh and resumed pacing.

"Why did you refuse him?" asked Kate.

"Because I don't want to marry him," I said, unable to stop myself from shrugging.

"Don't be impertinent," Lila snapped.

"It's the truth," I said.

"Whyever not? You could certainly do worse than Jim," said Kate.

I had a strange sense of unreality. I recalled scenes Constance had read to me from her books that ran along much the same line, but they were always mothers talking to their daughters, never madams talking to their whores.

"I don't love him," I said at last, lamely.

"Oh, for shit's sake, who told you that mattered?" Lila burst out.

"Lila, please," said Kate, holding up one hand. She turned back to me. "But Lila's right, that's a very childish answer."

"Well, it's not like it matters now," I said. "I already said no."

"How would you say he took it?" asked Kate.

I paused, remembering his great bulk sitting up on my bed, growing hotter and hotter like a steam engine preparing to scream out of the station.

"He seemed disappointed," I said.

Kate nodded. "Yes, I should say he is," she said. She reached over and poured some gin from the decanter on her end table, sipping birdlike from her little glass.

"Did you give us one fucking thought," said Lila. "Even one?"

That threw me. I looked at her, bewildered. "What do you mean?"

"You need another slap?" said Lila. "Because I'm not sure how much clearer I can make it that we need Jim. He looks after us, we show him a good time, everyone's happy. Or don't you remember how Kate introduced you to him all special, served you up like a pie?"

"I remember," I said quietly.

"Then what happened?"

"I told you, he asked me to marry him, and I said no."

"Is that really all?" asked Kate. I looked down at her and found I could hide not one scrap of truth.

"He said he loved me," I said, my voice flat.

Kate looked at Lila, whose eyes widened. I jumped in, words spilling out of my mouth before Lila could say anything. "But he don't know what he's talking about, he only thinks he loves me. He'll cool off, you'll see, or if he's tired of me he can take up with one of the other gals, and . . ."

"And nothing," said Kate. She and Lila exchanged another long look; Kate's lip puffed as she ran her tongue over her teeth. Lila threw her head back, hands on hips, and a loose pin fell from her hair onto the carpet.

"I told you," said Lila, still looking at the ceiling, "I expressly told you not to break his heart. To keep him happy, make him feel welcome. Easiest job in the goddamned world, and you still couldn't do it." Her chin dropped back to level and I flinched under the weight of her gaze. I heard Constance's voice in my head saying *I've seen things get messy in this place . . . worse than you've seen it.*

"But we don't need Jim," I said desperately. "We have Virgil to keep order."

"Not all on his fucking own," said Lila. "I'm truly astonished to be telling you this again—can you really think it's a coincidence that we get gamblers and officers instead of horse thieves and scalp-hunters? Or that we're not up to our necks in fines and permit fees from the damned respectability campaigns that run this town?"

I opened my mouth. "I don't . . . I didn't . . ."

"Of course you didn't," said Lila. "You never do, do you." She sighed and shook her head at the ceiling, one hand on her hip. "You've been nothing but trouble ever since I picked you up, you know that?" She threw up her hands. "I suppose it's my own damned fault, but why oh why did I see fit to bring such a one as you into our midst?"

"Lila, please," said Kate again. "But Bridget, dear, why didn't you say anything?"

I shrugged again. In truth, it simply hadn't occurred to me that they might be able to help. All my life I'd always had some dilemma to resolve on my own, and was long accustomed to just carrying unmade decisions around like stones in my pocket.

"It didn't seem to matter," I said simply.

"Why wouldn't it?" asked Kate.

"I don't know, it just . . ." I trailed off a moment, then found an argument that felt like a winner. "I mean, how much would it matter what I chose anyway? Wouldn't you rather have me stay here and work and keep Jim coming back? If we married he'd have took me away and then you'd be in the same spot you're in now." I ended with a nod of triumph.

Kate shook her head soberly. "Not necessarily. It's a good proposal, and we would have understood if you'd wanted to take it."

"There's other arrangements can be made," said Lila. "If he really had his heart set on you we could've worked something out."

Kate nodded. "And if the answer really was no, if you'd talked it over with us, we could have come up with some way to let him down gently. As it is, you've broken his heart, and so yes, we're in quite a spot."

"What do you mean?"

"She means we've had two decency committees up here just today levying fines on us, with their fucking wives standing around with their Bibles trying to get our gals on religion. Constance threw those bitches out—she understands what's at stake at least."

I swallowed and said nothing.

"You been told to change your ways once already," spat Lila. "And I'm telling you again. You make up with Bonnie the next time he's in here, you tell him absolutely anything he wants to hear, you fuck him 'til he can't see straight, and you get things back to normal around here." She took a step toward me so we were all but nose-to-nose. "You're new to this game so you don't know, but give it a month or so, when the drives are done and the cavalry in before the snow—ain't no one coming through our doors then. You add in the worst of the worst, the ones no one else will let in? And now you chased off the best protection we could've had. Who are we going to look to now if things get real bad? And what do you think would've happened to Sallie if Bonnie weren't so inclined to overlook your obvious shortcomings?"

She looked me up and down and sniffed, just as Sallie had when telling me off for the same thing. "Thank God for his limited imagination or she'd be up in that jailhouse by now, or probably hung. Or did you think whores are really allowed to shoot the sons of rich men whenever they get rough?"

My lashes were stinging bad but I willed the tears to stay inside my eyes. I tried to hold Lila's gaze but couldn't, and looked down at the dusty imprints my boots left in the carpet.

"I'll be good," I said. I was out of arguments, and wanted only to be gone from this close room where the air reeked of laudanum and disappointment.

"Damn fucking right you'll be good," said Lila. She grabbed me by the wrist and pulled me in close; behind her, I caught a glimpse of Kate's axe-head profile as she turned aside from the scene. "You be good as fucking gold, you hear me? You smile and play nice, you make up to that deputy the moment he walks through that door.

You keep that gunfighter coming back to play cards, and you two keep your shit well out of sight 'til she gets tired of you. And if I catch you idling one goddamned minute, so help me God you'll be out of here so fast it'll make your head spin." Up close I could smell her breath, that signature musk of strong coffee and rye. She let me go and I lost my balance, stumbling forward so I trod on the hem of Kate's wide skirt; she reflexively tugged at it and I froze in horror at the sound of ripping taffeta. I didn't dare look at Lila; instead my eyes met Kate's as the line of her mouth grew tighter. She huffed softly in frustration and gave one small shake of her head to dismiss me. I all but ran from the madams, letting the door fall shut behind me and covering the distance to my own room in what felt like a single step.

"What's gotten into you?" asked Constance from her seat at the bar. After Lila's tongue-lashing I'd got straight into my red dress and turned a steady stream of tricks. Now it was the midpoint of the evening, when it turned from early to late. It struck at a different hour every night—or at least I thought it did, as there were no clocks in the barroom—but it was an unmistakable turning point, like the cresting of a small hill, and a good time to snatch a word with a friend.

"Oh, I'm in Dutch with Kate and Lila," I said.

"Again?"

I sighed. "It does seem like a regular feature," I said. "But Lila's always mad at someone."

Constance shook her head. "Not at me."

"Well, of course not at you, you work hard, plus you and Pierre keep things busy."

"Well, you've got your deputy, isn't that enough for Lila?"

"I don't have the deputy no more, is the thing."

"Oh, I see. Did he go off you?"

"It seems I went off him," I said. "He asked me to marry him and I said no."

She drew back, the little F-shape of a frown drawing in between her eyebrows. "You didn't tell me that," she said.

"I know. I'm sorry," I said.

"Why didn't you tell me?" Her voice took a soft undercurrent that I knew meant I'd hurt her feelings.

"Oh, I don't know, I guess I just wanted to think it out my own self."

She nodded. "I can understand that," she said. She leaned in closer and spoke in a low voice.

"Was it because of her?" she asked.

I felt my face going as red as my dress.

"Why would it be," I muttered.

Constance half shrugged one shoulder. "Come on, everyone knows she struck a deal with Kate. An appearance fee *and* a girl? She drives a hard bargain."

My throat twisted. "I ain't part of any bargain," I hissed.

She looked at me. "Yes, you are. You were part of the bargain with a benevolent deputy, and now you're part of the bargain with an infamous gunfighter. Or did you forget what you are?"

"And what's that?" I asked, a little too loudly.

"A rather pretty whore in a rather nice whorehouse," she said, keeping her voice low but adding a little edge along the bottom. "Just like the rest of us."

I opened my mouth to say something back, but no words came out. The truth was that I had forgotten the rules, the formation in which we moved like figures in a square dance. I felt stupid for having fallen for my own song and dance, when in fact Spartan was only allowed in my room because of Kate's largesse and her own reputation; I was just a dusting of powdered sugar over the cake. I wanted to snarl at Constance to show her how wrong she was, but she just sighed and thumbed the edge of her book, smoothing a scratch in the binding.

"I don't want to quarrel with you," she said, sensing my mood. "I just want you to see sense. When you got here, you'd been down so long that everything looked like up, right?"

I nodded. "That about sums it up."

"Well, now that you've gotten used to looking up, you're forgetting how far down you can still fall. All of us, you, me, Arabella, Henrietta, even Sallie, wherever she is, we chose this life. Not that we had much else to choose from, mind you, but we came through that door"—she pointed at the saloon door behind her—"and in a certain sense we're never going to walk out. We'll work in other parlors or open our own, or we'll buy a boardinghouse in some new town and run a couple of girls out of the back, but this is it, my dear. You're a whore now, and a whore you'll stay. A man who'll open the door and invite you to step back outside is a rare thing. You should have thought twice before refusing, and you shouldn't have kept it secret from me."

I felt a version of the sadness I'd felt when Sallie had dressed me down—how long ago that felt—that sense of overwhelming foolishness. But under it was also the same bristling indignation that had been building in me ever since Jim had proposed. Everywhere I went, it seemed, someone was after me for something, asking for this or that piece of my life. I'd gotten used to selling off my time in chunks, used to letting strangers paw and thrust at me like I was a mattress with a heartbeat. Those were simple exchanges, well-defined and countable. But the thing that Jim and Lila and Constance were talking about, that was my whole life. The fact that they were all telling me to use it sensibly was infuriating, as if life were money to be prudently invested and wisely spent. What if I wanted to blow it, the way cowboys blew their wages on pokes and games of chance?

"Bridget?" said Constance. She was still looking at me. I returned her gaze.

"I know you're right, but I can't seem to summon up any regret," I said. "At least not for saying no. I am sorry I didn't tell you any of it."

Constance reached out and gave my hand a quick squeeze. "It's all right," she said. "For what it's worth, I don't regret your refusing either, not really."

I smiled, but worry still dug at me.

"One thing I don't understand," I said. "They kept saying I've put us all in danger or something, like Jim was keeping all sorts of outlaws away."

"He may have been," said Constance. "Or it may have just been talk. I did have to chase off some moral-decency sorts, but that may have just been a coincidence. Only time will tell, I suppose."

I looked around the room. So far everything seemed normal. Roscoe was clattering away at the keys, Henrietta was following a cowboy down the staircase, Pierre was shuffling his deck. A man sidled up to me and asked to buy me a drink. Remembering my promise to Lila that I'd be good and thinking I ought to keep it for at least a night or two, I smiled at him and let myself be drawn into conversation, though as of its own accord my eye never stopped scanning the room for signs that I hadn't done wrong.

But my hopes were misplaced, and things went downhill quickly. The speed of change wasn't the surprise, for everything moved fast in Dodge—gossip fastest of all—and within a few days it was all over town that Deputy Bonnie didn't give a rat's whisker for Kate and her girls anymore. Rather, it was the filling in of things I'd previously tried and failed to imagine; the aspects of whoring from which I'd been relatively insulated started to work their way in. Halfway through the first week, as I looked around at the faces of the men in the bar, I already marked a change. As Lila had predicted, there were fewer soft-jawed cowhands, twitching little grins under their new-minted mustaches; fewer cavalrymen gallantly slapping their gloves against their thighs; the spaces they had left were filled by scalp-hunters with dark streaks ground into their clothes or gunfighters with deep, hollow eyes. The card players who pulled up chairs at Pierre's table were in threadbare coats, hats blotched with ghostly salt stains.

I came down the stairs and leaned on the bar a moment to survey the room and wait for a man to approach me. I didn't have long to wait: before I could so much as sigh in imaginary ennui—a term Pierre had injected into the parlance of the Queen—I was looking into a pair of dull brown eyes, and I realized that he wasn't the relatively clean cowboy type I was used to seeing, but a scalp-hunter in filthy buckskins so stiff with grime that they flaked when he moved; by the time I started to actually listen to what he was saying, he'd reached the part of his tale where he'd had no choice but to slit his now ex-partner's throat for trying to steal his buffalo gun. I made a sound that he took for approving and let him rattle on while I scanned the room, looking for a better prospect to whom I could turn my attentions as, I tried not to remember, I had sometimes done with Jim. My eyes briefly found Grace, who was leaning for a moment in the kitchen doorway with her arms crossed; she looked back at me and shrugged one shoulder, expressionless.

My scalp-hunter whipped out his knife to make a point in his story, laughing and turning the blade before my eyes as though he were a milliner trying to sell me a new hat. I gasped theatrically and said, "Oh my!" without the vaguest notion of what he was actually telling me.

He held out the blade and invited me to feel the edge; I ran my thumb across the blade and felt where it had been honed finer than paper by someone who knew what they were doing.

"Good edge," I said. He grasped my hand, pinching my palm between his fingers. I tugged a little and gave a yelp of pain that was only half-joking, but he held tight, eyes fixed on my face as he raised my still-extended thumb and placed it in his mouth up to the first knuckle, pausing to suck long enough for me to feel a rut of slimy gum where he'd once had a canine.

"That's just about the sweetest thing I ever tasted," he said.

Still gripping tight on my hand, he asked what it would take to get upstairs with me. Hoping to drive him off, I quoted an outrageous figure and he nodded, sliding his hand up my arm and slipping it around my waist. He was a tall man but rangy, and somewhere between his grip and his eyes I knew that he wouldn't be paying me a dime.

As he turned me toward the staircase—for I could find no reason to refuse him, nor any better alternative—I saw Spartan making her way toward the bar. We often caught eyes throughout a night's action, trading silent promises that she'd be up later, but something in my face must have been different, for she crossed the space between us in a few quick strides and slipped her arm around my waist from the other side.

"Why there you are, Red, I had just about given up hope."

My scalp-hunter looked up, startled.

"Just what do you think you're up to?" he growled.

"Oh, I ain't up to nothing," said Spartan, voice light. Her hand fell above the scalp-hunter's on my back, and I tried to lean on it, savoring the difference between the two touches. While the scalp-hunter gripped at me, her hand was still and warm, steady as a tree on which the sun had shone all day. I longed to lean against her, fold myself into her arms as under the wing of a great big bird, but I held still, afraid that any movement could tip things out of control.

"Then get your hands off my gal," he said.

"She ain't your gal," said Spartan. I could have sworn she stopped herself before adding *She's mine.*

"I suppose she ain't for sale, then?"

"Not to you." She gestured with her free hand at the various unsatisfactory parts of his person. "Filthier than most mules, you are, and I heard that story you were telling, ain't no call for that sort of bloody talk in a nice place like this, and certainly not for laying hands on her the way you was just now."

"I'll talk how I like." His grip tightened on me.

"Talk all you want, but I already paid for her company this evening, a good deal more than you did I'll wager, so I believe I'll take my turn with the lady." Her hand on my back tensed.

"That ain't no lady," he snarled.

Spartan laughed. "Neither am I." With the grace of a dancer, she snatched me from the scalp-hunter's grip and twisted us away from him.

As we turned, Roscoe shouted, "Look out!"

Spartan ducked and pulled me down with her as the scalp-hunter's fist sang through the air above us. She shoved me out of the way in one smooth motion, then followed her own momentum around to smash her fist up into the scalp-hunter's jaw. He staggered back but didn't fall, reaching instead for his knife, with which he slashed the air between them even before he'd regained his footing. Keeping low, Spartan rushed the man, punching her shoulder into his belly so that he flew backward. What she hadn't seen was Virgil coming up behind the scalp-hunter, presumably to break up the fight. They both slammed into Virgil, whose head hit the bar with a sickening crack before he slid to the floor. Without waiting to see if Virgil was all right, Spartan grabbed the scalp-hunter by the front of his jacket and dragged him toward the door, kicking it open with one booted foot to fling him out into the darkness.

"What was that?" called Lila, emerging from the upstairs parlor as Kate trailed after her, watching the scene from above. She ran down the stairs and shoved aside the small crowd that had gathered around Virgil. Bart was already kneeling over him, pressing a filthy bar rag to the back of his brother's head. Lila drew up short and gasped at the sight: Bart's rag was already soaked in blood, but it was the twist of his mouth, the fear that reduced his eyes to blank stones that froze me in place.

"What happened here?" Lila snapped at the assembled.

Everyone started talking at once, tumbling over each other to tell her what they'd seen. I stayed still, heart floating up in my chest on a foamy tide of guilt, thinking about how I should have just stuck it out with the scalp-hunter until Spartan slid her arm back around my waist.

"Come on, Red," she said, breath warm on my ear. "We'd best get you upstairs."

She pulled me along beside her away from the scene; I knew it was only a stall for the trouble coming my way, but I took the gift she offered.

That was the only time I went to bed with her that I can't recall in all of its detail, just flashes of warm skin and sighs of hot breath, the way her voice snagged in her throat whenever I moved from one part of her to the next. When we were finally spent, we slid away into sleep, mine fretful and uneven, and when I woke to full daylight, it was as if no time at all had passed.

"That shouldn't have happened," I said, as though mid-conversation.

"What shouldn't have happened?" Still half-asleep, Spartan stretched, pulling one wrist over her head, then slid her hand up my side.

"Last night," I said. I warmed in the places she touched me, but as soon as her hand moved on I felt cold again. "With Virgil."

"He'll be all right in a week or two," she said.

"How do you know that?"

She shrugged. "Seen a lot of head wounds. And anyway, it was an accident."

"But it shouldn't have happened."

"I should have let you go with that ruffian who was breathing in your face like that?"

I gulped, recalled the scalp-hunter's knife, realizing I did not know how much danger I had truly been in, how much to trust my own judgment. Perhaps, I told myself, I'd just been spoiled by months of clean-enough men who feared the wrath of two madams.

I recalled Sallie telling me she'd rode out worse than the trick who beat her, and that I would as well.

"Maybe it comes with the territory," I said. "I'm in trouble enough as it is."

"Trouble enough to let a son of a bitch like that lay his hands on you?"

I bit the inside of my cheek. "It's the job," I heard myself say.

"Jesus, Red." I caught a note of disdain in her voice and bristled.

"You would've done different? If you was me, I mean."

"I wouldn't be you."

I sat up. "Oh, you never found yourself in dire straits? You ain't seen me when I first got here but I was a real sorry sight. Lila may not be easy to get along with, but she has always done right by me." I folded my arms around my legs and pulled myself in small, chin atop my knees. "I oughtn't to buck her so much."

She sat up and looked me over, then reached up to brush my hair back from my bare shoulder. "You're right, I ain't seen you then," she said. "But I can't imagine you've ever been a sorry sight."

My heart swelled a little, despite everything. "I think I just have to get used to fellows like him is all," I said. "No use getting precious about it, if that's the type of trick that comes in here now."

"What do you mean?"

"It's a long story," I said. I found myself hesitant to recount the tale of Jim Bonnie's broken heart; alone with her I hated to so much as recall the existence of other people.

"Something to do with that deputy who's been after you?"

"How'd you guess?"

She shrugged again and leaned back to light up a smoke, exposing one long flank as she twisted and stretched for her matches. I ran my hand down it, then followed with my mouth, leaving a trail of kisses that ended just above her knee.

"He asked me to marry him," I said, talking to her kneecap. "And I told him no. Now he's all in a huff and don't come around here no more, and he don't send his men neither."

"All on account of you?"

"Looks that way," I said.

Spartan laughed, a series of short barks. "Serves him right for falling in love with a whore," she said. My heart sank to hear her dismiss his feelings so lightly, but I couldn't place why.

"Look," she said, recovering herself, "I ain't been in the same situation you are, but that's just because I can't bear to stay still. Whenever I tire of a place, I just light out."

"Just like that?"

"Just like that." She made a gesture like she was flinging a handful of dust away into the wind; I could almost see it twist and dance as it disappeared. I remembered the cold air stinging my face and the tireless rhythm of Little Blue's feet on the earth, the icy pinpricks that worked their way through my clothes.

"Just go?"

"Just go," she said. "Just get on my horse and ride." She looked off dreamily into the distance.

There came a rap at my door and I got up, throwing my shawl over my naked body. I opened the door a crack to see Lila. I'd have expected a murderous gleam in her eye, but instead she just looked tired; I realized she must have been up all night.

"Is Virgil all right?" I asked.

"He'll be fine in a few days," she said. She craned her neck to look past me. "Let me in, I need to talk to her."

I stepped back to admit Lila into my room and shut the door behind her. "You get dressed, I got a job for you too," Lila muttered at me, moving toward the bed. Spartan stayed where she was, making no move to cover herself.

"Virgil can't work tonight and Bart can't hold the fort by himself," she said. She stood with her arms crossed, twisting the fingers of her tucked hand.

Spartan sighed. "It was an accident," she said again.

"So you ain't good for it?" said Lila.

"What do you mean?"

"We need help for the night. For a few nights, maybe, until Virgil's back on his feet." I paused, corset half-hooked up my front, for I'd never heard Lila make a request before; her voice dropped a few notes from the sharp pitch she used to give orders. I couldn't tell if it was humility or if she was just taking care not to be overheard.

"What did you have in mind?"

"More than losing at cards, but not by much—just sit there and look menacing, keep the peace so everyone else can have a good time."

"How much?"

Lila shook her head. "You're already getting forty dollars a night from Kate—that's more than enough considering the damage you caused."

Spartan sat up straighter. "The damage *I* caused?"

"You broke my bartender's brother," said Lila. "Can't pay that back in cash."

"It was an accident—wasn't my fault he stepped up behind that scalp-hunter."

"Accident or no accident, the result is the same," Lila spat, voice rising to the tone I was used to. "You gonna work for a living for once in your life or just laze around?"

Spartan shook her head and laughed softly. "You really that desperate?"

Lila drew herself up, arms crossed, and I couldn't suppress a glimmer of pride at the way she stood her ground. "You gonna help us or no?" she said.

Spartan looked at me, but I didn't look back. She sighed again. "Hell, why not, I'm already here anyway."

"And you," she said, pointing at me with her chin. "Before you get working I need you to go shine those big, innocent doe eyes of yours at Doc Merriweather, fetch him up here."

"I thought you said Virgil was fine," I said.

"Mostly, but he's seeing double and I'd rather he was looked at. I'd go myself, but I ain't got the time."

The thousand things that Lila had to see to seemed to buzz around her head like a swarm of flies, and I all but reached out to bat them away. "Where's he live?" I asked instead.

"Up the main drag, just over the tracks. His name's on the sign, you can't miss it."

I blushed as I tried to predict what the word Merriweather would look like, hesitant to ask. About to turn away, Lila noticed my failure to leap into action and paused to take in the color that flared up over my face and neck.

"Starts with an *M,*" she said simply. "Big blue sign, next to a hardware outfit always has all those plows stacked out front—you know the one?"

Heat receding from my hairline, I nodded—I knew the one she meant.

Lila nodded tersely. "Go 'round the back door when you get there, he don't like us coming up to the front. I'll see you both downstairs," she said, and left.

"Thanks," I said to Spartan, hoping to make up for Lila's poor manners. I was used to getting barked at but hated to see Spartan treated so roughly.

"It's just for one night," said Spartan.

Like the jerk of a rein, her words drew me up short. One night wasn't what she'd arranged with Kate or Lila, and it was far from enough for me.

"But what about Virgil's laying up?"

She shook her head. "I have to be getting along tomorrow." I opened my mouth in horror at the thought of her leaving—much less at what Lila would have to say about it—and she brought her hands up to clasp mine. "Calm down, Red, it's just for a few days. They're trying a bandit I caught up in Abilene, I gotta go testify. I'll be back before you know it."

"I'd go with you if you wanted," I said, mind flashing to the two of us riding side by side, her turning to look at me as the plains unfurled before us.

She shook her head, searching my face. I couldn't read what lay behind her expression; it was like there was a shade she'd drawn to keep herself to herself. Then she leaned in quick and kissed me, just once.

"I know you would," she said. "But don't you fret, I'll be back real soon."

She wasn't looking at me unkindly, but her face was closed, and I could see no recourse. I pulled my hands from hers and scooted to the edge of the bed.

"Where are you going?" asked Spartan.

"You heard Lila, I gotta go fetch the doctor," I said, not looking at her but searching instead for my clothes. "Get dressed, will you?"

I didn't turn around when I heard the sheets sliding around, but waited until her arms closed around me from behind.

"Don't fret," she said. "And don't you worry about this place neither, it'll all come right in the end." She kissed me on the shoulder and let me go, stubbing out her cigarillo and searching for her clothes.

Doc Merriweather worked out of a small house just on the north side of the railroad tracks; I found it, as promised, next to a hardware store whose portion of sidewalk was half-blocked by a stack of bladeless plows, all tangled up together. The sign, with its tall, straight-legged *M,* was the same shade of blue that peeked through shreds in the clouded afternoon sky above. Something in me felt sobered, chastened by Lila's asking for help, so I followed her instructions and forbore to rap on the front door, instead snaking down the side alley to let myself into the yard. The yard was small, with room for little more than a washtub and an outhouse. There weren't even any chickens, though I heard a dog barking a few lots over and an answering crow from a neighbor's rooster.

Doc Merriweather opened the door in his shirtsleeves, cuffs pushed up above his elbows as he dried his hands on a towel. His apron might once have been white but was now a map of rusty stains that varied only in shape and lividity. He was far from old—if I'd had to guess his age I'd have put him just north of thirty—but there was a distant look in his eye, as though he were struggling to hold the world at arm's length. I'd heard someone say once that he'd had a very bad war, forced to master his trade at too young an age in too bloody of circumstances.

"Yes?" he said, taking me in. I was already rouged and dressed for the night under my shawl; in the unforgiving afternoon light I looked exactly like what respectable people mean when they talk about whores.

"Lila sent me," I said.

The doc nodded. "I've seen you before," he said. A gust of wind swirled the hem of my skirt up around my ankles.

"Well, listen, we had a fight last night and Virgil—one of the men who works up at the Queen—he got hurt pretty bad. Hit his head on the bar and he's seeing two of everything. Can you come take a look at him?"

"Not for a while yet," he said, beginning to close the door even as he resumed wiping his hands on his towel, and I saw for the first time that he was trying to work blood out from under his nails before it dried.

"Why not?" I protested, putting my hand on the door to stop him.

He sighed. "If you must know, it's because I just finished cutting off some poor cowboy's crushed leg, and in my front parlor Mrs. Tippet's oldest boy is waiting to take me home to his ma, whose ninth baby is hesitant to make his entrance into this world."

"Well," I sputtered a moment, wondering what Lila would do at such a juncture. "Well, can't you at least stop by? Please," I added, hating the reedy, fibrous taste of the word in my mouth, but what did he know? He wasn't the one who would be getting his ears boxed if he turned up empty-handed, or have to slink past the room where Virgil lay up, spinning and alone.

"Lila's . . . establishment," he said, pronouncing the word as if it were the name of a foreign city rather than the place he passed his leisure time, "is in the opposite direction of Mrs. Tippet's house. And anyway, I can't take her boy there. Virgil will have to wait."

"But—"

"But nothing. Keep his hands and feet warm, and keep him awake. No coffee, someone will just have to sit up with him. I'll be there later, if I'm able."

"But what'll I tell Lila?" My voice was thin and an itchy panic prickled up under my hair as I thought of the scene that would await my failure.

He shook his head lightly and closed the door softly in my face without a word.

Alone in the yard, I pulled my shawl tighter around me as the wind changed direction, hating the thought of returning to the Queen in defeat, but knowing I had no other choice.

Rather than go home down the main drag, I took the long way, snaking through yards and back streets like the stray dog I was. I walked slowly, catching glimpses of the open plains between buildings. When I had first arrived, Dodge City had seemed to happen all at once, as if I had crossed an invisible line from the wild, empty plains to the world of men. Now I saw that there was no such boundary, that the town simply petered out into the grass that waved beyond, tall and mindless as ever it was and ever it would be. I paused for half a moment to watch an especially strong gust of wind give stir to the last tufted stems, which dipped and swayed with an almost maidenly languor. Spartan's voice spoke low and even at the back of my mind: "Whenever I tire of a place, I just light out." I half wondered what would happen if, instead of returning to Lila's ire and my drafty little room at the Buffalo Queen, I turned my feet toward that sea of waving grass and let them carry me as far as they could or wanted to. Would it be like the last time I'd been alone on the prairie? I couldn't help but think that somehow, after all that had passed between us, the plains would recognize me—that they'd know me from other humans—and protect me as one of their own. The cold fall air whipped toward me in a sudden blast but when it pushed the hair back from my cheeks, its touch felt gentle; I expected it to remind me of Spartan again, but instead I found myself thinking of the way Kate had cupped my face when first she'd looked me over in the heavy gloom of her parlor. I turned away from the prairie, putting the wind at my back and allowing it to prod me toward home.

Lila was waiting for me at the bar. When I repeated the doc's message, she didn't shout at me as I'd expected. Instead, I watched a veil of bitter disappointment—but no hint of surprise—draw itself over her eyes, whether with me or Merriweather I could not say.

I worked the rest of the night as best I could, resuming my habit of trying to catch Spartan's eye whenever possible, but she only ever looked up from her game to glower at potential trouble, and didn't seem to glance my way more than once or twice. She didn't let herself into my room at the end of the night, and when I woke up the next morning, she had already left town.

Spartan didn't return for three nights, each as long and dreadful as the storm that had accompanied her arrival in Dodge. Whenever I looked out a window, I was astonished to see that the skies were not roiling with angry clouds. Nor was rain pelting down, nor hail clattering against the panes, nor snow hissing into great wispy piles in the street. At first I assumed it was simply that I missed her; I remembered a similar pall after Sallie had left, the way that all the colors had dulled while the lamplight became brassy and flat. I couldn't even pass the time amusing myself with the men, for as the nights passed those paying for our time were grimier, more likely to have that edgy gleam in their eye that implied they'd been too long away from warm rooms and pleasant company. The tales they regaled us with were a bloody mishmash of scalpings and shootings; each story seemed to end with the teller's Bowie knife going into the belly or the heart or the eyeball of some unfortunate stranger. We kept the conversations short and left our bedroom doors propped open an inch or two while we plied our trade.

Early on the first night I paused for a quick drink, savoring the fiery harshness of real whiskey, though not the good stuff. Before I could so much as set my glass down, Lila appeared at my elbow.

"You don't look like you're working—that real?" She jerked her head at the cup in my hand.

"Only a little," I said. "Look at this bunch, you really expect us to face 'em sober?"

She snorted. "Maybe not the other gals, but this is more your doing than the season's. I hope you're happy."

"Jim ain't the only lawman in town," I said. "We'll find us another one."

"Yeah, but when?"

I shrugged. Though Doc Merriweather had never arrived, Virgil's wound hadn't turned out to be serious enough to create any lasting guilt in me—he had stayed awake long enough to go back to seeing one of everything, needing only now to rest—and so all I could summon up was heavy weariness of other people's problems.

"What about that famous outlaw-catcher of yours? We've got some braggarts by the fire who I'd love to see lose to her," said Lila.

"She rode out, said she'll be back in a couple days."

Lila's head whipped around to look at me. "The hell does that mean?"

"Going up to Abilene to testify on some outlaw she brung in there."

"Why didn't you say anything?"

"To who? You?" I heard the words jump out of my mouth and fully expected Lila to slap me across the face, but instead she just sucked her teeth and looked at me for a long moment before reaching over the bar for a bottle and another glass. She poured herself a shot, tossed it back, and returned the bottle to its post without offering me any.

"It's just a couple of days," I repeated.

"A couple of days when Virgil's laid up. A couple of days where we had a deal," she said, looking at me hard. "Or don't it mean nothing to you when people break their word."

"She don't work for you," I heard myself saying.

"No, but you do. So get to it—since I can't box her ears I've half a mind to box yours."

I stood up a little straighter and smoothed down the front of my dress. "Hers would be the last ears you'd ever box," I said, hoping my face looked as hard as her own.

Before Lila could answer there was a crash across the room as an entire table flipped over, glasses and bottles smashing, and then there was a quick flurry of movement and two shots, and one of the men fell dead. He lay like a gutted fish, his mouth flopped open and blood oozing out over the floorboards. Bart fought his way forward and looked at the shooter, whose gun was still raised and smoking.

"He was going for his gun," said a bystander. There was a rumble of agreement from the onlookers.

"I'll send for the sheriff," said Bart. He picked out the youngest and most fresh-faced of the shooter's companions and sent him out down the road.

Lila sighed heavily. "You just keep your wits about you," she said to me.

Turning to face the room, she called out, "Roscoe, more music!" She lacked the booming gaiety that filled Kate's voice when she called out the same order, but the parlor door had remained closed. Roscoe rumbled back to life and started pounding away again, with the same brittle quality that had animated Lila's voice a moment before.

The second night was even worse, its peace shattered early by a fight at Pierre's table, usually a beacon of calm where serious men played a serious game. Over the music I heard some shouting behind me and turned around to see a skinning knife flash and twist before it stabbed into the table with a *thunk,* straight through Pierre's left hand. His eyes bulged out like turnips and he made a high, strangled sound. He yanked at the knife handle with his remaining hand until the stabbed one and the blade came away as one, livid and gleaming.

Pierre held his ruined hand up to his attacker, still gulping, as though shocked to the core and demanding an explanation for such rudeness. Constance and Bart surged across the room to either side of him. Bart didn't even make a pretense of looking for law or order this time around. He punched the man in the side of his head so his jaw stuck out to one side, and didn't let him stagger more than a step or two before he was dragging the miscreant to the door. From my bar-side perch I could see him fly out and slide to a halt in the mud, where he just managed to scramble to his feet before getting trampled by a double team of mules.

"Don't look at it," I heard Constance say. When I looked back, she was helping Pierre up to her room. His face was grub-white and he stared at her obediently, holding his stabbed hand by the wrist. I glanced at it but quickly turned away, an awful, buglike curling sensation running up the backs of my legs. I'd seen plenty of cuts and scrapes in my life but hadn't seen before how blood flows like water if you give it enough room to do so. It must have shown in my face, for Bart placed a glass of something strong before me that I downed without tasting. Up on the balcony, I saw Grace hurrying toward Constance's room with her sewing kit and a roll of gauze, door shutting behind her in a way that was not inviting.

Feeling useless, I slipped out the back door to breathe the night air. I'd never seen the Queen in such a sorry state. Lila didn't even try to get the doc for Pierre's hand, just as the sheriff had never sent anyone about the previous night's gunfight. The shooter, whether from swagger or civic duty, had stuck around long enough to finish his game, which he lost. But when his pockets were empty and still no law in sight, he'd just put his hat on and walked out the door without so much as a by-your-leave, and no one knowing his name. We all watched him go, each person waiting for someone else to point out that he ought to stay, but I don't think anyone could think of a reason why; a dozen sets of eyes followed the man's departure, all of us reduced to bystanders in our own place of business.

The yard was dark and vaguely muddy, a mottled patchwork of blue and black under a sky where I could just make out the movements of high-up clouds getting pushed and chivvied along on their endless travels. There was a bleak, unyielding quality to it that I found comforting; I soaked it in, letting the wind hit me with gust after icy gust that blasted straight through my clothes and raised humming gooseflesh all up and down my body. Even my scalp felt the cold, the hairs on my head lifting as though electrified by the iron hardness of the night.

Lila's point that Spartan had broken her word stuck in my craw, and I kept returning to it, turning the question over in my mind. Was getting some bandit hung really more important than looking after us? After me? Whatever I was up to, I tried to picture what she might be doing at the exact same moment. While I was pinning up my hair, or sipping cold tea from a shot glass, or gazing at the ceiling while some stranger set to on me, I tried to imagine her life, but there was some vagueness I could not break through. I would picture her leaning back in the witness box to look some puffed-up lawyer in the eye as she talked back to him, but what was she saying? Would she laugh at the end? Or I'd imagine her cleaning her gun, but was it day or night? Was she in shelter, or camped under the open sky? And did she clean the barrel first or the chamber? I tried to fill in details with memories of the wind stinging my face, the weight of her gun in my hand, but the knot of her absence never loosened, just kept pulling tighter. I stayed out in the yard, hands open, face lifted, until a sudden shiver racked me from back to front, and I took myself back inside to finish the night's work.

The next evening when they came down at sunset, Constance and Pierre looked stricken and thoughtful. She plied her trade and he plied his, albeit more slowly with one mightily bandaged hand, shuffling by spilling the cards out facedown on the table and stirring them about before he gently pushed them back into a deck for dealing.

Between tricks, Constance and I watched the painstaking operation from across the room. "He all right?" I asked.

"He'll mend. Grace said the blade didn't break any bones, so only time will tell on the rest. He took it well, all told."

I could imagine it: Pierre wincing, muttering curses, and trying heroically to make jokes with Constance while Grace stitched him up, scowling.

"Still, he shouldn't have had to take it at all," I said. "That's no way to behave, damned disgrace if you ask me." I had never seen Constance so disconsolate. Through all previous trials and misfortunes, she'd always been able to pluck herself up, focus on the task at hand, or at least cheerfully kill time until she could get back to her book. This time, however, she looked worn out, and I couldn't tell whether I was seeing a frown between her eyebrows or just the shadow of previous disappointments.

Constance chewed the inside of her cheek as she surveyed the evening's prospects. The crowd was thin and ragged; as predicted, both the season and the loss of Jim's good graces were showing themselves. It's always amazed me how quickly one can sour on a place, how a house can go from home to prison in the blink of an eye, or a town can change from a cherished dream to a sea of regrets in the space of a day or two. When I'd first arrived, I'd been so relieved to find a place where I could get by on my own two feet, make things work through sheer force of will. It was the first time I'd felt a part of something, even something as simple as a whorehouse. But now it was all falling apart around me: I felt a growing sense of fragmentation as I chafed against the rules of this little world, worsened by the prospect of making less money in the coming months.

Almost as though she read my mind, Constance suddenly said, "Come outside with me, let's get some fresh air." She led me through the back door to the alley that ran along the side of the place from the yard to the street. It stank of sour beer mash and emptied chamber pots, but Constance liked it for being out of the wind.

"Pierre's leaving, and asked me to go with him," she said almost immediately.

I gasped, drew up short as if physically pushed.

"You said he was going to overwinter here," I said.

"Not after last night he isn't," she said.

"But I thought you were through with traveling," I said, ashamed of the little whine that crept into my voice.

"I was, but I've got a chance to move on, and I'm too afraid not to take it," said Constance. "He's heading back to New Orleans in a few days, and he asked me to go along."

I felt myself shrinking smaller and smaller, as if the world were stretching out in all directions. New Orleans might as well have been the moon. I wanted to reach out and grab at her arm, clutch at her like a child, but held myself still.

"Are you going to marry him?" I asked just to keep her talking, to keep her standing there with me.

She laughed, that easy, bell-ringing laugh that made me miss her already. "Oh heavens, no. He offered, but it was an offer, not a proposal." She raised her eyebrows. "After all that guff over Jim, perhaps I should have taken it. But I prefer to be a free agent."

"What'll you do in New Orleans?" I asked in a small voice.

"Gamble, mostly. Whore if I have to, maybe get a parlor of my own going if the mood takes me." She looked around. "I've got a good nest egg saved up, you know, in Kate's safe. It'll stake me awhile, and give me some time to think about what to do next."

"What about me?" I asked.

Constance pursed her lips, looking impatient. "What indeed?"

The question hit me like a smack in the jaw. She saw my face fall and stepped forward, clasping my hand between her two. "I didn't mean anything by that, I'm sorry. Just, I have a chance to go someplace—I have to take it or I may never leave, and I don't want to die here. I hope you'll be glad for me."

Looking into her face, I ached already. I'd seen her and Pierre together so many times, just casually talking, playing cards, smiling, joking quietly. They'd never looked quite like lovers, and this didn't sound like some lovers' escape. It sounded like friends setting out on an adventure together; a warm flush of envy worked up through my ache.

"I am glad for you," I said. "I'll just miss you is all." I was grateful for the darkness that hid my stinging eyes.

"I'll miss you too," she said. "But we'll meet again, you'll see."

I nodded. A gust of wind made the hard turn around the corner and I felt Constance shiver through our clasped hands. "Let's go inside," she said.

"You go on, I'll be right there."

She turned to go back in, but paused before the door and looked back. "I haven't said anything to Lila yet. You won't, will you?"

Without looking back at her I shook my head. "No, I won't say anything."

She opened her mouth as if to add more, but instead she just said "Thank you" before going in. Alone again, I looked once more at the sky. The loneliness was like a clutch of eggs that some bird kept laying in my chest; I wondered what would happen when they cracked.

CHAPTER 15

At last, on the following day and not a moment too soon, Spartan Lee returned. It was midday, and I was in my room, sitting before the mirror and glumly brushing my hair. But for the rules, I could think of no reason on this earth to take care of myself or make myself pretty. An idea had come to me the night before, and I twisted my hair into a tight rope at the back of my neck and held it up against my head, twisting and retwisting, trying out what I'd look like without it. I pinned my hair up high and tight; as I set my brush down I imagined it with a barrel, more weight, and an ivory handle. Then I reached behind me for a black hat that a light-boned young cowboy had left behind in the brighter days of summer and pulled it low over my eyes, looking in the mirror with a serious expression.

"Not bad," said a voice from the doorway, and I twisted around to see Spartan leaning against the doorframe with her arms crossed as though she owned the place.

I leapt up and halfway toward her, then pulled myself up short as I spied the open door. She laughed at my sudden restraint. "You don't really think there's such a thing as a secret in a whorehouse, do you?" Still, she stepped inside before pushing the door shut behind her, and this time I flung myself straight into her arms.

I don't think I could have told her in words how much had changed in the time she'd been gone. I'd lived through multiple tongue-lashings, several fights, and the news that my best friend was abandoning me for the better life she so richly deserved. Instead, I gave one kiss for each tragedy, and then one more just in case.

She broke my embrace. "Whoa there, Red, you're liable to burn this whole place down." She untwined my arms from her neck and cupped my face in one hand, as she had on the plains. "Now then, what's all this?"

I looked into her eyes and expected to see impatience, a glimmer of some expected reply, but instead she just waited, brown eyes cool and still. I had that same sense of being seen as a single, entire being, and felt open as a barn door.

I swallowed. "Nothing," I said. "I just missed you is all."

"Well, okay then," she said, and walked me backward toward the bed. There was none of the ravenous tearing this time around. Instead, she took her time, unbuttoning my dress and sliding me out of it, which I mirrored with her shirt. We took turns searching out new little scraps and corners of each other to marvel at. With her shirt off, I could see the dip where her neck joined onto her shoulder, and when I undid the top button on her union suit there was the porcelain cup of her collarbone above a soft sliver of bare skin that widened until I got down to the waist and slipped one hand under the cloth, thrilling to see her belly jump at my touch. She untied the top of my chemise and kissed the top of my breast, which drew a quiver and a gasp from me.

We both took this as a signal to pick up the pace, and we grew searching, anxious for more of each other, each grabbing fistfuls of clothing to pull at and shove aside. I slid a hand down the inside of her trousers and matched my movements to the stiffening of her grasp on me, keeping one step ahead of the waves that passed over her. She shut her eyes and pulled me in so close, thoughtlessly grasping at me, and I was overwhelmed by her smell of sweat and tobacco and cold wind. At the last moment she opened her eyes again and pulled my head back so she could meet my gaze, then bit her lip hard and melted like sugar. She put her forehead to my breastbone, panting a moment, then kissed me again, and then it was my turn.

After, we lay side by side in my bed. We were still close, still running our hands over each other, but something in the ease of our closeness had shifted. I started to relate the events of the last few days but found myself slipping into the showgirl style I used with men I wanted to keep at arm's length, stripping out the fear and sadness and lashing it all with bright paint and lacquer. I left out Constance's imminent departure.

"Shit, Red, sounds like you've had quite a time," she said after I finished.

"Lila said it's the season," I said. "And that it's my fault for driving Jim off, but what was I supposed to do?"

She shrugged. "I don't see as you had any choice." A little, hazy silence fell between us.

"What about you," I said at last. "You aren't leaving too, are you?"

She looked away, and then back again. "Well, as it happens, I probably am," she said. "I just came back to resupply—I'd rather overwinter down in San Antone where it ain't so chilly."

I wasn't surprised, but still, when she said it I felt myself falling like a stone dropped into a well. I recalled Constance from the night before saying she didn't want to die here, this time hearing the fear in her voice, and understanding it. If Spartan Lee rode off without me, I'd be just another abandoned, brokenhearted girl, whiling away the long winter with nothing to do but brood over my own mistakes.

"Then I'm going with you," I said. The words surprised me, but as soon as they were out I realized they'd been brewing in me for days.

"You're what?" She blinked at me, leaned back a little.

"I'm going with you," I said again. "I can keep up, and you said I was a good shot, didn't you?"

"That ain't the point. Why on earth would you want to come with me?"

"Isn't that obvious?" I said.

She let it hang in the air while I tried to think of anything to say besides the truth.

"I fell in love with you" is what I said at last. I hated the words, the way they bloomed through the air like the miasma before an outbreak of fever.

She snapped her gaze over to me. "Oh, Red" was all she said. Tenderly, she took my face in her hands, pulled me down, and kissed my forehead. "You don't want this. You think you do, but you don't."

I bristled, felt my face flush scarlet. "Everyone keeps saying that to me," I said. "Bridget, you ought to do this, that, and the other thing. Every time I turn around it's 'you oughtn't to done this' or 'you better keep your nose clean' or 'you get back on the straight and narrow, missy' and not one person has ever asked me if I give a shit. And now I do, and you don't even believe me."

"I believe you," she said, "but I also don't believe you have the slightest idea what you're asking for."

"Well, how the hell else am I supposed to find out than if you let me come along and see for myself?"

She sighed and threw her hands up, exasperated. Then she got up and started dressing in silence. I watched her yank her clothes on, churning with a mixture of fury at her reaction and regret that I'd said anything at all.

As she rose to take her hat from the peg I spoke. "Well?" My voice sounded so thin.

"Well?"

"What about it?"

She sighed again, softer this time, and looked at me. "Fuck it, why not."

I felt a huge grin leap out on my face and bit my lip to bring it under control. For a moment my mind's eye flashed to the gaping, endless horizon, the blue smudge of distant mountains, the sandpaper sting of sleet on the backs of my hands; I swatted away the small, doubtful whisper that "fuck it" was awfully far from "yes."

"But I travel hard," she continued. "Not a mattress or a plate of beefsteak to be had between here and Texas."

I nodded so eagerly I felt my jawbone rattle up and down. "Of course."

"All right, then," she said. She reached for the door.

"What about . . ." I began before I could stop myself, and paused.

"What about what?"

Too late now, I'd already begun. "What about the rest of what I said?"

She shook her head impatiently. "You're coming with me, ain't you?"

"Yes."

"Then let that be enough for you," she said. She shut the door behind her, just a little too hard.

As soon as she was gone I jumped up and wriggled into Constance's old dress. It was still only midafternoon, and I felt a feverish urgency to act before I changed my mind. I hurried down the catwalk and rapped on Kate's door, which was opened by Grace.

"Hush," she said. "Kate's poorly."

"Just tell Lila I want my box," I said.

Grace flattened her mouth, suspicious, but she shut the door and reopened it a minute later to pass my cigar box of money out through the crack. I tucked it under my arm and marched out of the Queen before anyone could so much as say hello to me.

First I went down to the livery, where I struck a good deal for Little Blue, the dark-coated gelding. I stopped to feed him an apple, stroking the salt-and-pepper velvet at the end of his nose.

"We're going traveling," I told him softly. "You and me, and

Spartan and Davey. You'll love it." I petted his face and he flicked his ears at me, bright eyes shining.

Then I headed for the north side of town and went into the first place I saw that sold men's clothes. I told the clerk that I was shopping for my brother, who happened to be about my size. With a somewhat skeptical twitch of his mustache, the clerk held up a few jackets against my back before selling me a suit of sturdy black serge.

"He'll need a shirt and a tie as well," I said. "And a good coat and gloves."

"Is he going somewhere?"

"Yes," I said, embellishing with a fluency built up over a lifetime of telling men what they wanted to hear. "He's headed to San Francisco. We've got an uncle in shipping, promised him a job."

"What an enterprising young man," the clerk said evenly. "Is he redheaded like you?"

I nodded. The clerk held a purple silk tie up next to my face and tilted a looking-glass up to show me the effect, which was quite rakish. The back of his hand just ghosted past my cheek as he went to wrap everything up, and I bit back a reflexive instinct to charge him for the touch.

Next I went to a dry goods and fixed myself up for travel: bedroll, canteen, tin plate, cup and spoon, a short-bladed knife with a little curve at the tip that reminded me of Spartan's lazy sneer. I wondered how different my last journey would have been if my pa had had even half the money I now splashed around like water. Watching the cigar box empty, I recalled how I had cared for my money when it was new, how I had imagined it was my own little army of dollars and cents. Now I sent that army out on the march; this felt like the battle they'd been drilled for, and if I kept them bivouacked for so much as another day I'd have a mutiny on my hands. I bought a set of saddlebags and filled them with crackers, jerky, a wedge of hard cheese, a pound of coffee and a little pot to boil it in, dried apples, cornmeal, and a dear little jar of molasses, no bigger than a walnut. There was a frantic quality to my buying. It was like the money had grown mold and rotted, and I suddenly wanted nothing to do with it, would have thrown it into the fire to free myself up for something new. For the first time in my life I felt a flicker of understanding for my pa and his recklessness with cash, the chattering thrill of letting everything I had slip from my grasp.

The last of it was spent on a revolver and a box of shells. It wasn't much of a gun, in bad need of a cleaning and oiling—the supplies for which the shopkeeper was happy to sell me—but it would get the job done. What job I had in mind was impossible to say.

"What's a little gal like you need with a pistol anyhow?" the shopkeeper asked me.

"A lady ought to be able to protect herself," I said simply. "Don't you agree?"

He harrumphed his disapproval, but I was spending so lavishly that he didn't care to push. Finally, I was down to twelve cents that rattled like teeth. I tipped the pennies and nickels out onto the counter and received a little sack of hard candy, lumpy and half stuck together in the bag.

As the shop boy wrapped the last of my purchases, the shopkeeper said, "You know, it's a hard trail this time of year. You sure you wouldn't rather wait until spring? My missus rents a room above here, you'd be snug as a bug 'til it thaws."

I shook my head. "No, thank you. I'm anxious to be going. You know how it gets, once you're sick of a place there's nothing for it but to get up and go."

The shopkeeper harrumphed again so his white whiskers jumped, but out of the corner of my eye I could see the shop boy looking at me, and I twitched the corner of my mouth just enough so that he could spend the rest of the day wondering if I'd smiled at him.

So laden, I made my way back to the Buffalo Queen, where I slid my heap of shopping under my bed and wriggled into my work dress. It felt tight and tawdry, and my face looked tighter still as I pinched my cheeks and rouged my lips; though Spartan and I had made no plan for our departure, somehow I couldn't help but feel like this was my last night. Finding myself with a little time to kill, I took out my new gun and set to cleaning it. As I worked, I pictured myself coming down the stairs, but this time I was in Spartan's seat by the fire, watching a lost girl preparing herself to turn one last spate of tricks. For a moment I wondered what had possessed her to agree to take me along but quickly pushed away the question. Instead, I thrilled at the prospect of being the one to watch someone else descend the stairs, of being the one to spend the night drinking and playing cards, sitting careless and wide-legged, blowing smoke right in men's faces and laughing as loud as they did. I holstered the oiled gun and tucked it back under my bed. Outside my door, Roscoe was at the keys playing "Red River Valley" so mournfully I almost burst into tears when I opened the door to go down.

CHAPTER 16

Despite everything, or perhaps because of it all, peace descended upon the Queen the next day. It was as if we were all on our best behavior, or perhaps just worn out from the preceding days' various disasters; either way, we got a full day of harmony with each other. Lila relaxed after a night with Spartan back in her seat and pulling in a little extra trade. Pierre's hand seemed unlikely to fester, which in turn lifted some weight from Constance's brow. Meanwhile, I had my own upcoming travel to daydream about, which kept me bright-eyed and cheerful.

It was the last of the afternoon, when the sun finally gave up trying and relaxed its grip, and deep-orange light would spill in through the windows, hatching the floor and the far walls with black lines from the window braces. Very little was happening; there was always a dip right around then, and in the patch of quiet that appeared, the Queen's residents had scattered for the afternoon. With Kate shut up in her parlor, Lila had let half the girls run off to the bathhouse with strict orders to return before dusk when business picked up, while she herself leaned on the balcony watching the sun ease down through the high windows; Roscoe declared he was going for a smoke, only for Grace to quietly let herself out the back door moments later, coat and bonnet fastened; Langley was out on one of his sprees, and with Virgil still laid up in his back bedroom it was just Bart polishing glasses behind the bar while Constance and I dawdled over coffee with Arabella, watching the room. Spartan was by the hearth, playing stud poker with Pierre and a freight man who I knew by his bowler hat but not by name. Spartan and Pierre usually presided over separate tables; Pierre didn't generally like to waste time with amateurs, while Spartan profited by pulling in tin-horns and skinning them of their wages. But if the evening happened to be slow, Spartan would plunk down at Pierre's table to play a hand and maybe learn something. That afternoon she sat facing the bar and the door while I mooned over her, waiting for fresh business.

"Would you knock that off," said Arabella, elbowing me.

"Knock what off?" I said.

"You're preening."

"I am not."

"You are. You're dipping your head this way and that and fussing at your hair, and I won't have it. Don't be so obvious."

"I'll do whatever I like, even if I were doing that," I said. "And anyway, since when it bad for a whore to be obvious?"

"You ain't being whore obvious, you're being regular girlish obvious," she said crossly. "It's irritating."

"Oh, everything irritates you," I said, but all the same tried to keep still. Behind me I heard Bart stumping slowly back and forth, while in the corner of my eye Constance flipped the page of her book with one thumb. Up on the balcony, Lila lit another cigarette. Pierre flipped his hole card and murmured something that twitched his mustache, and the freight man threw down his own card with a sigh while Spartan swore in her low tone that rolled across the barroom like a smooth, round stone.

Then the doors opened and a puff of cool air brought in two men; they wore new-looking, dark wool coats, but their mud-caked boots and dusty hems spoke of hard riding. One of the men had a muffler wrapped so high up under his chin it almost rubbed against his spectacles, so you mostly had to take it on faith that he had a face at all, while the other was handsome in his high-shouldered coat. As they surveyed the room, I turned away to put down my coffee cup and saw Constance's book shut around her finger, when from behind me a high voice said, "Why, hello gals."

All my insides went rigid and I steeled myself to turn around. It was Sallie.

She looked like the prairie sunset itself as the two men parted to reveal her, the layer of dust on her black coat only serving to highlight the gold of her hair, which was looped up under a hat with yellow silk flowers pinned to it, all of her aglow in the last tendrils of amber light streaming in from behind.

"Hello, Sallie," said Arabella. She lifted her chin to gaze at Sallie evenly from her naturally high vantage point. "What are you doing back?"

Sallie laughed. "Well, you haven't changed a bit, have you, old sourpuss," she said. Her eyes and voice were bright, cutting through the room like blades. "Bart!" she called out as she approached the bar. "Give me a glass of gin, will you?"

She leaned forward to accept a glass, her arm brushing mine and raising silver needles along my skin. I heard some money land on the bar behind me.

"Hello, Sallie," said Constance from my other side. "We're just surprised to see you. Last we heard, you were in Cheyenne."

"Oh, Cheyenne was all right," she said airily. "Wild as all get-out, but you sure can charge for pussy." She winked at Constance and turned to me. "And how's Miss Strawberry-Rhubarb? Who're you sweet on these days?"

I didn't know why, but I felt frozen, rabbit-scared. There'd been a time when I would have given anything to have Sallie come back to the Queen. But now that she had, it felt as though I had slipped out the back door at night, expecting to see the world bathed in blue moonlight and dancing with cricket-song, but finding it instead cold, pitch-black, and rustling. I glanced left and right, hoping for some clue to the tension all around me, but my friends made no move. "Hi, Sallie," I stammered. "Welcome back."

"Why, thank you," she said, dipping one shoulder in her lazy half-curtsey. Up on the balcony I saw Lila disappear silently into Kate's parlor.

"You come in with these fellas?" said Arabella, nodding toward the door, though the two men who'd stood there had now parted. The handsome one was at the other end of the bar, ordering a glass of whiskey from Bart, and the one in the muffler was warming himself at the hearth, hands out to the flames.

"Sure did," she said cheerfully. "That's Hector," she said toward the one at the bar. "And that's Jason, but we call him Jack," she said toward the one in the muffler. "Not that it matters since he don't hardly talk none. Their daddy was an educated man, it seems. Not that it does much good."

She half smirked at Constance when she said this, but Constance didn't take the bait. My breath shallowed and my eyes kept flicking over Sallie's companions. Hector was one of those men who only seems tall from far away. I marked the delicate way he curled his hand around the whiskey glass and fingered the rim, for something in it tugged at me, just as I kept glancing at the way his brother's chin tucked just a little into his shoulder as he warmed his fingers at the fireside.

"What are you doing here?" Arabella said again, more abruptly this time. "You know Kate can't take you back."

"I ain't looking for work, just passing through. Wanted to say hello to my long-lost friends—what could possibly be wrong with that?"

There was a moment's silence. I felt something must be happening, for I could see Constance's and Arabella's eyes moving slowly over the room behind Sallie, but sitting between them I felt stumpy and useless, like a child listening to the grown-ups talk politics.

"Well, I'll be goddamned!" came a shout from the stairway. Lila stood halfway up the steps with her biggest smile on. Once we all turned to look at her, she swept down the stairs and caught Sallie in a pale re-creation of the same embrace we'd all witnessed at their last reunion, though this time neither one closed her eyes.

They broke apart and Lila held Sallie out at arm's length. "What the hell are you doing here? Shouldn't you be queen of the Wyoming Territory by now?"

Sallie laughed again—it was getting strangely hard to listen to, like the tightening of a rusty bolt. "Just about was," she said. "But then this disarming fellow took to me, and we decided to see the world."

She held out a hand to the man at the bar, who came up and slid his arm around her waist. He looked Lila up and down as though she were no better than the rest of us, then muttered something in Sallie's ear that made her giggle.

"Come on, Lila," said Sallie. "Why don't you take us upstairs and we can say hello to Kate? Me and Hector are fixing to open up a place of our own when we get back to Wyoming, and I'm sure they would love to talk shop."

Lila cocked her head to one side and seemed to be appraising Sallie and Hector. "All right," she said. "I'd like a chance to visit with you a spell anyhow." She turned and led the way up the stairs, Sallie and Hector following like twin shadows.

"What's going on?" I asked Constance as soon as they were out of sight.

"I don't know," said Constance. "But I don't like it." She looked at Arabella. "What the hell is Sallie doing back here? It's a rough road out of the Territory—why come here? Why not just keep going west?"

I looked over at Arabella for her response but received none. Her lips were pursed and her eyes were fixed on the closed door of Kate's parlor. I looked back over at the card table where Spartan and Pierre were still playing, having cleaned out the freight man. The man in the muffler opened his coat to warm himself more directly for a moment before he sidled around the table, apparently seeking to compare the contents of the players' hands. They had looked up when Lila had shouted from the staircase but had returned to their game and seemed engrossed. I tried to catch Spartan's eye, but she was shuffling the cards and didn't look up. As she fanned out her cards with one hand, she curled her fingers gently around her coffee cup with the other and pulled her chin down slightly into her shoulder. It came to me in a flash.

"They're her brothers," I said quietly.

"Whose?" said Constance. "Sallie's?"

"Spartan's," I said. My heart began to hammer.

Constance squinted at me. "But they didn't even look at each other. They can't be kin." She looked at Spartan, then the man in the muffler, then back again, forehead bunched as she tried to think fast enough.

Arabella seemed to look harder at the parlor door. It opened and Lila came down, Sallie's high laugh sounding shrilly from within. She ducked under the heavy wooden flap to let herself behind the bar and bent down to poke around among the bottles.

"What're you looking for?" asked Arabella.

"Remember that Irishman, sold us that case of whiskey?" came Lila's voice from below. "There ought to be a bottle left, Kate sent me to bring it up."

"I think I got it over here," said Bart, moving to the other end of the bar.

"What's going on up there? Why's she back?" asked Constance.

Lila straightened up, brow furrowed, and looked at Constance. "What's any of that to you?" she asked. The words were something she might say any night of the week, but her tone was soft, supple with real curiosity, for Constance rarely questioned her. A cool shadow fell over my back as mufflered Jack worked his way around to the windows beside the door.

At that moment there came sounds from upstairs, muffled

thumps, and a cry. All of us, Lila included, whipped our gaze upward. The door to Kate's parlor opened and Sallie came out with a bulging carpetbag, followed by Hector, coat thrown back and hand resting on the ivory handle of his gun. They shut the door behind them and made for the staircase with smooth, controlled steps.

"Where are you off to?" called Lila, too loud.

Sallie started to make some reply when the door opened behind them. Kate leaned in her own doorway, pressing one hand to her side. Blood coated her hand like a scarlet glove, and she bent like a hinge to one side, mouth spread in a grimace showing what seemed to be dozens of teeth.

"The safe!" she gasped. "Lila, they got the safe!"

Before anyone could move, Hector drew and pointed his long, blue Colt at Lila where she stood behind the bar.

"Nobody move," he thundered. He had a deep voice like a boulder rolling down a hill. "We just want to get out of here."

My stomach dropped into my shoes. There was a crash as Bart dropped a tray that held the good Irish whiskey and a set of glasses, which smashed around his feet. He reached under the bar for his shotgun but Sallie shouted, "Bart, you keep still now!"

I heard more hammers cocking—Sallie raised a pistol from her skirts, while Jack raised his own gun from his position by the door to cover their escape. Frantically I tried to trace the paths their bullets would take if everyone fired, while my heart clanged faster, like the bell on a fire wagon. A scream gathered in my chest, but my mouth stayed shut.

Hector and Sallie started coming down the stairs. "You let us go," said Sallie. "You just let us go on, now."

There was a sound of chairs sliding, then the cock of one more pistol, and I heard Spartan say, "You just stay right where you are, Pierre." It was the same low, steady tone she always used, but hard along the bottom. I looked to see her standing up, holding her gun on Pierre, who lifted his hands to show they were empty before placing them on the tabletop. For a moment, I became my own ghost. My mouth opened, but no sound came out. I leaned forward as if to rise, but Constance stuck her arm out and blocked my chest, which was swelling horribly between the clamoring din building within and the iron bands of fear that bound me up.

"You set that money down!" Lila shouted.

"Now don't be greedy," said Sallie. She was pointing her pistol toward the bar. Its muzzle gaped like a mouth that sought to swallow all of us—Lila, Constance, Arabella, Bart, me—whole. "I'm just collecting my back pay is all."

"We don't owe you shit," Lila snarled.

"Lila, will you please shut up," said Sallie. "I really would hate to have to shoot you." The gun should have looked too big in her hand, but instead it looked natural. She and Hector kept coming down the stairs and had only to cross the bar before they'd be gone.

With a loud crack, the banister by Sallie's hand popped with a scatter of wood chips. We all looked up in time to see Kate, still clutching the doorway, one half of her dress soaked with blood, pointing Sallie's old confiscated derringer. There came a second crack and Hector shouted something unintelligible and lurched down the stairs, pushing Sallie ahead of him.

"Get back here, you worthless cunt," Kate rasped.

The roar of a revolver filled the room and I heard a single, barking cry from Kate. The shot had come from Jack; up above, Kate crumpled in a sigh of taffeta. Her arm dropped forward and the derringer fell through the rails of the balcony to land with a thump on the barroom floor.

Lila shrieked, leaping forward. Sallie swung the gun toward her and fired, missing but hitting a liquor bottle, which exploded into a silvery firework of glass.

"I said don't make me shoot you!" shouted Sallie. She shot and missed again, but with less of a margin this time, then continued down the stairs, Hector right behind her, his hand bleeding; one of

Kate's shots must have found its mark. Bart reached forward to clasp the sobbing Lila in a bear hug, dragging her to the floor while she squalled and clawed at him.

I looked over at Spartan, who was moving toward the door, though I still couldn't figure out why. My whole body felt full of boiling oil, but I found I could not move from my seat.

"What're you doing?" I asked in a small, bewildered voice.

She paid me no mind, so I forced the question out again, louder. "What're you doing?"

She looked at me and tipped her hat, gave me a version of her crooked half smile so cold I barely recognized her. "Aw hell," she said. "It's been fun, Red, but I told you I had to be moving on."

"Wait," I said.

On the ground floor now, Sallie laughed again, hard as stone, and nodded at Spartan. "Well, you sure did your bit."

Spartan shrugged. "I do like to mix business with pleasure."

I looked back and forth between them. "What's she talking about?" I said to both at once. Sallie and Hector were almost to the door, which Jack had propped open. Hector still had his gun raised, but the elbow of his coat was dripping steadily onto the floor and he tilted drunkenly toward Sallie.

"Normally we'd have sent one of the boys on ahead, but, well, this seemed like the better play," Sallie called from the threshold. "It sure wasn't Hector who'd turn your eye away from that deputy and leave this place ripe for the picking." She winked at me; I wished I could have erupted into a spout of fire and brimstone to bury us all.

"You won't get away with this, Sallie," said Constance. She was on her feet, standing beside me with clenched fists. For a moment I wondered vaguely what she was so worked up about, before I remembered she was being robbed from too.

Sallie swung around and pointed her gun at Constance. "We'll see about that," she said.

"You leave her alone!" Pierre called out from the card table, rising to his feet.

Without a word, Jack fired twice, then once more, and Pierre collapsed behind the table. Constance screamed.

"So long, Red," said Spartan. Jack covered the door while the whole gang disappeared. The doors shut behind them, and just like that, my life at the Buffalo Queen was over.

PART THREE

HARD RIDING

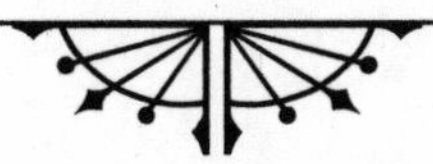

CHAPTER 17

A lot of things happened very quickly after that, and I would be hard-pressed to pick out the worst one. Word of the robbery shot through Dodge like lightning; just after the other girls returned breathless and frightened from the bathhouse, Roscoe ushered Grace in through the back way as they returned from whatever secret place they'd run off to. He locked the doors of the saloon and kept all of us inside, retreating to the kitchen now and then to brew pots of coffee. Bart carried Lila to her room. She was totally undone, sobbing like a child. Most people I've seen in the throes of grief have had to wait to be overtaken by it, like a storm that takes all day building at the far horizon; for Lila it was more like a flash flood that swept her up and carried her off downstream immediately.

Bart and Roscoe moved Kate into her parlor, then carried Pierre's body upstairs and laid him out on Constance's bed, where she pulled up the chair from her dressing table and sat at her own bedside. I offered to let her sleep in my room, but she just shook her head. She was like a cast-iron version of herself, cool to the touch and answering questions in a low, even voice that only now and then trailed up high and sharp. When I passed by at some later hour of the night, I pushed on the unlocked door to see her stretched out beside him in the darkness, half-curled on her side, touching no part of him.

I myself felt snuffed out, smothered like a fire. It was like a dream, and just as in a dream strange things suddenly occur to the dreamer, I would periodically recall that all of this had happened because those I had loved had been false, had played me hard, but then a moment later I would be unable to grasp it. It was the kind of shimmering trouble that's impossible to look at straight on but is always dancing and twinkling in the corner of your eye.

Instead, I worked; when the girls started waking up the next day I sent Grace off to check on Virgil, then organized everyone to wash and dress Kate. Like muses at a riverbank, we moved through her parlor in a ripple of low voices amid the sounds of water splashing in the washbasin, cloths dipped and wrung out dripping, smoothing the blood from her skin, combing her long hair out to burnish its pale brown to a gleaming bronze, buttoning her cold, slack body into her best dress of ruby-colored brocade. We slid her rings onto her fingers, daubed rouge onto the bow of her lips, and fastened her good garnet brooch high up under her papery chin.

After Kate was ready I went and knocked gently on Constance's door. She was sitting up again, facing away from me in the chair she'd pulled close to the bed. There was a chasteness to the scene, like a sister attending at her brother's sickbed, and I marked that it was the first time I'd ever seen her sitting anywhere without a book or a drink or a hand of cards. At some point in the night she had changed out of her work clothes into the dark calico I'd last seen the night of the hanging party.

"Would you like some help?" I asked her.

She looked up from the body and turned toward me. Her face looked dislocated, as though someone else were wearing it.

"You know, I couldn't say," she said at last.

I took one tentative step into the room and saw her tense up like a horse about to bolt. I stopped in the doorway.

"Why don't you go down and have Bart get you some coffee," I said after a moment. "We'll see to him." I gestured toward the bed.

She paused, then smoothed her skirt and rose, mouth set. I

stepped back from the door to let her pass. She stopped in the doorway and looked at her clasped hands.

"In the suitcase, there's a blue gabardine. It'll need brushing, but there's a brush in the valise." She looked at me with wide, wet eyes. "I don't know if he has any clean collars left."

"We'll find something," I said. I wanted very badly to reach out to her, to stroke her face and hold her tight against me, to let her sorrow flow into me so that I might carry it, whether as an act of love or an act of penance it wouldn't have mattered. But she was pulled in tighter than I'd ever seen, and I dared not risk breaking her brittle composure.

She nodded again and re-clasped her hands. I waited for her to get to the bottom of the stairs before rounding up the girls. It was a quicker job than Kate had been, for men wear so many fewer clothes than women do. Henrietta brushed Pierre's good blue suit while Arabella and I washed the body, and then the three of us dressed him. When I looked in the valise there were still a half-dozen crisp, white starched collars, nested inside each other in their round pasteboard box.

Bart and Roscoe laid Kate and Pierre out on the bar, head-to-head, and we all sat up together through the night to mourn. The whores wept, the men twisted their hats in their hands. Lila and Constance, the presumptive widows, sat side by side in the center. Langley, who had slunk back while we were all working, read a psalm and we sang a hymn, and then Bart passed around full glasses of whiskey. Grace helped Virgil down the stairs, then tucked herself up beside Roscoe on the piano bench while he played all of Kate's and Pierre's favorite songs, one after the other, while we drank and sang. It was the strangest funeral I've ever been to.

Around me, the girls were swaying and singing, leaning on each other like they were about to board a ship that would take them away to the promised land. I sat by the hearth and stewed through the proceedings, finally having time to indulge in selfish anger. Like a bookkeeper I worked my way through everyone who'd led us to this point, totting up the wrongs done like deficits in a ledger. Sallie, swanning into the place as though she still belonged here, as though any of us owed her anything, and after all anyone had done was try to help her. Kate, with her reckless dependence on a first-time whore, as if she could think of no better way to protect her business than some young gal making nice to a low-rent lawman. Lila, for closing her eyes to the dope creeping up through Kate's mind, allowing her to get feeble just when we needed her the most. Jim, watching over us only when it suited his purpose, and never letting us forget it. It was all ruined, and for what? For money. For a bit of cash that wouldn't see their pathetic little gang through 'til springtime, certainly not the way Spartan gambled and Sallie drank.

At the thought of Spartan Lee, my jaw clenched up again. I could have pulled down the whole saloon board by board, one rip for each kiss, one crack for each look, one axe-blow for every hand she'd ever laid upon me. I'd have liked to tear the whole place down into a heap and set fire to the wreckage: one great, roaring blaze for all the love she'd made to me, for letting me fall in love with her, for picking up my heart and putting it in her pocket with all the careless ease of a matchbook. Not just for what she'd taken, but for what she'd let me believe, for all the work she'd put into lying to me. Instead I poured liquor through my clenched teeth and snarled my way through the songs while rage scrabbled in my chest like a pack of wolves all caught in one trap, biting each other's legs and howling in each other's faces.

Morning crept upon us and I watched through the window as the saloons snuffed out their torches and surrendered to the light of day; I found it impossible that life had gone on as usual in every place but this one. Struck with a sudden impulse, I ran upstairs and tore through the packages of shopping from just three days before, back when I'd had hope for the future, until I found my new warm overcoat. I threw it on and ran out of the saloon in a wild, furious huff, turning north. I must have looked a fright: it didn't occur to me until I was halfway down the sidewalk how drunk I was, having taken nothing but whiskey for a day and a night. Blind to the faces that blurred past me, I moved with that strange, lurching swiftness that comes over the inebriated. The sidewalk unfurled beneath my feet and I drew power from the clacking of my heels over the boards. I almost passed the jailhouse but spotted it at the last moment and swung myself into the front office.

"Jim!" I shouted into the gloom.

A junior deputy looked up from the desk. "Yes, ma'am?" he said, leaning too hard on the *ma'am* for my liking.

"Where's Jim? Jim Bonnie?" I demanded.

"What do you want with Deputy Bonnie?" he asked.

"To talk to him! Now!"

"Now you hold on a minute," said the junior deputy, holding up one hand. The door to the back opened, and out came Jim in all his big, bearish solidity. He seemed to barely fit through the doorframe.

"It's all right, Stan," he said. "I'll talk with her."

He took his hat off its peg and steered me outside, around the side of the building to a sheltered spot next to the little stable they kept. I sat on a crate and he perched beside me, legs out long to brace him up, and asked what had happened in his most solicitous voice. The low, gentle tone of it was so unexpected that I burst out sobbing.

After an awkward moment he pulled me in close and let me cry a spell, my tears soaking into the shaggy collar of his buffalo coat. When I finally started to slow, he sat me up and fished in his pocket for a red bandanna with which I mopped at my face.

"Oh, Jim, it's all fallen apart," I said. "Sallie came back with these bad outlaws, they were brothers with—with Spartan Lee, you remember her?"

"I remember," he said softly.

"And they shot up the place and they killed Kate—"

"Aw, hell," he said. His brow dropped into his hand for a moment and he shook his head while I kept on.

"—and all she ever was was nice to people, and then they stole everyone's money, and they killed Pierre—you know Pierre?"

"I know Pierre," he said.

"He was about the gentlest man alive, and so friendly, and they killed him! How could they do that? Poor Constance's heart is broken."

He shook his head. "I heard there was some bad business down at the Queen."

"There's been bad business ever since you stopped coming around," I said.

"I'm sorry to hear that," he said. He recrossed the legs that were supporting him.

"Why'd you leave us like that?" I asked, still crying. "I'd have kept on with you—didn't we always have fun together? Or if you didn't want me no more, there's plenty of other gals you could have spent time with."

"I don't want plenty of other girls," he said. "Anyway, you gave me to believe you didn't want me around, so I stayed away."

"Oh, that's not true." I put my hand on his arm but he jerked it away.

"What do you want, Bridget?" he asked, arms folded.

I snuffled and picked at the crumpled bandanna. "To get 'em, of course. Can't you send your boys to round 'em up? Like you did with those bank robbers at the Emerald?"

He looked at his feet a long moment. "When'd this gang of outlaws ride out?" he said.

"Hector Lee and them?" I couldn't bring myself to say Spartan's name again.

"Yep."

"They was in the day before yesterday, but one of 'em's hurt, pretty bad, so they ain't traveling fast."

He looked up at the sky. It was pale, but the sun was paler—snow coming.

Jim shook his head. "No, I don't think it's possible," he said at last.

I felt the breath puff out of my lungs. "Why not?"

"We don't know which way they went, so we'd spend half a day looking for a trail if we don't get lucky." He pointed at the sky. "Besides, you really think I can raise a posse before the snow, to catch some bandits with over a day's head start? And for what cause?"

"You'd do it if they'd robbed the bank," I said.

He nodded. "I might do, yes. But the bank has everyone's money."

"You think Kate doesn't? Didn't?"

"It ain't the same and you know it. You're telling me that me and my deputies and a bunch of volunteers should risk our lives three different ways to go after the killers of a gambler and a whoremistress? That's really what you think we ought to do?" He looked at me with the same sullenness I'd last seen when I turned him down.

I could think of no answer, just gulped like a drunk catfish.

"Go on home, Bridget," he said after a moment.

"You ain't going to do nothing about any of this, are you."

"Go on home. You're drunk."

I leapt to my feet. "You're goddamned right I'm drunk. And you ought to be too, the amount of time you spent down there. Don't you give a single rat's whisker for all the good times you had because of Kate? All the work you didn't have to do on account of Pierre's honest game? Who do you think brought us together in the first place? God?"

He raised his hand and for a moment I feared he'd strike me, but then I realized he was just waiting to get his bandanna back. I plunked it down, making sure the wettest part hit his palm first.

"Your luck done run out, hasn't it," he said, quietly.

I wished he had struck me rather than say such a thing, and I think he wished it too. I reared back and staggered a little, then turned on my heel and fled from the cold weariness of his gaze.

CHAPTER 18

Back at the Queen, the girls were drifting about, too drunk to keep singing but too sad to go to bed. The air within was thick and cottony, as if everyone's exhalations were sticking to each other's skin. The bodies had been taken away and the bar looked oddly bare; Constance and Lila were still in place before it, though they seemed to be leaning toward each other a little, listing like ships in port.

"Where've you been?" said Arabella sharply when I came in.

"Went to see Jim," I said. Behind her I saw Constance and Lila look up.

"Whatever for?" she asked.

I waved my hand at the room. "To do something about this, of course."

Arabella snorted. "What on earth could he possibly do about any of this?"

"Go after 'em, get the money back, bring 'em back to hang for what they done," I said. Arabella drew her head back and looked at me, snakelike, from atop her long neck; I was suddenly aware of the silence that had collected around us.

"And what, pray tell, did dear old Jim have to say about this request?" she asked. The mockery in her voice was unmistakable now.

I shook my head and tried to speak but forgot to open my mouth.

"I beg your pardon, what was that?" she asked.

"Nothing," I said. "He ain't going to do a damned thing."

"We made our bed, we get fucked in it, something to that effect?"

I felt hot shame rising into my cheeks. "Something like that." I looked past her. "I'm sorry," I said, to Constance now, desperate for her to know that at least I'd tried. "I just thought he might . . . I don't know. Do something."

Constance opened her mouth, took a breath, and paused. "You're a sweet girl, Bridget," she said at last.

Next to her, Lila looked away from me in disgust and took a long drink from her tumbler. I wanted to say something but found that I was out of words. There was a pressure coming from the rest of the room, eyes like so many sweaty fingertips bruising my skin. I turned on my heel, thinking to escape up the stairs, but smacked instead into a big wad of sheets that tumbled to the floor, revealing Grace behind them.

"Why don't you watch where you're going?" she snapped at me. She shifted her feet to ease down and pick them back up; in my embarrassment I all but threw myself down on the floor to collect the scattered linens. They were damp, and I realized they must have been the sheets from the beds where we had washed the bodies yesterday. Bundling them tight, I hoisted the load up on my hip.

"Where do you want them?" I asked.

Grace looked past me, scanning the swollen, doughy faces of the other girls, and sniffed. "Out back," she said, and led the way to the yard. My skin burned under their eyes, and I was grateful for a reason to turn my back to them at last.

The yard was just as windy and unforgiving as the street had been, but now it felt right. What had been dust or mud through the summer had frozen around tooth-yellow tufts of grass under a dishwater sky that I sneered at appreciatively, for we deserved each other. Grace was working the pump in a lopsided two-step of splashing water and screeching iron. She jerked her chin at the tub, already half-full.

"In there," she said. I dumped the sheets inside and watched the water seep up through the thick-spun cotton.

"You gonna cry?" asked Grace. I looked up, startled. When Sallie had first left, I had felt torn through, ripped stem to stern and unable to do anything but howl; it seemed only right that now, with so very much more damage to account for, I should be entirely undone. But instead of welling up to spill out unbounded, something in me seemed to cool and harden like a piece of iron drawn from the forge and plunged into the water-barrel, red glow fading down to black.

I looked at Grace and shook my head. "Doesn't seem worth it," I said.

She nodded tersely. "Waste of good tears," she said.

Grace came around to the side of the tub, rolling up her sleeves and dropping to her knees. Instinctively I did the same, slipping off my coat first to drape it over the pump handle.

"I probably ought to, but I feel too stupid," I said.

"Sounds about right," said Grace as I knelt across from her. She threw a handful of soap flakes into the water and picked up two handfuls of cloth, rubbing them against each other. I opened my mouth to snap back at her, but when I looked up, she just ran one finger up the cut side of her face, leaving a thin trail of suds in the groove of her scar. "Felt real stupid after this," she continued.

"Like you should have fought harder?"

She gave me a long, hard look. "If I'd have fought him, he'd have killed me," she said, as though talking to a child she'd already whipped once and who yet insisted on misbehaving. Grace let me sit looking down at the half-submerged sheets, shame-faced, until she was ready to continue. "It was that he got away with it," she said. "He got to ruin me and ride away to live out the rest of his life doing

God knows what else, leave me to sit and rot. Hurt worse than my face did, I'll tell you that much."

"They didn't help you?"

"Who would have?"

I tried to shrug but felt almost physically weighted down with what she was telling me; her words piled on me like heavy snow.

"The other girls? Hugh?"

She laughed. "Hugh Montgomery ain't never done for a gal once in his life. I may as well have been a horse with a snapped leg—barely worth the bullet to shoot. But we had this new gal who'd come over from the Queen—couldn't make her cut, if I remember—and she told me to come here, that the madam, or one of 'em anyway, loved a sad story."

She paused again and her hands fell still, dangling over the edge of the tub. I watched soapsuds collect along her forearms, slide over the backs of her hands to drip into water that now looked like milky tea.

"I couldn't turn tricks, obviously, but Kate said she'd let me stay awhile if I pulled my weight around the place, and now here I am."

"What'll you do now?" I asked.

"Wait and see," she said, leaning forward to resume her work. "Best not to react too fast to something like this."

"Better to ride it out?"

"Just give it time to settle," she said. "There's some things happen in this life you can't do a thing about 'em, you just have to get through." A silence fell between us; to ease it, I pushed my sleeves up and sat forward to help with the washing, grabbing two fistfuls of linen and scrubbing them together. The icy water nipped at the backs of my hands, stung in the dry creases of my knuckles; the wind made me tear up but I couldn't lift a hand to wipe my eyes without rubbing soap in them.

"I don't know if I can just get through," I said.

"Doesn't matter what you know," said Grace.

I shrugged. "Told you I felt stupid."

She nodded. "You ought to," she said simply.

I wanted to say something sharp back to her, but she was right. Before I could reply, she changed the subject. "That's a real nice coat."

"It's new," I said.

"It's a boy's coat, though. Was it for you?"

I nodded.

"You were gonna leave with her, is that it? Be wild outlaws together?"

I blushed and plunged my hands into the water, which felt almost warm compared with the wind blowing down from the north.

"Just my luck to cast my lot with a double-crosser," I said by way of an answer to her question.

Grace scoffed and spat on the stone-hard dirt. "Luck," she said. I was reminded of Sallie spitting on the floor of her room, that same mixture of scorn and disbelief that I could hold such childish ideas.

"Well, who asked you anyway," I muttered.

"No one. But you're old enough to know luck's no more real than Santa Claus. I heard about what she said on the way out—how do you think she picked you out?"

My hands went still and I looked at her, startled. Truth was, I'd forgotten, or been trying to forget, everything they'd said that day. "What do you mean?"

Grace picked up a new section of sheet to work on. I wasn't really helping and she knew it. "You think you had some dear little secret, first Sallie, then that gunfighter, but you're about as secretive as a thunderstorm. Not that anyone cares, we've all been in this business a long time. Hell, you probably have more sympathizers than you realize—or would have had if it hadn't come to what it did."

The wind plucked at my teeth, bringing out a piano-wire hum at the tender spots, and I realized my mouth was open. Grace shrugged and shifted her grip again.

"But even if you weren't listening, you have to ask yourself, what are the odds that of all the gals on the south side of Dodge, hell, of all the gals in the Queen, that she'd pick you out? How do you think she might have known to do something like that?" She peered at me, mouth screwed up and eyebrows puckered together in mock bafflement.

I sat back on my heels, giving up all pretense at work as my wet hands stung in the air. The face of Spartan Lee rose up before my mind's eye, tilting up from under her hat brim in a cloud of cigarillo smoke tinted blue and gold by the torchlight behind her, low voice drowning out the music and revelry all around us. Sallie had said that they would have sent Hector on ahead, but then she'd had this little piece of extra information, a way to make her fortune, get one back at Kate and Lila, and rebreak my mending heart all at once. Spartan had slid right in like a freshly whetted knife, hit me right where it couldn't possibly hurt more. Prying Jim out of the Queen had been as simple as leading me away from that dance floor, and absorbing my attention had been the work of a few evenings. Like falling off a log.

"It was easy," I said.

"Or anyway, you made it easy," said Grace. Her words were a slug in the guts, a fist right under the rib cage. She was right, and I knew it. Suddenly I was hot all over, and if I'd had the power, I'd have burnt myself to ash, or crumbled into a pile of dust and let the wind whisk me away into nothingness. Instead I covered my face with my hands, eyes stinging from the soap pressing into my lashes.

"There it is," said Grace, half-softly. "You ain't even begun to count the cost yet." She seemed to be thinking aloud, as if she were doing household accounts in her head. "Lila'll recover eventually. Shit, she might even be better off in the long run. There's still some crates of whiskey in the back, and the boys'll work for room and board if they have to, same as me—ain't no better work to be had in Dodge this time of year anyhow. Still, we're in for a rough patch." She flicked one eye up to fix on me. "You seen the trade we're doing without the law on our side. What about your friend Constance—you want her working these ruffians? I saw you the other night, looking for better tricks as if you're the one who can pick and choose—those days are gone, sweetheart. Winter's coming and we got some long nights to get through. You ever seen hungry whores? Like drowned cats too dumb to catch a fish. Lucky you've got some good clothes to sell, maybe you can buy her a train ticket, do something for someone else for a change."

She continued scrubbing, steady and unhurried as though she had all day, though a threatening scrim of cloud was thickening over the sun and her face mottled into shadow. I felt no smarting against her, in fact a part of me loved hearing what I really deserved to hear. I recalled my ungrateful laughing at Jim Bonnie's proposal, the haughtiness with which I'd refused to listen to Kate's concerns, the pride I'd taken in hitting the same spot on a creek bank a few times in a row with a borrowed gun, the childish heap of new clothes and supplies stacked under my bed, reduced now to toys.

"My money's gone," I said.

"So's everyone's," she said acidly.

"No, I mean, I spent it all." I gestured toward my coat. "You were right, I was going to go with her. Not the robbery, just, she said she was leaving and I said take me with you, and she said okay." I bowed my head as though waiting to be struck about the shoulders, despite knowing that Grace would not oblige me.

Instead she scoffed again and continued scrubbing. "What earthly use did you think you could be to someone like that?"

"I can ride and shoot," I said, wondering what I was trying to convince her of. "And, well, I don't know. I just wanted to so badly."

Grace drew in her breath to say more, then paused. Her hands dropped into the water with a splash.

"You wide-eyed types. Kate likes—liked—to take on innocent-looking gals to make the place seem classier, and I suppose it works for some, but I for one don't care for it. Too hard to tell if you're really green or just have big eyes, and then you let the tricks get away with anything they want."

I shook my head. She was right again, but something in her words struck against whatever had been settling within me as I took my tongue-lashing. Grace had unknowingly hit upon the most galling thing of all, and a wave of half-drunk nausea swept over me as I realized that as far as Spartan knew, she'd gotten away with everything. I thought about the girls inside, getting as drunk as they could to put off thinking about the future they didn't have. I recalled Lila looking me over by the cattle pens, how she'd noted all my flaws and still given me the benefit of the doubt, and all I'd done was sass and argue and bring her to ruin. And Constance, well, I could hardly bear to think of what I had cost her. Hanging over all of it was the image of Spartan Lee waiting out the winter in some other sporting house. For all I knew, by now she could be scandalizing some new madam, curling her fingers around a fresh glass of whiskey and holding the place in thrall with a tale of her own daring. Somehow I doubted that I'd be more than a footnote in the drama, for in the end I'd been just a doll for her as well, to pick up and play with and toss aside once my purpose had been served.

The burning sensation on my skin turned to an electric hum, and I stood up, wishing I could grab the dishwater sky and tear it down like moldy curtains.

"They ain't getting away with it this time," I said.

Grace laughed, mouth so wide I could see her pink tongue dancing. "Yeah, you get 'em," she said. "Watch out, everyone, Bridget's on the loose!" She laughed so hard that tears streamed from her eyes and she rocked forward. I reached over her and grabbed my coat before I went inside.

I couldn't face the saloon again, so from the yard I went up to my room and tried to think of what to do next, drifting through the day until the sun set and left me in darkness at last. Guilt clung to me like a stink, soaking up from my skin into the fibers of my clothes. I kept thinking of Constance and Pierre sitting together at the bar just days earlier, the lights in her eyes turned down low not to hide but to listen and learn while their hands and voices overlapped in two parallel conversations. It twisted my gut like a wet rag to know she'd never get to do that again.

At first light, I heard voices through the wall. I felt hazy, lost in time the way one does after falling asleep unexpectedly, sprawled out atop my still-made bed. I had grown used to waking and sleeping to a shifting collage of sounds, voices of the girls waking up and complaining over their coffee, little rumbles as the male staff conferred over the coming day, the constant opening and closing of doors, the steady tattoo of footsteps on all the many wood floors of the house. All of that was still and silent now. Any other morning, I never would have heard Constance and Lila talking quietly in the next room. But now, in the heavy silence, their voices rang out, cutting through the last of my sleepiness and forcing me awake.

I lay still and strained but couldn't quite make out their words. Constance's voice was pitched a shade higher than usual but still had her smooth, practical rhythm; her mind seemed only to move at one rapid pace, and it sounded as if she had finally found a situation that called for speed. Lila's answers, cutting in here and there, were sharp as usual, but there was a throaty depth to her remarks, like she was talking business from deep inside a mine shaft. All through it, I could hear Constance's feet moving back and forth, opening and closing Pierre's suitcase, crossing and recrossing the room, pausing in the center before the bed. Then her feet drew nearer and I heard the gentle thump of the suitcase being set down against our shared wall.

"This one's very warm—with your coat you'll be fine," I made out from Constance.

I held very still, like they were a couple of rabbits I didn't want to scare off. Fine for what? A second set of footsteps as Lila approached her.

"Yeah, that looks good," Lila answered. "What about you?"

"I'll wear the traveling suit—it's warm as well, and anyhow cold doesn't bother me much."

"When was the last time you were outside for more than half an hour at a stretch, if you're so rough and ready?" said Lila.

Slowly I let the pieces come together. They were headed somewhere, but where?

"Bart gave you the shells for that shotgun?" said Constance.

"Yeah, only half a box left, but I ain't gonna need many."

With a stomach-drop I understood what they were about: they were leaving, together. They were going to go after the Lee gang themselves, and leave me behind. I gulped—they couldn't, could they? And what would they do when they caught up to the gang anyhow? I wasn't worried about Lila—I assumed she could and would kill anyone she had a mind to—but who would look after Constance? She was tough as nails in most of the ways that count, but when I tried to imagine her pointing a gun at a man and pulling the trigger my mind jammed up and I couldn't complete the image. I felt twin rushes of jealousy and protectiveness: jealousy that she might get revenge without me, and protectiveness not toward her person but toward her heart. Constance had already lost so much on my account; why add to her burden with the taking of lives?

I don't recall making a decision, only that one moment I was lying on my bed, eavesdropping, and the next I was on my feet and looping around the doorway to her room. I opened the door without knocking and said, "I'm going along too."

They looked up in only mild surprise. Lila had sat back down and was perched at the head of the bed, one leg braced on the floor under Bart's snapped-open shotgun while she oiled it with a blackened rag. Constance, closer to me, was standing over Pierre's open suitcase, holding up a pair of wool trousers, reinforced with suede patches inside the knees.

"I beg your pardon?" said Constance.

"I said I'm going along too," I repeated. Under Lila's gaze I twisted my hands together, felt a desire to shrink back, but I willed my feet to stay where they were.

"Going along where?" Constance asked. She reached over to the washstand and picked up a cigarette lying in a saucer, pulled on it, and exhaled twin puffs through her nose.

"Since when do you smoke?" I asked.

"Since today," she said.

I shrugged. "Well anyway. Look, I know you're going after 'em, so I'm going too."

"You can't," said Lila from the back of the room.

"Why not?" I said.

"Because you're not wanted," she said.

"I don't care if I'm wanted or not," I said. "I'm still going along."

"We're going to get the money back, yours included," said Constance wearily. "So you really aren't needed."

"It ain't about the money," I said. "I got to go with you."

"Why?"

I looked at both of them. "I want to help—"

"—Oh, for shit's sake," Lila interrupted.

"But I do," I said. "I ruined everything, I know, but this . . . you . . ." I trailed off.

"Us what?" Lila took a slug from a bottle by her feet and clunked it back down onto the floorboards.

"You're all I got left."

Silence fell. They glanced at each other, then Constance took another puff of her cigarette and looked down at the floor.

"It'll be hard going," said Lila. She meant to put me off but I took it as an opening; I drew my shoulders back to stand up straight as she was always telling me to.

"You know I walked here practically from Abilene, right?" I said. "Alone. And a fair piece before that. So what else have you got?"

"You ain't comin' along just to help out—whatever that means. We're getting our cash back. What're you gonna hit 'em with, your good looks and charm?"

"I got a gun."

"Cute little derringer for shooting mule skinners with?"

"A revolver," I said. "Know how to use it too."

"Well, that certainly could have helped before," said Constance, not meanly. I felt myself go scarlet but held my ground.

"We ain't got supplies for you," said Lila. I saw a hint of the crow-like curiosity in her face that I had first seen last summer by the cattle pens. She was interested, leveling arguments at me one at a time like a teacher running through a list of spelling words.

I too was warming to the fight, enjoying an argument after so much grief. "I got my own. I had planned to go on with . . . with her when she left, but she got the jump on me."

"You don't say," said Lila, with a scoff they heard all the way in Montana. But she resumed bickering with me, which I took for a good sign.

"You can't travel in those clothes," she said.

"Got me a suit, overcoat too."

"You need a horse."

"Bought one just the other day."

"You can't shoot."

"I told you already, I can too, pretty good."

"You ain't never killed a man."

"Have you?"

"Lots of times." Here a very faint shadow of a smile rippled past, just a flash like a face in the window of a passing train. I almost laughed; sensing that Lila was softening, I changed targets.

"Constance," I said, "you don't know the first thing about any of this—"

She opened her mouth to reply but I cut in before she could say anything.

"—I don't mean the Queen, I mean hard riding. You even know how to shoot? You think Lila's going to have time to teach you?" I turned back to Lila. "Once you clap eyes on Sallie you're going to plug her six ways from Sunday and ain't no one getting a word in edgewise then. Who'll look after Constance while you avenge yourself on those that wronged you?"

Constance bit her lip. I could see her thinking. "How do we know what you'll do when we find them?" she asked.

The question drew me up short. It wasn't that I hadn't thought that far—though I hadn't—so much that something told me I wouldn't know for sure until I saw Spartan Lee's face. For a half a second I cast about for an argument I could make. But Constance's eyes were jewel-bright, sharp and gleaming as the light crept in slowly from outside.

"Right now the only thing I want in the world is to shoot her right in the heart," I said. "But I suppose I can't be certain until I see her again."

Constance nodded. She took another long drag off her smoke and stubbed it out, then turned to Lila, holding up the butt. "These are disgusting—I don't know how you stand it." She laid it in the saucer and looked at me again. "But we could use one more gun."

"No," said Lila firmly.

I looked at Constance, but her face was closed tight, lips pursed. She shook her head once and then turned away from me. I felt the wind go out of me and the floor seemed to tilt like a ship at sea as I staggered from the room. I paused at my own doorway but the thought of my bed repulsed me. I felt as though I might throw up, gorge rising as I ran down the stairs through the empty barroom and back out into the yard. The wind steadied me, brought me back to myself as the sky stayed flat above me, refused to take me in its arms.

And then at last, after all my other tears had fallen, I cried for Spartan Lee. I didn't fall to my knees, or howl, or bury my face in my hands. Instead I stood upright, arms hanging down at my sides, face upturned to the marble sky. I closed my eyes and shook while hot rivers poured down over my cheekbones, curved under my chin, and fell from my jaw like the slow drip of rainwater in a cave. Tears cupped my face in all the places she had done; I ached so badly for the feel of her hands and hated myself for it, which only made me cry harder, but the effort failed to dispel even an ounce of my longing for her scratchy voice in my ear while her arm slid low and easy around my waist. Every little nip of the wind hurt, but it was hurt I welcomed, hoping that it would chisel me down to nothing. Perhaps then, even for a moment, I could stop thinking about her. Even the sting of my own tears growing cold and tacky around my collar only reminded me of her touch, her thumb sliding along the bone before her hand traveled lower.

I would have given anything to go back to any one of those moments, for now they were all I had. Constance and Lila were going to ride off and vanish into the plains just like she had, never to be seen again. I pictured them, side by side, riding away from me to be swallowed by the tall grass. I let out a single, wretched gulp of a sob and fell back against the side of the building, covering my face with my hands. For all they were tough as nails, Constance and Lila had no notion of what they were getting into. Not that I knew so much more about outlaws than they did, but I knew a damn sight more about Spartan Lee, and I knew she wouldn't hesitate to shoot them down and leave their bodies to rot away in an unknown spot under a patch of empty sky.

The thought was too awful to contemplate, so awful that in a strange way it calmed me, settled my shoulders down from around my ears, brought my breathing back to a somewhat steady rise and fall. I looked at the patch of dirt between my feet and listened to my breath, my mind drifting back to the last time I had felt so totally alone in this world. For a moment, the cold stabbing air transformed into the whisper of summer wind; the bedsheets flapping wetly on the line became the dappled shadows of the cottonwood branches playing over the surface of a lovely little spring. I closed my eyes and could almost hear my pa whisper *Just bad luck, Bridget,* before he slipped away from shade to shade. I recalled wading into the water and the promise I had made to myself there, that I would live a better life than his, that I would not be whipped about by the winds of misfortune as he had done, and realized it was a promise I had yet to keep.

Now I longed for the resolve I had felt in that moment, the way my heart had closed like a fist around the handle of a knife. It seemed strange that the moment in which I had felt most sure of myself had been the moment when I was most alone, lost on a road that, by all rights, should have ended there. Spartan's voice rang out in my mind: "Jesus, Red, you're lucky to be alive." I screwed my eyes up tighter, trying to hold on to the sound of her voice, but it seemed I could keep hold of nothing, that everything I reached for found a way to wrest itself from my grasp. I tried to wring out a few more tears, hoping to recall her touch once more, but none came, and the wetness at my throat now felt cold and useless. Defeated, I relinquished my grip on the memory of her, not through any sense of nobility or sacrifice, but from simple exhaustion, knowing that just as all my past efforts had been for naught, so too would any attempt to keep her close to me, even in deep places of my heart. And then, just as I resolved to turn away, her voice came back to me again. *Last good place to stop,* she'd said. *Only water for miles.* I saw again her hands, made graceful not by their beauty but by all they had done, lifting in the air to sketch the contours of the cottonwood grove she'd told me about our very first night together. I was ashamed that I'd thought she was talking to me as lovers do, that when I'd told her about Pa and she'd told me about her fight with her brothers it was meant to bring us closer, when her story of parting with Hector and Jack had just been another lie. Still, my mind's eye followed her hands once more over the trees to the spring and then snagged on something she hadn't mentioned but that I could see, plain as day: a little wooden door, worn to cloudy gray, in the hairy face of a sod house. *You know what boys are like,* I heard her saying. *They do so love to be right.*

My eyes snapped open and I straightened up. For half a moment I was shocked to see the yard still before me, that I hadn't actually been transported to that old sod house where my pa had met his end, but it didn't matter. With a clatter of boots I ran back inside and up the stairs, door banging as I barged back into Constance's room. They were as they had been when I'd left, though Lila had finished cleaning the gun and was now counting out shells.

"Which way are you going?" I asked, breathless.

Lila said nothing and flicked her eyes at Constance, who returned her gaze.

It was Lila who answered. "We'll ask around, I'm sure someone saw which way they left."

"And you think they'll tell you? You think a shop boy or, I know, that blacksmith down the way, you think they'll say which way they saw some killers going?"

"They'll tell me," said Lila.

I did laugh then, just one quick bark. "Don't be funny," I said. "The minute you step out of here anyone who might know anything'll be acting like they can't even see you, much less help you out. Once a whore, always a whore, isn't that right?"

I looked at Constance, who opened her mouth, then caught her lip between her teeth.

"I know where they're headed," I said, triumphant, but Lila looked unimpressed.

"How do you know?" asked Constance.

"We did find time for conversation, here and there," I said.

Constance threw up her hands, exasperated, and Lila took over. "Why don't you just tell us, then," she said.

I shook my head and squared my jaw. "Couldn't really describe it is the thing."

"Try."

"No." My tears had dried to tacky streaks all down my face, and I swallowed as I looked at Lila straight on. She cocked her head to one side and looked at the shells lined up on the bedspread.

"I mean it, Lila," I said. "It really is hard to describe, but I could show it to you if you let me come along."

"Bullshit. You found your way to Dodge, didn't you?"

"That was pure damned luck. That prairie's the biggest place there is," I said, realizing halfway through that I was repeating something I'd heard from Spartan. "Get a few miles from town and there's nothing but yourself between the grass and the sky."

"Don't give me any of that fuckin' cowboy poetry, you're not a trick."

"Neither is this," I said. "I swear I can find 'em."

"But what if we don't want you along at all?"

"Then I'll go myself," I said. "I'll ride off right to where they're going and catch them up before you've even decided which way to try first."

"They'll kill you," said Constance.

"Maybe they will, but what on earth have I got left to lose?" I asked her. "I got no home, no money, no . . ." I swallowed. "I got no friends. I may as well try my luck on the plains."

Constance looked over at Lila, her face a tangled knot of pain and loss, woven through with a single strand of softness that she'd somehow managed to keep after all this time.

Lila sighed, snapped the shotgun to, looked down the barrel with both eyes. "Let's understand one thing," she said. "I can come home with or without you, but I ain't coming back without Kate's money." She looked up. "You got that, Red?"

I winced under the borrowed pet name, but nodded. "Yeah, I got it."

"All right, then. Be ready in an hour," said Constance.

"I'll be ready," I said, and shut the door behind me with a snap, leaving them to stare.

CHAPTER 19

Before I returned to my room, I went downstairs and got myself a pitcher of cold wash-water from the rain barrel, pausing in the kitchen to boost Bart's poultry shears. Upstairs, I stood before the mirror and held out my long red braid. I looked at it a moment, the fiery copper strands that shone even in the pallid morning light, and thought about how much trouble it had caused me just by being so pretty. Armed with the shears, my right hand reached back behind my head and chewed through it, scissors chomping at the hair like a dog working the last gristle from a beef rib. When the braid came away in my hand, I looked at it one last time, then went to the window, pried it open, and flung my forlorn locks out into the muddy yard. Good riddance.

In bad need of a wash, I slunk Constance's old dress down into a pile around my feet, then pulled off my stockings, balling them up into black wads. With a series of pops I unhooked my corset at the front and paused for a moment, taking a wide, deep breath. I felt like I was pulling all the air in the Queen into my lungs: all of the smoke from the fire, the lamps, the torches, all of the tobacco ash and raked-out cinders, all the hazy vapors from the liquor bottles and empty glasses, all of the glances that had been cast and not received and now lay dead in the air, all of the disappointment, all of the grief, all of the merriment, all of the music. I pulled it all in and held my breath a moment, savoring all of the things that Sallie's greed and Spartan's deception and my own stupidity had broken. When my lips started to tingle and pulse, I parted them softly to let it all go.

I stripped off the last bits and pieces, then, naked, went to work on myself with a rough cloth. I scrubbed and rasped with the cold water in my basin, rubbed myself down top to toe so that when I caught a glimpse of myself in the mirror, the skin of my thighs and backside, arms and shoulders, breastbone and neck was all streaked red and pink. Shivering in the cold now, I patted myself dry with a flannel towel and dressed as I had intended to in a previous life, just a few days earlier.

First came the new union suit, crimson wool flannel that felt wonderfully warm after my cold scrubbing. Then the shirt, black calico with a purple stripe, that the shopkeeper had said would complement my fictional brother's red hair, then the trousers. I'd never worn pants before, but I immediately saw what there was to like, never having felt such freedom of movement. Then my cravat, tied in a sloppy four-in-hand, then the black wool waistcoat, buckling it only loosely at the back so that my bust didn't show. Not that disguise mattered, as I was riding after people who knew me, but as long as I was traveling, I thought might as well travel far. At least for the moment, the thought of coming back to this room repulsed me. I unwrapped all of my packages and parcels from the other day, making a great, rustling heap of paper in the corner of the room, and folded Constance's old dress, leaving it on the bed. I buckled on my new-yet-aged revolver so that it hung low and intimate against my hip, right on the spot where Spartan Lee had gripped to pull me into her. Sliding into my suit jacket and overcoat, I tucked my new leather gloves into my coat pocket, slung the saddlebags over my shoulder, and picked up the bedroll under the other arm.

I opened the door and looked back at my room. There on the wall were the pegs from which my work dress and shawl still hung, red and brown together like a barrel of apples that were starting to turn. There was the window that had rattled when the wind hit it just right, that let in enough light to tell me what time it was but not enough to shine in my eyes. There was the mirror in which I had watched myself transform from dust-covered prairie foundling to rouged-up whore, then into a girl in love, then into whatever I was now. There was the bed where I had slept and daydreamed and plied my trade, where I had sold pokes to more strangers than I could count, where I had sat and watched them wrestle their cocks out of their pants beforehand and tuck themselves sheepishly back in after, and where I had fallen in love. I pulled the door shut behind me and went to find the others.

They looked magnificent. Constance had donned Pierre's traveling suit of deep stone gray, topped with his long, sweeping overcoat, while Lila was in a collage of cast-off tweeds under a long black duster. Pulling on her gloves, she looked like a clothes-chest had turned itself out and come to life, but somehow the mishmash suited her even more than her usual stylish getup.

Roscoe was the only one awake downstairs. He looked out of place, sitting in a chair in the middle of the room, watching the street outside the window. Lila held up one finger in front of her lips to signal quiet, and he nodded. She pointed toward the door, and he stood up to meet us at the entrance. Lila took the key to the Queen from her pocket to let us out, then pressed it into Roscoe's hand.

"Tell Grace not to worry, I'll be back in a few days at most," she said.

"You need any help?" asked Roscoe.

"You just watch over the place 'til I get back," said Lila.

Roscoe hesitated a moment, then nodded. He looked past her to me. "Bye, Bridget, Constance," he said. "You girls be careful now."

I smiled at him quickly, and as we turned to go I heard the door shut and lock behind us with a clatter.

Shoulder to shoulder now, we strode up the main street, walking straight down the middle where once we might have minced in a line along the sidewalk. Another colorless day had fully broken, pale white light leaking out overhead like cracks spreading over the surface of a frozen lake. Winter had come, laying itself cold and unmoving over the landscape.

We woke the liveryman with our knocking. I quickly saddled Little Blue and led him outside ahead of the others, pausing to look behind us down the main street. Shuttered, I could barely pick out the Buffalo Queen among the rest of the buildings. The street was all but empty, the cold having chased everyone inside, but after a moment I did pick out a figure coming toward me up the way.

It was Jim. He materialized from the various mottled grays as though pulling himself together piece by piece as he slogged up the muddy street. I had pushed my hat back to get in close and adjust one stirrup, and my hair must have stood out a mile. He drew back a little when he spotted me, but then approached.

"That's some getup," he said. He stood a little ways away from me, a half pace back from how we had been before; I was startled to feel that the distance pained me a little, pinged like a plug hitting a spittoon.

I dropped the saddle flap and straightened up. "Do you like it?" I asked.

He looked me up and down, mustache twitching once. "Not one bit."

I smoothed my hair back with one gloved hand and replaced my hat, not sure whether I was supposed to laugh or not.

"You going after 'em, then?" he said.

I nodded.

"I thought you might," he said.

"You did?"

"Well, you never could keep still," he said simply. I nodded again; for once he was right about me.

"Constance and Lila are going too," I said.

"That's good. That bunch you're after sound like pretty rough customers—you be careful," he said.

"Ain't I always careful?"

"You've never been careful a day in your life."

We both laughed at that. It felt very strange, but not terrible.

"Wish me luck?" I said.

"I'll do you better than that," he said. He reached under his coat and brought out a gun belt of good black leather, tooled with a pattern of flowering vines. In the holster was a short-barreled revolver, oiled to a dark sheen, with a gleaming mother-of-pearl handle.

I reached out and took it, clasping the rig in both hands.

"I got it from a Ranger, who took it off a Mexican bandit," said Jim. "Or that's what he told me, but you know how Rangers like to talk."

"Is this for me?" I said, ignoring the story.

Jim nodded. "I wish to God I could think of something to say that'd stop you, but I doubt you'd listen anyway."

I took off the gun I'd bought from the dry goods and rolled it into my saddlebag, strapping on Jim's gift. It too hugged right up under my hip bone, heavier than my old one, but it was the weight of good craftsmanship.

When I looked up at Jim his face twitched a little under one eye. "You're sure?" he said.

"I wish I weren't," I said by way of forgiving us both for not being what the other was looking for.

We stood like that a moment, until a fresh gust of wind blew up and the door of the livery opened again, admitting Constance and Lila out onto the street, leading a pair of saddled horses.

"What's he doing here?" asked Lila.

"Nothing," said Jim. "Just out walking."

"*Hmph.* You ready, Bridget?"

"Yeah, let's go," I said. We mounted up and started out toward the prairie. When I looked back, Jim was still standing there, melting back into the muddy street.

As soon as we left Dodge I pointed us out toward the spring. Though I'd wandered in circles coming into town, now that we were leaving, the direction was clear as day. I was driven more by instinct than true knowledge, but even if I'd had a printed map I could have taken us no other way. It was like an arrow coming out of my heart and pointing me straight toward them, as if I could see through all the many miles between us, and with one good, level shot they'd be done and gone forever.

The question was not which way to go, but whether they would still be there at the end of the journey. The suspense was ten times worse than the cold, and if my horse could have stood it I'd have pushed him into a gallop and held him there until I closed the gap, but some practical impulse held me to the top end of a manageable pace. It was the same gut sense that had told me to hide every time I stopped when crossing the prairie, to dip my head and laugh no matter what any man said to me. But still, I kept catching myself leaning forward as I rode, drawn by the fishhook in my heart. Intention crackled between the three of us like heat lightning; the horses must have picked up our mood, for though they kept us together, they broke in and out of step with each other, nickering and blowing as though gossiping about us in their own language.

As soon as we got going it was clear that, as she said, Lila had done some hard traveling in her time and kept the knack of endurance. Though she never wearied or dropped her gaze from the horizon, she held her mount to a steadier pace than the rest of us. Constance, on the other hand, was a town girl through and through, with no experience on this sort of journey. After a while I could see her drooping in her saddle like a daisy dropping its petals around the vase. I called to her and poked at her with my quirt, and she jerked upright, but it was clear that she was worn past her limits. I called a halt after the fourth or fifth jab, and as the sun arced toward its midday zenith we set down in the grass to rest a spell. Lila was sullen and restive as she munched on some crackers and a hunk of cheese, casting glances over her shoulder while Constance stared into the roots of the grasses before her and chewed with the steady intensity of a cow at her cud.

"What will we do when we find them?" she said when her strength was restored.

Lila and I looked at each other. I wasn't sure when Constance had become a passenger, and clearly neither was Lila, but when our eyes met there passed between us an understanding that the decisions were ours to make.

"We're going to kill them and get our money back," said Lila. She stood up and brushed off her seat, then unhobbled and re-mounted her horse. She looked down from her saddle. "Is that all right with you?"

"It was a fair question," said Constance, pushing herself upright.

Lila said nothing and swung her horse around to point northeast again. By the time we mounted up she was already almost a quarter mile ahead of us. Constance and I rode side by side in silence for a spell.

"What do you want to do?" I asked Constance after a little bit.

She sighed. "I don't know what I want," she said. "But I couldn't just keep sitting there in my room—I've never felt anything so bad in all my life."

I glanced at her from under the brim of my hat, but she kept her head high and her gaze forward. "What about you?" she asked.

I thought a moment. "I want her to rue the day she left me behind."

I looked at the prairie spread around us. We'd gone far enough to lose sight of Dodge, so the land stretched out infinite in all directions. We were but three scattered crumbs on a handkerchief, waiting for some great hand to shake us out into the wind. The grass was all dead, brown and broken, lying inert under a featureless white sky. For a moment I was transported back to the Queen, to the moment not long ago when I had stood halfway down the stairs and felt Spartan look up at me, take me all in at once, when for perhaps the first time in my life I had been a full creature in the eyes of another. But here, now, there was nothing left to see, no matter where I looked or how I strained my eyes. I spurred Little Blue and he leapt forward, seeming almost relieved to be allowed to run. I gave him his head but he never strayed, and for a time my thoughts were drowned out by the beating of hooves against the earth and the rushing wind that whistled past my ears until they stung and throbbed with cold.

The days were getting short; after covering most of the distance we stopped for the night and built a little fire. Constance fell asleep almost before she finished eating. She curled up tight in all her borrowed clothes and pulled Pierre's coat up tight so only her face showed.

Lila poked at the fire as though to bank it down, but neither of us made any move to sleep. She pulled a bottle from her saddlebag and yanked at the cork with her teeth. For the first time I could see the years on her face, not that she'd had so very many more than I, but that each one had been long, and memorable.

"You really doing all this for Kate?" I asked her.

She looked past my shoulder into the night, so much blacker beyond the firelight than it had been outside the windows of the saloon. "Do you know how we came to work together?" she said.

I shook my head. She passed me the bottle and I took a swig before handing it back.

"We're both from Missouri," she said. "Though she was better stock than I, as anyone could tell from how she talked—that wasn't affected. But I came up poor, in a passel of twelve young'uns. My folks tried, but you know how it is."

"I do," I said.

She pointed the mouth of the bottle at me and nodded. "Our place was just off the road to St. Louis, and one night this traveling man stops by. Silk tie, clean hands, nicest manners I'd ever seen. Well, he liked the look of me right off, and I'll admit I liked him too. He paid my folks twenty dollars to take me with him the next day, though I was but fourteen at the time." I suppressed a shudder, recalling the morning in Dodge when I'd sold my broken-down mule for twenty dollars and felt slighted at the price. Lila took a swig and passed me the bottle again, waiting for me to return it before she went on.

"Well, you can guess how that went. Third time he backhanded me I hauled off and socked him in the jawbone, which set us more or less straight for a while. Though I suppose he wasn't all bad. He put us up in a hotel room so he could play cards, bought me a couple nice dresses and a few good meals, even made like we was sweethearts for a week or two. Then he hit a dry spell at the tables, and you'll never guess what he came up with to pay off the loss." She raised an eyebrow at me over the flames. "That's how I got to be a sporting woman. Anyway, I got the hang of that pretty quick. But what I didn't get the hang of was how to keep from getting in the family way, nor did I know how to get out of it—you don't learn those parts working on your own. Hooper—that was his name—might've known some gal who could've helped, but I waited too long, and I was already starting to show by the time he figured the state I was in. Smacked me on the head with a set of fire-tongs—to this day I can tell a storm coming by the way it buzzes." She wiggled her fingers under her left earlobe.

"And so there I was, out on my ass with one busted ear, two black eyes, and three dollars to my name. One of Kate's gals found me, much as I found you, and brought me back with her to work. Good work too: looking after the girls, mending their clothes and doing their hair, light tasks. She had a fine place back in St. Louis, nothing like the Queen. That's where I knew Sallie from—she came through a few months when I was older, and we sure had us some fun. I couldn't believe the place when I first saw it: thick carpets and heavy drapes, sweet girls too. I was their pet for a while, new and young and knocked up as I was. When the baby came, Kate took him to the sisters for me. You ain't never had one so you don't know how it feels to give one up. I knew it was best for him, of course. But if I'd had to go and lay him in that foundling box my hands would've frozen up, and he and I would've been stuck together forever. So Kate did it. She waited until I was asleep and wrapped him up in her cloak and sent him on to what I have to believe is a better life." She took another slug from the bottle. "He'll be almost nine by now. Ought to be handsome, at least—his daddy had good, thick hair like mine."

She looked up at me with long blue shadows under her eyes. "My point is, anyone can take in a half-starved gal and teach her to lie on her back. It don't take much to learn this trade, as you well know. But anyone else would have either turned us out or made me walk to that convent my own self. Kate spared me that, spared me having to say goodbye. That's the kind of person she was, especially before you knew her: to see another staggering under their load, to come up beside them and shift it onto your own shoulders so swiftly and so lightly that they don't even notice what you've done until they suddenly find themselves straightening up and feeling the sun on their face again. She cared for others without making it another way to care for herself." A silence fell between us. I nodded and held out my hand for the whiskey.

"What happened to the house in St. Louis?" I asked after a long drink.

"Burned down," she said simply. "Someone knocked over a lamp, caught those fine curtains and up she went. Word was out by then about cheap land and a booming cow trade, so Kate figured it best if we set down an early stake, be among the first to sell those cattlemen any pleasure." She looked at the last flames of the fire and laughed softly. "We did good for a while there, I must say. And I'll do good again, just you wait." She corked the bottle and gave it a thump with the heel of her hand. "But first I'm going to get Kate's money back. She may be dead, but I won't have her stolen from by any upstart prairie harlot."

CHAPTER 20

We came upon the sod house midmorning. The wind was at our backs; we crested a rise so gradual we didn't notice our own ascent until we reached the negligible summit, and there was the cottonwood grove, tilting over the spring at the head of the creek. We paused and looked down at the little crease in the earth.

The sod house was right where I'd left it, wooden door chipped around the edges. The trees before it were bare and black-barked, branches rattling as the wind shifted from its usual prairie moan to the high whine of an oncoming blizzard. Footprints led from the door down to the spring, where a messy pile of slush showed that someone had been fetching water regularly for at least a day. Beside the house, four horses were clustered together in a shaggy muddle of twitching ears and tails blowing out long in the wind. As the first flakes of snow melted into my cheeks, I spotted Davey, Spartan Lee's big bay mare. At the sight of the horse my insides tightened and grew rigid as I realized that my luck had held: for once in my life I was in the right place at the right time.

"Well, I'll be damned," said Lila. "You really did know the way."

"Told you," I said, annoyed.

We were upwind from the sod house and Davey must have smelled us, for as we paused on that pitiful little ridge she raised her pony-keg head and took a snuff of the freezing wind. Little Blue whinnied, shuffling his feet under me, and I held the reins tighter. We drew back a few yards to talk.

"Well, now what?" hissed Constance.

Lila looked at me. "There any other doors to that house?"

I shook my head. "No other doors, but there's a window in the wall above the horses."

"Okay then." Lila looked past my shoulder toward the house, chin lifted in the wind, snow drawing a thin veil between us.

"Shit, I don't know. What do you say we go through the damned door?" I said.

Lila nodded, chewing the inside of her cheek. "Fuck it, I ain't got any better ideas. You and me go through the front door. Constance, you go around the side and untie their horses, then stay outside and cover the window."

"Cover the window?" asked Constance.

Lila sighed and pointed. "See that window? You stand outside it, and if anyone comes out who isn't me or Bridget, shoot 'em."

"Okay. Give me the shotgun," she said.

"Then what'll I use?" Lila hissed.

"You said shoot them, but all I have is that skinning knife."

"Christ," said Lila through gritted teeth. She handed over the shotgun and a box of shells. "At least give me the knife."

"Hang on," I said. I twisted around and dug in my saddlebag until I came out with the revolver I'd bought in town and handed it to Lila.

"Why didn't you give this to me before?" she said.

"Forgot," I said sheepishly. "Anyway, you could have asked me."

"Good lord," she muttered as she buckled it on. "Are we the dumbest whores on this entire fuckin' prairie?"

"I don't know," said Constance. "There's a lot of prairie."

"And a lot of whores," I added.

Lila rolled her eyes. "Well, come on, then, before they get the drop on us again. Don't forget, that yellow-haired bitch is mine."

She kicked her horse into a trot over the rise and down the slope toward the spring.

I held back a moment and looked at Constance, then leaned over and squeezed her gloved hand with mine, and spurred Little Blue to catch up with Lila. Behind me I heard Constance's horse trot around in a wide arc toward where the others were stamping in their misty cloud.

Lila and I dismounted in the grove, looping our horses' reins to the branch of a tree. We moved slowly up to the house, careful not to crunch on the dead grass or patchy snow, and stood to either side of the door. There was an argument going on inside. It was stranger than most dreams to hear voices I knew so well, so out of place.

"Come on, ain't we laid up long enough? I want to get to a town." That was Sallie, whining.

"Want to get to a saloon is what you mean," Spartan interjected. Somehow I hadn't expected to hear her voice; it was like a hand reaching straight into my chest to scrounge around, squeezing everything it touched.

"It's your brother I'm worried about," Sallie snapped.

"He's had worse," said Spartan. "Besides, you ain't concerned on his behalf, you're just edgy on account of the whiskey's gone."

"Don't tell me what I'm edgy about!"

"Calm down, the both of you," came Hector's rumble. "You ain't heard that blizzard that's coming up out there? Like to blow the damn door in. We ain't going anywhere 'til it clears."

"I wish it would blow the door in," Sallie said. "All we've done is sit and stare at the walls."

Lila looked at me, and I looked back. My heart was pounding hard; my whole body was vibrating so evenly that I found myself unexpectedly steady. I unholstered my gun and pulled back the hammer. Lila did the same, and when our eyes met, hers had turned to little slabs of black ice. I nodded once and stepped back; she raised one booted foot and kicked the door in.

Sallie was sitting on the pallet in the corner next to Hector, who was laid out flat upon it, bandaged about his shooting arm where Kate had got him. Near the window Spartan and mufflered Jack were playing cards at the table. Everyone looked up when the door flew in and crashed to the floor, but only Sallie looked at all surprised.

"Aw, shit," said Spartan, in the same tone she used whenever she laid down a losing hand. Before she hit the *t* in *shit* every gun in the room was drawn, muzzles pointing all directions. Everyone looked glassy-eyed and greasy; there were empty bottles scattered around, and an acrid tang from some feathers that had burned off a turkey whose blackened bones lay scattered on a plate before the hearth.

"Aw shit is right," I said, aiming my gun at the space between Spartan and her brother, undecided as to who to shoot first.

"You can't be serious," said Spartan.

"The hell I'm not," I said. My thumb looped out, looking for the hammer; I'd forgotten it was already cocked.

"Everyone shut up," shouted Lila. She pointed her gun straight at Sallie. "Give me my money, you drunk, lying bitch."

"Fuck your money," said Sallie. And then the room exploded.

Lila and I both fired at the same time. I fired twice and missed, wood chips flying up from the tabletop. Shots came from the pallet and Lila screamed; I swung my gun to the right, squeezed the trigger twice more and was astonished to see Hector fling himself backward, good arm flying up like he'd lost his balance crossing a creek. My breath came ragged in my chest but I couldn't hear it in my ears. From the corner of my eye, I saw Jack climb out through the window, then heard Constance's shotgun fire from both barrels. There was a cascade of terrified whinnying from the horses outside, and I looked over just in time to see Spartan scrambling out the window after her brother. I fired my last two shots at her back, but they thudded into the sod beside the shutter, the sound overlaid with pounding hooves.

"Fuck!" Constance shouted. There came the snap of the shotgun being reloaded, followed by two more shots. I looked over at Lila, who was crouched beside the open doorway. She was gripping at her left arm just below the shoulder, teeth bared and clenched tight.

"You all right?" I asked her.

"I'll deal with this in a minute," she grunted. She staggered and heaved herself through the open doorway; a chair clattered to the floor as I followed her inside, gun drawn.

Hector and Sallie were splayed out on the pallet; Hector had clearly traveled, unearthly stillness having settled over his body, but I could see that Sallie was still breathing.

"Watch out, she ain't dead yet," I said.

"Won't be long," said Lila; I heard her voice before my eyes adjusted to the gloom.

"Where is it, you motherless bitch, what have you done with our stake?" she muttered, rummaging through a pile of rags near the hearth in which a low fire still flickered under an iron pot. I couldn't see her shoulder but there was an unsettling glisten to the entire left half of her body.

I turned back to Sallie. Her curdled-cream face was smeared red up from the neck of her dress; her whole torso glistened in the same way as Lila's left side. I approached slowly and knelt down on one knee beside her. She turned her head slowly toward me and opened her eyes halfway.

"Well howdy, mister," she said weakly. "You look like you could use some company."

"It's me, Bridget, from the Buffalo Queen," I said, taking off my hat. I touched the back of my neck to loose my hair but remembered that it was gone.

Her eyes had gone almost completely colorless, like the sky outside. They swam in circles around my face before fixing in. "Well I'll be damned, it is Bridget," she rasped at last. "The hell you doing here?"

"Looking for the money," I said.

"Oh, was that yours?" She smiled her curling drunkard's smile and I leaned in instinctively.

"It was everyone's," I said.

"Too bad for everyone, then," said Sallie. Her eyes knocked together like beads on a string. Perhaps I should have pitied her, but instead all I felt was a curl of irritation: even now, at the end of her life, she would still insist on being selfish. She was hit in the chest, right where she'd once showed me her derringer. I placed one hand above a rip in her dress that was leaking blood in weak, steady pulses. She winced.

"I wouldn't have minded if you'd robbed only me," I said. "But you stole from my friends, and I won't have it." I leaned forward just a hair and she gasped, high and sharp like a train braking. The palm of my hand was warm and wet; I glanced down to see scarlet pooling up between my fingers.

Her eyes flicked over to the hearth. My gaze followed hers to rest on the poorly set stones. "It's mine," she whispered. "I'm owed."

"What's she saying?" asked Lila.

I glanced up at her, then back down at Sallie. She had stopped breathing. I closed her eyes with fingers that left red streaks in their wake, shocked that the lids were still soft as butterfly wings.

"She's dead," I said.

Lila didn't answer right away. She eased herself up to half-standing and staggered over, then sat down beside me. She looked at her former friend.

"She never could settle down," she said. "Never could accept her lot in life."

The silence that should have fallen was broken by a single, short sob from outside followed by a sharp retch and heave.

Lila jerked her head toward the window. "Go see what that's about, will you?" she said.

I nodded and went outside, around the side of the house. Constance was standing beside a tumble of arms and legs that made up Jack Lee's body; his spectacles had fallen off and lay beside Constance's feet in a pool of blood and bile that was already starting to freeze.

"Constance?" I said gently.

She whipped her head around at the sound of my voice.

"You all right?" I asked.

"Am I all right?" she said, then whirled her body to face me and repeated herself at a shout. "Am I all right?" Waving the shotgun like a walking stick, she looked like a madwoman: she'd lost her hat and her curls had sprung loose around her head.

"Would you put your gun down?" I said.

"Oh, fuck you, Bridget!" she yelled.

"Yeah, fuck me is right," I said. "But could you put the gun down anyway?"

"It's empty, stupid!"

I held out my hands to Constance. She looked spooked, rolling her eyes like a horse.

"Easy," I said. "Be easy, Constance. Tell me what happened."

"I shot him, just like you told me to," she said.

"That's good," I said. "What about Spartan?"

"She got away. I meant to kill her too, but I ran out of shells. She was able to catch her horse before it bolted with the others. By the time I reloaded she was gone, so I shot this one again, just to be sure."

I nodded again. "You did real good," I said. "We'll go after her presently, but first I think we'd better check on Lila."

Constance nodded.

"Can you give me the gun, please?" I asked her.

She looked at it in bewilderment and then, with a head-to-toe shiver like a dog getting out of a stream, she passed it to me and smoothed back her hair.

"What about the others?" she asked.

"Hector and Sallie are dead," I said. "But Lila got one in the shoulder—I think it was Sallie."

Constance sprang to life. "Why didn't you say so?" In one graceful motion she bent to pick up her hat and pushed past me back toward the house, casting a reproving look over her shoulder as if I'd been idling. Before following her I couldn't help but scan the plains, looking for some sign, some flicker of Spartan like a distant flame, but all I saw was grass and endless sky.

Inside, Constance was already kneeling beside Lila, examining her layers of mushy, blood-soaked clothing.

"I'm sorry, Lila, it shouldn't have come to that," she was saying.

Lila grunted and shifted her weight. "You hit anything with all that blasting?"

Constance nodded. "The one who shot Pierre."

Lila nodded. "Well, good riddance," she said.

"Were you the one who shot Hector too?" said Constance.

"That was me," I said. Then, "I think I know where the money is."

Lila sat up like Lazarus. "Where?"

"In the hearth. Must be a loose stone or a burying place."

"Looks like you paid your freight after all," said Lila. She half rose again, then groaned and sank down. "Fuck me, but that hurts."

"Bridget, get them out of here," said Constance, pointing at the corpses. "Lila has to lie down and this is the only bed in the place."

"What about my money?" said Lila.

"You waited four days, you can wait four more minutes," said Constance sharply. To have her assume authority over the situation was a welcome relief; I could see Lila's face relaxing a little as Constance peeled back the sodden lapel of her duster. I grabbed Sallie by the ankles and drug her toward the door. Her dress rode up and bunched around her hips as I pulled her, skinny knees knocking together. Even dead, the shape of each leg was still perfect in its glide and curve from ankle to calf. As I pulled her body outside into a wash of white light from the oncoming storm, it all felt like such a waste: a waste of time, of life, the waste of a beautiful girl.

I left Sallie's corpse beside the house and went back for Hector. He was hard work and slow-going to move; I gripped his legs under my arms and pulled him outside. Wrestling with his unwieldy bulk, I struggled to recall that I was the one who had killed him; he seemed just another burden. I wondered if my conscience was waiting for more stillness to assault me, but then I recalled that his good arm had been too hurt to shoot, and I was grateful it was me pulling him and not the other way around. Behind me I could hear Constance moving the table and chairs, flipping and shaking out the pallet, muttering. By the time I got Hector outside, Sallie's corpse was already dusted with snow. I left them side by side next to the door, like the dregs of a woodpile, blackened with seepage from the ground below. I considered dragging Jack around to the same pile as his brother, but the cold was getting vicious, and I couldn't see what good it would do.

Straightening up, I turned toward the spring to where the cottonwoods stood bare, branches rattling in the wind. For a few seconds I searched the ground before them for any sign of my pa's grave, but there was nothing: neither a hump over his body nor a pit where coyotes might have dug him up. Instead, the ground was covered with untrod-upon snow, smooth as a freshly made bed. It scared me worse than if he'd still been there or clearly been gone; the way things stood it was as if he, and therefore I, had never been there in the first place. Now my only proof of having seen this place was my memory, and the fresh bodies stacked outside the house.

I barely darkened the doorway before Constance was giving more orders. At her behest I gathered up our three horses and tied them up just outside the door where the face of the sod house would shelter them from the worst of the wind. They gathered together, looking on through the open door. The fire had been fed and was crackling merrily, and Constance knelt over Lila, whose shoulder she had managed to clean and bandage while I'd been dragging corpses around. Altogether it was like some strange nativity; though Lila would have made a poor Christ child, Constance shone in the firelight with a gentle calm. I took what was left of the door and propped it back in place, plugging the chinks with bits and pieces from the rag pile until we were as snug as we were going to get while we waited for the storm to pass.

CHAPTER 21

The money was right where Sallie's glance had given it away—it took only a few minutes' tapping at the hearthstones to find a little group that were only wedged in, not mud-cemented like the rest. Behind them, the cluster of stacked bills and small canvas bags looked just as content in its little cave as it had in Kate's safe. I stuffed the booty into a gunnysack pulled from the rag pile while Lila craned her neck to watch.

"Give it to me," she said when I had the money all collected, reaching out with her good arm from where she lay nestled up on the pallet. I tucked it under her arm, and she pulled it close like a babe.

"Thanks," she said simply. Her wound wasn't a bad one, Constance told me. Nothing broken, and no organs up there to speak of, so as long as it didn't fester Lila would likely knit up just fine and live to enjoy telling the tale.

I nodded and sat down at the little table, where Constance had laid out provisions from my saddlebags. We ate, then rested a moment, listening to the storm howl outside.

"What do you want to do now?" Constance asked me.

"Wait for the storm to clear," I said.

"And after that?"

A bullet I'd fired was still lodged in the table, and I picked at it like a scab. "Go after her," I said. I worried at the back of the lead piece, thinking how it had been meant to bury itself in her neck, where she liked to tuck her chin, or right up at the top of her chest where shoulder muscle gave way to the downslope of her tits. I worked the bullet loose with my thumbnail and held it up, observing how the nose was just slightly blunted from hitting the table.

"You sure?" she asked. I looked past the bullet to see Constance watching me. She looked tired.

"You didn't like shooting the one that killed Pierre, did you."

She folded her arms, biting at a chapped spot on her bottom lip.

"It could have been worse," she said. "But it certainly could have been better. I somehow hadn't anticipated all the mess."

I couldn't help but laugh at that as I set the shell down on the table with a small click.

"I know, I know," she continued, "but all the same. I will say this: Pierre is still dead. It comes to me now that my heart may never recover, and maybe it never should. But I can't tell you how glad I am that that faceless fuck isn't riding around spending my money, making whores laugh with some wild story of how he shot a French gambler back in Dodge. Pierre's life may have come to nothing, but now Jack Lee's has come to nothing too, and richly deserved."

I nodded. Nothing, that was what it all came to. And maybe that was true, but I couldn't bring myself to believe it. I looked around us, and for a moment it was as if all the events that had ever taken place in this room were happening again, layered on top of each other like panes of glass. My hand pressing ever so gently into Sallie's wounded shoulder to draw a sharp cry; behind that, the brief but furious gunfight, in which I'd shot a man I cared so little about it was already hard to recall doing it. Behind that, my pa dancing in the feeble glow of banked coals, twisting and shrieking and yanking at the rattlesnake clamped to his neck, before I had to drag him outside too, before his eyes also slid away from mine, seeking some point of focus in the far, far distance. Nothing, indeed.

"You know this is where my pa died?" I said.

Constance looked up, startled. "No, I didn't know that."

"We was on our way out someplace and we camped the night in this house. He was a restless sleeper and must've scared a rattlesnake in the night with his shuffling around, for it come out and bit him, bad. I drug him out by the spring yonder and waited all day for him to die. Wound up walking most of the way to Dodge, though I kept getting lost following those damned creek beds." I gestured vaguely southward.

"I'm so sorry," said Constance. "That's dreadful."

"And then you know, Lila found me and brought me in, and I thought, hell, why not. Rather whore than chore, is what I say, or at least what I say now." I laughed but was greeted with silence. "And it was actually all right there for a while." I was trying not to talk too fast, but I felt myself racing some awful, cottony tightness in my throat.

"And then there was . . . there was Sallie, who left, on account of me and my own fucking strangeness."

"She would have annoyed Lila into throwing her out sooner or later," said Constance.

"Probably," I conceded, "but it broke my heart just the same. And then just as it's starting to mend, of all the people to walk into my stupid little life, there comes this . . . this woman." I had never said the word before, and it filled my whole mouth. "I know it probably just looked indecent, or at least very silly, from the outside, and I should've kept my cool, I know. But I'd never met anyone quite like her. Never will again, most likely."

Constance didn't move. "It didn't seem silly," she said.

I looked at her. Her eyes were soft.

"She told me she'd had enough of her brothers, but I suppose that was a lie," I continued. "I doubt she'd let the gals who killed 'em roam free."

"No," Constance agreed. "But you don't think being alone in that storm will stop her for good?"

"It might," I said. "Then again, it might not."

"And we can't have her turning up at the Queen," added Constance.

I shook my head in assent; there really was nothing else for it. "You know, you're supposed to be chasing me now too. Not that I would've helped knock over the Queen, but she said she'd take me with her. Why'd she say that if she didn't mean it?" I said.

Constance shook her head. "I don't know. But she shouldn't have said it."

"She shouldn't have said it," I said. The whole room was dissolving around me into points of light and streaks of color. I laid my head on the tabletop.

"But she did," said Constance.

"But she did," I repeated.

We stayed in our places, Lila asleep, Constance keeping watch, me with my forehead pressed against the rough-hewn boards. After a few minutes the crackling of the fire and the smell of warm earth coming off the walls brought me back to myself, and when I looked up again everything was right where I'd left it.

The storm was not a long one. I drifted in my chair, feet up before the fire like I'd built that house myself, until the wind shifted and died back down to its usual mania. When I opened the shutter to look outside, the snowfall was already petering out.

"It's now or never," I said to Constance.

She sat up from where she'd lain down on the pallet next to Lila. "Is the storm over?"

I nodded. "Yeah, it's over. And I ain't much of a tracker, so if we're going, we have to go now."

"You're more of a tracker than I am."

"Well, I know which way's the easiest to go from here, since I went that way myself without knowing what I was doing. We'll start there, and if it ain't the way I'll know soon enough." What I didn't say was that I was starting to remember all the things I'd let myself forget: the twists and turns of the creek bed where I'd been so lost were coming back to me in bits and pieces. Though I couldn't have laid out a plan for us to follow, the arrow in my heart was still pointing at Spartan Lee; I was certain that as soon as we started moving again, the landscape would render her up to me, for she was my due.

Constance didn't know enough not to take this at face value, and she nodded her assent. Beside her, Lila stirred. She pulled herself up onto the elbow of her unshot side.

"You gonna go kill that bitch that broke your heart?" she asked.

"Probably."

She rolled her head like a drunk until it pulled itself steady, then fixed me with one eye. "Well, you let me know which way it goes."

She sank back down with a sigh while I gathered up most of the food, stacking it with a canteen on the pallet within Lila's reach.

"This ought to hold you," I said. "If we ain't back in a day or two, you go on home."

She nodded while Constance pulled on her gloves and buttoned herself into Pierre's overcoat.

"He'd be right proud of you, you know," said Lila from her sprawl.

"He wouldn't, but thank you for saying so all the same," said Constance.

"You two don't get killed," said Lila, already half-asleep. "Come on back before I have to go off and leave you. And give me my gun."

I laid Lila's revolver and a box of shells within easy reach of her good hand. Laid out on the pallet, surrounded by supplies, she looked like some unknown prairie saint, haloed in hardtack and bullets.

"The second time you wake up, if we ain't back, you haul yourself up on that horse and get out of here," I said firmly, staring at her closed eyes. She nodded sleepily and turned away.

"Come on," said Constance, leading me toward the door; off its hinges, she could lift the whole thing and move it to one side. "The sooner we go, the sooner we can get back." She put the door back in place behind us and went to saddle her horse.

"You say it like we was going down to the dry goods," I said, throwing my saddle over Little Blue and tightening the girth under his belly.

Constance merely shrugged in reply. We mounted up and I swung Little Blue's head around to point past the side of the house. I looked back at my friend.

"You sure about this?"

"Why wouldn't I be?"

"You didn't seem to care much for the last gunfight, if you don't mind my saying so."

"You'd do the same for me," she said. "So can we please go?"

Without another word I put spur to Little Blue, who, as always, jumped forward as if he'd been waiting all day for this very request. He broke into a long, easy lope in the exact direction I would have chosen, as if he too could feel the aching pull under my breastbone, pointing us northwest. My eyes strained forward to seek out my quarry—though the snow had been brief, the wind had been bad, and she couldn't have gotten far. We traveled alongside the creek bed, broadside to its thickets and clusters of bare trees, and for a time I let us be carried as if in a dream over the stark, white ground. Under the wind, the only sound was Little Blue's heavy breathing, the creak of the saddle, the crunch and puff of his feet striking the snow and kicking it up as he ran.

The storm had chopped the day in half so that it was barely afternoon when suddenly hoofprints leapt out like bad omens from the ground ahead, dark half circles pressed into the snow, looping out from and then back toward the creek bed. We dropped down into a walk and turned north. The fiery ache in my chest that had dragged me this far had grown and suffused all through me; I felt I could have set the dry grass ablaze with a brush of my fingertips.

The brush thickened as we approached the creek and I lost the trail of prints. When last I'd seen it, the creek bed had been lush, overgrown with leafy bushes and low-slung trees, all of which were now bare, scraggly heaps of gray and black branches that pointed and laced in every direction. I scanned hard, searching through the patchwork; anywhere I looked there was nothing but thicket, like the lace edge of the ground as it merged up into the sky. With no other bearing, I watched Little Blue closely for signs that we were nearing our target, marking every twitch of his ears and toss of his head.

And then I spotted Davey, tucked into the brush, ears twitching. I put out my hand and behind me Constance stopped. We slipped from our horses and tied them to a nearby tree.

Crouched near our mounts, I pointed down the creek to where I'd seen the horse. We unholstered our guns and went forward on foot. Though we moved with care, our feet crunched on the dead grass, scattered over with new snow, and I was grateful to the creek for not freezing, its merry voice chirping away as if nothing were amiss. I heard a rustling just off to my left and glanced behind me, spotting the hem of Constance's coat as she vanished into the brush to take a wider angle.

I took two more crouched steps forward. On my third I stepped on the rib cage of a dead prairie chicken and froze as the crunch echoed like a gunshot.

"Hold it," said Spartan. She was close by, but I couldn't see her through the brush. Even in a low tone, her voice cut right through the air, striking against me like a hammer on cold iron, and I was shocked that I didn't literally ring like a bell. I crouched lower and slowly pulled back the hammer of my gun.

The click was what finally gave me away. Even moving slowly as I was, even with the obliging chatter of the creek, that hammer-cock cracked like a whip in the freezing air.

"I said stop where you are," said Spartan.

CHAPTER 22

I couldn't see her. Still crouched, I looked around wildly, trapped like a rabbit who's heard the hawk's cry but hasn't been caught yet. There was a crackle of brush, and when she spoke again her voice was suddenly much too close.

"Put the gun down, Red."

I looked up into the muzzle of a Colt and followed its long, blue barrel up into Spartan Lee's face. It was still the most beautiful face I'd ever seen. For half a heartbeat I considered flinging myself into her arms right then and there, forgiving everything. I'd jump up on the back of her horse and we'd ride until we ground ourselves to dust. But then I saw the expression on that face of hers: how cool she looked, how in her element. I released the hammer of my pistol and tucked it into its holster.

"Good," she said. "Now stand up, nice and slow. Hands up, if you please."

I rose, hands by my ears. As I did so she took a step back, keeping the gun trained on me.

"What're you doing here?" she said.

"What's it look like?"

She shook her head. "It looks like you might be a little beyond your depth." She looked me up and down. "But at least you're dressed the part."

"It's better for riding this way," I said.

"Sure, sure. Shame about your hair, though."

I said nothing, filled with the same grinding, flat-chested fury that had driven me out of Dodge. Even now she couldn't keep that mocking edge out of her voice; though she acted relaxed, I marked that her gaze never left me. I recognized the same subtle tension in her shoulders that I'd seen at the hanging, and again at the fight back in Dodge. It telegraphed readiness, that, like a gun, she was ready to go off at any moment. And yet I couldn't fight the certainty that even now, she didn't take me at all seriously.

"What are you doing here, Red?" she said finally. "You killed my brothers, you got your money, what the fuck else do you want from me?"

I swallowed, suddenly searching for words. I wished my mouth would open and loose an endless swarm of biting flies—it would have been easier than trying to put everything into sentences.

I was suddenly struck by the absurdity of the situation. Here we were, freezing our tits off, me at gunpoint having thought, what? That I would sneak up and shoot her? Or that she would ever understand, much less own up to, all the wrong she had done?

"Can I ask you something?" I said after a moment.

Spartan shrugged. "If you must."

"Was it the whole time you was playing me? Or just part?"

Spartan shifted her weight slightly. Without taking her eyes off me she rummaged in her breast pocket for a smoke, which she placed in her mouth, then dug for a match, which she lit with a flick of her thumbnail. She took a long drag and exhaled so that she was wreathed in blue clouds, and all I wanted to do was wrench it out of her hand and stomp it into the wet ground. Her eyes moved from my hands up to my face, and then our eyes met for just a moment before she flicked her gaze back to watchfulness.

"No, not the whole time," she said.

"Some, or most, then?"

She shook her head and rolled her eyes. "The hell kind of a question even is that?" she said.

From the bushes came two heavy clicks, and behind Spartan, Constance stepped out, shotgun raised. She was glorious: wide-eyed, windburned, looking scared half to death and utterly determined.

"Answer the question," she said.

Spartan half twisted to glance at her. "Well, I'll be goddamned," she said. "You even know how to use that thing?"

Constance lowered the muzzle of the gun and fired one barrel at the ground between them, sending up a little bloom of snow and earth. The gun's report crackled off over the plains. "I'll own I'm new at this," said Constance, "but I tend to be a very quick study, so lower your gun."

Spartan sighed heavily, like a mother who's had quite enough of her children for one day, but she lowered the hammer of her gun and holstered it. "Will that satisfy mademoiselle?" she said acidly.

Constance ignored the jab and took half a step forward. "Answer the question: how much of that time in the Queen were you just working my friend?"

"Ah, hell" was all she said. She looked at me and I saw the barest flicker pass over her face, a flash of the eyes that had shone at me in the middle of the night, out of the darkness. Then it was gone, her face—her heart—once again impenetrable. So that was that.

I don't know what look crossed my own face, only that I felt the air sharper than steel in my nostrils and the quick, stubborn thud of my heart.

Beyond her shoulder, Constance looked at me. "Well?" she said at last.

"Well what?" said Spartan. Then, with a twist, she shot her arm out and spun so that one hand knocked the shotgun askew and the other grabbed it by the snout. Spartan yanked at the barrel, crouched and pulled, then suddenly shoved it back toward Constance, butting her hard in the chin. Constance stumbled backward, arms wheeling; as her hand slipped from the stock her grip tightened, and the second barrel exploded. A red spray shot out over the snowfall and Spartan let out a low, barking scream like the jaws of a trap closing over a bear's hind leg.

As it had at the hanging, my body clenched and a scream jumped out of me. Spartan whirled, still in a half crouch.

"Ain't you had enough?" she snarled. She had a hand clasped over her leg, just above the knee, and more blood was pouring out between her fingers, running down her pant leg to pock the snow with red. She looked wildly about for a second and plunged off, inexplicably away from the shelter of the creek bed and out toward the blank expanse, grunting and shuffling.

I looked over at Constance, who was already sitting up, rubbing her chin.

"Go," she said.

I pulled my gun from its holster and turned to follow Spartan Lee. Ahead of me, she tilted badly to one side, dragging a legful of buckshot. Her trail was messy, a welter of bootprints and scrapings in the snow, leaving a trail of blood as uneven as her ragged steps, long drips fringed about with lacy droplets that somehow reminded me of the way Langley liked to decorate the ends of verses when it was his turn at the keyboard, little notes trilled out to make the melody more lush.

I broke into a run. No rational part of me believed that she would get away, not really, but I couldn't slow down. In the space between us the wind blew the snow so that it swirled and eddied among tufts of grass.

"Stop!" I yelled at her back.

She kept going, though the space between us was closing. I was already hot from running in winter clothes, but the cold air burned in my lungs, made my breath come heavy. I recalled the gun in my hand and raised it into the air, firing once.

She made no move to slow. I suddenly feared that somehow the plains were on her side, that the prairie itself would just keep stretching between us to keep us apart, and felt a fresh plume of fury that the world might choose her over me. I stopped running, pointed the gun forward, and remembered what she had taught me: look only at the target, let everything else fall away. The sky, the snow, the trail of blood all blurred into darkness. I stopped where I was, breathed in, pulled the hammer back, breathed out, and fired.

She twisted and fell. The whole world I'd blocked out a moment before rushed back in a blaze of white and red, and I leapt forward again. I covered the distance in a few seconds, skidding down to a halt beside her, heart pounding.

"Spartan," I said, just her name, which I realized I had never called her by before. On my knees beside her I found myself casting about, panicky, suddenly unsure of my next move, or if it even mattered.

She was lying on her back, bleeding badly from two wounds now. Blood pooled underneath her with terrifying speed, her face whitening at the same rate. She placed a hand on my leg and for a split second her touch was the only thing I could feel. My breath came hard and fast, my whole body twisted and tightened up so that all the ropes that bound me together should have burst apart, but I remained whole.

"You should've took me with you," I said.

She took her hand from my leg and reached up, touched my cheek with one blood-soaked glove; I could feel a wet print and a smear from her hand. "Yeah, I suppose you're right," she said. Her eyes made a jerky survey of the sky beyond me, then came back to my face, her gaze feverishly bright. She tilted her chin up just a hair. "Kiss me goodbye?"

Without hesitation I leaned down, slipped my free hand around the back of her shoulders and pulled her up to me, tasting that sour twist of smoke and hard riding under the unnameable sweetness, the sweat, now shot through with the cold, metallic tang of blood. That taste held everything: that first slide of her hand up my thigh, her voice tracing clouds of smoke in the blue dark of my bedroom, the whip of wind off the prairie as I raised her gun, and the warm press of her front to my back as she taught me everything I'd ever need to know. She kissed me back, hard, one arm so tight around my waist I thought I'd break in half, and hoped I finally would.

And then I thought I might be getting my wish, for a sharp pain starred up through me, first hot, then colder than ice.

"Sorry, Red," she murmured into my mouth. "Should've been more careful." I'm not sure if I felt or heard the wet shuck of the knife drawing out of my side.

"Never been careful a day in my life," I said. I raised my gun one last time, slipped it between us. It must have gleamed in the light, or else she had just been waiting a long time for this very moment, for she gasped only slightly before I pulled the trigger. The gun kicked me hard in the chest and threw me backward. Blood poured out of my side, spreading and soaking through the snow like a blanket, ringing the tufts of grass in bright-red skirts. I fell onto my back and looked up at the blank, white sky as though turning to watch her go, to see her vanish over that one last horizon. But she was already gone.

EPILOGUE

It was Constance who got me and Lila back to the Queen; she tied us into our saddles and we humped along behind her, two piles of bloody laundry that hurt too much to complain. I don't recall much of the journey, beyond the pain in my side that alternated between a dull ache and a red-hot starburst, seemingly at will. My mind had gone to wool again, with no thoughts but to hang on to the saddle horn and let Constance take me someplace safe.

I overwintered at the Buffalo Queen. For the first few weeks, Lila and I convalesced side by side, tucked up in Kate's big bed where between naps we bickered like old maids at cribbage. She recovered faster than I did; arm still in a sling under her busted shoulder but otherwise resplendent in her best garnet silk dress, she threw open the doors of the saloon on Christmas Eve to welcome those who found tidings of neither comfort nor joy in the hymn-singing and family suppers on the north side of town. I lay upstairs and listened to Roscoe lustily banging out carols while the whores sang in clumsy chorus with their tricks. I pictured them all clumped up and tripping over each other while Virgil—head wound long since mended—passed around mugs of Bart's home-brewed wassail that sloshed and stained their clothes, wet kisses passed from face to face wreathed in dreamy smiles. Every now and then one of the gals would slip up to see me with a cookie or a fresh cup. Every one of them offered to bring me downstairs, but I preferred my solitude: Spartan's knife had sliced right into my liver, and even all these weeks later it hurt something awful if I taxed myself beyond sitting up to draw breath, and sometimes even then as well.

For once, the doc showed up and earned his fee. I had a short, thick scar like a jutting lower lip along my side, but as I watched it change from blackened scab to livid scarlet to glossy pink, I felt the organ and the muscles that supported it start to knit themselves back up, more inclined to be together than apart. Only after staring at it for weeks did I ruefully recall Sallie's warning that all tricks had a knife. I laughed when I remembered it, which only made the memory of Spartan Lee stab me once again.

By New Year's I moved down into the little room Pierre had pretended to occupy, and I passed the remainder of the winter learning how to play a decent game of poker. I turned out to be good for business: though my card game wasn't anything to write home about, playing with the gal who'd rode down and shot a notorious gunfighter and her no-account brothers certainly was. So I copied the way Constance used to read to me: speeding up and slowing down for the best parts, pausing in the right places, looking away over my listener's shoulder for half a moment too long. The first few times, I had to stop and wait for a hard tightness to pass out of my throat, dissolving it with whiskey that had grown warm at the hearth. But I got the hang of it after five or six times, and before long I'd worked up a carnival barker's rendition of my own life that I could roll out smoothly for strangers while keeping the knotted, heartsick version all to myself.

And then to my surprise, the more times I told it, the more I wanted it to happen again, the more my palm ached for the hard curve of my gun, the more my cheeks yearned to be stung by the cold wind instead of warmed by the fire, the more I itched to feel the miles piling up behind me through the steady beat of my running horse. I started taking an interest in the idle talk around me—rumors of new settlements in the Rockies where misfits and ne'er-do-wells were making all kinds of good—and slowly, an inch at a time, I thawed with the plains.

Just when I feared I could stand it no longer, the ground was pliant and ready to be sown, and the scar that Spartan had left was just another part of my skin. I started spending long periods of time sitting out on Lila's porch sniffing the wind and waiting for Dodge to wake up after its winter slumber; at last the day came when the grass burst forth from the plains, and when I craned my neck down the street I saw a sea of green lapping at the shores of the town. I leaned on the rail and let Dodge fall away until all I could see was the plains. Beyond them was a slate-colored smudge of mountains to the far west; I couldn't be sure whether I was seeing or imagining them, but either way, it was time to go.

Constance saw me off from the livery. She'd ensured that Little Blue passed a comfortable winter on the proceeds from selling Davey; when I went to saddle him he tossed his head and stamped at me for so rudely keeping him waiting. Watching from the doorway, Constance was a dark silhouette against the street, which was once again boiling over with life: outside there was already a racket as cattle, horses, people called to each other through morning air so thick with dust you could cut it just by waving your hand. I led my horse out and Constance turned to follow so that the wind whipped her curls back from her brow; the sun shone full on her face.

"You look very dashing," she said, reaching to stroke the back of my neck. Bart had given me a proper haircut, and from afar she must have looked like a mother seeing her favorite son off to school.

"Thank you," I said.

"We'll meet again," she said, squinting against the light. "I know I said it before—I meant it then, and I mean it now. But take my advice," she continued, rapping on my breastbone with two fingers. "The next time that heart of yours tells you to do something, try something else first."

I shook my head and couldn't help but smile at her. "I wouldn't put money on it," I said.

"I suppose I wouldn't either." She lifted one hand to shade her eyes and smiled back.

We paused a moment. I ached to be leaving her, but unlike the rope-twist I had grown accustomed to, now my chest was full of violin strings, each one carefully tuned to just the right pitch so that when next the fiddler took up her bow I would ring out clear and bittersweet to fill the room with music. I tried to think of something to say to Constance, but instead we just embraced for a long minute and I let myself bury my face in her neck. Then I swung up onto Little Blue and rode south, looking back just once to see her turning away to get back to the Queen.

At the edge of town I turned my horse to face due west—away from Dodge, the creek bed, the sod house, Arkansas—away from every place I'd ever been. Then I loosened my grip on the reins, and we started to run.

ACKNOWLEDGMENTS

There are so many people without whom this book would not be out in the world, and to whom I wish to extend my deepest thanks. My agent, Alexa Stark, for your immediate, total faith in this book and your tireless advocacy; my editor, Katy Nishomoto, for reading the book I wrote, only better, and knowing exactly how to close the gap between the two; the incredible team at The Dial Press: Whitney Frick, Maya Millett, Rose Fox, Andy Ward, Avideh Bashirrad, Debbie Aroff, Donna Cheng, Rebecca Berlant, Leah Sims, Michael Morris, Cara DuBois, Maria Braeckel, Ralph Fowler, Corina Diez, Michelle Jasmine, Sarah Feightner. You have all made this wild ride so much fun, and I'm so grateful for all of your hard work and support.

I was lucky not to have to write this book alone either; thank you to my teacher, Lynn Steger Strong; my endlessly patient and insightful classmates; the amazing team at Catapult who kept the novel generator going even through the worst of the pandemic. I could not have asked for or imagined better fellowship.

My parents, Mark and Mary Cravens, who believed in me from day one: thank you for always encouraging me to keep trying, and for giving me the copy of *Harriet the Spy* for my eleventh birthday that changed the whole course of my life! My sister, Katie Cravens, and my uncles, Mark Harbick and Jon Kastl: where would I be without your relentless, astonishing faith? To Kevin Gessner, who showed up late in the game and yet, as always, right on time: your immediate, total enthusiasm has been such a gift. To the friends who listened to me talk about this book endlessly, read early drafts, offered up ideas, and generally saw me through: Louise Bauso, Whittney Klann, Ryan Ruby, Theadora Tolkin, Emily Anne Vaughn, Lauren Wilkinson, Alex Zafiris. I don't even know where to begin.

While it may be true that there's more to this life than luck, when I think of everyone who helped and loved and supported me through writing this book, it's hard to imagine what that "more" could possibly be.

ABOUT THE AUTHOR

Claudia Cravens has a BA in literature from Bard College and participated in Catapult's yearlong novel generator. She lives in New York City. *Lucky Red* is her first novel.

claudiacravens.com
Twitter: @claudia_cravens
Instagram: @claudia.cravens

ABOUT THE TYPE

This book was set in Granjon, a modern recutting of a typeface produced under the direction of George W. Jones (1860–1942), who based Granjon's design upon the letterforms of Claude Garamond (1480–1561). The name was given to the typeface as a tribute to the typographic designer Robert Granjon (1513–89).